# The Net
# A Novel

*by*

Rex Beach

Double9
BOOKS

**The Net**
**A Novel**

**by Rex Beach**

ISBN: 978-93-57272-78-0

**Published by**

# DOUBLE 9 BOOKS

2/13-B, Ansari Road
Daryaganj, New Delhi – 110002
info@double9books.com
www.double9books.com
Tel. 011-40042856

# ABOUT THE AUTHOR

Rex Ellingwood Beach (September 1, 1877 - December 7, 1949) was an American novelist, playwright, and Olympic water polo player. He was born in Atwood, Michigan, but moved to Tampa, Florida, with his family where his father was growing fruit trees. Beach was educated at Rollins College, Florida (1891-1896), the Chicago College of Law (1896-97), and Kent College of Law, Chicago (1899-1900). In 1900 he was drawn to Alaska at the time of the Klondike Gold Rush. After five years of unsuccessful prospecting, he turned to writing. His second novel The Spoilers (1906) was based on a true story of corrupt government officials stealing gold mines from prospectors, which he witnessed while he was prospecting in Nome, Alaska. The Spoilers became one of the bestselling novels of 1906.

# CONTENTS

# I.
# THE TRAIN FROM PALERMO

The train from Palermo was late. Already long, shadowy fingers were reaching down the valleys across which the railroad track meandered. Far to the left, out of an opalescent sea, rose the fairy-like Lipari Islands, and in the farthest distance Stromboli lifted its smoking cone above the horizon. On the landward side of the train, as it reeled and squealed along its tortuous course, were gray and gold Sicilian villages perched high against the hills or drowsing among fields of artichoke and sumac and prickly pear.

To one familiar with modern Sicilian railway trains the journey eastward from Palermo promises no considerable discomfort, but twenty-five years ago it was not to be lightly undertaken—not to be undertaken at all, in fact, without an unusual equipment of patience and a resignation entirely lacking in the average Anglo-Saxon. It was not surprising, therefore, that Norvin Blake, as the hours dragged along, should remark less and less upon the beauties of the island and more and more upon the medieval condition of the rickety railroad coach in which he was shaken and buffeted about. He shifted himself to an easier position upon the seat and lighted a cheroot; for although this was his first glimpse of Sicily, he had watched the same villages come and go all through a long, hot afternoon, had seen the same groves of orange and lemon and dust-green olive-trees, the same fields of Barbary figs, the same rose-grown garden spots, until he was heartily tired of them all. He felt at liberty to smoke, for the only other occupant of the compartment was a young priest in flowing mantle and silk beaver hat.

Finding that Blake spoke Italian remarkably well for a foreigner, the priest had shown an earnest desire for closer acquaintance and now plied him eagerly with questions, hanging upon his answers with a childlike intensity of gaze which at first had been amusing.

"And so the Signore has traveled all the way from Paris to attend the wedding at Terranova. Veramente! That is a great journey. Many wonderful adventures befell you, perhaps. Eh?" The priest's little eyes gleamed from his full cheeks, and he edged forward until his knees crowded Blake's. It was evident that he anticipated a thrilling tale and did not intend to be disappointed.

"It was very tiresome, that's all, and the beggars at Naples nearly tore me asunder."

"Incredible! You will tell me about it?"

"There's nothing to tell. These European trains cannot compare with ours."

Evidently discouraged at this lack of response, the questioner tried a new line of approach.

"The Signore is perhaps related to our young Conte?" he suggested. "And yet that can scarcely be, for you are Inglese—"

"Americano."

"Indeed?"

"Martel and I are close friends, however. We met in Paris. We are almost like brothers."

"Truly! I have heard that he spends much time studying to be a great painter. It is very strange, but many of our rich people leave Sicily to reside elsewhere. As for me, I cannot understand it."

"Martel left when his father was killed. He says this country is behind the times, and he prefers to be out in the world where there is life and where things progress."

But the priest showed by a blank stare that he did not begin to grasp the meaning of this statement. He shook his head. "He was always a wild lad. Now as to the Signorina Ginini, who is to be his beautiful Contessa, she loves Sicily. She has spent most of her life here among us."

With a flash of interest Blake inquired: "What is she like? Martel has spoken of her a great many times, but one can't place much dependence on a lover's description."

"Bellissima!" the priest sighed, and rolled his eyes eloquently. "You have never seen anything like her, I assure you. She is altogether too beautiful. If I had my way all the beautiful women would be placed in a convent where no man could see them. Then there would be no fighting and no flirting, and the plain women could secure husbands. Beautiful women are dangerous. She is rich, too."

"Of course! That's what Martel says, and that is exactly the way he says it. But describe her."

"Oh, I have never seen her! I merely know that she is very rich and very beautiful." He went off into a number of rapturous "issimas!" "Now as for the Conte, I know him like a book. I know his every thought."

"But Martel has been abroad for ten years, and he has only returned within a month."

"To be sure, but I come from the village this side of San Sebastiano, and my second cousin Ricardo is his uomo d'affare—his overseer. It is a very great position of trust which Ricardo occupies, for I must tell you that he attends to the leasing of the entire estate during the Conte's absence in France, or wherever it is he draws those marvelous pictures. Ricardo collects the rents." With true Sicilian naivete the priest added: "He is growing rich! Beato lui! He for one will not need to go to your golden America. Is it true, Signore, that in America any one who wishes may be rich?"

"Quite true," smiled the young man. "Even our beggars are rich."

The priest wagged his head knowingly. "My mother's cousin, Alfio Amato, he is an American. You know him?"

"I'm afraid not."

"But surely—he has been in America these five years. A tall, dark fellow with fine teeth. Think! He is such a liar any one would remember him. Ebbene! *He* wrote that there were poor people in America as here, but we knew him too well to believe him."

"I suppose every one knows about the marriage?"

"Oh, indeed! It will unite two old families—two rich families. You know the Savigni are rich also. Even before the children were left as orphans it was settled that they should be married. What a great fortune that will make for Ricardo to oversee! Then, perhaps, he will be more generous to his own people. He is a hard man in money matters, and a man of action also; he does not allow flies to sit upon his nose. He sent his own daughter Lucrezia to Terranova when the

Contessa was still a child, and what is the result? Lucrezia is no longer a servant. Indeed no, she is more like a sister to the Signorina. At the marriage no doubt she will receive a fine present, and Ricardo as well. He is as silent as a Mafioso, but he thinks."

Young Blake stretched his tired muscles, yawning.

"I'm sorry Martel couldn't marry in France; this has been a tedious trip."

"It was the Contessa's wish, then, to be wed in Sicily?"

"I believe she insisted. And Martel agreed that it was the proper thing to do, since they are both Sicilians. He was determined also that I should be present to share his joy, and so here I am. Between you and me, I envy him his lot so much that it almost spoils for me the pleasure of this unique journey."

"You are an original!" murmured the priest, admiringly, but it was evident that his thirst for knowledge of the outside world was not to be so easily quenched, for he began to question his traveling companion closely regarding America, Paris, the journey thence, the ship which bore him to Palermo, and a dozen other subjects upon which his active mind preyed. He was full of the gossip of the countryside, moreover, and Norvin learned much of interest about Sicily and the disposition of her people. One phenomenon to which the good man referred with the extremest wonder was Blake's intimacy with a Sicilian nobleman. How an American signore had become such a close friend of the illustrious Conte, who was almost a stranger, even to his own people, seemed very puzzling indeed, until Norvin explained that they had been together almost constantly during the past three years.

"We met quite by chance, but we quickly became friends—what in my country we call chums—and we have been inseparable ever since."

"And you, then, are also a great artist?"

Blake laughed at the indirect compliment to his friend.

"I am not an artist at all. I have been exiled to Europe for three years, upon my mother's orders. She has her own ideas regarding a man's education and wishes me to acquire a Continental polish. My ability to tell you all this shows that I have at least made progress with the languages, although I have doubts about the practical value of anything else I have learned. Martel has taught me Italian; I have taught him English. We use both, and sometimes we understand each other. My three years are up now, and once I have seen my good friend safely married I shall return to America and begin the serious business of life."

"You are then in business? My mother's cousin, Alfio Amato, is likewise a business man. He deals in fruit. Beware of him, for he would sell you rotten oranges and swear by the saints that they were excellent."

"Like Martel, I have land which I lease. I am, or I will be, a cotton-planter."

This opened a new field of inquiry for the priest, who was making the most of it when the train drew into a station and was stormed by a horde of chattering country folk. The platform swarmed with vividly dressed women, most of whom carried bundles wrapped up in variegated handkerchiefs, and all of whom were tremendously excited at the prospect of travel. Lean-visaged, swarthy men peered forth from the folds of shawls or from beneath shapeless caps of many colors; a pair of carabinieri idled past, a soldier in jaunty feathered hat posed before the contadini. Dogs, donkeys, fowls added their clamor to the high-pitched voices.

Twilight had settled and lights were kindling in the village, while the heights above were growing black against a rose-pink and mother-of-pearl sky. The air was cool and fragrant with the odor of growing things and the open sea glowed with a subdued, pulsating fire.

The capo stazione rushed madly back and forth striving by voice and gesture to hasten the movements of his passengers.

"Partenza! Pronto!" he cried, then blew furiously upon his bugle.

After a series of shudders and convulsions the train began to hiss and clank and finally crept on into the twilight, while the priest sat knee to knee with his companion and resumed his endless questioning.

It was considerably after dark when Norvin Blake alighted at San Sebastiano, to be greeted effusively by a young man of about his own age who came charging through the gloom and embraced him with a great hug.

"So! At last you come!" Savigno cried. "I have been here these three hours eating my heart out, and every time I inquired of that head of a cabbage in yonder he said, 'Pazienza! The world was not made in a day!'

"'But when? When?' I kept repeating, and he could only assure me that your train was approaching with the speed of the wind. The saints in heaven—even the superintendent of the railway himself—could not tell the exact hour of its arrival, which, it seems, is never twice the same. And now, yourself? You are well?"

"Never better. And you? But there is no need to ask. You look disgustingly contented. One would think you were already married."

Martel Savigno showed a row of even, white teeth beneath his military mustache and clapped his friend affectionately on the back.

"It is good to be among my own people. I find, after all, that I am a Sicilian. But let me tell you, that train is not always late. Once, seven years ago, it arrived upon the moment. There were no passengers at the station to meet it, however, so it was forced to wait, and now, in order to keep our good-will it always arrives thus."

The Count was a well-set-up youth of an alert and active type, tall, dark, and vivacious, with a skin as smooth as a girl's. He had an impulsive, energetic nature that seldom left him in repose, and hence the contrast between the two men was marked, for Blake was of a more serious cast of features and possessed a decidedly Anglo-Saxon reserve. He was much the heavier in build, also, which detracted from his height and robbed him of that elegance which distinguished the young Sicilian. Yet the two made a fine-looking pair as they stood face to face in the yellow glare of the station lights.

"What the deuce made me agree to this trip, I don't know," the American declared. "It was vile. I've been carsick, seasick, homesick—"

"And all for poor, lovesick Martel!" The Count laughed. "Ah, but if you knew how glad I am to see you!"

"Really? Then that squares it." Blake spoke with that indefinable undernote which creeps into men's voices when friend meets friend. "I've been lost without you, too. I was quite ashamed of myself."

The Count turned to a middle-aged man who had remained in the shadows, saying: "This is Ricardo Ferara, my good right hand, of whom you have heard me speak." The overseer raised his hat, and Blake took his hand, catching a glimpse of a grizzled face and a stiff mop of iron-gray hair. "You will see to Signore Blake's baggage,

Ricardo. Michele! Ippolito!" the Count called. "The carretta, quickly! And now, caro Norvin, for the last leg of your journey. Will you ride in the cart or on horseback? It is not far, but the roads are steep."

"Horseback, by all means. My muscles need exercise."

The young men mounted a pair of compact Sicilian horses, which were held by still another man in the street behind the depot, and set off up the winding road which climbed to the village above. Blake regretted the lateness of the hour, which prevented him from gaining an adequate idea of his surroundings. He could see, however, that they were picturesque, for San Sebastiano lay in a tiny step hewed out of the mountain-side and was crowded into one street overlooking the railway far below and commanding a view of the sea toward the Calabrian coast. As the riders clattered through the poorly lighted village, Blake saw the customary low-roofed houses, the usual squalid side-streets, more like steep lanes than thoroughfares, and heard the townspeople pronouncing the name of the Count of Martinello, while the ever-present horde of urchins fled from their path. A beggar appeared beside his stirrup, crying, "I die of hunger, your worship." But the fellow ran with surprising vigor and manifested a degree of endurance quite unexampled in a starving man. A glimpse of these, and then the lights were left behind and they were moving swiftly upward and into the mountains, skirting walls of stone over which was wafted the perfume of many flowers, passing fragrant groves of orange and lemon trees, and less fragrant cottages, the contents of which were bared to their eyes with utter lack of modesty. They disturbed herds of drowsy cattle and goats lying at the roadside, and all the time they continued to climb, until their horses heaved and panted.

The American's impressions of this entire journey, from the time of his leaving Paris up to the present moment, had been hurried and unreal, for he had made close connections at Rome, at Naples, and at Palermo. Having the leisurely deliberateness of the American Southerner, he disliked haste and confusion above all things. He had an intense desire, therefore, to come to anchor and to adjust himself to his surroundings.

As Martel chattered along, telling of his many doings, Blake noted that Ricardo and the man who had held the horses were following closely Then, as the cavalcade paused at length to breathe their mounts, he saw that both men carried rifles.

"Why! We look like an American sheriff's posse, Martel," said he. "Do all Sicilian bridegrooms travel with an armed escort?"

Savigno showed a trace of hesitation. "The nights are dark; the country is wild."

"But, my dear boy, this country is surely old enough to be safe. Why, Sicily was civilized long before my country was even heard of. All sorts of ancient gods and heroes used to live here, I am told, and I supposed Diana had killed all the game long ago."

He laughed, but Savigno did not join him, and a moment later they were under way again.

After a brief gallop they drew up at a big, dark house, hidden among the deeper shadows of many trees, and in answer to Martel's shout a wide door was flung back; then by the light which streamed forth from it they dismounted and made their way up a flight of stone steps. Once inside, Savigno exclaimed:

"Welcome to my birthplace! A thousand welcomes!" Seizing Norvin by the shoulders, he whirled him about. "Let me see you once. Ah! I am glad you made this sacrifice for me, for I need you above all men." His eyes, though bright with affection, were grave—something unusual in him—and the other inquired, quickly:

"There's nothing wrong, I hope?"

Savigno tossed his head and smiled.

"Wrong! What could be wrong with me now that you are here? No! All is quite right, but I have been accursed with lonesomeness. Something was lacking, It was you, caro mio. Now, however, I am the most contented of mortals. But you must be famished, so I will show you to your room at once. Francesca has provided a feast for us, I assure you."

"Give me a moment to look around. So this is the castello? Jove! It's ripping!"

Blake found himself in a great hall similar to many he had seen in his European wanderings, but ruder and older by far. He judged the castello to be of Norman build, but remodeled to suit the taste of the Savigni. To the right, through an open door, he saw a large room where a fat Sicilian woman was laying the table; to the left was a drawing-room lighted only by a fire of fagots in a huge, black fireplace, the furniture showing curiously distorted in the long shadows. Other rooms opened towards the rear, and he realized that the old place was very large. It was unkempt also, and showed the lack of a woman's hand.

"You exaggerate!" said Savigno. "After Paris the castello will seem very mean. We Siciliani do not live in grand style, and, besides, I have spent practically no time here, since my father (may the saints receive him) left me free to wander. The place has been closed; the old servants have gone; it is dilapidated."

"On the contrary, it's just the sort of place it should be—venerable and overflowing with romance. You must rule like a medieval baron. Why, you could sell this woodwork to some millionaire countryman of mine for enough to realize a fortune."

"Per Dio! If taxes are not reduced I shall be forced to some such expedient," the Count laughed. "It was my mother's home, it is my birthplace, so I love it—even though I neglect it. As you perceive, it is high time I took a wife. But enough! If you are lacking in appetite, I am not, and Francesca is an unbearable tyrant when her meals grow cold."

He led his friend up the wide stairs and left him to prepare for supper.

"And so this ends it all," said Blake, as the two young men lounged in the big, empty drawing-room later that evening. They had dined and gossiped as only friends of their age can gossip, had relived their adventures of the past three years, and still were loath to part, even for sleep.

"How so?" queried Savigno. "You speak of marriage as if it were dissolution."

"It might as well be, so far as the other fellow is concerned."

"Nonsense! I shall not change."

"Oh, yes, you will! Besides, I am returning to America."

"Even so, we are rich; we shall travel; we shall meet frequently. You will come to Sicily. Perhaps the Contessa and I may even go to America. Friendship such as ours laughs at the leagues."

But Blake was pessimistic. "Perhaps she won't like me."

Martel laughed at this.

"Impossible! She is a woman, she has eyes, she will see you as I see you. More than that, I have told her that she must love you."

"Then that does settle it! You have hung the crepe on our future intimacy, for good and all. She will instruct your cook to put a spider in my dumpling or to do away with me by some characteristic Sicilian method."

Martel seemed puzzled by the Americanism of this speech, but Norvin merely smiled and changed to Italian.

"Do you really love her?" he asked.

"Of course! Since I was a boy so high I have known we would marry. She adores me, she is young, she is beautiful, she is—rich!"

"In Heaven's name don't use that tone in speaking of her wealth. You make me doubt you."

"No, no!" The Count smiled. "It would be the same if she were a peasant girl. We shall be so happy—oh, there is no expressing how happy we intend being."

"I've no doubt. And that makes it quite certain to end our comradeship."

"You croak like a raven!" declared the Sicilian. "What has soured you?"

"Nothing. I am a wise young man, that's all. You see, happiness is all-sufficient; it needs nothing to complete itself. It is a wall beyond which the owner does not care to wander, so, when you are quite happy with the new Countess, you will forget your friends of unmarried days."

"Would you then have me unhappily married?"

"By no means. I am full of regrets at losing you, nothing more."

"It is plain, then, that you also must marry. Is there no admirable American lady?"

"Any quantity of them, but I don't care much for women except in an impersonal sort of way, or perhaps I don't attract them. I might enjoy falling in love if it were not such a tedious process."

"It is not necessarily tedious. One may love with the suddenness of an explosion. I have done so, many times."

"I know you have, but you are a Sicilian; we go about such things in a dignified and respectable manner. Love is a serious matter with us. We don't explode."

"Yes. When you love, you marry; and you marry in the same way you buy a farm. But we have blood in our veins and lime in our bones. I have loved many women to distraction; there is only one whom I would marry."

Ricardo entered at the moment, and the Count arose with a word of apology to his guest. He spoke earnestly with his overseer, but, as they were separated from him by the full width of the great room, Blake overheard no more than a word now and then. They were speaking in the Sicilian dialect, moreover, which was unfamiliar to him, yet he caught the mention of Ippolito, one of the men who had met him at the station, also of an orange-grove, and the word "Mafioso." Then he heard Martel say:

"The shells for the new rifle—Ippolito is a bad shot—take plenty."

When Ricardo had gone and the Count had returned to his seat, Norvin fancied he detected once more that grave look he had surprised in his friend's countenance upon their arrival at the castello.

"What were you telling Ricardo about rifles and cartridges?" he inquired.

"Eh? It was nothing. We are forced to guard our oranges; there are thieves about. I have been too long away from Martinello."

Later, as Norvin Blake composed himself to sleep he wondered idly if Martel had told him the whole truth. He recalled again the faint, grave lines that had gathered about the Count's eyes, where there had never been aught but wrinkles of merriment, and he recalled also that word "Mafioso." It conjured memories of certain tales he had heard of Sicilian outlawry and brigandage, and of that evil, shadowy society of "Friends" which he understood dominated this island. There was a story about the old Count's death also, but Martel had never told him much. Norvin tried to remember what it was, but sleep was heavy upon him and he soon gave up.

# II.
# A CONFESSION AND A PROMISE

Norvin Blake slept soundly, as befitted a healthy young man with less than the usual number of cares upon his mind, and, notwithstanding the fact that he had retired at a late hour, somewhat worn by his journey, he awoke earlier than usual. Still lacking an adequate idea of his surroundings, he arose and, flinging back the blinds of his window, looked out upon a scene which set him to dressing eagerly.

The big front door of the hall below was barred when he came down, and only yielded to his efforts with a clanging which would have awakened any one except Martel, letting him out upon a well-kept terrace beneath which the hills fell away in majestic sweeps and curves to the coast-line far beneath.

It was a true Sicilian morning, filled with a dazzling glory of color, and although it was not early, from a countryman's point of view, the dewy freshness had not entirely faded, and rosy tints still lingered in the valleys and against the Calabrian coast in the distance. An odor of myrtle and jessamine came from a garden beneath the outer terrace wall, and on either side of the manor rose wooded hills the lower slopes of which were laid out in vineyards and groves of citrus fruits.

Having in full measure the normal man's unaffected appreciation of nature, Blake found himself wondering how Martel could ever leave this spot for the artificialities of Paris. The Count was amply able to live where he chose, and it was no love for art which had kept him in France these many years. On the contrary, they had both recognized the mediocrity of his talent and had often joked about it. It was perhaps no more than a youthful restlessness and craving for excitement, he concluded.

Knowing that his luxurious host would not be stirring for another hour, he set out to explore the place at his leisure, and in time came around to the stables and outhouses. It is not the front of any residence which shows its real character, any more than a woman's true nature is displayed by her Sunday attire. Norvin made friends with a surly, stiff-haired dog, then with a patriarchal old goat which he found grazing atop a wall, and at last he encountered Francesca bearing a bundle of fagots upon her head.

She was in a bad temper, it appeared, for in answer to his cheerful greeting she began to revile the names of Ippolito and Michele.

"Lazy pigs!" she cried, fiercely. "Is it not sufficient that old Francesca should bare her bones and become a shadow with the cares of the household? Is it not sufficient that she performs the labor of twenty in caring for the padrone? No! Is it not the devil's task to prepare the many outlandish delicacies he learned to eat in his travels? Yes! Ha! What of that! She must also perform the duties of an ass and bear wood for the fires! And what, think you, those two young giants are doing all the day? Sleeping, Si'or! Up all night, asleep all day! A fine business. And Francesca with a broken back!"

"I'll carry your wood," he offered, at which the mountainous old woman stared at him as if she did not in the least comprehend his words. Although her burden was enough to tax a man's strength, she balanced it easily upon her head and made no move to go.

"And the others! May they all be blinded—Attilio, Gaspare, Roberto! The hangman will get them, surely. Briganti, indeed!" She snorted like a horse. "May Belisario Cardi roast them over these very fagots." Slowly she moved her head from side to side while the bundle swayed precariously. "It is a bad business, Si'or. The padrone is mad to resist. You may tell him he is quite mad. Mark me, Ricardo knows that no good will come of it, but he is like a bull when he is angry. He lowers his head and sees blood. Veramente, it is a bad business and we shall all lose our ears." She moved off majestically, her eyes rolling in her fat cheeks, her lips moving; leaving the American to speculate as to what her evil prediction had to do with Ippolito and the firewood.

He was still smiling at her anger when Ippolito himself, astride a horse, came clattering into the courtyard and dismounted stiffly, giving him a good morning with a wide yawn.

"Corpo di Baccho!" exclaimed the rider. "I shall sleep for a century." He stretched luxuriously and, unslinging a gun from his shoulder, leaned it against the wall. Blake was surprised to find it a late model of an American repeating rifle. "Francesca!" he called loudly. "Madonna mia, I am famished!"

"Francesca was here a moment ago," Norvin volunteered. "In a frightful temper, too."

"Just so! It was the wood, I presume." He scowled. "One cannot be in ten places unless he is in ten pieces. I am glad to be here, and not here and there."

"Well, she wants you roasted by some fellow named Cardi—"

"Eh? What?" Ippolito started, jerking the horse's head by the bridle rein, through which he had thrust his arm. "What is this?"

"Belisario Cardi, I believe she said. I don't know him."

The Sicilian muttered an oath and disappeared into the stable; he was still scowling when he emerged.

Prompted by a feeling that he was close to something mysterious, Blake tried to sound the fellow.

"You are abroad early," he suggested.

But Ippolito seemed in no mood for conversation, and merely replied:

"Si, Signore, quite early."

He was a lean, swarthy youth, square-jawed and well put up. Although his clothes were poor, he wore them with a certain grace and moved like a man who is sure of himself.

"Did you see any robbers?"

"Robbers?" Ippolito's look was one of quick suspicion. "Who has ever seen a robber?"

"Come, come! I heard the Count and Ricardo talking. You have been away, among the orange-groves, all night. Am I right?"

"You are right."

"Tell me, is it common thieves or outlaws whom you watch? I have heard about your brigands."

"Ippolito!" came the harsh voice of Ricardo, who at that moment appeared around the corner of the stable. "In the kitchen you will find food."

Ippolito bowed to the American and departed, his rifle beneath his arm.

Blake turned his attention to the overseer, for his mind, once filled with an idea, was not easily satisfied. But Ricardo would give him no information. He raised his bushy, gray eyebrows at the American's question.

"Brigands? Ippolito is a great liar."

Seeing the angry sparkle in the old fellow's eyes, Norvin hastened to say:

"He told me nothing, I assure you."

"Thieves, yes! We have ladri here, as elsewhere. Sometimes it is well to take precautions."

"But Francesca was quite excited, and I heard you and Martel mention La Mafia last night," Blake persisted. "I see you all go armed. I am naturally curious. I thought you might be in trouble with the society."

"Children's tales!" said Ricardo, gruffly. "There is no society of La Mafia."

"Oh, see here! We have it even in my own country. The New Orleans papers have been full of stories about the Mala Vita, the Mafia, or whatever you choose to call it. There is a big Italian population there, you know, and they are causing our police a great deal of worry. I live in Louisiana, so I ought to know. We understand it's an offshoot of the Sicilian Mafia."

"In Naples I hear there is a Camorra. But this is Sicily. We have no societies."

"Nevertheless, I heard you say something about 'Mafioso' last night," Blake insisted.

"Perhaps," grudgingly admitted the overseer. "But La Mafia is not a man, not a society, as you say. It is—" He made a wide gesture. "It is all Sicily. You do not understand."

"No, I do not."

"Very well. One does not speak of it. Would the Signore care to see the horses?"

"Thank you, yes."

The two went into the stables together, and Blake for the time gave up the hope of learning anything further about Sicilian brigandage. Nor did Martel show any willingness to enlighten him when he tentatively introduced the subject at breakfast, but laughingly turned the conversation into another channel.

"To-day you shall see the star of my life," he declared. "Be prepared to worship as all men do."

"Assuredly."

"And promise you will not fall in love."

"Is that why you discouraged my coming until a week before your wedding? Really, if she is all you claim, we might have been such delightful enemies."

"Enemies are never that," said the Count, gravely.

"I know men in my country who cherish their enemies like friends. They seem to enjoy them tremendously, until one or the other has passed on to glory. Even then they are highly spoken of."

"I am impatient for you to see her. She, of course, has many preparations to make, for the wedding-day is almost here; but it is arranged that we are to dine there to-night with her and her aunt, the Donna Teresa. Ah, Norvin mine, seven days separate me from Paradise. You can judge of my ecstasy. The hours creep, the moments are leaden. Each night when I retire, I feel faithless in allowing sleep to rob my thoughts of her. When I awake it is with the consolation that more of those miserable hours have crept away. I am like a man insane."

"I am beginning to think you really are so."

"Diamine! Wait! You have not seen her. We are to be married by a bishop."

"No doubt that will insure your happiness."

"A marriage like this does not occur every day. It will be an event, I tell you."

"And you're sure I won't be in the way this evening?"

"No, no! It is arranged. She is waiting—expecting you. She knows you already. This morning, however, you will amuse yourself—will you not?—for I must ride down to San Sebastiano and meet the colonel of carabinieri from Messina."

"Certainly. Don't mind me."

Martel hesitated an instant, then explained:

"It is a matter of business. One of my farm-hands is in prison."

"Indeed! What for?"

"Oh, it is nothing. He killed a fellow last week."

"Jove! What a peaceful, pastoral place you have here! I arrive to be met by an armed guard, I hear talk of Mafiosi, men ride out at night with rifles, and old women predict unspeakable evil. What is all the mystery?"

"Nonsense! There is no mystery. Do you think I would drag you, my best friend, into danger?" Savigno's lips were smiling, but he awaited an answer with some restraint. "That would not be quite the—quite a nice thing to do, would it?"

"So, that's it! Now I know you have something on your mind. And it must be of considerable importance or you would have told me before this."

"You are right," the Count suddenly declared, "although I hoped you would not discover it. I might have known. But I suppose it is better to make a clean breast of it now. I have enemies, my friend, and I assure you I do not cherish them."

"The Countess Margherita is a famous beauty, eh? Well! It is not remarkable that you should have rivals."

"No, no. This has nothing to do with her, unless our approaching marriage has roused them to make a demonstration. Have you ever heard of—Belisario Cardi?"

"Not until this morning. Who is he?"

"I would give much to know. If you had asked me a month ago, I would have said he is an imaginary character, used to frighten people—a modern Fra Diavolo, a mere name with which to inspire terror—for nobody has ever seen him. Now, however, he seems real enough, and I learn that the carabinieri believe in his existence." Martel pushed back the breakfast dishes and, leaning his elbows upon the table, continued, after a pause: "To you Sicily is all beauty and peace and fragrance; she is old and therefore civilized, so you think. Everything you have seen so far is reasonably modern, eh?" He showed his white teeth as Blake assured him:

"It's the most peaceful, restful spot I ever saw."

"You see nothing but the surface. Sicily is much what she was in my grandfather's time. You have inquired about La Mafia. Well, there is such a thing. It killed my father. It forced me to give up my home and be an exile." At Norvin's exclamation of astonishment, he nodded. "There's a long story behind it which you could not appreciate without knowing my father and the character of our Sicilian people, for, after all, Sicilian character constitutes La Mafia. It is no sect, no cult, no secret body of assassins, highwaymen, and robbers, as you foreigners imagine; it is a national hatred of authority, an individual expression of superiority to the law."

"In our own New Orleans we are beginning to talk of the Mafia, but with us it is a mysterious organization of Italian criminals. We treat it as somewhat of a joke."

"Be not so sure. Some day it may dominate your American cities as it does all Sicily."

"Still I don't understand. You say it is an organization and yet it is not; it terrorizes a whole island and yet you say it is no more than your national character. It must have a head, it must have arms."

"It has no head, or, rather, it has many heads. It is not a band. It is the Sicilian intolerance of restraint, the individual's sense of superiority to moral, social, and political law. It is the freemasonry that results from this common resistance to authority. It is an idea, not an institution; it is Sicily's curse and that which makes her impossible of government. I do not mean to deny that we have outlawry and brigandage; they are merely the most violent demonstrations of La Mafia. It afflicts the cities; it is a tyranny in the country districts. La Mafia taxes us with blackmail, it saddles us with a great force of carabinieri, it gives food and drink and life to men like Belisario Cardi. Every landholder, every man of property, contributes to its support. You still do not understand, but you will as I go along. As an instance of its workings, all fruit-growers hereabouts are obliged to maintain watchmen, in addition to their regular employees. Otherwise their groves will be robbed. These guards are Mafiosi. Let us say that one of us opposes this monopoly. What happens? He loses his crop in a night; his trees are cut down. Should he appeal to the law for protection, he is regarded as a weakling, a man of no spirit. This is but one small example of the workings of La Mafia; as a matter of fact, it permeates the political, the business, and the social life of the whole island. Knowing the impotence of the law to protect any one, peaceable citizens shield the criminals. They perjure themselves to acquit a Mafioso rather than testify against him and thus incur the certainty of some fearful vengeance. Should the farmer persist in his independence, something ends his life, as in my father's case. The whole country is terrorized by a conspiracy of a few bold and masterful men. It is unbearable. There are, of course, Capi-Mafia—leaders—whose commands are enforced, but there is no single well-organized society. It is a great interlocking system built upon patronage, friendship, and the peculiar Sicilian character."

"Now I think I begin to understand."

"My father was not strong enough to throw off the yoke and it meant his death. I was too young to take his place, but now that I am a man I intend to play a man's part, and I have served notice. It means a battle, but I shall win."

To Martel's hasty and very incomplete sketch of the hidden influences of Sicilian life Blake listened with the greatest interest, noting the grave determination that had settled upon his friend; yet he could scarcely bring himself to accept an explanation that seemed so far-fetched. The whole theory of the Mafia struck him as grotesque and theatrical.

"And one man has already been killed, you say?" he asked.

"Yes, I discharged all the watchmen whom I knew to be Mafiosi. It caused a commotion, I can tell you, and no little uneasiness among the country people, who love me even if, to them, I have been a more or less imaginary person since my father's death. Naturally they warned me to desist in this mad policy of independence. A week ago one of my campieri, Paolo—he who is now in prison—surprised a fellow hacking down my orange-trees and shot him. The miscreant proved to be a certain Galli, whom I had discharged. He left a family, I regret to say, but his reputation was bad. Notwithstanding all this, Paolo is still in prison despite my utmost efforts. The machinery of the Mafia is in motion, they will perjure witnesses, they will spend money in any quantity to convict my poor Paolo. Heaven knows what the result will be."

"And where does this bogey-man enter—this Belisario Cardi?"

"I have had a letter from him."

"Really?"

"It is in the hands of the carabinieri, hence this journey of my friend, Colonel Neri, from Messina."

"What did the letter say?"

"It demanded a great sum of money, with my life as the penalty for refusal. It was signed by Cardi; there was no mistaking the name. If it had been from Narcone, for instance, I would have paid no attention to it, for he is no more than a cattle-thief. But Belisario Cardi! My boy, you don't appreciate the significance of that name. I should not care to fall into his hands, I assure you, and have my feet roasted over a slow fire—"

"Good heavens!" Norvin cried, rising abruptly from his chair. "You don't really mean he's that sort?"

"As a matter of fact," the Count reassured his guest, "I don't believe in his existence at all. It is merely a name to be used upon occasion. But as for the punishment, that is perhaps the least I might expect if I were so unfortunate as to be captured."

"Why, this can't be! Do you realize that this is the year 1886? Such things are not possible any longer. In your father's time—yes."

"All things are possible in Sicily," smiled Savigno. "We are a century behind the times. But, caro mio, I did wrong to tell you—"

"No, no."

"I shall come to no harm, believe me. I am known to be young, rich, and my marriage is but a few days off. What more natural, therefore, than for some Mafioso to try to frighten me and profit by the dreaded name of Cardi? I am a stranger here in my own birthplace. When I become better known, there will be no more feeble attempts at blackmail. Other landholders have maintained their independence, and I shall do the same, for an enemy who fears to fight openly is a coward, and I am in the right."

"I am glad I came. I shall be glad, too, when you are married and safely off on your wedding journey."

"I feared to tell you all this lest you should think I had no right to bring you here at such a time—"

"Don't be an utter idiot, Martel."

"You are an American; you have your own way of looking at things. Of course, if anything should happen—if ill-fortune should overtake me before the marriage—"

"See here! If there is the slightest danger, the faintest possibility, you ought to go away, as you did before," Norvin declared, positively.

"I am no longer a child. I am to be married a week hence. Wild horses could not drag me away."

"You could postpone it—explain it to the Countess—"

"There is no necessity; there is no cause for alarm, even. All the same, I feel much easier with you here. Margherita has relatives, to be sure, but they are—well, I have no confidence in them. In the remote possibility that the worst should come, you could look out for her, and I am sure you would. Am I right?"

"Of course you are."

"And now let us think of something pleasanter. We won't talk of it any more, eh?"

"I'm perfectly willing to let it drop. You know I would do anything for you or yours, so we needn't discuss that point any further."

"Good!" Martel rose and with his customary display of affection flung an arm about his friend's shoulders. "And now Ricardo is waiting to go to San Sebastiano, so you must amuse yourself for an hour or two. I have had the billiard-table recovered, and the cushions are fairly good. You will find books in the library, perhaps a portfolio of my earlier drawings—"

"Billiards!" exclaimed the American, fervently, whereupon the Count laughed.

"Till I return, then, a riverderci!" He seized his hat and strode out of the room.

# III.
# THE GOLDEN GIRL

Shortly after the heat of the day had begun to subside the two friends set out for Terranova. Ricardo accompanied them—it seemed he went everywhere with Martel—following at a distance which allowed the young men freedom to talk, his watchful eyes scanning the roadside as if even in the light of day he feared some lurking danger.

The prospect of seeing his fiancee acted like wine upon Savigno, and from his exuberant spirits it was evident that he had completely forgotten his serious talk at the breakfast table. His disposition was mercurial, and if he had ever known real forebodings they were forgotten now.

It was a splendid ride along a road which wound in serpentine twinings high above the sea, now breasting ridges bare of all save rock and spurge, and now dipping into valleys shaded by flowering trees and cloyed with the scent of blooms. It meandered past farms, in haphazard fashion, past vineyards and gardens and groves of mandarin, lime, and lemon, finally toiling up over a bold chestnut-studded shoulder of the range, where Blake drew in to enjoy the scene. A faint haze, impalpable as the memory of dreams, lay over the land, the sea was azure, the mountains faintly purple. A gleam of white far below showed Terranova, and when the American had voiced his appreciation the three horsemen plunged downward, leaving a rolling cloud of yellow dust behind them.

The road from here on led through a wild and somewhat forbidding country, broken by ravines and watercourses and quite densely wooded with thickets which swept upward into the interior as far as the eye could reach; but in the neighborhood of Terranova the land blossomed and flowered again as on the other side of the mountains.

Leaving the main road by a driveway, the three horsemen swung through spacious grounds and into a courtyard behind the house, where an old man came shuffling slowly forward, his wrinkled face puckered into a smile of welcome.

"Ha! Aliandro!" cried the Count. "What do I see? The rheumatism is gone at last, grazie Dio!"

Aliandro's loose lips parted over his toothless gums and he mumbled:

"Illustrissimo, the accursed affliction is worse."

"Impossible! Then why these capers? My dear Aliandro, you are shamming.

Why, you came leaping like a goat."

"As God is my judge, carino, I can sleep only in the sun. It is like the tortures of the devil, and my bones creak like a gate."

"And yet each day I declare to myself: 'Aliandro, that rascal, is growing younger as the hours go by. It is well we are not rivals in love or I should be forced to hate him!'" The old man chuckled and beamed upon Savigno, who proceeded to make Norvin known.

Aliandro's face had once been long and pointed, but with the loss of teeth and the other mysterious shrinkages of time it had shortened until in repose the chin and the nose seemed to meet like the points of calipers. When he moved his jaws his whole countenance lengthened magically, as if made of some substance more elastic than flesh. It stretched and shortened rapidly now, in the most extraordinary fashion, for the Count had a knack of pleasing people.

"And where are the ladies?" Savigno inquired.

Aliandro cocked a watery eye at the heavens and replied:

"They will be upon the loggiato at this hour, Illustrissimo. The Donna Teresa will have a book." He squinted respectfully at a small note which Martel handed him, then inquired, "Do you wish change?"

"Not at all. It is yours for your courtesy."

"Grazie! Grazie! A million thanks." The old fellow made off with surprising agility.

"What a sham he is!" the Count laughed, as he and Norvin walked on around the house. "He will do no labor, and yet the Contessa supports him in idleness. There is a Mafioso for you! He has been a brigand, a robber. He is, to this day, as you see. Margherita has an army of such people who impose upon her. Every time I am here I tip him. Every time he receives it with the same words."

Although the country-seat of the Ginini was known as a castello, it was more in the nature of a comfortable and pretentious villa. It had dignity, however, and drowsed upon a commanding eminence fronted by a splendid terraced lawn which one beheld through clumps of flowering shrubs and well-tended trees. Here and there among the foliage gleamed statuary, and the musical purl of a fountain fell upon the ear.

As the young men mounted to the loggiato, or covered gallery, a delicate, white-haired Italian lady arose and came to meet them.

"Ah, Martel, my dear boy! We have been expecting you," she cried.

It was the Donna Teresa Fazello, and she turned a sweet face upon Mattel's friend, bidding him welcome to Terranova with charming courtesy. She was still exchanging with him the pleasantries customary upon first meetings when he heard the Count exclaim softly, and, looking up, saw him bowing low over a girl's hands. Her back was half turned toward Norvin, but although he had not seen her features clearly, he felt a great surprise. His preconceived notion of her had been all wrong; It seemed, for she was not dark—on the contrary, she was as tawny as a lioness. Her hair, of which there was an abundance, was not the ordinary Saxon yellow, but iridescent, as if burned by the fierce heat of a tropical sun. The neck and cheeks were likewise golden, or was it the light from her splendid crown?

He was still staring at her when she turned and came forward to give him her hand, thus allowing her full glory to flash upon him.

"Welcome!" she said, in a voice as low-pitched as a cello string, and her lover, watching eagerly for some sign from his friend, smiled delightedly at the emotion he saw leap up in Norvin's face. That young man was quite unconscious of Martel's espionage—unconscious of everything, in fact, save the splendid creature who stood smiling at him as if she had known him all her days. His first impression, that she was all golden, all gleaming, like a flame, did not leave him; for the same warm tints that were in her hair were likewise present in her cheeks, her neck, her hands. It was like the hue which underlies old ivory. Her skin was clear and of unusual pallor, yet it seemed to radiate warmth. Something rich and vivid in her voice also lent strength to the odd impression she had given him, as if her very speech were gold made liquid. Except for the faintest tinge of olive, her cheeks were colorless, yet they spoke of perfect health, and shone with that same pale, effulgent glow, like the reflection of a late sun. Her lips were richly red and as fresh as a half-opened flower, affording the only contrast to that puzzling radiance. Her unusual effect was due as much perhaps to the color of her eyes as to her hair and skin, for while they were really of a greenish hazel they held the fires of an opal in their depths. They were Oriental, slumbrous, meditative, and the black pupils were of an exaggerated size. Her brows were dark and met above a finely chiseled nose.

All in all, Blake was quite taken aback, for he had not been prepared for such a vision, and a sort of panic robbed him of speech. But when his halting tongue had done its duty and his eyes had turned once more to the aunt, some irresistible power swept them back to the young woman's face. The more he observed her the more he was puzzled by that peculiar effect, that glow which seemed to envelop her. Even her gown, of some shimmering material, lent its part to the illusion. Yellow was undeniably her color; she seemed steeped in it.

He had to make a determined effort to recover his composure.

Savigno fell quickly into a lover's rhapsody, devouring the girl with ardent glances under which she thrilled, and soon they began to chatter of the wedding preparations.

"It was very good of you to come so long a way," said the Countess at last, turning to the American for a second time. "Martel has told us all about you and about your adventures together."

"Not all!" cried Savigno, lightly. "We have pasts, I assure you."

"Martel tries so hard to impress us with his wickedness," the aunt explained. "But we know him to be jesting. Perhaps you will confound him here before us."

"I shall do nothing of the sort," Blake laughed. "Who am I to rob him of a delightfully wicked past upon which he can pretend to look back in horror? It is the only past he will ever have, so why spoil it for him? On the contrary, I am prepared to lend a hand and to start him off with a list of damning disclosures which it will require years to live down."

"Pray begin," urged the Count with an air of intense satisfaction. "Eh? He hesitates. Then I shall begin for him. In the first place, Margherita, he openly declares that I covet your riches."

The Countess joined in the laughter at this, and Norvin could only say:

"I had not met you then, Signorina."

"He was quite serious, nevertheless, and predicted that marriage would end our friendship, arguing that supreme happiness is but another term for supreme selfishness."

"At least I did not question the certainty of your happiness."

The girl spoke up gravely:

"I don't agree with you, Signor Blake. I should hate to think it will make us selfish. It seems to me that such—love as we share will make us very good and sweet and generous."

When she spoke of love she hesitated and lowered her eyes until the quivering lashes swept her cheeks, but no flush of embarrassment followed. Norvin realized that with all her reserve she could not blush, had probably never blushed.

"You shouldn't place the least dependence on the words of a man's best friend under such conditions," he told her, "for he covers his chagrin at losing a comrade by a display of pessimism which he doesn't really feel."

Norvin suddenly wished the Countess would not allow her glance to linger upon him so long and searchingly. It filled him with a most disturbing self-consciousness. He was relieved when the Donna Teresa engaged him in conversation and the lovers were occupied with each other. It was some time later that the Countess addressed her aunt excitedly:

"Listen! What do you think of this, zia mia? The authorities will not admit poor Paolo to bail, and he is still in prison."

"Poor fellow!" cried the Donna Teresa. "It is La Mafia."

"Perhaps it is better for him to remain where he is," Martel said. "He is at least safe, for the time being. Here is something you may not know: Galli's wife is sister to Gian Narcone."

"The outlaw?"

"Then she will probably kill Paolo," said the Countess Margherita, calmly.

Blake exclaimed wonderingly: "I say—this is worse than Breathitt County, Kentucky. You talk of murders and outlaws as we discuss the cotton crop or the boll-weevil. This is the most fatal country I ever saw."

"It is a great pity that such things exist," the Donna Teresa agreed, "but one grows accustomed to them in time. It has been so ever since I was a child—we do not seem to progress, here in Sicily. Now in Italy it is much more civilized, much more restful."

"How hard it must be to do right," said the Countess, musingly. "Look at Paolo, for instance; he kills a wretched thief quite innocently, and yet the law holds him in prison. It is necessary, of course, to be severe with robbers like this Galli and his brother-in-law, who is an open outlaw, and yet, I suppose if I were that Galli's wife I should demand blood to wash my blood. She is only a wife."

"You sympathize with her?" exclaimed Martel in astonishment.

"Deeply! I am not so sorry the man was killed, but a wife has rights. She will doubtless follow him."

"Do you believe in the vendetta?" Norvin asked, curiously.

"Who does not? The law is full of tricks. There is a saying which runs, 'The gallows for the poor, justice for the fool!'"

"You are a Mafiosa," cried the scandalized aunt.

"It is one of Aliandro's sayings. He has lived a life! He often tells me stories."

"Aliandro is a terrible liar," Martel declared. "I fear his adventures are much like his rheumatism."

"You do not exact a reckoning from your enemies in America?" queried Margherita.

"Oh, we do, but not with quite so much enthusiasm as you do," Blake answered her. "We aren't ordinarily obliged to kill people in order to protect our property, and wives don't go about threatening vengeance when their husbands meet with accidents. The police take care of such things."

"A fine country! It must be so peaceful for old people," ejaculated the aunt.

"We have some outlaws, to be sure, like your notorious Belisario Cardi—"

"Cardi is but a name," said the girl. "He does not exist."

Intercepting a warning glance from Martel, Blake said no more, and the talk drifted to more agreeable subjects.

But the Count, being possessed of a nervous temperament which called for constant motion, could not long remain inactive, and now, having poured his extravagant devotion into his sweetheart's ears, he rose, saying:

"I must go to the village. The baker, the confectioner, the butcher, all have many things to prepare for the festa, and I must order the fireworks from Messina. Norvin will remain here while Ricardo and I complete the arrangements. I tell you it will be a celebration to awaken the countryside. For an hour then, addio!" He touched his lips to Margherita's fingers and, bowing to her aunt, ran down the steps.

"Some gadfly stings him," said the Donna Teresa, fondly. "He is like a child; he cannot remain seated. He comes, he goes, like the wind. There is no holding him."

"So there's to be a festa?" Blake observed with interest.

"Oh, indeed! It will be a great event. It was Mattel's idea." Margherita arose and the young man followed. "See, out there upon the terrace there will be dancing. You have never seen a Sicilian merrymaking? You have never seen the tarantella! Then you will be interested. On the night before the ceremony the people will come from the whole countryside. There will be music, games, fireworks. Oh, it will be a celebrazione. My cousins from Messina will be here, the bishop, many fine people. I—I am more excited than Martel. I can scarcely wait." The girl's face mirrored her emotion and her eyes were as deep as the sea. She seemed for the moment very far away, uplifted in contemplation of the great change so soon to occur in her life, and Norvin began to suspect her of a tremendous depth of feeling. Unknown even to herself she was smouldering; unawakened fires were stirred by the consciousness of coming wifehood. Out here in the sun she was more tawny than ever, and, recalling the threat against her lover, the young man fell to wondering how she would take misfortune if it ever came. Feeling his eyes upon her, she met his gaze frankly with a smile.

"What is it? You have something to say."

He recovered himself with an effort.

"No! Only—you are so different from what I expected."

"And you also," she laughed. "You are much more agreeable; I like you immensely, and I want you to tell me all about yourself."

That was a wonderful afternoon for Blake. The Sicilian girl took him into her confidence without the slightest restraint. There was no period of getting acquainted; it was as if they had known each other for a lifetime. He never ceased marveling at her beauty and his ears grew ever more eager for her voice. Martel made no secret of his delight at their instantaneous liking for each other, and the dinner that evening was the gayest that had brightened Terranova for years.

Inasmuch as the ride to San Sebastiano was long, the young men were forced to leave early, but they were scarcely out of hearing before Martel drew his horse in beside Norvin and, laying a hand upon his friend's arm, inquired, breathlessly:

"Well? Come, come, brother of mine! You know I perish of eagerness. What have you to say? The truth, between man and man."

Blake answered him with an odd hesitation:

"You must know without asking. There's nothing to say— except that she—she is like a golden flame. She sets one afire. She is different—wonderful. I—I—"

"Exactly!" Savigno laughed with keenest contentment. "There is no other."

When Blake retired that night it was not to sleep at once, for he was troubled by a growing fear of himself that would not be lightly put aside.

# IV.
# THE FEAST AT TERRANOVA

During the next few days Norvin Blake saw much of the Countess Margherita, for every afternoon he and Martel rode to Terranova. The preparations for the wedding neared completion and the consciousness of a coming celebration had penetrated the countryside. Among all who looked forward to the big event, perhaps the one who watched the hours fly with the greatest degree of suspense was the American. He had half faced the truth on that night after his first meeting with the girl, and the succeeding days enforced the conviction he would have been glad to escape. He could no longer doubt that he was in love, madly infatuated with his best friend's fiancee, and the knowledge came like some crushing misfortune. It could scarcely be called a love at first sight, for he felt that he had always known and always loved this girl. He had never believed in these sudden obsessions, and more than once had been amused at Martel's ability to fall violently in love at a moment's notice, and to fall as quickly out again, but in spite of his coolest reasoning and sternest self-reproach he found the spell too strong for him. Every decent instinct commanded him to uproot this passion; every impetuous impulse burst into sudden flame and consumed his better sense, his judgment, and his loyalty, leaving him shaken and doubtful. Although this was his first serious soul conflict, he possessed more than average self-control, and he managed to conceal his feelings so well that Martel, who was the embodiment of loyalty and generosity, never for a moment suspected the truth. As for the girl, she was too full of her own happiness to see anything amiss. She took her lover's comrade into her heart with that odd unrestraint which characterized her, and, recognizing the bond which united the two young men, she strove to widen it sufficiently to include herself. It spoke well for her that she felt no jealousy of that love which a man bears for his life's best friend, but rather strove to encourage it. Her intense desire to be a part of her lover and share all his affections led her to strive earnestly for a third place in the union, with the result that Blake saw even more of her than did Savigno. She deliberately set herself the task of winning the American, a task already more than accomplished, had she but known it, and, although for some women such a course would have been neither easy nor safe, with her a misconception of motive was impossible.

She had an ardent, almost reckless manner of attacking problems; she was as intense and yet as changeful as a flame. Blake watched her varying moods with the same fascination with which one regards a wind-blown blaze, recognizing, even in her moments of repression, that she was ready to burst forth anew at the slightest breath. She was the sort of woman to dominate men, to inspire them with tremendous enthusiasm for good or for evil as they chanced to lean toward the one or the other. While she seemed wholly admirable, she exercised a damnable effect upon Norvin. He was tortured by a thousand devils, he was possessed by dreams and fancies hitherto strange and unrecognized. The nervous strain began to tell in time; he slept little, he grew weary of the struggle, things became unreal and distorted. He longed to end it all by fleeing from Sicily, and had there been more time he would have arranged for a summons to America. His mother had not been well for a long time, and he was tempted to use this fact as an excuse for immediate departure, but the thought that Martel needed him acted as an effective restraint. The vague menace of La Mafia still hung over the Count and was not lessened by the receipt of a second threatening letter a few days after Blake's arrival.

Cardi wrote again, demanding instant compliance with the terms contained in his first communication. Savigno was directed to send Ricardo Ferara at a given hour to a certain crossroads above San Sebastiano with ten thousand lire. In that case candles would be burned and masses said for the soul of the murdered Galli, so the writer promised. The letter put no penalty upon a failure to comply with these demands, beyond a vague prediction of evil. It was short and business-like and very much to the point.

As this was the first document of the kind Norvin had ever seen, he was greatly interested in it.

"Don't you think it may be the work of this fellow Narcone?" he inquired. "I understand he is the brother-in-law of Galli."

"Narcone would scarcely undertake so bold a piece of blackmail," the Count declared. "I knew him slightly before he gave himself to the campagna. He was a butcher; he was brutal and domineering, but he was a coward."

"It is not from Narcone," Ricardo pronounced, positively—they had called in the overseer for the discussion—"he is grossolano. He can neither read nor write. This letter is well spelled and well written."

"Then you think it is really from Cardi?"

Ricardo shrugged his square shoulders. "Who knows? Some say there is no such person, others declare he went to America years ago."

"What is your belief?"

"I know a man who has seen him."

"Who?"

"Aliandro."

"Bah! Aliandro is such a liar!" exclaimed Savigno.

"However that may be, he has seen things in his time. He says that Cardi is not what people suppose him to be—a brigand—except when it suits his desires. That is why he comes and goes and the carabinieri can never trace him. That is why he is at home in all parts of Sicily; that is why he uses men like Narcone when he chooses."

"It would please me to capture the wretch," said Martel.

"Let's try it," Norvin suggested, and accordingly a trap was laid.

Four carabinieri were sent to the appointed place, ahead of time, with directions to conceal themselves, and Ferara carried out his part of the programme. But no one came to meet him, he encountered no one coming or going to the crossroads, and returned greatly disgusted. However, at his suggestion Colonel Neri stationed the four soldier policemen at the castello to prevent any demonstration and to profit by any development which might occur.

The young men did not permit this diversion to interrupt their daily trips to Terranova, although as a matter of precaution they added Ippolito to their party. He was delighted at the change of duty, because, as Norvin discovered, it brought him to the side of Lucrezia Ferara. Thus it happened that Martel had reason to regret the choice of his bodyguard, for on the very first visit Ippolito began to strut and swagger before the girl and allowed the secret to escape him, whereupon it was carried to the Countess.

She appealed to Martel to leave San Sebastiano for the time being, to postpone the wedding, or at least to go to Messina for it; but of course he refused and tried to laugh down her misgivings, and of course she appealed privately to Blake for assistance.

"You must use your influence to change his mind," she said, earnestly. "He declares he will not be overawed by these ruffians. He says that to pay them the least attention would be to encourage them to another attempt when we return, but—he does not know the Mafia as I know it. You will do this for me?"

"Of course, if you wish it, although I agree with Martel, and I'm sure he won't listen to me. He can't play the coward. The wedding is only two days off now. Why, to-morrow is the gala-day! How could he notify the whole district, when all his preparations have been completed? What excuse could he give without confessing his fear and making himself liable to a later and stronger attack?"

"The country people need not know anything about it. Let them come and make merry. He can leave now, tonight. We will join him at Messina."

Norvin shook his head. "I'll do what I can, since you wish it, but I'm sure he won't consent to any change of plan. I'm sure, also, that you are needlessly troubled."

"Perhaps," she acknowledged, doubtfully. "And yet Martel's father—"

"Yes, yes. But conditions are not what they were fifteen years ago. This is merely a blackmailing scheme, and if he ignores it he'll probably never hear of it again. On the other hand, if he allows it to drive him away it will be repeated upon his return."

She searched his face with her eyes, and his wits reeled at her earnest gaze. He was conscious of a single wild desire that such anxiety might be for him. How gladly he would yield to her wishes— how gladly he would yield to any wish of hers! He was a foreigner; he hated this island and its people, for the most part, and yet if he stood in Martel's place he would willingly change his life to correspond with hers. He would become Sicilian in body and soul. She had the power to dissolve his habits, his likes and dislikes, and reconstruct him through and through.

"I hope you are right," she said at last. "And yet—it is said that no one escapes the Mafia."

"This isn't the Mafia. It is the work of some brigand—"

"What is the difference? The one merges into the other. Blood has been spilled; the forces are at work."

Suddenly she seized him by the arm, and her eyes blazed. "Look you," she cried, "if Martel should be injured, if these men should dare—all Sicily would not hold them. No power could save them, no hiding-place could be so secret, no lies so cunning, that I would not know. You understand?"

Blake saw that the girl was at last aroused to that intensity of feeling which he had recognized as latent in her. Love had caused her to glow, but it had required this breath of fear to fan the fire into full strength. He was deeply moved and answered simply: "I understand. I—never knew how much you loved him."

Her humor changed, and she smiled.

"One is foolish, perhaps, to be so frank, but that is my nature. You would not have me change it?"

"You couldn't if you tried."

"Martel has always known I loved him. I could never conceal it. I never wished to. If he had not seen it I would have told him. Just now, when I heard he was threatened—well, you see."

"Ippolito had no business to mention the matter. I suppose his tongue ran away with him. Tongues have a way of doing such things when their owners are in love."

"He is not for Lucrezia."

"Why? He's a fine fellow."

"Oh, but Lucrezia is superior. I have taught her a great many things. She is more like a sister to me than a servant, and I could not see her married to a farm-hand. She can do much better than to marry Ippolito."

"Love goes where it pleases," said the American with so much feeling that Margherita's eyes leaped to his.

"You know? Ah, my good friend, then you have loved?"

He nodded. "I have. I do."

She was instantly all eagerness, and beamed upon him with a frank delight that stabbed him.

"Martel? Does he know?"

"No, You see, there's no use—no possibility."

"I'm sorry. There must be some great mistake. I cannot conceive of so sad a thing."

"Please don't try," he exclaimed, panic-stricken at thought of the dangerous ground he was treading and miserably afraid she would guess the truth in spite of him.

"I should think any woman might love you," she said, critically, after a moment's meditation. "You are good and brave and true."

"Most discerning of women!" he cried, with an elaborate bow. "Those are but a few of my admirable traits." He was relieved to see that she had no suspicion of his feelings, for she was extremely quick of wit and her intuition was keen. No doubt, her failure to read him was due to her absorption in her own affairs. He had arrived at a better knowledge of her capabilities to-day and began to realize that she was as changeable as a chameleon. One moment she could be like the sirocco in warmth and languor, the next as sparkling as the sunlit ocean. Again she could be steeped in a dreamy abstraction or alive with a pagan joy of life. She might have been sixteen or thirty, as her mood chanced to affect her. Of all the crossed strains that go to make up the Sicilian race she had inherited more of the Oriental than the Greek or Roman. Somewhere back in the Ginini family there was Saracen blood, he felt sure.

Blake was as good as his word, and made her wishes known to Martel, who laughingly accused him of a lack of faith in his own arguments. The Count was bubbling with spirits at the immediate nearness of his nuptials, and declined to consider anything which might interfere with them. He joyfully told Blake that the tickets were already bought and all arrangements made to leave for Messina immediately after the ceremony, which would take place in the church at Terranova. They would catch the boat for Naples on the evening after the wedding, he explained, and Blake was to accompany them at least that far on his way to America. Meanwhile, he had no intention of foregoing the pleasure of to-morrow's celebration, even if Belisario Cardi himself should appear, to dispute his coming. It was the first, the last, and the only time he intended marrying, and he had promised himself to enjoy the occasion to the utmost, despite those letters, which, after all, were not to be taken seriously. So the matter was allowed to stand.

The country people had begun to assemble when Martel and his friend arrived at the Ginini manor on the following afternoon, and the grounds were filling with gaily dressed peasants. The train from Messina had brought Margherita's relatives, and the bishop had sent word that he would arrive in ample time for the ceremony on the next morning. The contadini were coming in afoot, astride of donkeys and mules, or in gaily painted carts pictured with the miracles of the saints and the conquests of the Moors. There were dark-haired men and women, wild-haired boys with roses above their ears, girls with huge ear-rings and fringed shawls which swept the ground as they walked. As yet they had not entirely lost their restraint, but Martel went among them with friendly hand-clasps and exuberant greetings, renewing old acquaintances and welcoming new until at last their shyness disappeared and they began to laugh and chatter unaffectedly.

Savigno had traveled, he told them. He had arranged many surprises for his friends. There would be games, dances, music, and a wonderful entertainment in the big striped tent yonder, supplied by a troupe of players which he had brought all the way from Palermo. As for the feast, well, the tables were already stretched under the trees, as they could see, and if any one wished to tantalize his nostrils just let him wander past the kitchen in the rear, where a dozen women had been at work since dawn. But that was not all; there would be gifts for the children and prizes for the best dancers. The handsomest woman would receive a magnificent shawl the like of which had never been dreamed of in Terranova, and then to prevent jealousy the others would receive presents also. But he would not say too much. Let them wait and see. Finally there would be fireworks, enough to satisfy every one; and all he asked of them was that they drink the health of the Countess Margherita and wish her lifelong happiness. It was to be a memorable occasion, he hoped, and if they did not enjoy themselves as never before, then he and his bride would feel that their wedding had been a great, a colossal failure.

But it seemed, as night approached, that Martel had no reason to doubt the quality of his entertainment, for the guests gave themselves up to joy as only southerners can, forgetting poverty, hardship, and all the grinding cares of their barren lives. They yielded quickly to the passion of the festa, and Blake began to see Sicily for the first time. He would have liked to enter into their merrymaking, but felt himself too much a stranger.

The feast was elaborate; no ristorante could have equaled it, no one but a spendthrift lover like Martel would have furnished it. But it was not until darkness came and the trees began to twinkle and glow with their myriad lights that the fun reached its highest pitch. Then there was true Sicilian dancing, true Sicilian joking, love-making. Eyes were bright, cheeks were flushed, lips were parted, and the halls of Terranova echoed to a bacchanalian tumult.

There had been an elaborate supper inside also, to which the more prominent townspeople had been invited and from which Norvin Blake was only too eager to escape as it drew to an end. The strain to which he had been subjected for the past week was growing unbearable, and the sight of Margherita Ginini clad like a vision in some elaborate Parisian gown so intensified his distress that he was glad to slip away into the open air at the first opportunity. He found Ricardo leaning against the bole of a eucalyptus-tree, observing the throng with watchful eyes.

"Why aren't you making merry?" Blake inquired.

The overseer shrugged his shoulders, replying, somberly, "I am waiting."

"For what?"

"Who knows? There are strangers here."

"You mean,"—Blake's manner changed quickly—"there may be enemies?"

"If Cardi is in the mountains behind Martinello, may he not be here at Terranova? I am looking for a thick, black man. Aliandro has described him."

"Cardi would scarcely come to a wedding feast," said Blake, with a certain feeling of uneasiness.

"Scarcely," the overseer agreed.

"Have you seen anything?"

"Nothing."

"Where is Ippolito?"

Ricardo grunted. "Asleep in the stable. The imbecile is drunk."

To the American these Sicilian people looked very much alike. They were all a bit fantastic, and the scene reminded him of a fancy-dress ball where all the men represented brigands. Many of them were, or seemed to be, of truculent countenance; some wore piratical ear-rings, others had shawls wrapped about their heads as if for concealment. Any one of them might have been a brigand, for all he knew, and he saw how easy it would be for a handful of evil-intentioned persons to mingle unobserved with such a throng. Yet his better sense told him that he was silly to imagine such things. He had allowed old women's tales to upset his nerves.

A half-hour later, as he was watching the crowd from the loggiato, Margherita appeared, and he thought for a moment that she too might feel some vague foreboding, but her first words reassured him.

"My good friend, I missed you," she said, "but I had no chance of leaving until this moment." Coming close to him, she inquired: "Has something gone amiss? You have seemed sad all this evening. I do not know, but I fear your heart is—heavy."

He answered, unsteadily: "Perhaps it is. I—don't know."

"It is that certain woman."

"I dare say. I'm a great fool, you know."

"Don't say that. This is perhaps the only chance I shall have of seeing you alone."

"I'm glad," he broke out in a tone that startled her. "Glad for you. I have tried not to be a death's-head at your feast, but it has been a struggle."

"We women see things. Martel, boy that he is, does not suspect, and yet I, who have known you so short a time, have read your secret. It is our happiness which makes you sad."

"No, no. I'm not that sort. I share your happiness. I want it to continue."

"If I had one wish it would be that she might care for you as I care for Martel. And who knows? Perhaps she may. You say it is impossible, yet life is full of blind ways and unseen turnings. Somehow I feel that she will."

"You are very good," he managed to say. Then yielding to a sudden impulse, he took her hand and kissed it. A moment later she left him, but the touch of her cool flesh against his lips remained an unforgetable impression.

Savigno appeared, yawning prodigiously.

"Dio!" he exclaimed with a grimace. "Those cousins of hers are deadly dull; I do not blame you for escaping. And the judge, and the notary's wife, and that village doctor! Colonel Neri is a good chap, notwithstanding his mustache in which he takes so much pride. He nurses it like a child, and yet it is older than I. Poor friend of mine, you are a martyr, thus to endure for me."

"It's tremendously interesting, particularly this part out here," Norvin asserted. "I saw them dancing what I took to be the tarantella a moment ago. Those peasant boys are like leaping fauns."

"Yes, and they will continue to dance for hours yet. I fear the Donna Teresa will not retire at her usual hour. What a day it has been! It is fine to give people happiness. That is one of my new discoveries."

"Remember to-morrow."

"Believe me, I think of nothing else. That is why we must be going soon. We cannot wait even for the fireworks, as much as I would like to. It is a long road to Martinello and we must be up early in the morning. You do not object?"

"On the contrary, I was about to bear you off in spite of yourself."

"Then I will have Ippolito fetch the horses."

"Ippolito has been demonstrating the mastery of wine over matter. He is asleep in the manger."

"Drunk? Oh, the idiot! He has the appetite of a shark, but the belly of a herring. I ought to warm his soles with a cane," declared Savigno, angrily.

"Don't be too hard on him. I suspect Lucrezia would not listen to his suit, poor chap. He's sick from unrequited passion."

"Very well, we will leave him to sleep it off. I couldn't be harsh with him at this time. And now we had best begin presenting our good-nights, although I hate to go."

# V.
# WHAT WAITED AT THE ROADSIDE

To avoid the dampening effect of an early departure the three men rode out quietly from the courtyard at the rear of the house, leaving the merrymakers to their fun.

"So, this is our last ride together," Norvin said, as they left the valley and began the long ascent of the mountain that lay between them and Martinello.

"Yes. Henceforth we spare our horses. You see tomorrow we will take the morning train. Half of San Sebastiano will accompany us, too, and everybody will be dressed in his finest. Ricardo here, for instance, will wear his new brown suit—a glorious affair. Eh, Ricardo?"

"It would be as well to refrain from speaking," said the overseer, gruffly. "The road is dark. Who knows what may be waiting?"

"Nonsense! Be not always a bear. We are three armed men. I fancy Narcone, nay, even our dreadful Cardi himself, would scarcely dare molest us."

Ferara merely grunted and continued to hold his place abreast of his employer. Norvin observed that he carried his rifle across his saddle-bow, and involuntarily shifted the strap of his own weapon so that it might be ready in case of an emergency. He had rebelled, somewhat, at carrying a firearm, but Martel, after making a clean breast of his troubles that first morning, had insisted, and the American had yielded even though he felt ridiculous.

The sky was moonless to-night but crowded with stars which gave light enough so that the riders were able to follow the road without difficulty, although the shadows on either side were dense. The air was sweet, and so still that the sounds of revelry from Terranova were plainly audible. Strains of music floated up the hillside, the shouts of the master of ceremonies came distinctly as he issued his commands for a country dance. The many lights within the grounds shone cloudily among the tree-tops far below, like the effulgence from some well-lit city hidden behind a hill, now disappearing for a time, now shining out again as the road pursued its meanderings. The hurried footfalls of the horses thudded steadily in the soft dust; the saddles creaked with that music which lulls a horseman like a song.

"Youth! Youth! What a glorious thing it is!" exclaimed Martel after a fruitless attempt to hold his tongue. "Ricardo would have us go prowling like robbers when our hearts are singing loud enough for all the mountainside to hear. There is no evil in the world to-night, for the world is in love; to-morrow it bursts into happiness! And I am king over it all!"

"I shall be glad to be rid of you, just the same," grumbled the old man.

"Ricardo alone has fears, but he was never young. Think you that the gods would permit my wedding-day to be marred? Bah! One can see evil before it comes; it casts a shadow; it has a chilling breath which any one with sensibilities can feel. As for me, I see the future as clearly as if it were spread out before me in the sunshine, and there is no misfortune in it anywhere. I cannot conceive of misfortune, with all this gladness and expectancy inside me."

"They have begun the fireworks," said Blake. "It's too bad you couldn't stay to see them, Martel." He turned in his saddle, and the others reined in as a rocket soared into the night sky and burst with a shower of sparks. Others followed and a detonation sounded faintly.

"Poor people!" said the Count, gently. "I can hear them crying, 'Oh!' 'Ah!' 'Beautiful!' 'It is an angel from heaven!'"

"On the contrary, I'll warrant they're exclaiming, 'It is that angel from San Sebastiano.' You have given them a great night."

The Count laughed. "Yes. They will have much to talk and dream about. Their lives are very barren, you know, and I hope the Countess and I will be able to make them brighter as the years go by. Oh, I have plans, caro mio, so many plans I scarcely know where to begin or how to talk about them. I could never be an artist, no matter how furiously I painted, no matter how many beautiful women I drew; but I can paint smiles upon the faces of those sad women down yonder. I can bring happiness into their lives. And that will be a picture to look back upon, eh? Don't you think so? When they learn to know me, when they learn to love and trust me, there will be brighter days at Terranova and at San Sebastiano."

"They love you now, I am sure."

"I am too much a stranger yet. I have neglected my duties, but— well, in my travels I have learned some things that will be of benefit to us all. I see so much to do. It is delightful to be young and full of hopes, and to have the means of realizing them. Above all, it is delicious to know that there is one who will share those ambitions and efforts with you. I see Ricardo is disgusted with me, but he is a pessimist. He does not believe in charity and love."

"What foolish talk!" protested the old man with heat. "Do I not love my girl Lucrezia? Do I not love you, the Countess, and—and— perhaps a few others?"

Martel laughed. "I was merely teasing you."

They resumed their journey, leaving the showering meteors behind them, and the Count, in the lightness of his heart, began humming a tune.

As for Blake, he rode as silently as Ferara, being lost in contemplation of a happiness in which he had no part. Not until this moment had he realized how entirely unnecessary he was to the existence of Martel and Margherita. He longed to remain a part of them, but saw that his desire was vain. They were complete without him, their lives would be full. He began to feel like a stranger already. It was a new sensation, for he had always seemed to be a factor in the lives of those about him; but Martel had changed with the advent of new interests and ambitions. Sicily, too, was different from any land he knew, and even Margherita Ginini was hard to understand. She seemed to be the spirit of Sicily made flesh and blood. He wondered if the very fact that she was so unusual might not help him to forget her once he was away from her influence. He hoped so, for this last week had been the most painful period of his life. He had come south, somewhat against his will, for a kaleidoscopic glimpse of Europe, never dreaming that he would carry back to America anything more than the usual flitting memories of a pleasant trip; but instead he was destined to take with him a single vivid picture. He argued that he was merely infatuated with the girl, carried away by the allurement of a new and remarkable type of woman, and that these headlong passions were neither healthy nor lasting; but his reasoning brought him no real sense of conviction, and his life, as he looked forward to it, appeared singularly flat and stale. His one consolation, poor as it seemed, lay in the fact that he had played the man to the best of his ability and was really glad, even if a bit envious, of Martel's good-fortune.

He let his thoughts run free in this manner, sitting his horse listlessly, for he was tired mentally and physically, watching the gray road idly as it slipped past beneath the muffled hoofs, and lulled by Savigno's musical humming.

It was while he was still in this half-somnolent, semidetached frame of mind that he rode into a sudden white-hot whirl of events.

Norvin Blake was never clear in his mind regarding the precise sequence of the action that followed, for he was snatched too quickly from his mental relaxation to retain any well-defined impressions. He recalled vaguely that the road lay like a mysterious canon walled in with darkness, and that his thoughts were miles away when his horse shied without warning, nearly unseating him and bringing him back to a sense of his surroundings with a shock. Simultaneously he heard a cry from Ricardo; it was a scream of agony, cutting through Savigno's song like a saber stroke. For a moment Blake's heart seemed to stop, then began pounding crazily. A stream of fire leaped out at his left side, splitting the quiet night with a detonation. The wood which had lain so silent and deserted an instant before was lit by answering flashes, the blackness at an arm's-length on every side was stabbed by wicked tongues of flame, and the road swarmed with grotesque bodies leaping and tumbling and fighting. Blake's horse reared as something black rose up beneath its forefeet and snatched at its bridle; Martel's steed lurched into it, then fell kicking and screaming, sending its mate careening to the roadside. The unexpected movement wrenched Norvin's feet from the stirrups and left him clinging desperately to mane and cantle.

It all came with a terrifying swiftness—quite as if the three riders had crossed over a powder-train at the instant of its eruption, to find themselves, in the fraction of a second, involved in chaos.

Ricardo's horse thundered away, riderless, leaving a squirming, wriggling confusion of forms in the road where the overseer was battling for his life. Martel's voice rose shrilly in a curse, and then Norvin felt himself dragged roughly from his saddle, whether by human hands or by some overhanging tree-branch he never knew. The force of his fall bruised and stunned him, but he struggled weakly to his feet only to find himself in the grasp of a man whose black visage fronted his own. He tried to break away, but his bones were like rope, his muscles were flabby and shaking. He exerted no more force than a child. In front of him something sickening, something unspeakably foul and horrible, was going on, and in its presence he was wholly unmanned. More hands seized him quickly, but he lacked the vigor to attempt an escape. On the contrary, he hung limp and paralyzed with terror. The mystery, the uncertainty, the hideous significance of that wordless scuffle in the dusty road rendered him nerveless, and he cried out shakingly, like a man in a nightmare.

A voice commanded him to be silent, a hot breath beat against his cheek; but he could not restrain his hysteria, and one of his captors began to throttle him. He heard his name called and saw Savigno's figure outlined briefly against the gray background, saw another figure blend with it, then heard Martel's voice end in a rising cry which lived to haunt his memory. It rose in protest, in surprise, as if the Count doubted even at the last that death could really claim him. Then it broke in a thin, wavering shriek.

Blake may have fainted; at any rate, his body was beyond his control, and his next remembrance was of being half dragged, half thrust forward out into the lesser shadows. There was no longer any struggling, although men were speaking excitedly and he could hear them panting; some one was working the ejector of a rifle as if it had stuck. A tall man was wiping his hands upon some dried grass pluck'ed from the roadside, and he was cursing.

"Who is this?" he cried, thrusting his face into the American's and showing a brutal countenance bristly with a week's growth of beard.

"The stranger," one of Blake's captors answered, whereupon the tall man uttered a violent exclamation.

"Wait!" cried the other. "He is already dying. He cannot stand."

Some one else explained, "It is indeed the American, but he is wounded."

"Let me finish the work; he has seen too much," said the first speaker, roughly.

"No, no! He is the American. Do you not understand?"

"Remember the order, Narcone," cautioned another.

But Narcone continued to curse as if mastered by the craving to kill, and if the others had not laid hands upon him he might have made good his intention. They argued with him, all at once, and in the midst of the confusion which ensued a new voice called from the darkness:

"What have you there?"

"The American! He cannot stand."

A square figure came swiftly through the group, muttering angrily, and the others fell back to give him room, all but Narcone, who repeated, doggedly:

"Let me finish the work if you fear to do so."

His companions broke out at him again in a babble of argument, whereupon the new-comer shouted at them in a furious voice:

"Silenzio! Who did this?"

No one answered for a moment, but at length the brigand who held Blake's hands pinioned at his back with a sash or scarf ventured to suggest:

"I am not so sure he is injured. We pulled him down first; he may only be frightened."

"There was to be no shooting," growled the leader of the band.

"Eh? But you saw for yourself. There was nothing else to do," said Narcone. "That Ricardo was an old wolf."

The thick-set man, whom Norvin took to be the infamous Cardi himself, cried sharply:

"Come, come, Signore, speak! Are you hurt?"

The prisoner shook his head mechanically, although he did not know whether he was injured or not. His denial seemed to satisfy the chief, who said with relief:

"It is well. We did not wish to harm you. There would be consequences, you understand? And now a match, somebody."

"It is not necessary," Narcone assured him with a laugh. "Of what use to learn a trade like mine if one cannot strike true? The knife went home, twice—once for us, once for poor Galli, who was murdered. It was like killing sheep." Picking up the wisp of grass which he had dropped, he began to dry his hands once more.

A tiny flame flickered in the darkness. It was lowered until it shone upon the upturned face of Ricardo Ferara where he lay sprawled in the dust, his teeth showing beneath his gray mustache, then died away, and the black outlines of the bull-necked man leaped into relief again as he stooped to examine Martel.

Not until that instant did the full, crushing horror of the affair come home to the American, for events had crowded one another so closely that his mind was confused; but when, in the halting yellow glare, he saw those two slack forms and the crooked, unnatural postures in which death had left them, his consciousness cleared and he strained at his bonds like a fear-maddened horse.

His actual danger, however, was at an end. One of the band removed the rifle which still hung from his shoulders and which he had forgotten; another slipped the scarf from his wrists and directed him to go. He staggered away down the road along which he and Martel and Ricardo had come, walking like a sick man, for he was crippled with fright. After a few steps he began to run, heavily, awkwardly at first, stumbling as if his joints were loose; but as his body awoke and the blood surged through him he went faster and faster until he was fleeing like a wild animal. And as he ran his terror grew. He fell many times, goblin shapes pursued him or leaped forth from the shadows, but he knew that no matter how fast he fled he could never escape the thing he had met back there in the night. It was not the grisly sight of his murdered friend nor the bared teeth of Ricardo Ferara grinning upward out of the road which filled him with the greatest horror; it was the knowledge of his own foul, sickening cowardice. He ran wildly as if to leave it behind, but it trod in his tracks and kept step with him.

The pyrotechnics at Terranova were nearly over and the grounds echoed to the applause of the delighted spectators. The Donna Teresa was leaning upon the arm of Colonel Neri and saying:

"No one but that extravagant Martel would have entertained these poor people so magnificently, but there is no reasoning with him when he has an idea."

"It is the finest display since the fair at San Felice two years ago," the Colonel acknowledged. They had come out upon the open piazza which overlooked the lawn, and the other guests who had been present at the supper had followed suit and were gathered there to admire the spectacle.

"The country people will never finish discussing it. Why, it has been the greatest event this village ever witnessed. And Margherita! Have you ever seen her so beautiful?" The old lady spoke with pride, for she was very happy.

"Never!" Colonel Neri fondled his mustache tenderly. "She is ablaze with love. Oh, that Martel has broken all our hearts, lucky fellow! I could hate him if I did not like him so."

"You men, without exception, pretend to adore her but it is flattery; you know that she loves it and that it pleases me. Now Martel—Madonna mia! What is this?" She broke off sharply and pointed toward the main gateway to the grounds.

By the light that gleamed from the trees on each side of the driveway men could be seen approaching at a run; others were hurrying toward them across the terrace, calling excitedly to one another. A woman screamed something unintelligible, but the tone of her voice brought a hush over the merrymakers.

In the midst of the group coming up the road was one who labored heavily. He was bareheaded, gray with dust, and he staggered as if wounded.

"Some one has been hurt," exclaimed the Colonel. "Maledetto! There has been a fight." He dropped his companion's arm and hastened to the steps, then halfway down paused, staring. He whirled quickly and cried to the old lady: "Wait! Do not come."

But Madame Fazello had seen the white face of the runner, and screamed:

"Mother of God! The American!"

The other guests from the balcony pressed forward with alarmed inquiries. No one guessed as yet what had befallen, but the loud voices died away, a murmuring tide swept the merrymakers toward the castello.

"What has happened, Signore?" Colonel Neri was crying. "Speak!"

"The Mafia!" Blake gasped. "Martel—is—" His knees sagged and he would have pitched forward had not the soldier supported him. "We met them—in the woods. Cardi—"

"Cardi!" echoed the Colonel in a harsh voice.

"Cardi!" came from a dozen frightened throats. The Donna Teresa uttered a second shrill cry, and then through the ranks of staring, chalk-faced peasants the Countess came running swiftly.

"Cardi!" she cried. "What is this I hear?"

"Go away, Signorina, I beseech you," exclaimed the Colonel of carbineers. "Something dreadful has occurred." But she disregarded him and faced Norvin Blake.

He raised his dripping, dust-smeared face and nodded, whereat she closed her eyes an instant and swayed. But she made no outcry.

"Take her—away," he wheezed painfully. "God in heaven! Don't you—understand?"

Even yet there was no coherent speech and the people merely stared at one another or inquired, dully:

"What did he say? What is this about Cardi?"

"Take her away," Blake repeated. But the Countess recovered herself and with a little gesture bade him go on. He told his story haltingly, clinging to the Colonel to prevent himself from falling, his matted head rolling weakly from side to side. When he had finished a furious clamor broke forth from the men, the women, and the children. Neri commanded them roughly to silence.

"Run to the village, some one, and give the alarm," he ordered in the voice of a sick man. "Call Sandro and his men and bid them bring extra horses."

A half-dozen fleet-footed youths broke away and were off before he had finished speaking. Then Blake was helped into the hall of the castello, where the confusion was less.

Lucrezia Ferara, who had been in the rear of the house and was among the last to hear the evil tidings, came running to him with colorless lips and eyes distended, crying:

"The truth, Signore, for the love of Christ! They tell me he is murdered, but I know it is a lie."

The notary's wife attempted to calm her, but the girl began to scream, flinging herself upon her knees at the feet of the American, begging him to tell her it was all a mistake.

"My father would not die," she cried, loudly. "He was here but an hour ago and he kissed me."

She would not be calmed and became so violent that it required force to remove her. As soon as she was out of the way, Colonel Neri began questioning Norvin rapidly, at the same time striving by his own example to steady the young man, who was in a terrible condition of collapse. Bit by bit, the soldier learned all there was to learn of the shocking story, and through it all the Countess Margherita stood at his elbow, never speaking. Her eyes were glazed with horror, her lips were whispering something over and over, but when her cousin appealed to her to leave the scene she seemed not to hear him. She only stood and stared at the exhausted man until he could bear it no longer and, hiding his face in his hands, he began to shiver and cringe and sob.

It seemed to him that she must know; that all these people must know the truth, and see his shame as if it were blazoned in fire. Their horror was for him; their looks were changing even now to contempt and hatred. Why did they not accuse him openly instead of staring with wide, shocked eyes? Realization had come to him long before he had reached Terranova, and he was sick with loathing for himself. Now, therefore, in every blanched cheek, in every parted lip, he felt an accusation. He supposed all the world would have to know it, and it was a thing he could never live down. He wished he might have died as Martel had died, might die even now, and escape this torture; but with every breath life flowed back into him, his heart was no longer bursting, his lungs were no longer splitting.

"Why do you wait?" he queried at length, thinking of Martel out there on the lonely mountainside. "Why don't you go fetch him?"

Neri said, soothingly: "Help will be here in a few moments, Signore. You could not sit a horse yet a while."

"I?" Blake asked blankly, and shuddered. So they expected him to return through that darkness—to guide them to the horror from which he had just fled! He would not go! His mind recoiled at the thought and terror came upon him afresh. Nevertheless, he made an effort at self-control, lurched to his feet, and chattered through clicking teeth: "Come on! I'm ready."

"Presently! Presently! There will be men and horses here in a moment." In a lower tone the Colonel urged: "For the love of our Saviour, can you not send the Contessa away? I am afraid she is dying."

Blake went to the girl and laid a shaking hand upon her arm, stammering, wretchedly:

"Contessa, you—you—" He could not go on and turned appealingly to the others.

"You say he is dead?" she inquired dully. "How can that be when you told me there was no danger?"

"I did not know. Oh—" he lowered his working features. "If it had only been I, instead!"

She nodded. "That would have been better."

From somewhere to the rear of the house came the shrill screams of Lucrezia, and the Countess cried: "Poor child! They did not even spare Ricardo, but—after all, he was only a father."

Neri said, gently: "Let me help you, Signorina. The doctor is with your aunt, but I will call him."

"He cannot give me back Martel," she answered in the same dull, lifeless tone.

Voices, footsteps, sounded outside and a man in the cocked hat and uniform of a lieutenant of carbineers came briskly into the hall and saluted his superior.

"We are ready, sir."

The Countess roused herself, saying: "Then come! I too am ready."

"Heaven above us!" Neri faltered. "You are not going." He took her by the hand and led her away from the door. "No, my child, we will go alone. You must wait." His face was twitching, and the sweat dripped from his square jaw as he nodded to Blake.

They went out into the mocking glare of the garden lights, leaving her standing in the great hall like a statue of ivory, her lips dumbly framing the name of her lover.

# VI.
# A NEW RESOLVE

All Sicily blazed with the account of the assassination of the Count of Martinello and his overseer. All Italy took it up and called for vengeance. There went forth to the world by wire, by post, and through the public press a many-voiced and authoritative promise that the brigandage which had cursed the island for so many generations should be extirpated. The outrage was the one topic of conversation from Trapani to Genoa, from Brindisi to Venice, in clubs, in homes, upon the streets. Carbineers and soldiers came pouring into Terranova and San Sebastiano. They scoured the mountains and patrolled the roads; they searched the houses and farms, the valleys and thickets, and as the days dragged on, proving the futility of their efforts, still more carbineers arrived. But no trace of Cardi, of Narcone, or of the other outlaws was discovered. Rewards were offered, doubled, trebled; the north coast seethed with excitement.

The rank of the young Count and his fiancee enlisted the interest of the nobility, the lively-minded middle classes were romantically stirred by the picture of the lonely girl stricken on the eve of her wedding, and yet notwithstanding the fact that towns were searched, forests dragged as with a net, no quarry came to bay.

Colonel Neri explained it to Norvin, as he rode in to San Sebastiano after thirty-six hours in the saddle.

"It is this accursed Sicilian Mafia," he growled. "The common people are shocked, horrified, sympathetic, and yet they fear to show their true feelings. They dare not tell what they know. Mark you, those men are not hiding in the forests, they are here in San Sebastiano or the other villages under our very noses; perhaps they are strutting the streets of Palermo or Bagheria or Messina marked by a hundred eyes, discussed by a hundred tongues, and yet we cannot surprise a look or win the slightest hint. Fifty arrests have been made, but there will be fifty alibis proven. It is maddening, it is damnable, it is—Sicily!" He swore wearily beneath his breath, and twirled his mustache with listless fingers.

"Then you are losing hope?"

"No. I had none to begin with, for I know these people. But we are doing everything possible. God in heaven! The country is wild. From Rome has come the order, definite, explicit, to stamp out the banditti, if it requires an army; enough soldiers are coming to defeat the Germans. But the more we have the less we shall accomplish. 'Sweep Sicily!' 'Stamp out the Mafia!' What does Rome know about the Mafia? Signore, did we arrest one half of those whom we know to be Mafiosi, Rome would need to send us, not an army of soldiers, but regiments of stone masons to enlarge our prisons. No! Send back the armed men, give me ten thousand of your American dollars, and ten of my carbineers, and I will catch Cardi, though it would require the cunning of the devil. However, we may find something; who can tell? At any rate we will try."

"Can't you work secretly?"

"It is being done, but we are too many. We make too much noise. The Sicilian distrusts the law and above all he distrusts his neighbor. He will perjure himself to acquit a Mafioso rather than betray him and become a victim of his vengeance. He who talks little is wise. Of that which does not concern him he says neither good nor evil; that is a part of the Sicilians' training. But—miracles have happened, and God may intervene for that saintly girl at Terranova. And now tell me, how is the poor child bearing up?"

"I haven't seen her since we brought in Martel's body. I couldn't, in fact, although I have sent word for her to call me when she is ready. It seems a long time since—since—"

Neri shook his head in sorrowful agreement.

"I have never seen such grief. My heart bleeds. She was so still! Not a tear! Not an outcry! It was terrible! Weak women do not act in that manner. But you have suffered also, and I judge you have rested no more than I."

"I can't rest," Blake said, dully. "I can do nothing but think." He did not reveal the nature of the thoughts which in the short space of thirty-six hours had put lines into his face. Instead, he scanned the officer's countenance with fearful eyes to see if by any chance he had guessed the truth. Blake had found himself looking thus at every one since the tragedy, and it was a source of constant wonder to him that his secret had remained his own. It seemed that they must know and loathe him as he loathed himself. But on the contrary he was treated with sympathy on all sides, and it was taken merely as an example of the outlaws' cunning that they had refrained from injuring a foreigner. To illustrate how curiously the Sicilian mind works on these subjects, there were some who even spoke of it as demonstrating the fairness of the bandits, thus to exclude Savigno's friend from any connection with their quarrel.

During the long hours since the night of his friend's death Blake had looked at himself in all his nakedness of soul, and the sight was not pleasant. He could never escape the thought that if he had acted the part of a man, if he had resisted with the promptness and vigor of his companions, the result might have been different and Martel might at this moment be on his way to Rome with his bride, alive and well. On such occasions he felt like a murderer. But his mind was not always undivided in this self-condemnation; there were times when with some show of justice he told himself that the result would have been the same or even worse if he had fought; and he tried to ease his conscience by dwelling on the possibility that under other circumstances he might not have proved a coward. He had been physically tired, worn out; his nervous force had been spent. At the moment of ambush his mind had been far away and he had had no time in which to gather his wits. Moral courage, he knew, is quite different from physical courage, which may depend upon one's digestion, one's state of mind, or the amount of sleep one has had. It is sometimes present in physical weaklings, and men of great daring may entirely lack it. A man's behavior when suddenly attacked and overpowered is a test of his nerve rather than his true nature. Still, at the last, he was always faced by the stark, ugly fact that he had been tried and found wanting. Conversation with Neri he found rather a relief.

"I wonder what the Countess will do?" he said.

"What would any one do? She will grieve for a long while, but time will gradually rob her of her sorrow. She will remember Martel as a saint and marry some sinner like you or me."

"Marry? Never!"

"Never?" The Colonel raised his brows. "She is young, she is human, she is full of fire. It would be a great pity if she did not allow herself to love—a great pity indeed."

"I'm afraid she's thinking more of vengeance than of love."

"Perhaps, but hatred is short-lived, while love grows younger all the time. The world is full of great loves, but great hates usually consume themselves quickly. I hope she will leave all thoughts of such things to us who make a business of them."

"If you fail, as you fear, she might feel bound to take up the task where you leave it."

"And she might succeed. But—"

"But what?"

"Revenge is a cold bedfellow, and women are designed to cherish finer sentiments. As for Lucrezia, she will doubtless swear a vendetta, like those Sardinians."

"She has."

"Indeed! Well, she is the kind to nourish hatred, for she is like her father, silent, somber, unforgiving, whereas the Contessa is all sunshine. But hear me talk! I am dying of fatigue. The funeral is at twelve? It will be very sad and the poor girl will be under the greatest strain then, so we must be with her, you and I. And then I must be off again upon the trail of this infamous Cardi, who is, and who is not. Ah, well!" He yawned widely. "We may accomplish the impossible, or if not we may press him so closely that he will sail for your America, which would not be so bad, after all."

Of course the country people turned out for the funeral, but for the most part they came from curiosity. To Norvin the presence of such spectators at the last sacred rites for the dead seemed sacrilegious, indecent, and he knew that it must add to Margherita's pain. It was an endless, heart-rending ordeal, a great somber, impressive pageant, of which he remembered little save a tall, tawny girl crushed beneath a grief so great that his own seemed trivial in comparison.

She was in such a state of physical collapse after the service that she did not send for him until the second day following. He came timidly even then, for he was at a loss how to comfort her, vividly conscious as he was of his own guilt and shame. He found her crouched upon one of the old stone benches in the garden in the full hot glare of the sun. It relieved him to find that she had lost her unnatural self-control, having fallen, it seemed, into much the same mood he would have expected in any woman. It had been so hard to find what to say heretofore—for she was braver than those about her and her grief was so deep as to render words of comfort futile. Her eyes now were heavy and full of haunting shadows, her ivory cheeks were pale, her lips tremulous, and she seemed at last to crave sympathy.

"I do not know why I have summoned you," she said, leaving her hand in his, "unless it is because my loneliness has begun and I lack the courage to face it."

"I have been waiting. It will always be so, Contessa. I shall come from across the world whenever you need me."

She smiled listlessly. "You are very good. I knew you were waiting. It seems so strange to know that he is gone"—her voice caught, her eyes filled, then cleared without overflowing—"and that the world is moving on again in the same way and only I am left standing by the wayside. You cannot wait with me; you must move on with the rest of the world. You had planned to go home, and you must, for you have your work and it calls you."

"Please don't think of it. I sha'n't leave you for a long time. I promised Martel—"

"You promised? Then he had reason to suspect?"

"He would not acknowledge the possibility, and yet he must have had a premonition."

"Oh, why will men trust themselves when women know! If he had told me, if he had confided his fears to me, I could have told him what to do."

"I couldn't leave now, even if I wished, for I might be needed by the—the law. You understand? It isn't finished with me yet."

"The law will not need you," she told him bitterly. "The law will do nothing. The task is for other hands."

After a pause he said, "I had news from home to-day,—rather bad news." Then at her quick look of inquiry he went on: "Nothing serious, I hope, nothing to take me away. My mother is ill and has cabled me to come."

"Then you will go at once, of course?"

"No. I've tried to explain to her the situation here, and the necessity of my remaining for a time at least. Unless she grows worse I shall stay and try to help Neri in his search."

"It is a great comfort to have you near, for in you I see a part of— Martel. You were his other half. But there are other aching hearts, it seems. That mother calls to you, and you ought to go. Besides, I must begin my work."

"What work?"

She met his eyes squarely. "You know without asking. Neri will fail; no Italian could succeed; no one could succeed except a Sicilian. I am one."

"You mean to bring those men to justice?"

She nodded. "Certainly! Who else can do it?"

"But, my dear Signorina, think what that means. They are of a class with which you can have no contact. They are the dregs; there is the Mafia to reckon with. How will you go about it?"

"I will become one of them, if necessary."

He answered her in a shocked voice. "No, no! You are mad to think of it. If you were a man you might have some chance for success, but you—a girl, a gentlewoman!"

"I am a Sicilian. I am rich, too. I have resources." She took him by the arm as she had done that first time when the thought of Martel's danger had roused her. "I told you no power could save them; no hiding-place could be so secret, no lies so cunning that I would not know. Well! Those soldiers have failed and will continue to fail. But you see they did not love Martel. I shall live for this thing."

"I won't allow you to dwell on the subject; it isn't natural, and it isn't good for you. The desire to see justice done is commendable and proper, but the desire for revenge isn't. You must not sacrifice your life to it. There is a law of compensation; those men will be apprehended."

"Where is my compensation? What had Martel done to warrant this?"

He fell silent, and she shook her head as if to indicate the hopelessness of answering her. After a moment of meditation he began again, gravely:

"If you feel that way, I shall make you an offer. Give up your idea of taking an active personal part in this quest, and I will assume your place. We will work together, but you will direct while I face the risks."

"You are a stranger. We would be sure to fail. I thank you, but my mind is made up."

"If it becomes known, you will be in great danger. Think! Life is before you, and all its possibilities. Please let other hands do this."

"It is useless to argue," she said, firmly. "I am like rock. I have begun already and I have accomplished more than Colonel Neri and his carbineers. I see Aliandro coming now, and I think he has news. He knows many things of which the soldiers do not dream, for he is one of the people. You will excuse me?"

"Of course, but—I can't let you undertake so dangerous a task without a protest. I shall come back, if I may."

He rose as the old man shuffled down the path, and went in search of the Donna Teresa, for he was determined to offer every discouragement in his power to what struck him as an extremely rash and perilous course. Men like Belisario Cardi, or Narcone the Butcher, would hesitate no more in attacking a woman than a man. He knew the whole Sicilian country to be a web of intrigue and secret understandings, sensitive to the slightest touch and possessed of many means of communication. It was a great ear which heard the slightest stir, and its unfailing efficiency was shown by the ease with which the bandits had forestalled every effort of the authorities.

In the hall of the manor house he encountered Lucrezia and stopped to speak to her.

"You would do a great deal to protect the Countess, would you not?" he asked.

"Yes, Signore. She has been both a sister and a mother to me. But what do you mean?"

Ferara's daughter was a robust girl of considerable physical charm, but although her training at Terranova had done much for her, it was still evident that she was a country woman. She had nursed her grief with all the sullen fierceness of a peasant, and even now her face and eyes were swollen from weeping.

Blake explained briefly his concern, but when he had finished, the girl surprised him by breaking forth into a furious denunciation of the assassins. She surrendered to her passion with complete abandon, and began to curse the names of Cardi and Gian Narcone horribly.

"We demand blood to wash our blood," she cried. "I curse them and their souls, living and dead, in the name of God who made my father, in the name of Christ who died for him, in the name of the holy saints who could not save him. In the name of the whole world I curse them. May they pray and not be heard. May they repent unforgiven and lie unburied. May every living thing that bears their names die in agony before their eyes. May their women and unborn children be afflicted with every unclean thing until they pray for death at my hands—"

"Lucrezia!" He seized her roughly and clapped his hand over her mouth, for her voice was rising steadily and threatened to rouse the whole household. Her cheeks were white, she was shaking with long, tearless sobs. She would have broken out again when he released her had he not commanded her to be silent. He tried to explain that this work of vengeance was not for her or for the Countess, and to point out the ruin that was sure to follow any attempt on their part to take up the work of the carabinieri, but she shook her head, declaring stubbornly:

"We have sworn it."

The more he argued the more obstinate she became, until, seeing the ineffectiveness of his pleas, he gave up any further effort to move her, sorry that he had raised such a storm. He went on in search of Madam Fazello, with Lucrezia's parting words ringing ominously in his ears:

"If we die, we shall be buried; if we live, we shall give them to the hangman."

From Margherita's aunt he got but little comfort or hope of assistance.

"Oh, my dear boy, I agree with your every word," the old lady said. "But what can I do? I know better than you what it will lead to, but Margherita is like iron—there is no reasoning with her. She would sacrifice herself, Lucrezia, even me, to see Martel avenged, and if she does not have her way she will burn herself to ashes. As for Lucrezia, she is demented, and they do nothing all day but scheme and plan with Aliandro, who is himself as bad as any bandit. I have no voice with them; they do with me as they will." She hid her face in her trembling fingers and wept softly. "And to think—we were all so happy with Martel!"

"Nevertheless, somebody must dissuade them from this enterprise. It is no matter for two girls and an old man to undertake."

"I pray hourly for guidance, but I am frightened, so frightened! When Margherita talks to me, when I see her high resolve, I am ready to follow; then when I am alone I become like water again."

"What are her plans?"

"I do not know. I have begged her to take her sorrow to God. The bishop who came from Messina to marry Martel and remained to bury him has joined me. There is a convent at Palermo—"

"No, no!" Blake cried, vehemently. "Not that! That life is not for her. She must do nothing at all until her grief has had time to moderate."

"It will never be less. You do not know her. But you are the one to reason with her."

Realizing that the old lady was powerless, he returned to the garden and tried once more to weaken the girl's resolution, but without success. It was with a very troubled mind that he took the train back to San Sebastiano that afternoon.

The more he thought it over, the more certain he became that it was his duty to remain in Sicily until Margherita had reached her right senses. Martel had put a trust in him, and what could be more important than to prevent her from carrying out this fantastic enterprise? He would take up the search for the assassins in her place, allowing her to work through him and in that way satisfying her determination. What she needed above all things was distraction, occupation. If she remained persistent they would work side by side until justice had been done, and meanwhile he would become a part of her life. He might make himself necessary to her. At least he would prevent her from doing anything rash and perhaps fatal. In time he would prevail upon her to travel, to seek recreation, and then her youth would be bound to tell. That would be the work of a friend indeed, that would remove at least a part of the obligation which rested upon him. Some day, he reasoned, the Countess might even marry and be happy in spite of what had occurred. As he contemplated the idea, it began to seem less improbable. What if she should come to care for him? He would still be true to Martel, for how could he protect her better than by making her his wife? His heart leaped at the thought, but then his old self-disgust returned, reminding him that he had yet to prove himself a man.

As he stepped down from the train at San Sebastiano the station master met him with a telegram. Even before he opened it he guessed its contents, and his spirits sank. Was he never to escape these maddening questions of duty—never to be free to pursue his heart's desire?

It was a cablegram, and read:

"Come quickly.

**"KENEAR."**

He regarded it gravely for a moment, striving to balance his duty to Martel and the girl against his duty to his mother, but his hesitation was brief. He stepped into the little telegraph office with the mandarin-tree peering in at the open window and wrote his answer. He did not try to deceive himself; the mere fact that Dr. Kenear had been summoned from New Orleans showed as plainly as the message itself that his mother's condition was more serious than he had supposed. She was alone with many responsibilities upon her frail shoulders, and she was calling for her son. There was but one thing to do.

He stopped at the barracks to explain the necessity for his immediate departure to Colonel Neri, who was most sympathetic. "You are not needed here," the soldier assured him, "and you would have to go, even though you were. You made your statement at the inquest; there is nothing further for you to do until we accomplish the capture of somebody. Even then I doubt if you could identify any one of those bandits."

"I think I should know Narcone anywhere."

The Colonel shrugged. "Narcone has been swallowed by the earth. As for Cardi and the rest, they have become thin smoke and the wind has carried them away. We are precisely where we were at the start. Perhaps it is fortunate for you that you have not been called upon to testify against any of the band, for even the fact that you are a foreigner might not save you from—unpleasant results."

Norvin reasoned silently that if this were indeed true it more than confirmed his fears for the Countess, and after a brief hesitation he told the soldier what he had learned at his visit to Terranova. Neri rose and paced the room in agitation.

"Oh! She is mad indeed!" he exclaimed. "What can she do that we have not already done? Aliandro? Bah! He is a doddering old reprobate who will spread news instead of gather it. He has a bad record, and although he loved Martel and doubtless loves Margherita, I have no confidence in him whatever. She will accomplish nothing but her own undoing."

"I am afraid so, too. That is why I shall return to Sicily as soon as possible."

"Indeed? Then you plan to come back? Martel was fortunate to have so good a friend as you, Signore. We must both do all we can to prevent this folly on the part of his sweetheart. You may rest assured that I shall make every effort in your absence." The Colonel extended his hand, and Norvin took it, feeling some relief in the knowledge that there was at least one man close to the girl upon whose caution he could rely and upon whose good offices he could count. He had grown to like the soldier during their brief acquaintance, and the fact that Neri knew and appreciated the situation helped to reconcile him to the thought of going away.

He was not ready to leave Sicily, however, without one final appeal, and accordingly he stopped at Terranova on the following morning on his way to Messina, where a boat was sailing for Naples that night. But he found no change in the Countess; on the contrary, she told him gently but firmly that she had made up her mind once for all and that she would resent any further efforts at dissuasion.

"Won't you even wait until I return?" he inquired.

She shook her head and smiled sadly.

"Do not let us deceive ourselves, amico mio; you will not return."

"On the contrary, I shall. You make it necessary for me to return whether I wish to or not."

"The ocean is wide, the world moves. You are a foreigner and you will forget. It is only in Sicily that people remember."

"Will you give me time to prove you wrong?"

"I could not allow it. You have your own life to live; you have a multitude of duties. Martel, you see, was only your friend. But with me it is different. He was my lover; my life was a part of his and my duty will not let me sleep."

"You have no reason to say I will forget."

"It is the way of the world. Then, too, there is the other woman. You will see her. You will find a way, perhaps."

But he replied, doggedly, "I shall return to Sicily."

"When?"

"I can't tell. A month from now—two months at the longest."

"It would be very sweet to have you near," she said musingly, "for I am lonely, very lonely, and with you I feel at rest, at peace in a way. But something drives me, Signore, and I cannot promise. If you should not forget, if you should wish to join hands with me, then I should thank God and be very glad. But I sha'n't wish for it; that would be unfair."

His voice shook as he said, "I am going to prove to you that your life is not hopelessly wrecked, and to show you that there is something worth living for."

She laid her two cool hands in his and looked deeply into his eyes, but if she saw what lay in them she showed no altered feeling in her words or tone.

"Martel would be glad to have you near me, I am sure," she said, "but I shall only pray for your safety and your happiness in that far-off America. Good-by."

He kissed her fingers, vowing silently to devote his whole life to her, and finding it very hard to leave.

# VII.
# THE SEARCH BEGINS

It was ten months later when Norvin Blake landed at Messina and took the morning train westward to Terranova. As he disposed his travelling-bags in a corner of the compartment, and settled himself for the short journey, he felt a kind of irrational surprise at the fact that there had been no changes during his absence. The city was just as dirty and uninteresting as when he had left, the beggars were just as ragged and importunate, the street coaches were just as rickety. It required an effort to realize that ten months is, after all, a very short time, for it seemed ten years since he had sailed away. It had been a difficult period for him, one crowded with many changes, readjustments, and responsibilities. He had gone far, he had done much, he had been pressed by cares and anxieties on every side, and even at the last he had willfully abandoned urgent duties, to his own great loss and to the intense disgust of his friends, in order to come back according to his promise. His return had been delayed from week to week, from month to month, in spite of all he could do, and meanwhile his thoughts had not been in America at all, but in Sicily, causing him to fret and chafe at the necessities which bound him to his post. Now, however, the day upon which he had counted had arrived; he had taken his liberty regardless of consequences, and no dusty pilgrim ever longed more fiercely for a journey's end. He was glad of the impression of sameness he had received, for it made him feel that there would be no great changes in Terranova.

He had learned little from the Countess during the interim, for she had been slow in answering his frequent letters, while her own had been brief and non-commital. They contained hardly a suggestion of that warmth and intimacy which he had known in her presence. Her last letter, now quite old, had added to this impression of aloofness and rendered him somewhat timid as the time for meeting her approached. He re-read it for the hundredth time as the train crawled out of the city—

"MY DEAR FRIEND,—Your good letter was very welcome indeed, and I thank you for your sympathetic interest in our affairs at Terranova, but since fate has shown in so many ways that your life lies in Louisiana, and not in Sicily, I beg of you to let things take their course and give up any idea of returning here. There is nothing that you can do, particularly since time has proved your fears for our safety to be groundless. It is kind and chivalrous of you to persist in offering to take that long journey from America, but nothing would be gained by it, absolutely nothing, I assure you, and it would entail a sacrifice on your part which I cannot permit.

"Very little of interest or of encouragement had occurred here, but I am working. I shall always work. Some day I shall succeed. Meanwhile we talk of you and are heartened by your friendship, which seems very close and real, despite the miles that separate us. We shall cherish it and the memory of your loyalty to Martel. Meanwhile, you must not feel bound by your promise to come back, which was not a promise, after all, but merely an unselfish offer. Once again I repeat, it would do no good, and might only disappoint you. Besides, I am hoping that you have seen the woman of whom you told me and that she will need you.

"We are all well. We have made no plans.

"Yours gratefully, MARGHERITA GININI"

It was certainly unsatisfying, but her letters had all been of this somewhat formal nature. She persisted, too, in referring to that imaginary woman, and Blake regretted ever having mentioned her. If Margherita suspected the truth, she could not help feeling his lack of delicacy, his disloyalty to Martel, in confessing his love while the Count was still alive; if she really believed him to be in love with some other woman, it would necessitate sooner or later an explanation which he dreaded. At all events, he hoped that the surprise of seeing him unexpectedly, the knowledge that he had really crossed the world to help her, would tend to dissipate her melancholy and restore her old responsiveness.

During the months of his absence the girl had never been out of his mind, and he had striven hard to reconcile his unconquerable love for her with the sense of his own unworthiness. His unforgivable cowardice was a haunting shame, and the more he dwelt upon it the more unspeakably vile he appeared in his own sight; for the Blakes were honorable people. The family was old and cherished traditions common to fine Southern houses; the men of his name prided themselves upon an especially nice sense of honor, which had been conspicuous even in a country where bravery and chivalrous regard for women are basic ideals. Having been reared in such an atmosphere, the young man looked upon his own behavior with almost as much surprise as chagrin. He had always taken it for granted that if he should be confronted with peril he would behave himself like a man. It was inexplicable that he had failed so miserably, for he had no reason to suspect a heritage of cowardice, and he was sound in mind and body. He loved Margherita Ginini with all his heart and his resolution to win her was stronger than ever, but he felt that sooner or later he would have to prove himself as manly as Martel had been, and, having lost faith in himself, the prospect frightened him. If she ever discovered the truth—and such things are very hard to conceal—she would spurn him: any self-respecting woman would do the same.

He had forced himself to an unflinching analysis of his case, with the result that a fresh determination came to him. He resolved to reconstruct his whole being. If he were indeed a physical coward he would deliberately uproot the weakness and make himself into a man. Others had accomplished more difficult tasks, he reasoned; thieves had made themselves into honest men, criminals had become decent. Why, then, could not a coward school himself to become brave? It was merely a question of will power, not so hard, perhaps, as the cure of some drug habit. He made up his mind to attack the problem coldly, systematically, and he swore solemnly by all his love for Margherita that he would make himself over into a person who could not only win but hold her. As yet there had been no opportunity of putting the plan into operation, but he had mapped out a course.

Terranova drowsed among the hills just as he had left it, and high up to the right, among the trees, he saw the white walls of the castello. As he mounted the road briskly a goat-herd, flat upon his back in the sun, was piping some haunting air; a tinkle of bells came from the hillside, the vines were purple with fruit. Women were busy in the vineyards gathering their burdens and bearing them to the tubs for the white feet of the girls who trod the vintage.

Nearing his goal, he saw that the house had an unoccupied air, and he found the big gates closed. Since no one appeared in answer to his summons, he made his way around to the rear, where he discovered Aliandro sunning himself.

"Well, Aliandro!" he cried. "This is good weather for rheumatism."

The old man peered up at him uncertainly, muttering:

"The saints in heaven are smiling to-day."

"Where are the Contessa Margherita and her aunt?"

"They are where their business takes them, I dare say. Ma che?"

"Gone to Messina, perhaps?"

"Perhaps."

"Visiting friends?"

"Exactly." Aliandro nodded. "They are visiting friends in Messina."

"I wish I had known; I just came from there. Will they return soon?" Blake's hopes had been so high, his disappointment was so keen, that he failed to notice the old man's lack of greeting and his crafty leer as he answered:

"Si, veramente! Soon, very soon. Within a year—five years, at the outside."

"What?"

"Oh, they will return so soon as it pleases them." He chuckled as if delighted at his own secrecy.

Norvin said sharply: "Come, come! Don't jest with me. I have traveled a long way to see them. I wish to know their whereabouts."

"Then ask some one who knows. If ever I was told, I have forgotten, Si'or. My memory goes jumping about like a kid. It is the rheumatism." After an instant more, he queried, "You are perhaps a friend of that thrice-blessed angel, my padrona?"

With an exclamation of relief Norvin laid a hand upon the old fellow's shoulder and shook him gently.

"Have your eyes failed you, my good Aliandro?" he cried. "Don't you recognize the American?—the Signore Blake, who came here with the Count of Martinello? Look at me and tell me where your mistress has gone."

Aliandro arose and peered into his visitor's face, wagging his loose jaws excitedly.

"As God is my judge," he declared, finally, "I believe it is, Che Dio! Who would have expected to see you? Yes, yes! I remember as if it were yesterday when you came riding up with that most illustrious gentleman who now sits in Paradise. It is a miracle that you have crossed the seas so many times in safety."

"So! Now tell me what I want to know."

"They have gone."

"Where?"

"How do I know? Find Belisario Cardi—may he live a million years in hell! Find him, and you will find them also."

"You mean—"

"Find Belisario Cardi, that most infamous of assassins. My padrona has set out to say good morning to him. He may even now be on his way to purgatory."

Blake stared at the speaker, for he could not credit the words. Once more he asked:

"But where? Where?"

"Where, indeed? If I had known in time where this Cardi lived I would have knocked at his door some evening with the hilt of a knife. But he was never twice in the same place. He has the ears of a fox. So long as the soldiers went tramping back and forth he laughed. Then he must have heard something—perhaps it was Aliandro whetting his blade—at any rate he was gone in an hour, in a moment, in a second. Now I know nothing more."

"She took the Donna Teresa with her?"

"Yes, squealing like a cat. She is too old to be of use, but the Contessa could not leave her behind, I suppose."

Norvin felt some relief at this intelligence, reflecting that Margherita would hardly draw her aunt into an enterprise which promised to be dangerous. As he considered the matter further he began to doubt the truth of Aliandro's story, for the old fellow seemed half daft. Perhaps the Countess and her aunt were merely traveling and Aliandro had construed their trip into a journey of vengeance. He had doubtless spent all his time meditating upon the murder of his friend and benefactor, and that was a subject which might easily unbalance a stronger mind. Ten months had worked a change in Blake's viewpoint. When he left Sicily the idea of a girl's devoting her life to the pursuit of her lover's assassins had seemed to him extravagant, yet not wholly unnatural. Now it struck him as beyond belief that Margherita should really do this. Aliandro was continuing:

"It is work for young hands, Excellency. Old people grow weary and forget, especially women. Now that Lucrezia, she is a fine child; she can hate like the devil himself and she is as silent as a Mafioso. It was two months ago that they went away, and that angel of gold, that sweetest of ladies whom the saints are quarreling over, she left me sufficient money for the balance of my days. But I will tell you something, Excellency—a scandal to make your blood boil. She left that money with the notary. And now, what do you think? He gives me scarcely enough for tobacco! Once a week, sometimes oftener, I go down to the village and whine like a beggar for what is mine. A fine man to trust, eh? May he lie unburied! Sometimes I think I shall have to kill him, he is so hard-hearted, but—I cannot see well enough. If you should find him kicking in the road, however, you will know that he brought it upon himself. You are shocked? No wonder. He is a greater scoundrel than that Judas. Perhaps you—you are a great friend of the family—perhaps you might force the wolf to disgorge. Eh? What do you say? A word would do it. You will save his life in all probability."

"Very well, I'll speak to him, and meanwhile here is something to please you." Norvin handed the old ruffian a gold coin, greatly to his delight. "They have been gone two months and you have had no word?"

"Not a whisper. Once a week the notary comes up from the village to see that all is well with the house. Many people have asked me the same questions you asked. Some of them know me, and I know some who think I do not. They would like to trick me into betraying the whereabouts of the Contessa, but I lie like a lawyer and tell them first one thing, then another. Body of Christ! I am no fool."

When Norvin had put himself in possession of all that Aliandro knew he retraced his steps to the village, where the notary confirmed practically all the old man had said, but declared positively that the Countess and her admirable aunt were traveling for pleasure.

"What else would take them abroad?" he inquired. "Nothing! I have the honor to look after the castello during their absence and the rents from the land are placed in the bank at Messina."

"When do you expect them to return?"

"Privately, Signore, I do not expect them to return at all. That shocking tragedy preyed upon the poor child's mind until she could no longer endure Terranova. She is highly sensitive, you know; everything spoke of Martel Savigno. What more natural than for her to wish never to see it again? She consulted me once regarding a sale of all the lands, and only last week some men came with a letter from the bank at Messina. They were Englishmen, I believe, or perhaps Germans—I can never tell the difference, if indeed there is any. I showed them through the house. It would be a great loss to the village, however, yes, and to the whole countryside, if they purchased Terranova, for the Countess was like a ray of sunshine, like an angel's smile. And so generous!"

"Tell me—Cardi was never found?"

The notary shrugged his shoulders. "As for me, I have never believed there was such a person. Gian Narcone, yes. We all knew him, but he has not been heard from since that terrible night which we both remember. Now this Cardi, well, he is imaginary. If he were flesh and blood the carabinieri would certainly have caught him—there were enough of them. Per Baccho! You never saw the like of it. They were thicker than flies."

"And yet they didn't catch Narcone, and he's real enough."

"True," acknowledged the notary, thoughtfully. "I never thought of it in that light. Perhaps there is such a person, after all. But why has no one ever seen him?"

"Where is Colonel Neri?"

"He is stationed at Messina. Perhaps he could tell you more than I."

Dismayed, yet not entirely discouraged, by what he had learned, Blake caught the first train back to Messina and that evening found him at Neri's rooms. The Colonel was delighted to see him, but could tell him little more than Aliandro or the notary.

"Do you really believe the Countess left Sicily to travel?" Blake asked him.

"To you I will confess that I do not. We know better than that, you and I. She was working constantly from the time you left for America until her own departure, but I never knew what she discovered. That she learned more than we did I am certain, and it is my opinion that she found the trail of Cardi."

"Then you're not like the others. You still believe there is such a person?"

"Whether he calls himself Cardi or something else makes no difference; there has been an intelligence of a high order at work among the Mafiosi and the banditti of this neighborhood for many years. We learned things after you left; we were many times upon the verge of important discoveries; but invariably we were thwarted at the last moment by that Sicilian trait of secrecy and by some very potent terror. We tried our best to get to the bottom of this fear I mention, but we could not. It was more than the customary distrust and dislike of the law; It was a lively personal dread of some man or body of men, The fact that we have been working nearly a year now without result would indicate that the person at the head of the organization is no common fellow. No one dares betray him, even at the price of a fortune. I believe him to be some man of affairs, some well-fed and respected merchant, or banker, perhaps, the knowledge of whose identity would cause a commotion such as Etna causes when she turns over in her sleep."

"That was Ricardo's belief, you remember."

"Yes. I have many reasons for thinking he was right, but I have no proof. Cardi may still be in Sicily, although I doubt it. Gian Narcone has fled; that much I know."

"Indeed?"

"Yes! The pursuit became hot; we did not rest! I do not see, even yet, how we failed to capture him. We apprehended a number whom we know were in the band, although we have no evidence connecting them with that particular outrage. I think we will convict them for something or other, however; at any rate, we have broken up this gang, even though we have lost the two men we most desired. Narcone went to Naples. He may be there now, he may be in any part of Italy, or he may even be in your own America, for all I know. And this mysterious Cardi is probably with him. It is my hope that we have frightened them off the island for all time."

"And sent them to my country! Thanks! We're having trouble enough with our own Italians, as it is."

"You at least have more room than we. But now, before we go further, you must tell me about yourself, about your mother—"

Norvin shook his head gravely. "I arrived in time to see her, to be with her at the last, that is all."

"I am indeed full of sympathy," said Neri. "It is no wonder you could not return to Sicily as soon as you had planned."

"Everything conspired to hold me back. There were many things that needed attention, for her affairs had become badly mixed and required a strong hand to straighten them out. Yet all the time I knew I was needed here; I knew the Countess was in want of some one to lean upon. I came at the first opportunity, but—it seems I am too late. I am afraid, Neri—afraid for her. God knows what she may do."

"God knows!" agreed the soldier. "I pleaded with her; I tried to argue."

"But surely she can't absolutely disappear in this fashion. She will have to make herself known sooner or later."

"I'm not so certain. Her affairs are in good shape and Terranova is for sale."

"Doesn't the bank know her whereabouts?"

"If so, she has instructed them to conceal it."

"Nevertheless I shall go there in the morning and also to her cousins. Will you help me?"

"Of course!" Neri regarded the young man curiously for an instant, then said, "You will pardon this question, I hope, but since she has taken such pains to conceal herself, do you think it wise to—to—"

"To force myself upon her? I don't know whether it is wise or foolish; all I know is that I must find her. I must!" Blake met the older man's eyes and his own were filled with a great trouble. "You told me once that revenge and hatred are bad companions for a woman and that it would be a great pity if Margherita Ginini did not allow herself to love and be loved. I think you were right. I'm afraid to let her follow this quest of hers; it may lead her into something—very bad, for she has unlimited capabilities for good or evil. I had hoped to—to show her that God had willed her to be happy. You see, Neri, I loved her even when Martel was alive."

The Colonel nodded. "I guessed as much. All men love her, and there lies her danger. I love her, also, Signore. I have always loved her, even though I am old enough to be her father, and I would give my life to see her—well, to see her your wife. You understand me? I would help you find her if I could, but I am a soldier. I am chained to my post. I am poor."

"Jove! You're mighty decent," said the American with an odd breathlessness. "But do you think she could ever forget Martel?"

"She is not yet twenty."

"Do you think there is any possibility of my winning her? I thought so once, but lately I have been terribly doubtful."

"I should say it will depend largely upon your finding her. We are not the only good men who will love her. They sailed from here to Naples on the trail of Narcone; that much I believe is reasonably certain. I will give you a letter to the police there, and they will help you. It is possible that we excite ourselves unduly; perhaps you will have no difficulty whatever in locating her, but in the mean time we will do well to talk with her relatives and with the officials of the bank. I look for little help from those quarters, however."

Colonel Neri's misgivings were well founded, as the following day proved. At the bank nothing definite was known as to the whereabouts of the Countess. She had left instructions for the rents to be collected until Terranova was sold and then for all moneys to be held until she advised further. Her cousins were under the impression that she had taken her aunt to northern Italy for a change of climate and believed that she could be found in the mountains somewhere. Blake was not long in discovering that while the relations between the two branches of the family were maintained with an outward show of cordiality they were really not of the closest. Neri told him, as a matter of fact, that Margherita had always considered these people covetous and untrustworthy.

Having exhausted the clues at Messina, Norvin hastened to Naples and there took up his inquiry. He presented his letter, but the police could find no trace of the women and finally told him that they must have passed through the city without stopping, perhaps on their way to Rome. So to Rome he went, and there met a similar discouragement. By now he was growing alarmed, for it seemed incredible that a woman so conspicuous and so well known as the Countess of Terranova should be so hard to find unless she had taken unusual pains to hide her identity. If such were the case the search promised many difficulties. Nevertheless, he set about it energetically, sparing no expense and yet preserving a certain caution in order not to embarrass the Countess. He reasoned that if Cardi and Narcone had fled their own island they would be unlikely to seek an utterly foreign land, but would probably go where their own tongue was spoken; hence the Countess was doubtless in one of the Italian cities. When several weeks had been spent without result the young man widened the scope of his efforts and appealed to the police of all the principal cities of southern Europe.

Two months had crept by before word came from Colonel Neri which put an end to his futile campaign. The bank, it seemed, had received a letter from the Countess written in New York. It was merely a request to perform certain duties and contained no return address, but it sent Norvin Blake homeward on the first ship. Now that he knew that the girl was in his own country he felt his hopes revive. It seemed very natural, after all, that she should be there instead of in Europe, for Cardi and his lieutenant, having found Sicily too hot to hold them, had doubtless joined the tide of Italian emigration to America, that land of freedom and riches whither all the scum of Europe was floating. Why should they turn to Italy, the mother country, when the criminals of Europe were flocking across the westward ocean to a richer field which offered little chance of identification? It seemed certain now that Margherita had taken up the work in earnest; nothing less would have drawn her to the United States. Blake gave up his last lingering doubt regarding her intentions, but he vowed that if her resolve were firm, his should be firmer; if her life held nothing but thoughts of Martel, his held nothing but thoughts of her; if she were determined to hide herself, he was equally determined to find her, and he would keep searching until he had done so. The hunt began to obsess him; he obeyed but one idea, beheld but one image; and he cherished the illusion that once he had overtaken her his task would be completed. Only upon rare occasions did he realize that the girl was still unwon—perhaps beyond his power to win. He chose to trust his heart rather than his reason, and in truth something deep within him gave assurance that she was waiting, that she needed him and would welcome his coming.

# VIII.
# OLD TRAILS

Mr. Bernard Dreux was regarded by his friends rather as an institution than as an individual. He was a small man, but he wore the dignity of a senator, and he possessed a pride of that intense and fastidious sort which is rarely encountered outside the oldest Southern families. He was thin, with the delicate, bird-like mannerisms of a dyspeptic, and although he was nearing fifty he cultivated all the airs and graces of beardless youth. His feet were small and highly arched, his hands were sensitive and colorless. He was an authority on art, he dabbled in music, and he had once been a lavish entertainer—that was in the early days when he had been a social leader. Now, although harassed by a lack of money which he considered degrading, he still mingled in good society, he still dressed elegantly, his hands were still white and sensitive, contrasting a little with his conscience, which had become slightly discolored and calloused. He no longer entertained, however, except by his wit; he exercised a watchful solicitude over his slender wardrobe, and his revenues were derived from sources so uncertain that he seemed to maintain his outwardly placid existence only through a series of lucky chances. But adversity had not soured Mr. Dreux; it had not dimmed his pride nor coarsened his appreciation of beauty; he remained the gentle, suave, and agreeably cynical beau. Young girls had been known to rave over him, despite their mother's frowns; fathers and brothers called him Bernie and greeted him warmly—at their clubs.

But aside from Mr. Dreux's inherited right to social recognition he was marked by another and peculiar distinction in that he was the half-brother and guardian of Myra Nell Warren. This fact alone would have assured him a wide acquaintance and a degree of popularity without regard to his personal characteristics.

While it was generally known that old Captain Warren, during a short and riotous life, had dashed through the Dreux fortune at a tremendous rate, very few people realized what an utter financial wreck he had left for the two children. There had been barely enough for them to live upon after his death, and inasmuch as Myra Nell's extravagance steadily increased as the income diminished, her half-brother was always hard pressed to keep up appearances. She was a great responsibility upon the little man's shoulders, particularly since she managed in all innocence and thoughtlessness to spend not only her own share of the income, but his also. He was many times upon the point of remonstrating with her, but invariably his courage failed him and he ended by planning some additional self-sacrifice to offset her expanding necessities.

The situation would have been far simpler had Bernie lacked that particular inborn pride which forbade him to seek employment. Not that he felt himself above work, but he recoiled from any occupation which did not carry with it a dignity matching that of his name. Since the name he bore was as highly honored as any in the State, and since his capabilities for earning a living were not greater than those of an eighteen-year-old boy, he was obliged to rely upon his wits. And his wits had become uncommonly keen.

The winter climate of New Orleans drew thither a stream of Northern tourists, and upon these strangers Mr. Dreux, in a gentlemanly manner, exercised his versatile talents. He made friends easily, he knew everybody and everything, and, being a man of leisure, his time was at the command of those travelers who were fortunate enough to meet him. He understood the good points of each and every little cafe in the foreign quarters; he could order a dinner with the rarest taste; it was due largely to him that the fame of the Ramos gin-fizz and the Sazerac cocktail became national. His grandfather, General Dreux, had drunk at the old Absinthe House with no less a person that Lafitte, the pirate, and had frequented the house on Royal Street when Lafayette and Marechal Ney were there. It was in this house, indeed, that he had met Louis Philippe. His grandson had such a wealth of intimate detail at his finger tips that it was a great pleasure and privilege to go through the French quarter with him. He exhaled the atmosphere of Southern aristocracy which is so agreeable to Northern sensibilities, he told inimitable stories, and, as for antiques, he knew every shop and bargain in the city. He was liberal, moreover, nay, ingenuous in sharing this knowledge with his new-found friends, even while admitting that he coveted certain of these bargains for his own slender collection. As a result of Mr. Dreux's knack of making friends and his intimate knowledge of art he did a very good business in antiques. Many of his acquaintances wrote him from time to time, asking him to execute commissions, which he was ever willing to do, gratuitously, of course. In this way he was able to bridge over the dull summer season and live without any unpleasant sacrifice of dignity. But it was at best a precarious means of livelihood and one which he privately detested. However, on the particular day in the summer of 1890 on which we first encounter him Mr. Dreux was well contented, for a lumber-man from Minneapolis, who had come South with no appreciation whatever of Colonial antiques, had just departed with enough worm-eaten furniture to stock a museum, and Bernie had collected his regular commission from the dealer.

Now that his own pressing necessities were taken care of for the moment, he began, as usual, to plan for Myra Nell's future. This would have required little thought or worry had she been an ordinary girl, but that was precisely what Miss Warren was not. The beaux of New Orleans were enthusiastically united in declaring that she was quite the contrary, quite the most extraordinary and dazzling of creatures. Bernie had led them to the slaughter methodically, one after another, with hope flaming in his breast, only to be disappointed time after time. They had merely served to increase the unhappy number which vainly swarmed about her, and to make Bernie himself the target of her satire. Popularity had not spoiled the girl, however; her attitude toward marriage was very sensible beneath the surface, and Bernie's anxious efforts at matchmaking, instead of relieving their financial distress, merely served to keep him in the antique business. Miss Warren loved admiration; she might be said to live on it; and she greeted every new admirer with a bubbling gladness which was intoxicating. But she had no appreciation of the sanctity of a promise. She looked upon an engagement to marry in the same light as an engagement to walk or dine, namely, as being subject to the weather or to a prior obligation of the same sort. Bernie was too much a gentleman to urge her into any step for which she was not ready, so he merely sighed when he saw his plans go astray, albeit confessing to moments of dismay as he foresaw himself growing old in the second-hand business. But a change had occurred lately, and although no word had passed between brother and sister, the melancholy little bachelor had been highly gratified at certain indications he had marked. It seemed to him that her choice, provided she really had chosen, was excellent; for Norvin Blake was certainly very young to be the president of the Cotton Exchange, he was free from any social entanglements, and he was rich. Moreover, his name had as many honorable associations as even Bernie's own. All in all, therefore, the little man was in an agreeable frame of mind to-day as he strolled up Canal Street, nodding here and there to his acquaintances, and turned into Blake's office.

He entered without announcing himself, and Norvin greeted him cordially. Bernie seldom announced himself, being one of those rare persons who come and go unobtrusively and who interrupt important conversations without offense.

"Do I find you busy?" he inquired, dropping into one of Blake's easy-chairs and lighting a perfumed cigarette.

"No. Business is over for the day. But I am glad to see you at any time; you're so refreshingly restful."

"How are the new duties and responsibilities coming on?"

"Oh, very well," said Blake, "Although I'm absurdly self-conscious."

"The Exchange needed new blood, I'm told. I think you are a happy choice. Opportunity has singled you out and evidently intends to bear you forward on her shoulders whether you wish or not. Jove! you *have* made strides! Let me see, you are thirty—"

"Two! This makes me look older than I am." Norvin touched his hair, which was gray, and Bernie nodded.

"Funny how your hair changed so suddenly. I remember seeing you four years ago at the Lexington races just after you returned from Europe the second time. You were dark then. I saw you a year later and you were gray. Did the wing of sorrow brush your brow?"

Blake shrugged. "They say fear will turn men gray."

Dreux laughed lightly. "Fancy! You afraid!"

"And why not? Have you never been afraid?"

"I? To be sure. I rather like it, too! It's invigorating—unusual. You know there's a kind of fascination about certain emotions which are in themselves unpleasant. But—my dear boy, you can't understand. We were talking about you the other night at the Boston Club after your election, and Thompson told about that affair you had with those niggers up the State, when you were sheriff. It was quite thrilling to hear him tell it."

"Indeed?"

"Oh, yes! He made you out a great hero. I never knew why you went in for politics, or at least why, if you went in at all, you didn't try for something worth while. You could have gone to the legislature just as easily. But for a Blake to be sheriff! Well, it knocked us all silly when we heard of it, and I don't understand it yet. We pictured you locking up drunken men, serving subpoenas, and selling widows' farms over their heads."

"There's really more to a sheriff's duties than that."

"So I judged from Thompson's blood-curdling tales. I felt very anaemic and insignificant as I listened to him."

"It doesn't hurt a gentleman to hold a minor political office, even in a tough parish. I think men ought to try themselves out and find what they are made of."

"It isn't your lack of exclusiveness that strikes one; it's your nerve."

"Oh, that's mostly imaginary. I haven't much, really. But the truth is I'm interested in courage. They say a man always admires the quality in which he is naturally lacking, and wants to acquire it. I'm interested in brave men, too; they fascinate me. I've studied them; I've tried to analyze courage and find out what it is, where it lies, how it is developed, and all about it, because I have, perhaps, a rather foolish craving to be able to call myself fairly brave."

"If you hadn't made a reputation for yourself, this sort of modesty would convict you of cowardice," Dreux exclaimed. "It sounds very funny, coming from you, and I think you are posing. Now with me it is wholly different. I couldn't stand what you have; why, the sight of a dead man would unsettle me for months and, as for risking my life or attempting the life of a fellow creature—well, it would be a physical impossibility. I—I'd just turn tail. You are exceptional, though you may not know it; you're not normal. The majority of us, away back in the woodsheds of our minds, recognize ourselves as cowards, and I differ from the rest in that I'm brave enough to admit it."

"How do you know you are a coward?"

"Oh, any little thing upsets me."

"Your people were brave enough."

"Of course, but conditions were different in those days; we're more advanced now. There's nothing refined about swinging sabers around your head like a windmill and chopping off Yankee arms and legs; nor is there anything especially artistic in two gentlemen meeting at dawn under the oaks with shotguns loaded with scrap iron." Mr. Dreux shuddered. "I'm tremendously glad the war is over and duels are out of fashion."

"Well, be thankful that antiques are not out of fashion. There is still a profit in them, I suppose?"

Dreux shook his head mournfully. "Not in the good stuff. I just sold the original sword of Jean Lafitte to a man who makes preserved tomatoes. It is the eighth in three weeks. The business in Lafitte sabers is very fair lately. General Jackson belt-buckles are moving well, too, not to mention plug hats worn by Jefferson Davis at his inauguration. There was a fabulous hardwood king at the St. Charles whom I inflamed with the beauties of marquetrie du bois. It was all modern, of course, made in Baltimore, but I found him a genuine Sinurette four-poster which was very fine. I also discovered a royal Sevres vase for him, worth a small fortune, but he preferred a bath sponge used by Louis XIV. I assured him the sponge was genuine, so he bought a Buhl cabinet to put it in. I took the vase for Myra Nell."

"Do you think Myra Nell would care to be Queen of the Carnival?" Norvin inquired.

"Care?" Bernie started forward in his chair, his eyes opened wide. "You're—joking! Is—is there any—" He relaxed suddenly, and after an instant's hesitation inquired, "What do you mean?"

"I mean what I say. She can be Queen if she wishes."

Dreux shook his head reluctantly. "She'd be delighted, of course; she'd go mad at the prospect, but—frankly, she can't afford it." He flushed under Blake's gaze.

"I'm sorry, Bernie. I've been told to ask her."

"I am very much obliged to you for the honor, and it's worth any sacrifice, but—Lord! It is disgusting to be poor." He prodded viciously with his cane.

"It is a great thing for any girl to be Queen. The chance may not come again."

Dreux made a creditable effort to conceal his disappointment, but he was really beside himself with chagrin. "You needn't tell me," he said, "but there is no use of my even dreaming of it; I've figured over the expense too often. She was Queen of Momus last year—that's why I've had to vouch for so many Lafitte swords and Davis high hats. If those tourists ever compare notes they'll think that old pirate must have been a centipede or a devilfish to wield all those weapons."

"I would like to have her accept," Blake persisted.

Bernie Dreux glanced at the speaker quickly, feeling a warm glow suffuse his withered body at the hint of encouragement for his private hopes. What more natural, he reasoned, than for Blake to wish his future wife to accept the highest social honor that New Orleans can confer? Norvin's next words offered further encouragement, yet awoke a very conflicting emotion.

"In view of the circumstances, and in view of all it means to Myra Nell, I would consider it a privilege to lend you whatever you require. She need never know."

Involuntarily the little bachelor flushed and drew himself up.

"Thanks! It's very considerate of you, but—I can't accept, really."

"Even for her sake?"

"If I didn't know you so well, or perhaps if you didn't know us so well, I'd resent such a proposal."

"Nonsense! Don't be foolish." Realizing thoroughly what this sacrifice meant to Miss Warren's half-brother, Norvin continued: "Suppose we say nothing further about it for the time being. Perhaps you will feel differently later."

After a pause Dreux said: "Heaven knows where these carnivals will end if we continue giving bigger pageants every year. It's a frightful drain on the antique business, and I'm afraid I will have to drop out next season. I scarcely know what to do."

"Why don't you marry?" Blake inquired.

"Marry?" Dreux smiled whimsically. "That lumber king had a daughter, but she was freckled."

"Felicite Delord isn't freckled."

Bernie said nothing for a moment, and then inquired quietly:

"What do you know about Felicite?"

"All there is to know, I believe. Enough, at any rate, to realize that you ought to marry her."

As Dreux made no answer, he inquired, "She is willing, of course?"

"Of course."

"Then why don't you do it?"

"The very fact that people—well, that I know I ought to, perhaps. Then, too, my situation. I have certain obligations which I must live up to."

"Don't be forever thinking of yourself. There are others to be considered."

"Exactly. Myra Nell, for instance."

"It seems to me you owe something to Felicite."

"My dear boy, you don't talk like a—like a—"

"Southern gentleman?" Blake smiled. "Nevertheless, Miss Delord is a delightful little person and you can make her happy. If Myra Nell should be Queen of the Mardi Gras it would round out her social career. She will marry before long, no doubt, and then you will be left with no obligations beyond those you choose to assume. Nobody knows of your relations with Felicite."

"*You* know," said the bachelor stiffly, "and therefore others must know, hence it is quite impossible. I'd prefer not to discuss it if you don't mind."

"Certainly. I want you to keep that loan in mind, however. I think you owe it to your sister to accept. At any rate, I am glad we had this opportunity of speaking frankly."

"Ah," said Bernie, suddenly, as if seizing with relief upon a chance to end the discussion, "I think I heard some one in the outer office."

"To be sure," exclaimed Blake. "That must be Donnelly. I had an appointment with him here which I'd forgotten all about."

"The Chief of Police? He's quite a friend of yours."

"Yes, we met while I was sheriff. He's a remarkably able officer—one of those men I like to study."

"Well, then, I'll be going," said Bernie, rising.

"No, stay and meet him." Blake rose to greet a tall, angular man of about Dreux's age, who came in without knocking. Chief Donnelly had an impassive face, into which was set a pair of those peculiar smoky-blue eyes which have become familiar upon our frontiers. He acknowledged his introduction to Bernie quietly, and measured the little man curiously.

"Mr. Dreux is a friend of mine, and he was anxious to meet you, so I asked him to stay," Norvin explained.

"If I'm not intruding," Bernie said.

"Oh, there's nothing much on my mind," the Chief declared. "I've come in for some information which I don't believe Blake can give me." To Norvin he said, "I remembered hearing that you'd been to Italy, so I thought you might help me out."

Mr. Dreux sat back, eliminated himself from the conversation in his own effective manner, and regarded the officer as a mouse might gaze upon a lion.

"Yes, but that was four years ago," Norvin replied.

"All the better. Were you ever in Sicily?"

Blake started. The sudden mention of Sicily was like a touch upon an exposed nerve.

"I was in Sicily twice," he said, slowly.

"Then perhaps you can help me, after all. I recalled some sort of experience you had over there with the Mafia, and took a chance."

The Chief drew from his pocket a note-book which he consulted. "Did you ever hear of a Sicilian named—Narcone? Gian Narcone?" He looked up to see that his friend's face had gone colorless.

Blake nodded silently.

"Also a chap named—some nobleman—" He turned again to his memorandum-book.

"Martel Savigno, Count of Martinello," Norvin supplied in a strained, breathless voice.

"That's him! Why, you must know all about this affair."

Blake rose and began to pace his office while the others watched him curiously, amazed at his agitated manner and his evident effort to control his features. Neither of his two friends had deemed him capable of such an exhibition of feeling.

As a matter of fact, Norvin had grown to pride himself upon his physical self-command and above all upon his impassivity of countenance. He had cultivated it purposely, for it formed a part of his later training — what he chose to call his course in courage. But this sudden probing of an old wound, this unexpected reference to the most painful part of his life, had found him off his guard and with his nerves loose.

After his return from Europe he had set himself vigorously to the task of uprooting his cowardice. Realizing that his parish had always been lawless, it occurred to him that the office of sheriff would compel an exercise of whatever courage he had in him. It had been absurdly easy to win the election, but afterward — the memory of the bitter fight which followed often made him cringe. Strangely enough, his theory had not worked out. He found that his cowardice was not a sick spot which could be cauterized or cut out, but rather that it was like some humor of the blood, or something ingrained in the very structure of his nervous tissue. But although his lack of physical courage seemed constitutional and incurable, he had a great and splendid pride which enabled him to conceal his weakness from the world. Time and again he had balked, had shied like a frightened horse; time and again he had roweled himself with cruel spurs and ridden down his unruly terrors by force of will. But the struggle had burned him out, had calcined his youth, had grayed his hair, and left him old and tired. Even now, when he had begun to consider his self-mastery complete, it had required no more than the unexpected mention of Martel Savigno's name and that of his murderer to awaken pangs of poignant distress, the signs of which he could not altogether conceal.

When after an interval of several minutes he felt that he had himself sufficiently in hand to talk without danger of self-betrayal, he seated himself and inquired:

"What do you wish to know about — the Count of Martinello and Narcone the bandit?"

"I want to know all there is," said Donnelly. "Perhaps we can get at it quicker if you will tell me what you know. I had no idea you were familiar with the case. It's remarkable how these old trails recross."

"I—I know everything about the murder of Martel Savigno, for I saw it. I was there. He was my best friend. That is the story of which you read. That is why the mention of his name upset me, even after nearly five years."

Bernie Dreux uttered an exclamation and hitched forward in his chair. This new side of Blake's character fascinated him.

"If you will tell me the circumstances it will help me piece out my record," said the Chief, so Blake began reluctantly, hesitatingly, giving the facts clearly, but with a constraint that bore witness to his pain in the recital.

When he had finished, it was Donnelly's turn to show surprise.

"That is remarkable!" he exclaimed. "To think that you have seen Gian Narcone! D'you suppose you would know him again after four years?" He shot a keen glance at his friend.

"I am quite sure I would. But come, you haven't told me anything yet."

"Well, Narcone is in New Orleans."

"What?" Blake leaned forward in his chair, his eyes blazing.

"At least I'm informed that he is. I received a letter some time ago containing most of the information you've just given me, and stating that there are extradition papers for him in New York. The letter says that some of his old gang have confessed to their part in the murder and have implicated Narcone so strongly that he will hang if they can get him back to Sicily."

"I believe that. But who is your informant?"

"I don't know. The letter is anonymous."

A sudden wild hope sprang up in Blake's mind. He dared not trust it, yet it clamored for credence.

"Was it written by a—woman?" he queried, tensely.

"No; at least I don't think so. It was written on one of these new-fangled typewriting machines. I left it at the office, or you could judge for yourself."

"If it is typewritten, how do you know whether—"

"I tell you I don't know. But I can guess pretty closely. It was one of the Pallozzo gang. This Narcone—he calls himself Vito Sabella, by the way—is a leader of the Quatrones. The two factions have been at war lately and some member of the Pallozzo outfit has turned him up."

The light died out of Norvin's face, his body relaxed. He had followed so many clues, his quest had been so long and fruitless, that he met disappointment half-way.

Up to this moment Bernie Dreux had listened without a word or movement, but now he stirred and inquired, hesitatingly:

"Pardon me, but what is this Pallozzo gang and who are the Quatrones? I'm tremendously interested in this affair."

"The Pallozzos and the Quatrones," Donnelly explained, "are two Italian gangs which have come into rivalry over the fruit business. They unload the ships, you know, and they have clashed several times. You probably heard about their last mix-up—one man killed and four wounded."

"I never read about such things," Dreux acknowledged, at which the Chief's eyes twinkled and once more wandered over the little man's immaculate figure.

"You are familiar with our Italian problem, aren't you?"

"I—I'm afraid not. I know we have a large foreign population in the city—in fact, I spend much of my time on the other side of Canal Street—but I didn't know there was any particular problem."

"Well, there is, and a very serious one, too," Blake assured him. "It's giving our friend Donnelly and the rest of the city officials trouble enough and to spare. There have been some eighty killings in the Italian quarter."

"Eighty-four," said Donnelly. "And about two hundred outrages of one sort or another."

"And almost no convictions. Am I right?"

"You are. We can't do a thing with them. They are a law to themselves, and they ignore us and ours absolutely. It's getting worse, too. Fine situation to exist in the midst of a law-abiding American community, isn't it?" Donnelly appealed to Dreux.

"Now that will show you how little a person may know of his own home," reflected Bernie. "Has it anything to do with this Mafia we hear so much about?"

"It has. But the Mafia is going to end," Donnelly announced positively. "I've gone on record to that effect. If those dagos can't obey our laws, they'll have to pull their freight. It's up to me to put a finish to this state of affairs or acknowledge I'm a poor official and don't know my business. The reform crowd has seized upon it as a weapon to put me out of office, claiming that I've sold out to the Italians and don't want to run 'em down, so I've got to do something to show I'm not asleep on my beat. I've never had a chance before, but now I'm going after this Vito Sabella and land him. Will you look him over, Norvin, and see if he's the right party?"

"Of course. I owe Narcone a visit and I'm glad of this chance. But granting that he is Narcone, how can you get him out of New Orleans? He'll fight extradition and the Quatrones will support him."

"I'm blamed if I know. I'll have to figure that out," said the Chief as he rose to go. "I'm mighty glad I had that hunch to come and see you, and I wish you were a plain-clothes man instead of the president of the Cotton Exchange. I think you and I could clean out this Mafia and make the town fit for a white man to live in. If you'll drop in on me at eight o'clock to-night we'll walk over toward St. Phillip Street and perhaps get a look at your old friend Narcone. If you care to come along, Mr. Dreux, I'd be glad to have you."

Bernie Dreux threw up his shapely hands in hasty refusal. "Oh dear, no!" he protested. "I haven't lost any Italian murderers. This expedition, which you're planning so lightly, may lead to—Heaven knows what. At any rate, I should only be in the way, so if it's quite the same to you I'll send regrets."

"Quite the same," Donnelly laughed, then to Norvin: "If you think this dago may recognize you, you'd better tote a gun. At eight, then."

"At eight," agreed Blake and escorted him to the door.

# IX.
## "ONE WHO KNOWS"

Norvin Blake dined at his club that evening, returning to his office at about half-past seven. He was relieved to find the place deserted, for he desired an opportunity to think undisturbed. Although this unforeseen twist of events had seemed remarkable, at first, he began to feel that he had been unconsciously waiting for this very hour. Something had always forewarned him that a time would come when he would be forced to take a hand once more in that old affair. Nor was he so much disturbed by the knowledge that Narcone, the butcher, was here in New Orleans as by the memories and regrets which the news aroused.

Entering his private office, he lit the gas, and flinging himself into an easy-chair, gave himself over to recollections of all that the last four years had brought forth. It seemed only yesterday that he had returned from Italy, hot upon the scent which Colonel Neri had uncovered for him. He had been confident, eager, hopeful, yet he had failed, signally, unaccountably. He had combed New York City for a trace of Margherita Ginini with a thoroughness that left no possible means untried. As he looked back upon it now, he wondered if he could ever summon sufficient enthusiasm to attack any other project with a similar determination. He doubted it. Later experience had bred in him a peculiar caution, a shrinking hesitancy at exposing his true feelings, due, no doubt, to that ever-present necessity of watching himself.

Margherita had never written him after her first disappearance; his own letters had been returned from Sicily; the police of New York had failed as those of Rome and Naples and other cities had failed. He had wasted a small fortune in the hire of private detectives. At last, when it was too late to profit him, he had learned that the three women had been in New York at the time of his arrival, but evidently they had become alarmed at his pursuit and fled. It was this which had forced him to give up—the certainty that Margherita knew the motive of his search and resented it. He had never quite recovered from the sting of that discovery, for he was proud, but he had grown too wise to cherish unjust resentment. It merely struck him as a great pity that their lives had fallen out in such unhappy fashion. He never tried to deceive himself into believing that he could forget her, become a new man, and banish the joy and the pain of his past, impartially. There were other women, it is true, who attracted him strongly, aroused his tenderness and appealed to his manhood—and among them Myra Nell Warren. His power of feeling had not been atrophied, rather it had become deeper. Yet his loyalty was never really impaired. In the bottom of his heart he knew that that tawny, slumbrous yet passionate Sicilian girl was his first and his most sacred love.

As he sat alone now, with the evidences of his accomplishment about him, he realized that in spite of his material success, life, so far, at least, had been just as stale and flat as it had promised to be on that night when he and Martel had ridden away from the feast at Terranova. He had made good, to his own satisfaction, in all respects save one, and even in that he had gained the form if not the substance, for the world regarded him as a man of proven courage. It seemed to him a grim and hideous joke, and he wondered what his friends would think if they knew that the very commonplace adventure planned for this evening filled him with a cringing horror. The prospect of this trip into the Italian quarter with the probability of encountering Narcone turned him cold and sick. His hands were like ice and the muscles of his back were twitching nervously; he could feel his heart pound as he let his thoughts have free play. But these symptoms were only too familiar; he had conquered them too many times to think of weakening.

After five years of intimate self-study he was still at a loss to account for his phenomenal cowardice. He wondered again to-night if it might not be the result of a too powerful imagination. Donnelly had no imagination whatever, and the same seemed true of others whom he had studied. As for himself, his fancies took alarm at the slightest hint and went careering off into all the dark byways of supposition, encountering impossible shapes and improbable dangers. Whatever the cause, he had long since given up hope of ever winning a permanent victory over himself and had learned that each trial meant a fresh battle.

When he saw by the clock that the hour of his appointment had come, he arose, although his body seemed to belong to some one else and his spirit was crying out a mad, panicky warning. He opened the drawer of his desk and, extracting a revolver, raised it at arm's-length. He drew it down before his eye until the sights crept into alignment, and held it there for a throbbing second. Then he smiled mirthlessly, for his hand had not shown the slightest tremor.

Donnelly was waiting as Blake walked into headquarters, and, exhuming a box of cigars from the remotest depths of a desk drawer, he offered them, saying:

"I've sent O'Connell over to reconnoiter. There's no use of our starting out until he locates Sabella. You needn't be so suspicious of those perfectos; they won't bite you."

"The last one you gave me did precisely that."

"Must have been one of my cooking cigars. I keep two kinds, one for callers and one for friends."

"Then if this is a Flor de Friendship I'll accept," Blake said with a laugh.

"I see Mr. Dreux didn't change his mind and decide to join us."

"No, this is a little too rough for Bernie. He very cheerfully acknowledged that he was afraid Narcone might recognize me and make trouble."

"I thought of that," Donnelly acknowledged. "Is there any chance?"

In the depths of Blake's consciousness something cried out fearfully in the affirmative, but he replied: "Hardly. He never saw me except indistinctly, and that was nearly five years ago. He might recall my name, but I dare say not without an introduction, which isn't necessary."

"Do you think you will know him?"

"I-I have reason to think I will."

The Chief grunted with satisfaction.

"A funny little fellow, that Dreux!" he remarked. "Wasn't it his father who fought a duel with Colonel Hammond from Baton Rouge?"

"The same. They used shotguns at forty yards. Colonel Hammond was killed."

"Humph! And he was afraid to go with us to-night?"

"Oh, he makes no secret of his cowardice."

"Well, a mule is a mule, a coward is a coward, and a gambler is a—son-of-a-gun," paraphrased the Chief. "If he hasn't any courage he can't force it into himself."

"Do you think so?"

"I know so. I've seen it tried. Some people are born cowards and can't help themselves. As for me, I was never troubled much that way. I suppose you find it the same, too."

"No. My only consolation lies in thinking it's barely possible the other fellow may be as badly frightened as I am."

Donnelly scoffed openly. "I never saw a man stand up better than you. Why I've touted you as the gamest chap I ever saw. Do you remember that dago Misetti who jumped from here into your parish when you were sheriff?"

Blake smiled. "I'm not likely to forget him."

"You walked into a gun that day when you knew he'd use it."

"He didn't, though—at least not much. Perhaps he was as badly rattled as I was."

"Have it your own way," the Chief said. "But that reminds me, he's out again."

"Indeed! I hadn't heard."

"You knew, of course, we couldn't convict him for that killing. We had a perfect case, but the Mafia cleared him. Same old story— perjury, alibis, and jury-fixing. We put him away for resisting an officer, though; they couldn't stop us there. But they've 'sprung' him and he's back in town again. Damn such people! With over two hundred Italian outrages of various kinds in this city up to date, I can count the convictions on the fingers of one hand. The rest of the country is beginning to notice it."

"It is a serious matter," Blake acknowledged, "and it is affecting the business interests of the city. We see that every day."

"If I had a free hand I'd tin-can every dago in New Orleans."

"Nonsense! They're not all bad. The great majority of them are good, industrious, law-abiding people. It's a comparatively small criminal element that does the mischief."

"You think so, eh? Well, if you held down this job for a year you'd be ready to swear they're all blackmailers and murderers. If they're so honest and peaceable, why don't they come out and help us run down the malefactors?"

"That's not their way."

"No, you bet it isn't," Donnelly affirmed. "Things are getting worse every day. The reformers don't have to call my attention to it; I'm wise. So far, they have confined their operations to their own people, but what's to prevent them from spreading out? Some day those Italians will break over and tackle us Americans, and then there will be hell to pay. I'll be blamed for not holding them in check. Why, you've no idea of the completeness of their organization; it has a thousand branches and it takes in some of their very best people. I dare say you think this Mafia is some dago secret society with lodge-rooms and grips and passwords and a picnic once a year. Well, I tell you—"

"You needn't tell me anything about La Mafia," Blake interrupted, gravely. "I know as much about it, perhaps, as you do. Something ought to be done to choke off this flood of European criminal immigration. Believe me, I realize what you are up against, Dan, and I know, as you know, that La Mafia will beat you."

"I'm damned if it will!" exploded the officer. "The policing of this city is under my charge, and if those people want to live here among us—"

The telephone bell rang and Donnelly broke off to answer it.

"Hello! Is that you, O'Connell? Good! Stick around the neighborhood. We'll be right over." He hung up the receiver and explained: "O'Connell has him marked out. We'd better go."

It was not until they were well on their way that Norvin thought to mention the letter, which he had wished to see.

"Oh, yes, I meant to show it to you," said Donnelly.

"But there's nothing unusual about it, except perhaps the signature."

"I thought you said it was anonymous."

"Well, it is; it's merely signed 'One who Knows.'"

"Does it mention an associate of Narcone—a man named Cardi?"

"No. Who's he?"

"I dare say at least a hundred thousand people have asked that same question." Briefly Norvin told what he knew of the reputed chief of the banditti, of the terrors his name inspired in Sicily, and of his supposed connection with the murder of Savigno. "Once or twice a year I hear from Colonel Neri," he added, "but he informs me that Cardi has never returned to the island, so it occurred to me that he too might be in New Orleans."

"It's very likely that he is, and if he was a Capo-Mafia there, he's probably the same here. Lord! I'd like to get inside of that outfit; I'd go through it like a sandstorm."

By this time they had threaded the narrow thoroughfares of the old quarter, and were nearing the vicinity of St. Phillip Street, the heart of what Donnelly called "Dagotown." There was little to distinguish this part of the city from that through which they had come. There were the same dingy, wrinkled houses, with their odd little balconies and ornamental iron galleries overhanging the sidewalks and peering into one another's faces as if to see what their neighbors were up to; the same queer, musty, dusty shops, dozing amid violent foreign odors; the same open doorways and tunnel-like entrances leading to paved courtyards at the rear. The steep roofs were tiled and moss-grown, the pavements were of huge stone flags, set in between seams of mud, and so unevenly placed as to make traffic impossible save by the light of day. Alongside the walks were open sewers, in which the foul and sluggish current was setting not toward, but away from, the river-front. The district was peopled by shadows and mystery; it abounded in strange sights and sounds and smells.

At the corner of Royal and Dumaine they found O'Connell loitering in a doorway, and with a word he directed them to a small cafe and wine-shop in the next block.

A moment later they pushed through swinging doors and entered. Donnelly nodded to the white-haired Italian behind the bar and led the way back to a vacant table against the wall, where he and Norvin seated themselves. There were perhaps a half-dozen similar tables in the room, at some of which men were eating. But it was late for supper, and for the most part the occupants were either drinking or playing cards.

There was a momentary pause in the babble of conversation as the two stalked boldly in, and a score of suspicious glances were leveled at them, for the Chief was well known in the Italian quarter. The proprietor came bustling toward the new-comers with an obsequious smile upon his grizzled features. Taking the end of his apron he wiped the surface of their table dry, at the same time informing Donnelly in broken English that he was honored by the privilege of serving him.

Donnelly ordered a bottle of wine, then drew an envelope from his pocket and began making figures upon it, leaning forward and addressing his companion confidentially, to the complete disregard of his surroundings. Norvin glued his eyes upon the paper, nodding now and then as if in agreement. Although he had taken but one hasty glance around the cafe upon entering, he had seen a certain heavy-muscled Sicilian whose face was only too familiar. It was Narcone, without a doubt. Blake had seen that brutal, lust-coarsened countenance too many times in his dreams to be mistaken, and while his one and only glimpse had been secured in a half-light, his mind at that instant had been so unnaturally sensitized that the photograph remained clear and unfading.

He could feel Narcone staring at him now, as he sat nodding to the senseless patter of the Chief in a sort of breathless, terrifying suspense. Would his own face recall to the fellow's mind that night in the forest of Terranova and set his fears aflame? Blake's reason told him that such a thing was beyond the faintest probability, yet the flesh upon his back was crawling as if in anticipation of a knife-thrust. Nevertheless, he lit a cigar and held the match between fingers which did not tremble. He was fighting his usual, senseless battle, and he was winning. When the proprietor set the bottle in front of him he filled both glasses with a firm hand and then, still listening to Donnelly's words, he settled back in his chair and let his eyes rove casually over the room. He encountered Narcone's evil gaze when the glass was half-way to his lips and returned it boldly for an instant. It filled him with an odd satisfaction to note that not a ripple disturbed the red surface of the wine.

"Have you 'made' him?" Donnelly inquired under his breath.

Blake nodded: "The tall fellow at the third table."

"That's him, all right," agreed the Chief. "He doesn't remember you."

"I didn't expect him to; I've changed considerably, and besides he never saw me distinctly, as I told you before."

"You've got the policeman's eye," declared Donnelly with enthusiasm. "I wanted you to pick him out by yourself. We'll go, now, as soon as we lap up this dago vinegar."

Out in the street again, Blake heaved a sigh of relief, for even this little harmless adventure had been a trial to his unruly nerves.

"We'll drift past the Red Wing Club; it's a hang-out of mine and I want to talk further with you," said Donnelly.

They turned back towards the heart of the city, stopping a moment while the Chief directed O'Connell to keep a close watch upon Narcone.

The Red Wing Club was not really a club at all, but a small restaurant which had become known for certain of its culinary specialties and had gathered to itself a somewhat select clientele of bons vivants, who dined there after the leisurely continental fashion. Thither the two men betook themselves.

"I can't see what real good those extradition papers are going to do you, even now that you're sure of your man," said Norvin as soon as they were seated. "It won't be difficult to arrest him, but to extradite him will prove quite another matter. I'm not eager myself to take the stand against him, for obvious reasons." Donnelly nodded his appreciation. "I will do so, if necessary, of course, but my evidence won't counterbalance all the testimony Sabella will be able to bring. We know he's the man; his friends know it, but they'll unite to swear he is really Vito Sabella, a gentle, sweet soul whom they knew in

Sicily, and they'll prove he was here in America at the time Martel Savigno was murdered. If we had him in New York, away from his friends, it would be different; he'd go back to Sicily, and once there he'd hang, as he deserves."

Donnelly swore under his breath. "It's the thing I run foul of every time I try to enforce the law against these people. But just the same I'm going to get this fellow, somehow, for he's one of the gang that fired into the Pallozzos and killed Tony Alto. That's another thing I know but can't prove. What made you ask if that letter was written by a woman? Has Sabella a sweetheart?"

"Not to my knowledge. I—" Norvin hesitated. "No, Sabella has no sweetheart, but Savigno had. I haven't told you much of that part of my story. It's no use my trying to give you an idea of what kind of woman the Countess of Terranova was, or is—you wouldn't understand. It's enough to say that she is a woman of extraordinary character, wholly devoted to Martel's memory, and Sicilian to the backbone. After her lover's death, when the police had failed, she swore to be avenged upon his murderers. I know it sounds strange, but it didn't seem so strange to me then. I tried to reason with her, but it was a waste of breath. When I returned to Sicily after my mother died, Margherita— the Countess—had disappeared. I tried every means to find her—you know, Martel left her, in a way, under my care—but I couldn't locate her in any Italian city. Then I learned that she had come to the United States and took up the search on this side. It's a long story; the gist of it is simply that I looked up every possibility, and finally gave up in despair. That was more than four years ago. I have no idea that all this has any connection with our present problem."

Donnelly listened with interest, and for a time plied Blake with shrewd questions, but at length the subject seemed to lose its importance in his mind.

"It's a queer coincidence," he said. "But the letter was mailed in this city and by some one familiar with Narcone's movements up to date. If your Countess was here you'd surely know it. This isn't New York. Besides, women don't make good detectives; they get discouraged. I dare say she went back to Italy long ago and is married now, with a dozen or more little counts and countesses around her."

"I agree with you," said Blake, "that she can't be the 'One Who Knows.' There are too many easier explanations, and I couldn't hope—" He checked himself. "Well, I guess I've told you about all I know. Call on me at any time that I can be of assistance."

He left rather abruptly, struggling with a sense of self-disgust in that he had been led to talk of Margherita unnecessarily, yet with a curious undercurrent of excitement running through his mood.

# X.
# MYRA NELL WARREN

Miss Myra Nell Warren seldom commenced her toilet with that feeling of pleasurable anticipation common to most girls of her age. Not that she failed to appreciate her own good looks, for she did not, but because in order to attain the desired effects she was forced to exercise a nice discrimination which can be appreciated only by those who have attempted to keep up appearances upon an income never equal to one's requirements. She had many dresses, to be sure, but they were as familiar to her as family portraits, and even among her most blinded admirers they had been known to stir the chords of remembrance. Then, too, they were always getting lost, for Myra Nell had a way of scattering other things than her affections. She had often likened her dresses to an army of Central American troops, for mere ragged abundance in which there lay no real fighting strength. Having been molded to fit the existing fashions in ladies' clothes, and bred to a careless extravagance, poverty brought the girl many complexities and worries.

To-night, however, she was in a very happy frame of mind as she began dressing, and Bernie, hearing her singing blithely, paused outside her door to inquire the cause.

"Can't you guess, stupid?" she replied.

"Um-m! I didn't know he was coming."

"Well, he is. And, Bernie—have you seen my white satin slippers?"

"How in the world should I see them?"

"It isn't them, it is just him. I've discovered one under the bed, but the other has disappeared, gone, skedaddled. Do rummage around and find it for me, won't you? I think it's down-stairs—"

"My dear child," her brother began in mild exasperation, "how can it be down-stairs—"

The door of Myra Nell's room burst open suddenly, and a very animated face peered around the edge at him.

"Because I left it there, purposely. I kicked it off—it hurt. At least I think I did, although I'm not sure. I kicked it off somewhere."

Miss Warren's words had a way of rushing forth head over heels, in a glad, frolicky manner which was most delightful, although somewhat damaging to grammar. But she was too enthusiastic to waste time on grammar; life forever pressed her too closely to allow repose of thought, of action, or of speech.

"Now, don't get huffy, honey," she ran on. "If you only knew how I've— Oh, goody! you're going out!"

"I was going out, but of course—"

"Now don't be silly. He isn't coming to see you."

Bernie exclaimed in a shocked voice:

"MyraNell!YouknowIneverleaveyoutoentertainyourcallersalone. It isn't proper."

She sighed. "It isn't proper to entertain them on one foot, like a stork, either. Do be a dear, now, and find my slipper. I've worn myself to the bone, I positively have, hunting for it, and I'm in tears."

"Very well," he said. "I'll look, but why don't you take care of your things? The idea—"

She pouted a pair of red lips at him, slammed the door in his face, and began singing joyously once more.

"What dress are you going to wear?" he called to her.

"That white one with all the chiffon missing."

"What has become of the chiffon?" he demanded, sternly.

"I must have stepped on it at the dance. I—in fact, I know I did."

"Of course you saved it?"

"Oh, yes. But I can't find it now. If you could only—"

"No!" he cried, firmly, and dashed down the stairs two steps at a time. From the lower hall he called up to her, "Wear the new one, and be sure to let me see you before he comes."

Bernie sighed as he hung up his hat, for he had looked forward through a dull, disappointing day to an evening with Felicite Delord. She was expecting him—she would be greatly disappointed. He sighed a second time, for he was far from happy. Life seemed to be one long constant worry over money matters and Myra Nell. Being a prim, orderly man, he intensely disliked searching for mislaid articles, but he began a systematic hunt; for, knowing Myra Nell's peculiar irresponsibility, he was prepared to find the missing slipper anywhere between the hammock on the front gallery and the kitchen in the rear. However, a full half-hour's search failed to discover it. He had been under most of the furniture and was both hot and dusty when she came bouncing in upon him. Miss Warren never walked nor glided nor swayed sinuously as languorous Southern society belles are supposed to do; she romped and bounced, and she was chattering amiably at this moment.

"Here I am, Bunny, decked out like an empress. The new dress is a duck and I'm ravishing—perfectly ravishing. Eh? What?"

He wriggled out from beneath the horsehair sofa, rose, and, wiping the perspiration from his brow, pointed with a trembling finger at her feet.

"There! There it is," he said in a terrible tone. "That's it on your foot."

"Oh, yes. I found it right after you came downstairs." She burst out laughing at his disheveled appearance. "I forgot you were looking. But come, admire me!" She revolved before his eyes, and he smiled delightedly.

In truth, Miss Warren presented a picture to bring admiration into any eye, and although she was entirely lacking in poise and dignity, her constant restless vivacity and the witch-like spirit of laughter that possessed her were quite as engaging. She was a madcap, fly-away creature whose ravishing lace was framed by an unruly mop of dark hair, which no amount of attention could hold in place. Little dancing curls and wisps and ringlets were forever escaping in coquettish fashion:

Bernie regarded her critically from head to foot, absent-mindedly brushing from his own immaculate person the dust which bore witness to his sister's housekeeping. In his eyes this girl was more than a queen, she was a sort of deity, and she could do no wrong. He was by no means an admirable man himself, but he saw in her all the virtues which he lacked, and his simple devotion was touching.

"You didn't comb your hair," he said, severely.

"Oh, I did! I combed it like mad, but the hairpins pop right out," she exclaimed. "Anyway, there weren't enough."

"Well, I found some on the piano," he said, "so I'll fix you."

With deft fingers he secured the stray locks which were escaping, working as skilfully as a hair-dresser.

"Oh, but you're a nuisance," she told him, as she accepted his aid with the fidgety impatience of a restless boy. "They'll pop right out again."

"They wouldn't if you didn't jerk and flirt around—"

"Flirt, indeed! Bunny! Bunny! What an idea!" She kissed him with a resounding smack, squarely upon the end of his thin nose, then flounced over to the old-fashioned haircloth sofa.

Now, Mr. Dreux abhorred the name of Bunny, and above all things he abominated Myra Nell's method of saluting him upon the nose, but she only laughed at his exclamation of disgust, saying:

"Well, well! You haven't told me how nice I look."

"There is no possible hope for him," he acknowledged. "The gown fits very nicely, too."

"Chloe did it—she cut it off, and sewed on the doodads—"

"The what?"

"The ruffly things." Myra Nell sighed. "It's hard to make a dressmaker out of a cook. Her soul never rises above fried chicken and light bread, but she did pretty well this time, almost as well as—Do you know, Bunny, you'd have made a dandy dressmaker."

"My dear child," he said in scandalized tones, "you get more slangy every day. It's not ladylike."

"I know, but it gets you there quicker. Lordy! I hope he doesn't keep me waiting until I get all wrinkled up. Why don't you go out and have a good time? I'll entertain him."

"You know I wouldn't leave you alone."

She made a little laughing grimace at him and said:

"Well, then, if you must stay, I'll keep him out on the gallery all to myself. It's a lovely night, and, besides, the drawing-room is getting to smell musty. Mind you, don't get into any mischief."

She bounced up from the sofa and gave his ear a playful tweak with her pink fingers, then danced out into the drawing-room, where she rattled off a part of a piano selection at breakneck speed, ending in the middle with a crash, and finally flung open the long French blinds. The next instant he heard her swinging furiously in the hammock.

Bernie smiled fondly, as a mother smiles, and his pinched little face was glorified, then he sighed for a third time, as he thought of Felicite Delord, and regretfully settled himself down to a dull and solitary evening. The library had long since been denuded of its valuable books, in the same way that the old frame mansion had lost its finer furniture, piece by piece, as some whim of its mistress made a sacrifice necessary. In consequence, about all that remained now to afford Bernie amusement were certain works on art which had no market value. Selecting one of these, he lit a cigarette and lost himself among the old masters.

When Norvin Blake came up the walk beneath the live-oak and magnolia trees, Myra Nell met him at the top of the steps, and her cool, fresh loveliness struck him as something extremely pleasant to look upon, after his heated, bustling day on the Exchange.

"Bernie's in the library feasting on Spanish masters, so if you don't mind we'll sit out here," she told him.

"I'll be delighted," he assured her. "In that way I may be seen and so excite the jealousy of certain fellows who have been monopolizing you lately."

"A little jealousy is a good thing, so I'll help you. But—they don't have it in them. They're as calm and placid as bayou water."

Blake was fond of mildly teasing the girl about her popularity, assuming, as an old friend, a whimsically injured tone. She could never be sure how much or little his speeches meant, but, being an outrageous little coquette herself, she seldom put much confidence in any one's words.

"Tell me," he went on—"I haven't seen you for a week—who are you engaged to now?"

"The idea! I'm never really engaged; that is, hardly ever."

"Then there is a terrible misapprehension at large!"

"Oh, I'm always misapprehended. Even Bernie misapprehends me; he thinks I'm frivolous and light-minded, but I'm not. I'm really very serious; I'm—I'm almost morose."

He laughed at her. "You don't mean to deny you have a bewildering train of admirers?"

"Perhaps, but I don't like to think of them. You see, it takes years to collect a real train of admirers, and it argues that a girl is a fixture. That's something I won't be. I'm beginning to feel like one of the sights of the city, such as Bernie points out to his Northern tourists. Of course, you're the exception. I don't think we've ever been engaged, have we?"

"Um-m! I believe not, I don't care to be considered eccentric, however. It isn't too late."

"Bernie wouldn't allow it for a moment, and, besides, you're too serious. A girl should never engage herself to a serious-minded man unless she's really ready to—marry him."

"How true!"

"By the way," she chattered on, "what in the world have you done to Bernie? He has talked nothing but Mafia and murders and vendettas ever since he saw you the other day."

"He told you about meeting Donnelly in my office?"

"Yes! He's become tremendously interested in the Italian question all at once; he reads all the papers and he haunts the foreign quarter. He tells me we have a fearful condition of affairs here. Of course I don't know what he's talking about, but he's very much in earnest, and wants to help Mr. Donnelly do something or other—kill somebody, I judge."

"Really! I didn't suppose he cared for such things."

"Neither did I. But your story worked him all up. Of course, I read about *you* long ago, and that's how I knew you were a hero. When you returned from abroad I was simply smothered with excitement until I met you. The *idea* of your fighting with bandits, and all that! But tell me, did you discover that murderer creature?"

"Yes. We identified him."

"Oh-h!" The girl fairly wriggled with eagerness, and he had to smile at her as she leaned forward waiting for details. "Bernie said you asked him to go, but he was afraid. I—I wish you'd take me the next time. Fancy! What did he do? Was he a tall, dangerous-looking man? Did he grind his teeth at you?"

"No, no!" Norvin briefly explained the very ordinary happenings of his trip with the Chief of Police, to which she listened with her usual intensity of interest in the subject of the moment.

"You won't have to testify against him in those what-do-you-call-'em proceedings?" she asked as soon as he had finished.

"Extradition?"

"Why! Why, they'll blow you up, or do something dreadful!"

"I suppose I'll have to. Donnelly is bent on arresting him, and I owe something to the memory of Mattel Savigno."

"You mustn't!" she exclaimed with a gravity quite surprising in her. "When Bernie told me what it might lead to, it frightened me nearly to death. He says this Mafia is a perfectly awful affair. You won't get mixed up in it, will you? Please!"

The girl who was speaking now was not the Myra Nell he knew; her tone of real concern struck him very agreeably. Beneath her customary mood of intoxication with the joy of living he had occasionally caught fleeting glimpses of a really unusual depth of feeling, and the thought that she was concerned for his welfare filled him with a selfish gladness. Nevertheless, he answered her, truly:

"I can't promise that. I rather feel that I owe it to Martel"

"He's dead! That sounds brutal, but—"

"I owe something also to—those he left behind."

"You mean that Sicilian woman—that Countess. I suppose you know I'm horribly jealous of her?"

"I didn't know it."

"I am. Just think of it—a real Countess, with a castle, and dozens—thousands of gorgeous dresses! Was she—beautiful?"

"Very!"

"*Don't* say it that way. Goodness! How I hate her!"

Miss Warren flounced back into the corner of the hammock, and Norvin said with a laugh:

"No wonder you have a train of suitors."

"I've never seen a really beautiful Italian woman—except Vittoria Fabrizi, of course."

"Your friend, the nurse?"

"Yes, and she's not really Italian, she's just like anybody else. She was here to see me again this afternoon, by the way; it's her day off at the hospital, you know. I want you to meet her. You'll fall desperately in love."

"Really, I'm not interested in trained nurses, and I wouldn't want you to hate her as you hate the Countess."

"Oh, I couldn't hate Vittoria, she's such a dear. She saved my life, you know."

"Nonsense! You only had a sprained ankle."

"Yes, but it was a perfectly odious sprain. Nobody knows how I suffered. And to think it was all Bernie's fault!"

"How so? You fell off a horse."

"I did not," indignantly declared Miss Warren. "I was thrown, hurled, flung, violently projected, and then I was frightfully trampled by a snorting steed."

Norvin laughed heartily at this, for he knew the rickety old family horse very well by sight, and the picture she conjured up was amusing.

"How do you manage to blame it on Bernie?" he inquired.

"Well, he forbade me to ride horseback, so of course I had to do it."

"Oh, I see."

"I fixed up a perfectly ravishing habit. I couldn't ask Bernie to buy me one, since he refused to let me ride, so I made a skirt out of our grand-piano cover—it was miles long, and a darling shade of green. When it came to a hat I was stumped until I thought of Bernie's silk one. No mother ever loved a child as he loved that hat, you know. I twisted his evening scarf around it, and the effect was really stunning—it floated beautifully. Babylon and I formed a picture, I can tell you. I call the horse Babylon because he's such an old ruin. But I don't believe any one ever rode him before; he didn't seem to know what it was all about. He was very bony, too, and he stuck out in places. I suppose we would have gotten along all right if I hadn't tried to make him prance. He wouldn't do it, so I jabbed him."

"Jabbed him?"

Myra Nell nodded vigorously. "With my hat-pin. I didn't mean to hurt him, but—oh my! He isn't nearly so old as we think. I suppose the surprise did it. Anyhow, he became a raging demon in a second, and when they picked me up I had a sprained ankle and the piano cover was a sight."

"I suppose Babylon ran away?"

"No, he was standing there, with one foot right through Bernie's high hat. That was the terrible part of it all—I had to pretend I was nearly killed, just to take Bernie's mind off the hat. I stayed in bed for the longest time—I was afraid to get up—and he got Vittoria Fabrizi to wait on me. So that's how I met her. You can't linger along with your life in a person's hands for weeks at a time without getting attached to her. I was sorry for Babylon, so I had Chloe put a poultice on his back where I jabbed him. Now I'd like to know if that isn't Bernie's fault. He should have allowed me to ride and then I wouldn't have wanted to. Poor boy! he was the one to suffer after all. He'd planned to take a trip somewhere, but of course he couldn't do that and pay for a trained nurse, too."

Myra Nell's allusion to her brother's financial condition reminded Blake of the subject which had been uppermost in his mind all evening, and he decided to broach it now. Subsequent to his last talk with Dreux he had thought a good deal about that proffered loan and had come to regard Bernie's refusal as unwarranted. To be Queen of the Carnival was an honor given to but few young women, and one that would probably never come to Miss Warren again, so even at the risk of offending her half-brother he had decided to lay the matter before Myra Nell herself. She ought at least to have in later years the consoling thought that she had once refused the royal scepter. He hoped, however, that her persuasion added to his own would bring Dreux to a change of heart.

"If you'll promise to make no scene, refrain from hysterics, and all that," he began, warningly, "I'll tell you some good news."

"How silly! I'm an iceberg! I never get excited!" she declared.

"Well then, how would you like to be Queen of the next Mardi Gras?"

Myra Nell gasped faintly in the darkness, and sat bolt-upright.

"You—you're joking."

"That's no answer."

"I—I—Do you mean it? Oh!" She was out of the hammock now and poised tremblingly before him, like a bird. "Honestly? You're not fooling? Norvin, you dear duck!" She clapped her hands together gleefully and began to dance up and down. "I-I'm going to scream."

"Remember your promise."

"Oh, but Queen! Queen! Why I'm dreaming, I *must* scream."

"I gather from these rapt incoherences that you'd like it."

"*Like* it! You silly! Like it? Haven't I lived for it? Haven't I dreamed about it ever since T was a baby? Wouldn't any girl give her eyes to be queen?" She seemed upon the verge of kissing him, perhaps upon the nose, but changed her mind and went dancing around his chair like some moon-mad sprite. He seized her, barely in time to prevent her from crying the news aloud to Bernie, explaining hastily that she must breathe no word to any one for the time being and must first win her brother's consent. It was very difficult to impress her with the fact that the Carnival was still a long way off and that Bernie was yet to be reckoned with.

"As if there could be any question of my accepting," she chattered. "Dear, dear! Why shouldn't I? And it was lovely of you to arrange it for me, too. Oh, I know you did, so you needn't deny it. I hope you're to be Rex. Wouldn't that be splendid—but of course you wouldn't tell me."

"I can tell you this much, that I am not to be King. Now I have already spoken to Bernie—"

"The wretch! He never breathed a word of it."

"He's afraid he can't afford it."

"Oh, la, la! He'll have to. I'll die if he refuses—just die. You know I will."

"We'll bring him around, between us. You talk to him after I go, and the next time I see him I'll clinch matters. You'll make the most gorgeous of queens, Myra Nell."

"You think so?" She blushed prettily in the gloom. "I'll have to be very dignified; the train is as long as a hall carpet and I'll have to walk this way." She illustrated the royal step, bowing to him with a regal inclination of her dark head, and then broke out into rippling life and laughter so infectious that he felt he was a boy once more.

The girl's unaffected spontaneity was her most adorable trait. She was like a dancing ray of sunshine, and underneath her blithesome carelessness was a fine, clean, tender nature. Blake watched her with his eyes alight, for all men loved Myra Nell Warren and it was conceded among those who worshiped at her shrine that he who finally received her love in return for his would be favored far above his kind. She was closer to him to-night than ever before; she seemed to reach out and take him into her warm confidence, while he felt her appeal more strongly than at any time in their acquaintance. Of course she did not let him do much talking, she never did that, and now her head was full of dreams, of delirious anticipations, of splendid visions.

At last, when she had thanked him in as many ways as she could think of for his kindness and the time drew near for him to leave, she fell serious in a most abrupt manner, and then to his great surprise referred once again to his affair with the Mafia.

"It seems to me that my joy would be supreme to-night if I knew you would drop that Italian matter," she said. "The consequences may be terrible and—I—don't want you to get into trouble."

"I'll be careful," he told her, but as she stood with her hand in his she looked up at him with eyes which were no longer sparkling with fun, but deep and dark with shadows, saying, gently:

"Is there nothing which would induce you to change your mind?"

"That's not a fair question."

"I shall be worried to death—and I detest worry."

"There's no necessity for the least bit of concern," he assured her. But there was a plaintive wrinkle upon her brow as she watched him swing down the walk to the street.

As Blake strolled homeward he began to reflect that this charming intimacy with Myra Nell Warren could not go much farther without doing her an injustice. The time was rapidly nearing when he would have to make up his mind either to have very much more or very much less of her society. He was undeniably fond of her, for she not only interested him, but, what is far rarer and quite as important, she amused him. Moreover, she was of his own people; the very music of her Southern speech soothed his ear in contrast with the harsh accents of his Northern acquaintances. The thought came to him with a profound appeal that she might grow to love him with that unswerving faithfulness which distinguishes the Southern woman. And yet, strangely enough, when he retired that night it was not with her picture in his mind, but that of a splendid, tawny Sicilian girl with lips as fresh as a half-opened flower and eyes as deep as the sea.

# XI.
# THE KIDNAPPING

Bernie Dreux appeared at Blake's office on the following afternoon with a sour look upon his face. Norvin had known he would come, but hardly expected Myra Nell to win her victory so easily. Without waiting for the little man to speak, he began:

"I know what you're here for and I know just what you're going to tell me, so proceed; run me through with your reproaches; I offer no resistance."

"Do you think you acted very decently?" Dreux inquired.

"My dear Bernie, a crown was at stake."

"A crown of thorns for me. It means bankruptcy."

"Then you have consented? Good! I knew you would."

"Of course you knew I would; that's what makes your trick so abominable. I didn't think it of you."

"That's because you don't know my depravity; few people do."

"It would serve you right if I accepted your loan and never paid you back."

"It would indeed." Blake laughingly laid his hand upon his friend's shoulder. "What's more, that is exactly what I would do in your place. I'd borrow all I could and give my sister her one supreme hour, free from all disturbing fears and embarrassments; then I'd tell the impertinent meddler who was to blame for my trouble to go whistle for his satisfaction. Of course Miss Myra Nell doesn't suspect?"

"Oh, Heaven forbid!" piously exclaimed Dreuix.

"Now how much will you need?"

"I don't know; some fabulous sum. There will be gowns, and luncheons, and carriages, and entertaining. I will have to figure it out."

"Do. Then double it. And thanks awfully for coming to your senses."

"That's just the point—I haven't come to them, I'm perfectly insane to consider it," Bernie declared, savagely. "But what can I do when she looks at me with her eyes like stars and—and—" He waved his hands hopelessly. "It's mighty decent of you, but understand I consider it a dastardly trick and I'm horribly offended."

"Exactly, and I don't blame you, but your sister deserves a crown for her royal gift of youth and sweetness. As for being offended, since you are not one of the Mafia, I am not afraid."

"Do you know," said Bernie, "I have been thinking about this Mafia matter ever since I saw you. I'm tremendously interested and I—I'm beginning to feel the dawning of a civic spirit. Remarkable, eh? You know I haven't many interests, and I'd like to—to take a hand in running down these miscreants. I've always had an ambition, ever since I was a child, to be a—Don't laugh now. This is a confession. I've always wanted to be a—detective." He looked very grave, and at the same time a little shamefaced. "Do you suppose Donnelly could make me one?"

"Well! This is rather startling," said Blake, with difficulty restraining a desire to laugh.

"I—I can wear disguises wonderfully well," Bernie went on, wistfully. "I learned when I was in college theatricals. I was really very good. And you see I might earn a lot of money that way; I understand there are tremendous rewards offered for train-robbers and that sort of people. No one need know, of course, and no one would ever suspect me of being a minion of the law."

"That's true enough. But I'm afraid detectives in real life don't wear false beards. It's a pretty mean occupation, I fancy. Do you seriously think you are—er—fitted for it?"

"Heavens! I'm no good at anything else, and I'm perfectly wonderful at worming secrets out of people. This Mafia matter would give me a great opportunity. I—think I'll try it."

"These Italians have no sense of humor, you know. Something disagreeable might happen if you went prowling around them."

"Oh, of course I'd quit if they discovered my intentions—my game. When we were talking of such things, the other day, I said

I was a coward, but really I'm not. I've a frightful temper when I'm roused—really fiendish. As a matter of fact, I've"—he smiled sheepishly and tapped his slender, high-arched foot with his rattan cane—"I've already begun."

Blake settled back in his chair without a word.

"I'm taking Italian lessons from Myra Nell's nurse, Miss Fabrizi. She's a very superior woman, for a nurse, and she knows all about the Mafia. Quite an inspiration, I call it, thinking of her. I'm working her for informa—for a clue." He winked one eye gravely, and Norvin gasped. Bernie suddenly seemed very secretive, very different from his usual self. It was the first time Blake had ever seen him give this particular facial demonstration, and the effect was much as if some benevolent old lady had winked brazenly.

"Well!" he exclaimed. "I don't know what to say."

"There is nothing to say," Mr. Dreux answered in a vastly self-satisfied tone. "I'm going to offer my services to Donnelly—in confidence, of course. I'm glad you introduced us, for otherwise I'd have to arrange to meet him properly. If he doesn't want me, I'll proceed unaided."

When his caller had gone Blake gave way to the hearty laughter he had been smothering, dwelling with keen enjoyment upon the probable result of Bernie's interview with the Chief. Dan, he was sure, would not hurt the little man's feelings, so he felt no obligation to interfere.

Although he was expecting to hear from Donnelly at any moment regarding the Narcone matter, it was not until two weeks after their nocturnal excursion to the Italian quarter that the Chief came to see him. He brought unexpected news.

"We've had a run of luck," he began. "I've verified the information in that letter and found that those extradition papers for Narcone are really in New York. What's more, there's an Italian detective there on another matter, and he's ready to take our man back to Sicily with him."

"Really!"

"Narcone, it seems, was in New York for a year before he came here; that's why steps were taken to extradite him. Then he evidently got suspicious and came South. Anyhow, the plank is all greased, and if we land him in that city he'll go back to Sicily."

"I see. All that's necessary is to invite him to run up there and be arrested. It seems to me you're just where you were two weeks ago, Dan; unfortunately, this doesn't happen to be New York, and you've still got to solve the important problem of getting him there."

"I'm going to kidnap him," said the Chief, quietly.

"What? You're joking!"

"Not a bit of it."

"But—kidnapping—it isn't done any more! It's not even considered the thing in police circles, I believe. You'll be stealing children next, like any Mafioso."

Donnelly grinned. "That's where I got the idea. This same Narcone is mixed up in the Domenchino case. The kid has been gone nearly a month, now, but the father won't help us. He made a roar at the start, but they evidently got to him and now he declares that the boy must have strayed away to the river-front and been drowned. Well, it occurred to me to treat that Quatrone gang to some of its own medicine by stealing their ringleader."

"There's poetic justice in the idea—that is, if Narcone was really connected with the disappearance of the child."

"Oh, he was connected with it all right. Ordinary blackmail was getting too slow for the outfit, so they went after a good ransom. Now that old Domenchino has kicked up such a row, they're afraid to come through, and have probably murdered the child. That's what he fears, at any rate, and that's why he won't help us."

"It's shocking! But tell me, is this plan your own, or did Bernie Dreux suggest it?"

Donnelly laughed silently.

"So you knew he'd turned fly cop? I thought I'd split when he came to me."

"I hope you didn't offend him."

"Oh, not at all. Those little milliners are mighty sensitive. I told him he had the makings of another Le Coq, but the force was full. I suggested that he work on the outside, and set him to watching a certain dago fruit-stand on Canal Street."

"Why that particular stand?"

"Because it's owned by one of our men and he can't come to any harm there. He reports every day."

"But Narcone—Are you really in earnest about this scheme?"

"I am. It's our only chance to land him, and I've got to accomplish something or quit drawing my salary. Here's the layout; the Pinkertons have an operative who knew Sabella in New York; they were friends, in fact. This fellow arrived here two hours ago—calls himself Corte. He's to renew his acquaintance with our man and explain that he is returning to New York in a week. The day he sails we grab Mr. Narcone, hustle him aboard ship, and Corte will see to the rest. If it works right nobody'll know anything about it until Narcone is at sea, when it will be too late for interference. It's old stuff, but it'll work."

From what he knew of the Sicilian bandit, Blake felt a certain doubt as to the practicability of this plan, yet he was relieved to learn that he would not be called upon to testify. He therefore expressed himself as gratified at the change of procedure.

"It was partly to spare you," the Chief replied, "that I decided on this course. I want you to help me though."

"In what way?"

"Well, it will naturally take some force; Narcone won't go willingly. I want you to help me take him."

Instantly those fears which had been lulled in Norvin's breast leaped into turmoil; the same sick surge of emotions rose, and he felt himself quailing. After an instant's pause he said:

"I'll act any part you cast me for, but don't you think it is work for trained officers like you and this Corte?"

"That's exactly the point. Narcone may put up a fight, and I have more confidence in you, when it comes to a pinch, than in any man I know. Corte's job is to get him down to the dock, and I can't ask any of my men to take a hand with me, for it's—well, not exactly regular. Besides, I may need a witness." Donnelly hesitated. "If I do need one, I'll want some man whose word will carry more weight than that of a policeman. You understand?" He leveled his blue eyes at Blake and they looked particularly smoky and cold.

"You mean the Quatrones may try to break you?"

"Something like that."

"Suppose Narcone—er—resists?"

Donnelly shrugged, "We can't very well kill him, That's what makes it hard. I knew you had as much at stake as I, so I felt sure you'd help."

Blake heard himself assuring the officer that he had not been mistaken, but it was not his own voice that reached his ears, and when his caller had gone he found himself sitting limply in his chair, numb with horror at his own temerity.

As he looked back upon it, blaming himself for his too ready agreement, he realized that several mingling emotions had been at the root of it. In the first place, he had said "yes" because his craven spirit had screamed "no" so loudly. He felt that the project was not only dangerous, but impracticable, yet something, which he chose to term his over-will, had warned him that he must not upon any account give way to fear lest he weaken his already insecure hold upon himself. Again, Donnelly had appealed to him in a way hard to resist. He was not only flattered by the Chief's high regard for his courage, but grateful to him for having relieved him of the notoriety and possible consequences of a public proceeding. Most of all, perhaps, his final acquiescence had been an instinctive reaction of rage and disgust at the part of his nature that he hated. He struck at it as a man strikes at a snake.

But now that he was irrevocably pledged, his reason broke and fled, leaving him a prey to his imagination.

What, he wondered, would Narcone do when he saw his life at stake—when he recognized in one of his captors the man he had craved to kill in the forest of Terranova? There would in all probability be a physical struggle—perhaps he would find his own flabby muscles pitted against the mighty thews of the Sicilian butcher. At the thought he felt again the melting horror which had weakened him on that unspeakable night when Narcone had turned from wiping the warm blood from his hands to glare into his face. Blake feared that the memories would return to betray him at the last moment. That would mean that he would be left naked of the reputation he had guarded so jealously—and a far worse calamity—that his rebellious nature would finally triumph. One defeat, he knew, implied total overthrow.

He tried to reason that he was magnifying the danger—that Narcone would be easily handled, that other criminals as desperate had been taken without a struggle, but the instant such grains of comfort touched the healed terrors in his mind they vanished like drops of water sprinkled upon an incandescent furnace.

Nevertheless, he was pledged, and he knew that he would go.

He had barely gotten himself under a semblance of control, two days later, when Donnelly called him up by telephone to advise him in cautious terms that affairs were nearing a climax and to warn him to make ready.

This served to throw him into a renewed panic. It required a tremendous effort to concentrate upon his business affairs, and it took the genius of an actor to carry him through the inconsequent details of his every-day life without betrayal. Alone, at home, upon the crowded 'Change, in deadly-dull directors' meetings, that sinister shadow overhung him. These long, leaden hours of suspense were doing what nothing else had been able to do since he took himself definitely in hand. They were harder to bear than any of those disciplinary experiences which had turned his hair white and burned his youth to an ash.

At last Donnelly came.

"Corte has framed it for to-morrow," he announced with evident satisfaction.

"To-morrow?" Norvin echoed, faintly.

"Yes. He's sailing on the *Philadelphia* at eleven o'clock—no stops between here and New York. They'll be waiting for Narcone at Quarantine."

"I'm glad—it's time to do something."

Donnelly rubbed his palms together and showed his teeth in a smile, "Corte says he'll have him at the Cromwell Line docks without fail, so that will save us grabbing him on the street and holding him until sailing time. If we pull it off quietly, at the last minute, nobody'll know anything about it. You'd better be at my office by nine, in case anything goes wrong."

"You may count on me," Blake answered in a tone that gave no hint of his inward flinching. But once alone, he found that his nerves would not allow him to work. He closed his desk and went home. When the heat of the afternoon diminished he took out his saddle-horse and went for a gallop, thinking in this way to blow some of the tortured fancies out of his mind, but he did not succeed.

Despite his agitation, he ate a hearty dinner—much as a condemned man devours his last meal—but he could not sleep. All night he alternately tossed in his bed or paced his room restlessly, his features working, his body shivering.

He ate breakfast, however, with an apparent appetite that delighted his colored servant, and as the clock struck nine he walked into Donnelly's office, smoking a cigar which he did not taste.

"I haven't heard anything further from Corte, so we'll go down to the dock," the Chief informed him.

On the way to the river-front, Blake continued to smoke silently, giving a careful ear to Donnelly's final directions. When they reached their destination he waited while Dan went aboard the ship in search of the captain.

In those days, rail transportation had not developed into its present proportions, and New Orleans was even more interesting as a shipping-point than now. Along the levee stretched rows of craft from every port, big black ocean liners, barques and brigantines, fruit steamers from the tropics, and a tremendous flotilla of flat-nosed river steamers with their huge tows of barges. The cavernous sheds that lined the embankment echoed to a thunder of rumbling trucks, of clanking winches, of stamping hoofs, while through and above it all came the cries and songs of a multitude of roustabouts and deck-hands. Down the gangways of the *Philadelphia*, a thin, continuous line of dusky truckmen was moving. A growing chaos of trunks and smaller baggage on the dock indicated that her passenger-list was heavy.

Blake watched the shifting scene with little interest, now and then casting an unseeing eye over the ramparts of cotton bales near by; but although he was outwardly calm, his palms were cold and wet and his mind was working with a panicky swiftness.

Donnelly reappeared with the assurance that all was arranged with the ship's master, and, taking their stand where they could observe what went on, they settled themselves to wait.

Again the moments dragged. Again Blake fought his usual weary battle. He envied Donnelly his utter impassivity, for the officer betrayed no more feeling than as if he were standing, rod in hand, waiting for a fish to strike. An hour passed, bringing no sign of their men, although a stream of passengers was filing aboard and the piles of baggage were diminishing. Norvin struggled with the desire to voice his misgivings, which were taking the form of hopes; Donnelly chewed tobacco, and occasionally spat accurately at a knot-hole. His companion watched him curiously. Then, without warning, the Chief stirred, and there in the crowd Norvin suddenly saw the tall figure of Gian Narcone, with another man, evidently a Sicilian, beside him.

"That's Corte," Donnelly said, quietly.

The two watchers mingled with the crowd, gradually drawing closer to their quarry. But it seemed that Narcone refused to go aboard with his friend—at any rate, he made no move in that direction. The *Philadelphia* blew a warning blast, the remaining passengers quickened their movements, there was but little baggage left now upon the deck, and still the two Italians stood talking volubly. Donnelly waited stolidly near by, never glancing at his man. Blake held himself with an iron grip, although his heart-throbs were choking him. It was plain that Corte also was beginning to feel the strain, and Norvin began to fear that Donnelly would delay too long.

At last the Pinkerton man stooped and raised his valise, then extended his hand to the Mafioso. Donnelly edged closer.

Blake knew that the moment for action had come, and found that without any exercise of will-power he too was closing in. His mind was working at such high speed that time seemed to halt and wait. Donnelly was within arm's-length of Narcone before he spoke; then he said, quietly, "Going to leave the city, Sabella?"

"Eh?" The Sicilian started, his eyes leaped to the speaker, and the smile died from his heavy features. Recognizing the officer, however, he pulled at the visor of his cap, and said, brokenly: "No, no, Signore. My friend goes."

"Come, now," the Chief said, grimly. "I want you to tell me something about the Domenchino boy."

Narcone recoiled, colliding with Blake, who instantly locked his arm within his own. Simultaneously Donnelly seized the other wrist, repeating, "You know who stole the little Domenchino."

The tension which had leaped into the giant muscles died away; Narcone shrugged his shoulders, crying, excitedly, in his native tongue:

"Before God you wrong me."

It was the instant for which his captor had planned; the ruse had worked; there was a deft movement on Donnelly's part, something snapped metallically, and the manacles of the law were upon the murderer of Martel Savigno.

It had all been accomplished quietly, quickly; even those standing near by hardly noticed it, and those who did were unaware of the significance of the arrest. But once his man was safely ironed, the Chief's manner changed, and in the next instant the prisoner caught, perhaps from the eye of Corte, the stool-pigeon, some fleeting hint that he had been betrayed. Following that came the suspicion that he had been seized not for complicity in the Domenchino affair, but for something far more significant. With a furious, snarling cry he flung himself backward and raised his manacled hands to strike.

But it was too late for effective resistance. They took him across the gang-plank, screaming, struggling, biting like a maddened animal, while curious passengers rushed to the rails above and stared at them, and another crowd yelled and hooted derisively from the dock.

A moment later they were in Corte's stateroom, panting, grim, triumphant, with their prisoner's back against the wall and their work done.

Now that Narcone realized the deception that had been practised upon him he began to curse his betrayer with incredible violence and fluency. As yet he had no idea whither he was being taken, nor for which of his many crimes he had been apprehended. But it seemed as if his rage would strangle him. With the unrestraint of a lifetime of lawlessness he poured out his passion in a terrifying rush of vilification, anathema, and threat. He hurled himself against the walls of the stateroom as if to burst his way out, and they were forced to clamp leg-irons upon him. When Donnelly had regained his breath he savagely commanded the fellow to be silent, but Narcone only shifted his fury from his betrayer to the Chief of Police.

To the Pinkerton operative Donnelly said, gratefully: "That was good work, Corte. Wire me from New York. We'll have to go now, for the ship is clearing."

"Wait!" said Blake; then pushing himself forward, he addressed the captive in Italian, "Where is Belisario Cardi?"

The question came like a gunshot, silencing the outlaw as if with a gag. His bloodshot eyes searched his questioner's face; his lips, wet with slaver, were snarling like those of a dog, but he said nothing.

"Where is Belisario Cardi?" came the question for a second time.

"I do not know him," said the Sicilian, sullenly. "I am Vito Sabella, an honest man—"

"You are Gian Narcone, the butcher, of San Sebastiano," said Blake. "You are going back to Sicily to be hanged for the murder of Martel Savigno, Count of Martinello, and his man Ricardo."

"Bah!" cried the prisoner, loudly. "I am not this Narcone of which you speak. I do not know him. I am Vito Sabella, a poor man, I swear it by the body of Christ. I have never seen this Cardi. God will punish those who persecute me."

Blake leaned forward until his face was close to Narcone's.

"Look closely," he said. "Have you ever seen me before?"

They stared at each other, eye to eye, and the Sicilian nodded.

"You were drinking chianti in the cafe on Royal Street, but I swear to you I am an innocent man and I curse those who betray me."

"Think! Do you recall a night four years ago? You were waiting beside the road above Terranova. There was a feast of all the country people at the castello, and finally three men came riding upward through the darkness. One of them was singing, for it was the eve of his marriage, and you knew him by his voice as the Count of Martinello. Do you remember what happened then? Think! You were called Narcone the Butcher, and you boasted loudly of your skill with the knife as you dried your hands upon a wisp of grass. You left two men in the road that night, but the third returned to Terranova. I ask you again if you have ever seen my face."

The effect of these words was extraordinary. The fury died from the prisoner's eyes, his coarse lips fell apart, the blood receded from his purple cheeks, he shrank and shivered loosely. In the silence they could hear the breath wheezing hoarsely in his throat. Blake made a final appeal.

"They will take you back to Sicily, to Colonel Neri and his carbineers, and you will hang. Before it is too late, tell me, where is Belisario Cardi?"

Narcone moistened his livid lips and glared malignantly at his inquisitors. But he could not be prevailed upon to speak.

"Well, that was easy," said Donnelly, when the *Philadelphia* had cast off and the two friends were once more back in the rush and bustle of the water-front.

Norvin agreed. "And yet it seemed a bit unfair," he remarked. "There were three of us, you know. If he were not what he is, I'd feel somewhat ashamed of my part in the affair." Donnelly showed his contempt for such quixotic views by an expressive grunt. "You can take the next one single-handed, if you prefer. Perhaps it may be your friend Cardi."

"Perhaps," said Norvin, gravely. "If that should happen, I should feel that I had paid my debt in full."

"I'd like a chance to sweat Narcone," growled the Chief, regretfully. "I'd find Cardi, or I'd—" He heaved a sigh of relief. "Oh, well, we've done a good day's work as it is. I hope the papers don't get hold of it."

But the papers did get hold of it, and with an effect which neither man had anticipated. Had they foreseen the consequences of this morning's work, had they even remotely guessed at the forces they had unwittingly set in motion, they would have lost something of their complacency. Throughout the greater part of the city that night the kidnapping of Vito Sabella became the subject of excited comment. In the neighborhood of St. Phillip Street it was received in an ominous silence.

# XII.
# LA MAFIA

The surprising ease with which the capture of Narcone had been effected gratified Norvin Blake immensely, for it gave him an opportunity to jeer at the weaker side of his nature. He told himself that the incident went to prove what his saner judgment was forever saying—that fear depends largely upon the power of visualization, that danger is real only in so far as the mind sees it. Moreover, the admiration his conduct aroused was balm to his soul. His friends congratulated him warmly, agreeing that he and Donnelly had taken the only practical means to rid the community of a menace.

In our Southern and Western States, where individual character stands for more than it does in the over-legalized communities of the North and East, men are concerned not so much with red-tape as with effects, and hence there was little disposition to criticize.

Blake was amazed to discover what a strong public sentiment the Italian outrages had awakened. New Orleans, it seemed, was not only indignant, but alarmed.

His self-satisfaction received a sudden shock, however, when Donnelly strolled into his office a few days later, and without a word laid a letter upon his desk. It ran as follows:

DANIEL DONNELLY, Chief of Police,

**NEW ORLEANS, LA.**

DEAR SIR,—God be praised that Gian Narcone has gone to his punishment! But you have incurred the everlasting enmity of the Mala Vita, or what you term La Mafia, and it has been decided that your life must pay for his. You are to be killed next Thursday night at the Red Wing Club. I cannot name those upon whom the choice has fallen, for that is veiled in secrecy.

I pray that you will not ignore this warning, for if you do your blood will rest upon, ONE WHO KNOWS.

P. S. Destroy this letter.

The color had receded from Norvin's face when he looked up to meet the smoke-blue eyes of his friend.

"God!" he exclaimed. "This—looks bad, doesn't it?"

"You think it's on the level?"

"Don't you?"

Donnelly shrugged. "I'm blessed if I know. It may have come from the very gang I'm after. It strikes me that they wanted to get rid of Narcone, but didn't know just how to go about it, so used me for an instrument. Now they want to scare me off."

"But—he names the very place; the very hour."

"Sure—everything except the very dago who is to do the killing! If he knew where and when, why wouldn't he know how and who?"

"I—that sounds reasonable, and yet—you are not going to the Red Wing Club any more, are you?"

"Why not? I've got until Thursday and—I like their coffee. Here is the other letter, by the way." Donnelly produced the first communication. The paper was identical and the type appeared to be the same. Beyond this Norvin could make out nothing.

"Well," Dan exclaimed, when they had exhausted their conjectures, "they've set their date and I reckon they won't change it, so I'm going to eat dinner to-night at the Red Wing Club as usual, just to see what happens."

After a brief hesitation Norvin said, "I'd like to join you, if you don't mind."

Donnelly shook his gray head doubtfully. "I don't think you'd better. This may be on the square."

"I think it is, and therefore I intend to see you through."

"Suit yourself, of course. I'd like to have you go along, but I don't want to get you into any fuss."

Seven o'clock that evening found the two friends dining at the little cafe in the foreign quarter, but they were seated at one of the corner tables and their backs were toward the wall.

"I've had my reasons for eating here, and it wasn't altogether the coffee, either," the elder man confessed.

"I suspected as much," Norvin told him. "At least I couldn't detect anything remarkable about this Rio."

"You see, it's a favorite hang-out of the better Italian class, and I've been working it carefully for a year."

"What have you discovered?"

"Not much, and yet a great deal. I've made friends, for one thing, and that's considerable. Here comes one now. You know him, don't you?" Dan indicated a thick-necked, squarely built Italian who had entered at the moment. "That's Caesar Maruffi."

Norvin regarded the new-comer with interest, for Maruffi stood for what is best among his Americanized countrymen. Moreover, if rumor spoke true, he was one of the richest and most influential foreigners in the city. In answer to the Chief's invitation he approached and seated himself at the table, accepting his introduction to Blake with a smile and a gracious word.

"Ah! It is my first opportunity to thank you for the service you have done us in arresting that hateful brigand," he began.

"Did you know the fellow?" Norvin queried.

"Very well indeed."

"Maruffi knows a whole lot, if he'd only open up. He's a Mafioso himself—eh, Caesar?" The Chief laughed.

"No, no!" the other exclaimed, casting a cautious glance over his shoulder. "I tell you everything I learn. But as for this Sabella—I thought him a trifle sullen, perhaps, but an honest fellow."

"You don't really think there has been any mistake?"

"Eh? How could that be possible? Did not Signore Blake remember him?" Norvin was about to disclaim his part in the affair, but the speaker ran on:

"I fear you must regard all us Italians as Mafiosi, Signore Blake, but it is not so. No! We are honest people, but we are terrorized by a few bad men. We do not know them, Signore. We are robbed, we are blackmailed, and if we resist, behold! something unspeakable befalls us. We do not know who deals the blow, we merely know that we are marked and that some day we—are buried." Maruffi shrugged his square shoulders expressively.

"Do you suffer in your business?" Norvin asked.

"Per Dio! Who does not? I have adopted your free country, Signore, but it is not so free as my own. Maledetto! You have too damned many laws in this free America."

Maruffi spoke hesitatingly, and yet with intense feeling; his black eyes glittered wickedly, and it was plain that he sounded the note of revolt which was rising from the law-abiding Italian element. His appearance bore out his reputation for leadership, for he was big and black and dour, and he gave the impression of unusual force.

"Your home is in Sicily, is it not?" Blake inquired.

"Si! I come from Palermo."

"I have been there."

"I remember," said Maruffi, calmly.

Donnelly broke in, "What do you hear regarding our capture of Sabella?"

"Eh?"

"How do they take it?"

Again Maruffi shrugged. "How can they take it? My good countrymen are delighted; others, perhaps, not so well pleased."

"But Sabella has friends. I suppose they've marked me for revenge?"

"No doubt! But what can they do? You are the law. With a private citizen, with me, for instance, it would be different. My wife would prepare herself for widowhood."

"How's that? You're not married," said Donnelly.

"Not yet. But I have plans. A fine Sicilian girl."

"Good! I congratulate you."

"Speaking of Sabella," Blake interposed, curiously, "I had a hand in taking him, and I'm a private citizen."

"True!" Maruffi regarded him with his impenetrable eyes.

"You predict trouble for me, then?"

"I predict nothing. We say in my country that no one escapes the Mafia. No doubt we are timid. You are an American, you are not easily frightened. But tell me" — he turned to the Chief of Police — "who is to follow this brigand? There are others quite as black as he, if they were known."

"No doubt! But, unfortunately, I don't know them. Why don't you help me out, Caesar?"

"If I could! You have no suspicions, eh?"

"Plenty of suspicions, but no proofs."

Maruffi turned back to Norvin, saying: "So, you identified the murderer of your friend Savigno? Madonna mia! You have a memory! But were you not—afraid?"

"Afraid of what?"

"Ah! You are American, as I said before; you fear nothing. But it was Belisario Cardi who killed the Conte of Martinello."

"Belisario Cardi is only a name," said Norvin, guardedly.

"True!" Maruffi agreed. "Being a Palermitan myself, he is real to me, but, as you say, nobody knows."

He rose and shook hands cordially with both men. When he had joined the group of Italians at a near-by table, Donnelly said:

"There's the whitest dago in the city. I thought he might be the 'One Who Knows,' but I reckon I was mistaken. He could help me, though, if he dared."

"Have you confided in him?"

"Lord, no! I don't trust any of them. Say! The more I think about that letter, the more I think it's a bluff."

"You can't afford to ignore it."

"Of course not. I'll plant O'Connell and another man outside on Thursday night and see if anything suspicious turns up, but I'll take my dinner elsewhere."

The two men had finished their meal when Bernie Dreux strolled in and took the seat which Maruffi had vacated.

"Well, how goes your detecting, Bernie?" Norvin inquired.

"*Hist!*" breathed the little man so sharply that his hearers started. He winked mysteriously and they saw that he was bursting with important tidings. "There's something doing!"

"What is it?" demanded the Chief. But Mr. Dreux answered nothing. Instead he lit a cigarette, and as he raised the match looked guardedly into a mirror behind Donnelly's chair.

"I'm glad you took this table," he began in a low voice. "I always sit where I can get a flash."

"A *what*?" queried the astonished Blake.

"Pianissimo with that talk!" cautioned the speaker. "You'll tip him off."

"Tip who?" Donnelly breathed.

"My man! He's one of the gang. Do you see that fellow—that wop next to Caesar Maruffi?" Bernie did not lower his eyes from the mirror, "the third from the left."

"Sure!"

"Well!" triumphantly.

"Well?"

"That is he."

"That's who?"

"I don't know."

"What the—"

"He's one of 'em, that's all I know. I've been on him for a week. I've trailed him everywhere. He has an accomplice—a woman!"

The Chief's face underwent a remarkable change. "Are you sure?" he whispered, eagerly.

"It's a cinch! He comes to the fruit-stand every day. I think he's after blackmail, but I'm not sure."

"Good!" Dan exclaimed. "I want you to trail him wherever he goes, and, above all, watch the woman. Now tear back to your banana rookery or you'll miss something. Better have a drink first, though."

"I'll go you; it's tough work on the nerves. I'm all upset."

"I thought you never drank whiskey," Norvin said, still amazed at the extraordinary transformation in his friend.

"I don't as a rule, it kippers my stomach; but it gives me the courage of a lion."

Donnelly nodded with satisfaction. "Don't get pickled, but keep your nerve. Remember, I'm depending on you."

Dreux's slender form writhed and shuddered as he swallowed the liquor, but his eyes were shining when he rose to go. "I'm glad I'm making good," said he. "If anything happens to me, keep your eye skinned for that fellow; there's dirty work afoot."

When he had gone Donnelly stuck his napkin into his mouth to still his laughter. "'There's dirty work afoot,'" he quoted in a strangling voice. "Can you beat that?"

"I—can't believe my senses. Why, Bernie's actually getting tough! Who is this fellow he's trailing?"

"That? That's Joe Poggi, the owner of the fruit-stand. He's my best dago detective, and I sent him here to-night in case anything blew off. The woman is his wife—lovely lady, too. 'Blackmail!' Oh, Lord! I'll have to tell Poggi about this. I'll have to tell him he's being shadowed, too, or he'll stop suddenly on the street some day and Bernie will run into him from behind and break his nose."

Thursday night passed without incident. Donnelly set a watch upon the Red Wing Club, but nothing occurred to give the least color to the written warning. In the course of a fortnight he had well-nigh forgotten it, and when a third letter came he was less than ever inclined to believe it genuine.

"You forestalled the first attempt upon your life," wrote the informant, "but another will be made. You are to be shot at Police Headquarters some night next week. Your desk stands just inside a window which opens upon the street. A fight will occur at the corner near by and during the disturbance an assassin will fire upon you out of the darkness, then disappear in the confusion. Do not treat this warning lightly or I swear that you will repent it.

**"ONE WHO KNOWS"**

Donnelly showed this to Blake, saying, sourly, "You see. It's just as I told you. They're trying to run me out."

"What are you going to do?"

"I'm going to move my desk, for one thing, then I'm going to run down this writer. O'Connell is going through the stationery-stores now, trying to match the water-mark on the paper. The post-office is on the lookout for the next letter and will try to find which mail-box it is dropped into."

"Then you think there will be other letters to follow this one?"

"Certainly! When they see that I've moved away from that window they'll think they've got me going, then I'll be warned of another plot, and another, and another. It might work with some people." The speaker's lips curled in a wintry smile.

"You no longer think it came from one of the Pallozzo gang?"

"No! There's nobody in the outfit who can write a letter like that. It's from the Mafia."

"How can you say that when the same writer betrayed Narcone?"

"Oh, I've asked myself the same question," Donnelly answered with a trace of exasperation, "and I can't answer it unless that was merely a case of revenge. Take it from me, I'll get another letter inside of ten days. See if I don't."

True to his prediction, the tenth day brought another warning. The writer advised him that his enemies had changed their plans once more, but would strike, when the first opportunity offered. As to where or when this would occur, no information was given. The Chief was merely urged in the strongest terms to remove himself beyond the possibility of danger.

Naturally the recipient took this as proof positive that the whole affair was no more than a weak attempt to frighten him. Unfortunately, the postal authorities could not determine where the letter had been mailed, and O'Connell reported that the paper on which it was written was of a variety in common use. There seemed to be little hope of tracing the matter back to its source, so Donnelly dismissed the whole affair from his mind and went about his duties undisturbed.

Norvin Blake, however, could not bring himself to take the same view. As usual, he attributed his fears to imagination, yet they preyed upon him so constantly that he was forced to heed them. His one frightful experience with La Mafia had marked him, it seemed, like some prenatal influence, and now the more he dwelt upon the subject, the more his apprehension quickened. He was ashamed to confess to Donnelly, and at the same time he was loath to allow the Chief to expose himself unnecessarily. Therefore he made it a point to be with him as much as possible. This, of course, involved a considerable risk to himself, and he recalled with misgiving what Caesar Maruffi had said that night in the Red Wing Club. Donnelly alone had been warned, but that did not argue that vengeance would be confined to him.

October had come; the lazy heat of summer had passed and New Orleans was awakening under its magic winter climate. The piny, breeze-swept Gulf resorts had emptied their summer colonies cityward, the social season had begun.

The preparations for the great February Carnival were nearing completion, and Blake had the satisfaction of knowing that Myra Nell Warren was to realize her heart's desire. He had forced a loan upon Bernie sufficient to meet the requirements of any Queen, and had spent several delightful evenings with the girl herself, amused by her plans of royal conquest.

It was like a tonic to be with her. Norvin invariably parted from her with a feeling of optimism and a gayety quite reasonless; he had no fears, no apprehensions; the universe was peopled with sprites and fairies, the morrow was a glad adventure full of merriment and promise.

He was in precisely such a mood one drizzly Wednesday night after having made an inexcusably long call upon her. Nothing whatever had occurred to put him in this agreeable humor, yet he went homeward humming as blithely as a barefoot boy in springtime.

As he neared the neighborhood in which Donnelly lived he decided to drop in on him for a few moments and smoke a cigar. Business had lately kept him away from the Chief, and he felt a bit guilty.

But Donnelly had either retired early or else he had not returned from Headquarters, for his windows were dark, and Norvin retraced his steps, a trifle disappointed. In front of a cobbler's shop, across the street, several men were talking, and as he glanced in their direction the door behind them opened, allowing a stream of light to pour forth. He recognized Larubio, the old Italian shoemaker himself, and he was on the point of inquiring if Donnelly had come home, but thought better of it.

Larubio and his companions were idling beneath the wooden awning or shed which extended over the sidewalk, and in the open doorway, briefly silhouetted against the yellow light, Blake noted a man clad in a shining rubber coat. Although the picture was fleeting, it caught his attention.

The thought occurred to him that these men were Italians, and therefore possible Mafiosi, but his mood was too optimistic to permit of silly suspicions. To-night the Mafia seemed decidedly unreal and indefinite.

He found himself smiling again at the memory of an argument in which he had been worsted by Myra Nell. He had taken her a most elaborate box of chocolates and she had gleefully promised to consume at least half of them that very night after retiring. He had remonstrated at such an unhygienic procedure, whereupon she had confessed to a secret, ungovernable habit of eating candy in bed. He had argued that the pernicious practice was sure to wreck her digestion and ruin her teeth, but she had confounded him utterly by displaying twin rows as sound as pearls, as white and regular as rice kernels. Her digestion, he had to confess, was that of a Shetland pony, and he had been forced to fall back upon an unconvincing prophecy of a toothless and dyspeptic old age. He pictured her at this moment propped up in the middle of the great mahogany four-poster, all lace and ruffles and ribbons, her wayward hair in adorable confusion about her face, as she pawed over the sweets and breathed ecstatic blessings upon his name.

Near the corner he stumbled over a boy hiding in the shadows. Then as he turned north on Rampart Street he ran plump into Donnelly and O'Connell.

"I just came from your house," he told Dan. "I thought I'd drop in and smoke one of your bad cigars. Is there anything new?"

"Not much! I've had a hard day and there was a Police Board meeting to-night. I'm fagged out."

"No more letters, eh?"

"No. But I've heard that Sabella is safe in Sicily. That means his finish. I'll have something else to tell you in a day or so; something about your other friend, Cardi."

"No! Really?"

"If what I suspect is true, it'll be a sensation. I can't credit the thing myself, that's why I don't want to say anything just yet. I'm all up in the air over it."

A moment later the three men separated, Donnelly and O'Connell turning toward their respective homes, Blake continuing his way toward the heart of the city.

But the Chief's words had upset Norvin's complacency. His line of thought was changed and he found himself once more dwelling upon the tragedy which had left such a mark upon his life. Martel had been the finest, the cleanest fellow he had ever known; his life, so full of promise, had just begun, and yet he had been ruthlessly stricken down. Norvin shuddered at the memory. He saw the road to Martinello stretching out ahead of him like a ghost-gray canyon walled with gloom; he heard the creaking of saddles, the muffled thud of hoofs in the dust of the causeway, the song of a lover, then—

Blake halted suddenly, listening. From somewhere not far away came the sound again; it was a gunshot, deadened by the blanket of mist and drizzle that shrouded the streets. He turned. It was repeated for a third time, and as he realized whence it came he cried out, affrightedly:

"Donnelly! Donnelly! Oh, God!"

Then he began to run swiftly, as he had run that night four years before, with the lights of Terranova in the distance, and in his heart was that same sickening, horrible terror. But this time he ran, not away from the sound, but towards it.

As he raced along the slippery streets the night air was ripped again and again with those same loud reverberations. He saw, by the flickering arc-lamp above the crossing where he had just left Donnelly, another figure flying towards him, and recognized O'Connell. Together they turned into Girod Street.

They were in time to see a flash from the shed that stood in front of Larubio's shop, then an answering spurt of flame from the side of the street upon which they were. The place was full of noise and smoke. At the farther crossing a man in a shining rubber coat knelt and fired, then rose and scurried into the darkness beyond. Figures broke out from the shadows of the wooden awning in front of Larubio's shop and followed, some turning towards the left at Basin Street, others continuing on through the area lighted by the sputtering street light and into the night. One of them paused and looked back as if loath to leave the spot until certain of his work.

Side by side Blake and O'Connell raced towards the Chief, whom they saw lurching uncertainly along the banquette ahead of them. The detective was cursing; Blake sobbed through his tight-clenched teeth.

Donnelly was down when they reached him, and his empty revolver lay by his side. Norvin raised him with shaking arms, his whole body sick with horror.

"Are you badly—hit, old man?" he gasped.

"I'm—done for!" said the Chief, weakly. "And the dagos did it."

From an open window above them a woman began to scream loudly:

"Murder! Murder!"

The cry was taken up in other quarters and went echoing down the street.

Doors were flung wide, gates slammed, men came hurrying through the wet night, hurling startled questions at one another, but the powder smoke which hung sluggishly in the dark night air was sufficient answer. It floated in thin blue layers beneath the electric lights, gradually fading and melting as the life ebbed from the mangled body of Dan Donnelly.

It was nearing dawn when Norvin Blake emerged from the hospital whither Donnelly had been taken. The air was dead and heavy, a dripping winding-sheet of fog wrapped the city in its folds; no sound broke the silence of the hour. He was sadly shaken, for he had watched a brave soul pass out of the light, and in his ears the words of his friend were ringing:

"Don't let them get away with this, Norvin. You're the only man I trust."

# XIII.
# THE BLOOD OF HIS ANCESTORS

At the Central Station Norvin found a great confusion. City officials and newspaper men were coming and going, telephones were ringing, patrolmen and detectives, summoned from their beds, were reporting and receiving orders; yet all this bustling activity affected him with a kind of angry impatience. It seemed, somehow, perfunctory and inadequate; in the intensity of his feeling he doubted that any one else realized, as he did, the full significance of what had occurred.

As quickly as possible he made his way to O'Neil, the Assistant Superintendent of Police, who was deep in consultation with Mayor Wright. For a moment he stood listening to their talk, and then, at the first pause, interposed without ceremony:

"Tell me—what is being done?"

O'Neil, who had not seemed to note his approach, answered without a hint of surprise at the interruption:

"We are dragging the city."

"Of course. Have you arrested Larubio, the cobbler?"

"No!" Both men turned to Blake now with concentrated attention.

"Then don't lose a moment's time. Arrest all his friends and associates. Look for a man in a rubber coat. I saw him fire. There's a boy, too," he added, after a moment's pause, "about fourteen years old. He was hiding at the corner. I think he must have been their picket; at any rate, he knows something."

The Assistant Superintendent noted these directions, and listened impassively while Norvin poured forth his story of the murder. Before it was fairly concluded he was summoned elsewhere, and, turning away abruptly, he left the room, like a man who knows he must think of but one thing at a time. The young man, wiping his face with uncertain hand, turned to the Mayor.

"Dan was the second friend I've seen murdered by these devils," he said. "I'd like to do something."

"We'll need your help, if it was really the dagoes."

"What? There's no doubt on that score. Donnelly was warned."

"Well, we ought to have them under arrest in short order."

"And then what? They've probably arranged their alibis long ago. The fellows who did the shooting are not the only ones, either. We must get the leaders."

"Exactly. O'Neil understands."

"But he'll fail, as Donnelly failed."

"What would you have us do?"

Blake spoke excitedly, his emotions finding a vent.

"Do? I'd rouse the people. Awaken the city. Create an uprising of the law-abiding. Strip the courts of their red tape and administer justice with a rope. Hang the guilty ones at once, before delay robs their execution of its effect and before there is time to breed doubts and distrust in the minds of the people."

"You mean, in plain words—lynch them?"

"Well, what of that? It's the only—"

"But, my dear young man, the law—"

"Oh, I know what you're going to say, well enough, yet there are times when mob law is justified. If these men are not destroyed quickly they will live to laugh at our laws and our scheme of justice. We must strike terror into the heart of every foreign-born criminal; we must clean the city with fire, unless we wish to see our institutions become a mockery and our community overridden by a band of cutthroats. The killing of Dan Donnelly is more than a mere murder; it is an attack on our civilization."

"You are carried away by your personal feelings."

"I think not. If this thing runs through the regular channels, what will happen? You know how hard it is to convict those people. We must fight fire with fire."

"Personally, I agree with a good deal you say; officially, of course. I can't go so far. You say you want to help. Will you assume a large responsibility? Will you take the lead in a popular movement to help the enforcement of the law—organize a committee?"

"If you think I'm the right man?"

"Good! Understand"—the Mayor spoke now with determined earnestness—"we must have no lynchings; but I believe the police will need help in the search, and I think you are the man to stir up the public conscience and secure that aid. If you can help in apprehending the criminals we shall see that the courts do their part. I can trust you in so delicate a matter where I couldn't trust—some others."

O'Neil appeared at that moment with two strange objects in his hands.

"See what we've just found on the Basin Street banquette."

He displayed a pair of sawed-off shotguns the stocks of which were hinged in such a manner that the weapons could be doubled into a length of perhaps eighteen inches and thus be concealed upon the person. Blake examined them with mingled feelings. Having seen the body of the Chief ripped and torn in twenty places by buckshot, slugs, and scraps of iron, he had tried to imagine what sort of firearms had been used. Now he knew, and he began to wonder whether death would come to him in the same ugly form.

"Have you sent for Larubio?" he asked.

"The men are just leaving."

"I'll go with them."

O'Neil intercepted the officers at the door, and a moment later Norvin was hurrying with them toward Girod Street. Mechanically his mind began to review the events leading up to the murder, dwelling on each detail with painful and fruitless persistence. He repictured the scene that his eye had so swiftly and so carelessly recorded; he saw again the dark shed, the dumb group of figures idling beneath it, the open door and the flood of yellow light behind. But when he strove to recall a single face or form, or even the precise number of persons, he was at a loss. Nothing stood out distinctly but the bearded face of Larubio, the silhouette of a man in a gleaming rubber coat, and, a moment later, a slim stripling boy crouched in the shadows near the corner.

As the party turned into Girod Street he saw by the first streaks of dawn that the curious had already begun to assemble. A dozen or more men were morbidly examining the scene, re-enacting the assassination and tracing the course of bullets by the holes in wall and fence—no difficult matter, since the ground where Donnelly had given battle had been swept by a fusillade.

Larubio's shop was dark.

The officers tried the door quietly, then at a signal from Norvin they rushed it. The next instant the three men found themselves in an evil-smelling room furnished with a bench, some broken chairs, a litter of tools and shoes and leather findings. It was untenanted, but, seeing another door ahead of him, Blake stumbled toward it over the debris. Like the outer door, it was barred, but yielded to his shoulder.

It was well that the policemen were close upon his heels, for they found him locked in desperate conflict with a huge, half-naked Sicilian, who fought with the silent wickedness of a wolf at bay.

The chamber was squalid and odorous; a tumbled couch, from which the occupant had leaped, showed that he had been calmly sleeping upon the scene of his crime. Through the dim-lit filth of the place the cobbler whirled them, struggling like a man insane. A table fell with a crash of dishes, a stove was wrecked, a chair smashed, then he was pinned writhing to the bed from which he had just arisen.

"Close the front door—quick!" Norvin panted. "Keep out the crowd!"

One of the policemen dashed to the front of the hovel barely in time to bar the way.

Larubio, as he crouched there in the half-light, manacled but defiant, made a striking figure. He was a patriarchal man. His hairy, naked chest rose and fell as he fought for his breath, a thick beard grew high upon his cheeks, lending dignity to his fierce aquiline features, a tangled mass of iron-gray hair hung low above his eyes. He looked more like an Arab sheik than a beggarly Sicilian shoemaker.

"Why are you here?" he questioned, in a deep voice.

Blake answered him in his own language:

"You killed the Chief of Police."

"No. I had no part—"

"Don't lie!"

"As God is my judge, I am innocent. I heard the shooting; I looked out into the night and saw men running about. I was frightened, so I went to bed. That is all."

Norvin undertook to stare him down.

"You will hang for this, Larubio," he said.

The fierce gray eyes met his unflinchingly.

"You had a hand in the killing, for I saw you. But you acted against your will. Am I right?"

Still the patriarch flung back his glance defiantly.

"You were ordered to kill and you dared not disobey. Where is Belisario Cardi?"

The old man started. Into his eyes for the briefest instant there leaped a look of terror, then it was gone.

"I do not know what you are talking about," he answered.

"Come! The man with the rubber coat has confessed."

Larubio's gaze roved uncertainly about the squalid quarters; but he shook his head, mumbling:

"God will protect the innocent. I know nothing, your Excellency."

They dragged him, still protesting, from his den as dogs drag an animal from its burrow. But Norvin had learned something. That momentary wavering glance, that flitting light of doubt and fear, had told him that to the cobbler the name of Cardi meant something real and terrible.

Back at headquarters O'Neil had further information for him.

"We've got Larubio's brother-in-law, Caspardo Cressi. It was his son, no doubt, whom you saw waiting at the corner."

"Have you found the boy?"

"No, he's gone."

"Then make haste before they have time to spirit him away. These men won't talk, but we might squeeze something out of the boy. He's the weakest link in the chain, so you *must* find him."

The morning papers were on the street when Norvin went home. New Orleans had awakened to the outrage against her good name.

Men were grouped upon corners, women were gossiping from house to house, the air was surcharged with a great excitement. It was as if a public enemy had been discovered at the gates, as if an alien foe had struck while the city slept. That unformed foreign prejudice which had been slowly growing had crystallized in a single night.

To Norvin the popular clamor, which rose high during the next few days, had a sickening familiarity. At the time of Martel Savigno's murder he had looked upon justice as a thing inevitable, he had felt that the public wrath, once aroused, was an irresistible force; yet he had seen how ineffectually such a force could spend itself. And the New Orleans police seemed likely to accomplish little more than the Italian soldiers. Although more than a hundred arrests were made, it was doubtful if, with the exception of Larubio and Cressi, any of the real culprits had been caught. He turned the matter over in his mind incessantly, consulted with O'Neil as to ways and means, conferred with the Mayor, sounded his friends. Then one morning he awoke to find himself at the head of a Committee of Justice, composed of fifty leading business men of the city, armed with powers somewhat vaguely defined, but in reality extremely wide. He set himself diligently to his task.

There followed through the newspapers an appeal to the Italian population for assistance, and offers of tremendous rewards. This resulted in a flood of letters, some signed, but mostly anonymous, a multitude of shadowy clues, of wild accusations. But no sooner was a promising trail uncovered than the witness disappeared or became inspired with a terror which sealed his lips. It began to appear that there was really no evidence to be had beyond what Norvin's eyes had photographed. And this, he knew, was not enough to convict even Larubio and his brother-in-law.

While thus baffled and groping for the faintest clue, he received a letter which brought him at least a ray of sunshine. He had opened perhaps half of his morning's mail one day when he came upon a truly remarkable missive. It was headed with an amateurish drawing or a skull; at the bottom of the sheet was a dagger, and over all, in bright red, was the life-size imprint of a small, plump hand.

In round, school-girl characters he read as follows:

"Beware! You are a traitor and a deserter, therefore you are doomed. Escape is impossible unless you heed this warning. Meet me at the old house on St. Charles Street, and bring your ransom. "THE AVENGER."

At the lower left-hand corner, in microscopic characters, was written:

"I love chocolate nougat best."

Norvin laughed as he re-read this sanguinary epistle, for he had to admit that it had given him a slight start. Being a man of action, he walked to the telephone and called a number which had long since become familiar.

"Is this the Creole Candy Kitchen? Send ten pounds of your best chocolate nougat to Miss Myra Nell Warren at once. This is Blake speaking. Wait! I have enough on my conscience without adding another sin. Perhaps you'd better make it five pounds now and five pounds a week hereafter. Put it in your fanciest basket, with lots of blue ribbon, and label it 'Ransom!'"

Next he called the girl himself, and after an interminable wait heard a breathless voice say:

"Hello, Norvin! I've been out in the kitchen making cake, so I couldn't get away. It's in the oven now, cooking like mad."

"I've just received a threatening letter," he told her.

"Who in the world could have sent it?"

"Evidently some blackmailing wretch. It demands a ransom."

"Heavens! You won't be cowardly enough to yield?"

"Certainly. I daren't refuse."

He heard her laughing softly. "Why don't you tell the police?"

"Indeed! There's an army of men besieging the place now."

"Then you must expect to catch the writer?"

"I've been trying to for a long time."

"I'm sure I don't know what you are talking about," she said, innocently.

"Could I have sent the ransom to the wrong address?"

He pretended to be seized with doubt, whereupon Myra Nell exclaimed, quickly:

"Oh, not necessarily." Then, after a pause, "Norvin, how does a person get red ink off of her hands?"

"Use a cotton broker. Let him hold it this evening."

"I'd love to, but Bernie wouldn't allow it. It was his ink, you know, and I spilled it all over his desk. Norvin—is it really nougat?"

"It is, the most unhealthy, the most indigestible—"

"You *duck*! You *may* hold my gory hand for—Wait!" Blake heard a faint shriek. "Don't ring off. Something terrible—" Then the wire was dead.

"Hello! Hello!" he called. "What's wrong, Myra Nell?" He rattled the receiver violently, and getting no response, applied to Central. After some moments he heard her explaining in a relieved tone:

"Oh, *such* a fright as I had."

"What was it? For Heaven's—"

"The cake!"

"You frightened me. I thought—"

"It's four stories high and pasted together with caramel."

"You should never leave a 'phone in that way without—"

"Bernie detests caramel; but I'm expecting a 'certain party' to call on me to-night. Norvin, do you think red ink would hurt a cake?"

"Myra Nell," he said, severely, "didn't you wash your hands before mixing that dough?"

"Of course."

"I have my doubts. Will you really be at liberty this evening?"

"That depends entirely upon you. If I am, I shall exact another ransom—flowers, perhaps."

"I'll send them anyhow, Marechal Neils."

"Oh, you are a—Wait!"

For a second time Miss Warren broke off; but now Norvin heard her cry out gladly to some one. He held the receiver patiently until his arm cramped, then rang up again.

"Oh, I forgot all about you, Norvin dear," she chattered. "Vittoria has just come, so I can't talk to you any more. Won't you run out and meet her? I know she's just dying to—She says she isn't, either! Oh, fiddlesticks! You're not so busy as all that. Very well, we'll probably eat the cake ourselves. Good-by!"

"Good-by, Avenger," he laughed.

As he turned away smiling he found Bernie Dreux comfortably ensconced in an office chair and regarding him benignly.

"Hello, Bernie! I didn't hear you come in."

"Wasn't that Myra Nell talking?" inquired the little man.

"Yes."

"You called her 'Avenger.' What has she been up to now?"

Blake handed him the red-hand letter. To his surprise Bernie burst out angrily:

"How dare she?"

"What?"

"It's most unladylike—begging a gentleman for gifts. I'll see that she apologizes."

"If you do I'll punch your head. She couldn't do anything unladylike if she tried."

"I don't approve—"

"Nonsense!"

"I'll see that she gets her chocolates."

"Oh, I've sent 'em—a deadly consignment—enough to destroy both of you. And I've left a standing order for five pounds a week."

"But that letter—it's blackmail." Bernie groaned. "She holds me up in the same way whenever she feels like it. She's getting suspicious of me lately, and I daren't tell her I'm a detective. The other day she set Remus, our gardener, on my trail, and he shadowed me all over the town. Felicite thinks there's something wrong, too, and she's taken to following me. Between her and Remus I haven't a moment's privacy."

"It's tough for a detective to be dogged by his gardener and his sweetheart," Norvin sympathized. He began to run through his mail, while his visitor talked on in his amusing, irrelevant fashion.

"I'm rather offended that I wasn't named on that Committee of Fifty," Bernie confessed, after a time. "You know how the Chief relied on me?"

"Exactly."

"Well, I'm full of Italian mysteries now. What I haven't discovered by my own investigations, Vittoria Fabrizi has told me. For instance, I know what became of the boy Gino Cressi."

"You do?" Blake looked up curiously from a letter he had been eagerly perusing.

"He's in Mobile."

"Are you sure?"

"Certainly."

"I think you're wrong."

"Why am I wrong?"

"Read this. My mail is full of anonymous communications." He passed over the letter in his hand, and Mr. Dreux read as follows:

**NORVIN BLAKE,**

**NEW ORLEANS, LOUISIANA.**

The Cressi boy is hidden at 93 1/2 St. Phillip Street. Go personally and in secret, for there are spies among the police.

**ONE WHO KNOWS.**

"Good Lord! Do you believe it?"

"I shall know in an hour." In reality Norvin had no doubt that his informant told the truth. On the contrary, he found that he had been waiting subconsciously for a hint from this mysterious but reliable source, and now that it had come he felt confident and elated. "A leak in the department would explain the maddening series of checkmates up to date." After a moment's hesitation he continued: "If Gino Cressi proves to be the boy I saw that night, we will put the rope around his father's and his uncle's necks, for he is little more than a child, and they evidently knew he would confess if accused; otherwise they wouldn't have been so careful to hide him." He rose and, eying Dreux intently, inquired, "Will you go along and help me take him?"

Bernie fell into a sudden panic of excitement. His face paled, he blinked with incredible rapidity, his lips twitched, and he clasped his thin, bloodless hands nervously.

"Why—are you—really—going—and alone?"

Norvin nodded. "If they have spies among our own men the least indiscretion may give the alarm. Besides, there is no time to lose; it would be madness to go there after dark. Will you come?"

"You—b-b-bet," Mr. Dreux stuttered. After a painful effort to control himself he inquired, with rolling eyes, "S-say, Norvin, will there be any fighting—any d-d-danger?"

Blake's own imagination had already presented that aspect of the matter all too vividly.

"Yes, there may be danger," he confessed. "We may have to take the boy by force." His nerves began to dance and quiver, as always before every new adventure.

"Perhaps, after all, you'd better not go. I—understand how you feel."

The little man burst out in a forceful expletive.

"*Pudding!* I *want* to fight. D-don't you see?"

"No. I don't."

"I've never been in a row. I've never done anything brave or desperate, like—like you. I'm aching for trouble. I go looking for it every night."

"Really!" Blake looked his incredulity.

"Sure thing! Last night I insulted a perfectly nice gentleman just to provoke a quarrel. I'd never seen him before, and ordinarily I hesitate to accost strangers; but I felt as if I'd have hysterics if I couldn't lick somebody; so I walked up to this person and told him his necktie was in rotten taste."

"What did he say?"

"He offered to go home and change it. I was so chagrined that I—cursed him fearfully."

"Bernie!"

Dreux nodded with an expression of the keenest satisfaction. "I could have cried. I called him a worm, a bug, a boll-weevil; but he said he had a family and didn't intend to be shot up by some well-dressed desperado."

"I suppose it's the blood of your ancestors."

"I suppose it is. Now let's go get this dago boy. I'm loaded for grizzlies, and if the Mafia cuts in I'll croak somebody." He drew a huge rusty military revolver from somewhere inside his clothes and flourished it so recklessly that his companion recoiled.

Together the two set out for St. Phillip Street. Blake, whose reputation for bravery had become proverbial, went reluctantly, preyed upon by misgivings; Dreux, the decadent, overbred dandy, went gladly, as if thirsting for the fray.

# XIV.
# THE NET TIGHTENS

Number 93 1/2 St. Phillip Street proved to be a hovel, in the front portion of which an old woman sold charcoal and kindling. Leaving Bernie on guard, Blake penetrated swiftly to the rooms behind, paying no heed to the crone's protestations. In one corner a slender, dark-eyed boy was cowering, whom he recognized at once as the lad he had seen on the night of Donnelly's death.

"You are Gino Cressi," he said, quietly.

The boy shook his head.

"Oh, yes, you are, and you must come with me, Gino."

The little fellow recoiled. "You have come to kill me," he quavered.

"No, no, my little man. Why should I wish to do that?"

"I am a Sicilian; you hate me."

"That is not true. We hate only bad Sicilians, and you are a good boy."

"I did not kill the Chief."

"True. You did not even know that those other men intended to kill him. You were merely told to wait at the corner until you saw him come home. Am I right?"

"I do not know anything about the Chief," Gino mumbled.

But it was plain that some of his fear was vanishing under this unexpected kindness. Blake had a voice which won dumb animals, and a smile which made friends of children. At last the young Sicilian came forward and put his hand into the stranger's.

"They told me to hide or the Americans would kill me. Madonna mia! I am no Mafioso! I—I wish to see my father."

"I will take you to him now."

"You will not harm me?"

"No. You are perfectly safe."

But the boy still hung back, stammering:

"I—am afraid, Si'or. After all, you see, I know nothing. Perhaps I had better wait here."

"But you will come, to please me, will you not? Then when you find that the policemen will not hurt you, you will tell us all about it, eh, carino?"

He led his shrinking captive out through the front of the house, whence the crone had fled to spread the alarm, and lifted him into the waiting cab. But Bernie Dreux was loath to acknowledge such a tame conclusion to an adventure upon which he had built high hopes.

"L-let's stick round," he shivered. "It's just getting g-g-good."

"Come on, you idiot." Blake fairly dragged him in and commanded the driver to whip up. "That old woman will rouse the neighborhood, and we'll have a mob heaving bricks at us in another minute."

"That'll be fine!" Dreux declared, his pride revolting at what he considered a cowardly retreat. He had come along in the hope of doing deeds that would add luster to his name, and he did not intend to be disappointed. It required a vigorous muscular effort to keep him from clambering out of the carriage.

"I don't understand you at all," said Norvin, with one hand firmly gripping his coat collar, "but I understand the value of discretion at this moment, and I don't intend to take any chances on losing our little friend Gino before he has turned State's evidence."

Dreux sank back, gloomily enough, continuing for the rest of the journey to declaim against the fate that had condemned him to a life of insipid peace; but it was not until they had turned out of the narrow streets of the foreign quarter into the wide, clean stretch of Canal Street that Blake felt secure.

Little Gino Cressi was badly frightened. His wan, pinched face was ashen and he shivered wretchedly. Yet he strove to play the man, and his pitiful attempt at self-control roused something tender and protective in his captor. Laying a reassuring hand upon his shoulder, Blake said, gently:

"Coraggio! No harm shall befall you."

"I—do not wish to die, Excellency."

"You will not die. Speak the truth, figlio mio, and the police will be very kind to you. I promise."

"I know nothing," quavered the child. "My father is a good man. They told me the Chief was dead, but I did not kill him. I only hid."

"Who told you the Chief was dead?"

"I—do not remember."

"Who told you to hide?"

"I do not remember, Si'or." Gino's eyes were like those of a hunted deer, and he trembled as if dreadfully cold.

It was a wretched, stricken child whom Blake led into O'Neil's office, and for a long time young Cressi's lips were glued; but eventually he yielded to the kind-faced men who were so patient with him and his lies, and told them all he knew.

On the following morning the papers announced three new arrests in the Donnelly case, resulting from a confession by Gino Cressi. On the afternoon of the same day the friendly and influential Caesar Maruffi called upon Blake with a protest.

"Signore, my friend," he began, "you and your Committee are doing a great injustice to the Italians of this city."

"How so?"

"Already everybody hates us. We cannot walk upon your streets without insult. Men curse us, children spit at us. We are not Jews; we are Italians. There are bad people among my countrymen, of course, but, Signore, look upon me. Do you think such men as I—"

"Oh, you stand for all that is best in your community. Mr. Maruffi. I only wish you'd help us clean house."

The Sicilian shrugged. "Help? How can I help?"

"Tell what you know of the Mafia so that we can destroy it. At every turn we are thwarted by the secrecy of your people."

"They know what is good for them. As for me, my flesh will not turn the point of a knife, Signore. Life is an enjoyable affair, and if I die I can never marry. What would you have me tell?"

"The name of the Capo-Mafia, for instance."

"You think there is a Capo-Mafia?"

"I know it. What's more, I know who he is."

"Belisario Cardi? Bah! Few people believe there is such a man."

"You and I believe it."

"Perhaps. But what if I could lay hands upon him? Think you that I, or any Sicilian, would dare? All the police of this city could never take Belisario Cardi. It is to make laugh! Our friend Donnelly was unwise, he was too zealous. Now—he is but a memory. He took a life, his life was taken in return. This affair will mean more deaths. Leave things as they are, my friend, before you too are mourned."

Norvin eyed his caller curiously.

"That sounds almost as much like a threat as a warning."

"God forbid! I simply state the truth for your own good and for the good of all of us. Wherever Sicilians are found there your laws will be ignored. For my own part, naturally, I do not approve—I am an American now—but the truth is what I tell you."

"In other words, you think we ought to leave your countrymen alone?"

"Ah, I do not go so far. The laws should be enforced, that is certain. But in trying to do what is impossible you stir up race hatred and make it hard for us reputable Sicilians, who would help you so far as lies in our power. You cannot stamp out the Mafia in a day, in a week; it is Sicilian character. Already you have done enough to vindicate the law. If you go on in a mad attempt to catch this Cardi—whose existence, even, is doubtful—the consequences may be in every way bad."

"We have five of the murderers now, and we'll have the other man soon—the fellow with the rubber coat. The grand jury will indict them. But we won't stop there. We're on a trail that leads higher up, to the man, or men, who directed Larubio and the others to do their work."

Maruffi shook his head mournfully. "And the Cressi boy—it was you who found him?"

"It was."

"How did you do it?"

Norvin laughed. "If you'd only enlist in the cause I'd tell you all my secrets gladly."

"Eh! Then he was betrayed!"

For the life of him Norvin could not tell whether the man was pleased or chagrined at his secrecy, but something told him that the Sicilian was feeling him out for a purpose. He smiled without answering.

"Betrayed!" said Maruffi. "Ah, well, I should not like to be in the shoes of the betrayer." He seemed to lose himself in thought for a moment. "Believe me, I would help you if I could, but I know nothing, and besides it is dangerous. I am a good citizen, but I am not a detective. You American-born," he smiled, "assume that all we Sicilians are deep in the secrets of the Mafia. So the people in the street insult us, and you in authority think that if we would only tell—bah! Tell what? We know no more than you, and it is less safe for us to aid." He rose and extended his hand. "Of course, if I learn anything I will inform you; but there are times when it is best to let sleeping dogs lie."

Norvin closed the door behind him with a feeling of relief, for he was puzzled as to the object of this visit and wanted time to think it out undisturbed. The upshot of his reflection was that Donnelly had been right and that Caesar was indeed the author of the warning letters. As to his want of knowledge, the Sicilian protested rather like a man who plays a part openly. On the other hand, his fears for his own safety seemed genuine enough. What more natural, then, than that he should "wish to test Donnelly's successor with the utmost care before proceeding with his disclosures?" Blake was glad that he had been secretive, for if Maruffi were the unknown friend he would find such caution reassuring.

As if to confirm this view of the case, there came, a day or two later, another communication, stating that the assassin who was still at large (he, in fact, who had worn the rubber coat) was a laborer in the parish of St. John the Baptist, named Frank Normando. The letter went on to say that in escaping from the scene of the crime the man had fallen on the slippery pavement, and the traces of his injury might still be found upon his body.

Norvin lost no time in consulting O'Neil.

"Jove! You're the best detective we have," said the Acting Chief, admiringly. "I'd do well to turn this affair over to you entirely."

"Have you learned anything more from your prisoners?"

"Nothing. They refuse to talk. We're giving them the third degree; but it's no use. There was another murder on St. Phillip Street last night. The old woman who guarded the Cressi boy was found dead."

"Then they think she betrayed the lad?" Norvin recalled Maruffi's hint that it would go hard with the traitor.

"Yes; we might have expected it. How many men will you need to take this Normando?"

"I? You—think I'd better do the trick?" Blake had not intended to take any active part in the capture. He was already known as the head of the movement to avenge Donnelly; he had apprehended Larubio and the Cressi boy with his own hand. Inner voices warned him wildly to run no further risks.

"I thought you'd prefer to lead the raid," O'Neil said.

"So I would. Give me two or three men and we'll bring in Normando, dead or alive."

Six hours later the last of Donnelly's actual assassins was in the parish prison and the police were in possession of evidence showing his movements from early morning on the day of the murder up to the hour of the crime. His identification was even more complete than that of his accomplices, and the public press thanked Norvin Blake in the name of the city for his efficient service.

The anonymous letters continued to come to him regularly, and each one contained some important clue, which, followed up, invariably led to evidence of value. Slowly, surely, out of nothing as it were, the chain was forged. Now came the names of persons who had seen or had talked with some of the accused upon the fatal day, now a hint which turned light upon some dark spot in their records. Again the letters aided in the discovery of important witnesses, who, under pressure, confessed to facts which they had feared to make public—until at last the history of the six assassins lay exposed like an open sheet before the prosecuting attorney.

The certainty and directness with which the "One Who Knows" worked was a matter of ever-increasing amazement to Blake. He himself was little more than an instrument in these unseen hands. Who or what could the writer be? By what means could he remain in such intimate touch with the workings of the Mafia, and what reason impelled him to betray its members? Hour after hour the young man speculated, racking his head until it ached. He considered every possibility, he began to look with curiosity at every face. At length he came to feel an even greater interest in the identity of this hidden friend than in the result of the struggle itself. But investigations—no matter how cautious—invariably resulted in a prompt and imperative warning to desist upon pain of ruining everything.

Gradually in his mind the conviction assumed certainty that the omniscient informer could be none other than Caesar Maruffi. He frequented the Red Wing Club as Donnelly had done, and the more he saw of the fellow the more firm became his belief. He had recognized at their first meeting that Caesar was unusual—there was something unfathomable about him—but precisely what this peculiarity was he could never quite determine.

As for Maruffi, he met Norvin's advances half-way; but although he was apparently more than once upon the verge of some disclosure, the terror of the brotherhood seemed always to intervene. Feeling that he could not openly voice his suspicions until the other was ready to show his hand, Blake kept a close mouth, and thus the two played at cross-purposes. Maruffi—if he were indeed the author of those letters—had not shrunk from betraying the unthinking instruments of the Mafia. Would he ever bring himself to implicate the man, or men, higher up? Blake doubted it. A certain instinctive distrust of the Sicilian was beginning to master him when a letter came which put a wholly different face upon the matter.

"The men who really killed Chief Donnelly," it read, "are Salvatore di Marco, Frank Garcia, Giordano Bolla, and Lorenzo Cardoni." Blake gasped; these were men of standing and repute in the foreign community. "Larubio and his companions were but parts of the machine; these are the hands which set them in motion. These four men dined together on the evening of October 15th, at Fabacher's, then attended a theater where they made themselves conspicuous. From there they proceeded to the lower section of the city and were purposely arrested for disturbing the peace about the time of Donnelly's murder, in order to establish incontestable alibis. Nevertheless, it was they who laid the trap, and they are equally guilty with the wretches who obeyed their orders. It was they who paid over the blood money, and with their arrest you will have all the accessories to the crime, save one. Of him I can tell you nothing. I fear I can never find him, for he walks in shadow and no man dares identify him."

The importance of this information was tremendous, for arrests up to date had been made only among the lower element. An accusation against Di Marco, Garcia, Bolla, and Cardoni would set the city ablaze. O'Neil was aghast at the charge. The Mayor was incredulous, the Committee of Fifty showed signs of hesitation. But Blake, staking his reputation on the genuineness of the letter, and urging the reliability of the writer as shown on each occasion in the past, won his point, and the arrests were made.

The Italian press raised a frightful clamor, the prisoners themselves were righteously indignant, and Norvin found that he had begun to lose that confidence which the public had been so quick to place in him. Nevertheless, he pursued his work systematically, and soon the mysterious agent proceeded to weave a new web around the four suspected men, while he looked on fascinated, doing as he was bid, keeping his own counsel as he had been advised, and turning over the results of his inquiries to the police as they were completed.

Then came what he had long been dreading—a warning like those which had foreshadowed Donnelly's death—and he began to spend sleepless nights. His daylight hours were passed in a strained expectancy; he fought constantly to hold his fears in check; he began sitting with his face to doors; he turned wide corners and avoided side streets. He became furtive and watchful; his eyes were forever flitting here and there; he chose the outer edges of the sidewalks, and he went nowhere after nightfall unattended. The time was past when he could doubt the constancy of his purpose; but he did fear a nervous breakdown, and even shuddered at the thought of possible insanity. Being in fact as sane a man as ever lived, his irrational nerves alarmed him all the more. He could not conceive that an event was immediately before him which, without making his position safer, would rouse him from all thought of self.

Our lives are swayed by trifles; a feather's weight may alter the course of our destinies. A man's daily existence is made up of an infinite series of choices, every one of which is of the utmost importance, did he but know it. We follow paths of a million forkings, none of which converge. A momentary whim, a passing fancy, a broken promise, turns our feet into trails that wind into realms undreamed of.

It so happened that Myra Nell Warren yielded to an utterly reasonless impulse to go calling at the utterly absurd hour of 10 A.M. Miss Warren followed no set rules in her conduct, her mind reacted according to no given formula, and, therefore, when it suddenly occurred to her to visit a little old creole lady in the French quarter, she went without thoughtful consideration or delay.

Madame la Branche was a distant cousin on Bernie's side—so distant, in fact, that no one except herself had ever troubled to trace the precise relationship; but she employed a cook whose skill was celebrated. Now Myra Nell's appetite was a most ungovernable affair, and when she realized that her complete happiness depended upon a certain bouillabaisse, in the preparation of which Madame la Branche's Julia had become famous, she whisked her hair into a knot, jammed her best and largest hat over its unruly confusion, and went bouncing away in the direction of Esplanade Street.

It was in the early afternoon that Norvin Blake received a note from a coal-black urchin, who, after many attempts, had finally succeeded in penetrating to his inner office.

Recognizing the writing, Norvin tore open the envelope eagerly, ready to be entertained by some fresh example of the girl's infinite variety. He read with startled eyes:

"I send this by a trusted messenger, hoping that it will reach you in time. I am a prisoner. I am in danger. I fear my beauty is destroyed. If you love me, come.

"Your wretched

**"MYRA NELL."**

The address was that of a house on Esplanade Street.

"How did you get this?" he demanded, harshly, of the pickaninny.

"A lady drap it from a window."

"Where? Where was she?"

"In a gre't big house on Esplanade Street. She seemed mighty put out about something. Then a man run me away with a club."

A moment later Blake was on the street and had hailed a carriage. The driver, reading urgency in the set face of his fare, whipped the horses into a gallop and the vehicle tore across town, leaping and rocking violently. The thought that Myra Nell was in danger filled

Blake with a physical sickness. Her beauty gone! Could it be that the Mafia had taken this means of attacking him, knowing of his affection for the girl? Of a sudden she became very dear, and he was smothered with fury that any one should cause her suffering.

His heart was pounding madly as the carriage slowed into Esplanade Street, threatening to upset, and he saw ahead of him the house he sought. With a sharp twinge of apprehension he sighted another man approaching the place at a run, and leaping from his conveyance, he raced on with frantic speed.

# XV.
# THE END OF THE QUEST

Evidently the alarm had spread, for there were others ahead of Blake. Several men were grouped beneath an open window. They were strangely excited; some were panting as if from violent exertion; a young French Creole, Lecompte Rilleau, was sprawled at full length upon the grassy banquette, either badly injured or entirely out of breath. He raised a listless hand to the newcomer, as if waving him to the attack. Norvin recognized them all as admirers of Myra Nell—cotton brokers, merchants, a bank cashier—a great relief surged over him.

"Thank God! You're here—in time," he gasped. "What's happened to—her?"

Raymond Cline started to speak, but just then Blake heard the girl herself calling to him, and saw her leaning from a window, her piquant beauty framed with blushing roses which hung about the sill.

"Myra Nell! You're safe!" he cried, shakingly. "What have they done to you?"

She smiled piteously and shook her dark head.

"You were good to come. I am a prisoner."

"A prisoner!" Norvin stared at the young men about him. "Come on," he said, "let's get her out!"

But Murray Logan quieted him. "It's no use, old man."

"What d'you mean?"

"You can't go in."

"Can't—go—in?" As Blake stared uncomprehendingly at the speaker he heard rapid footsteps approaching and saw Achille Marigny coming on the wings of the wind. It was he who appeared in the distance as Norvin rounded the corner, and it was plain now that he was well-nigh spent.

Rilleau reared himself on one elbow and cried with difficulty:

"Welcome, Achille."

"Take it easy, Marigny," called Cline; "we've saved her."

Some one laughed, and the suspicion that he had been hoaxed swept over Blake.

"What's the joke?" he demanded. "I was frightened to death."

"The house is quarantined."

"I never dreamed you'd all come," Miss Warren was saying, sweetly. "It was very gallant, and I shall *never* forget it—never."

"She says her—beauty is—gone," wildly panted Marigny, who had run himself blind and as yet could hear nothing but the drumming in his ears.

"Judge for yourself." Cline steadied him against the low iron fence and pointed to the girl's bewitching face embowered in the leafy window above.

From where he lay flat on his back, idly flapping his hands, Rilleau complained: "I have a weak heart. Will somebody get me a drink?"

"It was *splendid* of you," Myra Nell called down to the group. "I love you for it. Please get me out, right away."

Norvin now perceived a burly individual seated upon the steps of the La Branche mansion. He approached with a view to parleying, but the man forestalled him" saying warningly:

"You can't go in. They've got smallpox in there."

"Smallpox!"

"Go away from that door!" screamed Myra Nell; but the fellow merely scowled.

"I hate to offend the lady," he explained to Norvin, in a hoarse whisper; "but I can't let her out."

Miss Warren repeated in a fury:

"Go away, I tell you. These are friends of mine. If you were a gentleman you'd know you're not wanted. Norvin, make him skedaddle."

Blake shook his head. "You've scared us all blue. If you're quarantined I don't see what we can do."

"The idea! You can at least come in."

"If you go in, you can't come out," belligerently declared the watchman. "Them's orders."

"*Oh-h!* You monster!" cried his prisoner.

"She says herself she's got it," the man explained.

"I never did!" Myra Nell wrung her hands. "Will you stand there and let me perish? Do you refuse to save me?"

"Where is Madame la Branche?" Norvin asked.

"Asleep. And Cousin Montegut is playing solitaire in the library."

"Then who has the smallpox?"

"The cook! They took her screaming to the pest-house an hour after I came. I shall be the next victim; I feel it. We're shut up here for a *week*, maybe longer. Think of that! There's nothing to do, nobody to talk to, nothing to look at. We need another hand for whist. I—I supposed somebody would volunteer."

"I'd love to," Rilleau called, faintly, from the curb, "but I wouldn't survive a week. My heart is beating its last, and besides—I don't play whist."

Mr. Cline called the attention of his companions to two figures which had appeared in the distance, and began to chant:

"The animals came in two by two, The elephant and the kangaroo,"

"Gentlemen, here come the porpoise and the antelope. We are now complete."

The new arrivals proved to be Bernie Dreux and August Kulm, the latter a fat Teutonic merchant whose place of business was down near the river. Mr. Kulm had evidently run all the way, for he was laboring heavily and his gait had long since slackened into a stumbling trot. His eyes were rolling wildly; his fresh young cheeks were purple and sheathed in perspiration.

Miss Warren exclaimed, crossly:

"Oh, dear! I didn't send for Bernie. I'll bet he's furious."

And so it proved. When her half-brother's horrified alarm had been dispelled by the noisy group of rescuers it was replaced by the blackest indignation. He thanked them stiffly and undertook to apologize for his sister, in the midst of which Rilleau, who had now managed to regain his feet, suggested the formation of "The Myra Nell Contagion Club."

"Its object shall be the alleviation of our lady's distress, and its membership shall be limited to her rejected suitors," he declared. "We'll take turns amusing her. I'll appoint myself chairman of the entertainment committee and one of us will always be on guard. We'll sing, we'll dance, we'll cavort beneath the window, and help to while the dreary hours away."

His suggestion was noisily accepted, then after an exchange of views Murray Logan confessed that he had bolted a directors' meeting, and that ruin stared him in the face unless he returned immediately. Achille Marigny, it appeared, had unceremoniously fled from the trial of an important lawsuit, and Raymond Cline was needed at the bank. Foote, Delavan, and the others admitted that they, too, must leave Miss Warren to her fate, at least until after 'Change had closed. And so, having put themselves at her service with extravagant protestations of loyalty, promising candy, books, flowers, a choir to sing beneath her window, they finally trooped off, half carrying the rotund Mr. Kulm, who had sprinted himself into a jelly-like state of collapse.

Rilleau alone maintained his readiness to brave the perils of smallpox, leprosy, or plague at Miss Warren's side, until Bernie informed him that the very idea was shocking, whereupon he dragged himself away with the accusation that all his heart trouble lay at her door.

"Oh, you spoiled it all!" Myra Nell told her brother, indignantly. "You might at least have let *him* come in. Cousin Althea would have chaperoned us."

"The idea! Why *did* you do such an atrocious thing?"

"Where you frightened, Norvin?" The girl beamed hopefully down upon him.

"Horribly. I'm not over it yet. I'm half inclined to act on Lecompte's suggestion and break in."

She clapped her hands gleefully, whereupon the watchman arose, saying:

"No you don't!"

"I wouldn't allow such a thing," said Bernie, firmly. "It would mean a scandal."

"I—I can't stay here *alone*, for a whole *week*. I'll die."

"Then I'll join you myself," her brother offered.

Myra Nell looked alarmed. "Oh, not *you*! I want some one to nurse me when I fall ill."

"What makes you think you'll catch it? Were you exposed?"

"Exposed! Heavens! I can feel the disease coming on this very minute. The place is full of germs; I can spear 'em with a hat-pin." She shuddered and managed to counterfeit a tear.

"I've an idea," said Norvin. "I'll get that trained nurse who saved you when you fell off the horse."

"Vittoria? She might do. But, Norvin, the horse threw me." She warned him with a grimace which Bernie did not see. "He's a frightful beast."

"I can't afford a trained nurse," Dreux objected, "and you don't need one, anyhow."

"All right for you, Bernie; if you don't care any more for my life than that, I'll sicken and die. When a girl's relatives turn against her it's time she was out of the way."

"Oh, all right," said her brother, angrily. "It's ruinous, but I suppose you must have it your way."

Myra Nell shook her head gloomily. "No—not if you are going to feel like that. Of course, if she were here she could cut off my hair when I take to my bed; she could bathe my face with lime-water when my beauty goes; she could listen to my ravings and understand, for she is a—woman. But no, I'm not worth it. Perhaps I can get along all right, and, anyhow, I'll have to teach school or—or be a nun if I'm all pock-marks."

"Good Lord!" Bernie wiped his brow with a trembling hand. "D'you think that'll happen, Norvin?"

"It's bound to," the girl predicted, indifferently. "But what's the odds?" Suddenly a new thought dilated her eyes with real horror. "Oh!" she cried. "*Oh!* I just happened to remember. I'm to be Queen of the Carnival! Now, I'll be scarred and hideous, even if I happen to recover; but I won't recover. You shall have my royal robe, Bunny. Keep it always. And Norvin shall have my hair."

"Here! I—don't want your hair," Blake asserted, nervously. "I mean not without—"

"It is all I have to give."

"You may not catch the smallpox, after all."

"We'll—have Miss Fabrizi b-by all means," Bernie chattered.

"You stay here and talk to her while I go," Norvin suggested, quickly. "And, Myra Nell, I'll fetch you a lot of chocolates. I'll fetch you anything, if you'll only cheer up."

"Remember, It's against my wishes," the girl said. "But she's not at the hospital now; she's living in the Italian quarter." She gave him the street, and number, and he made off in all haste.

On his way he had time to think more collectedly of the girl he had just left. Her prank had shocked him into a keen realization of his feeling for her, and he began to understand the large part she played in his life. Many things inclined him to believe that her regard for him was really deeper than her careless levity indicated, and it seemed now that they had been destined for each other.

It was dusk when he reached his destination. A nondescript Italian girl ushered him up a dark stairway and into an old-fashioned drawing-room with high ceiling, and long windows which opened out upon a rusty overhanging iron balcony. The room ran through to a court in the rear, after the style of so many of these foreign-built houses. It had once been the home of luxury and elegance, but had long since fallen into a state of shabby decay. He was still lost in thoughts of the important step which he contemplated when he heard the rustle of a woman's garment behind him and rose as a tall figure entered the room.

"Miss Fabrizi?" he inquired. "I came to find you—"

He paused, for the girl had given a smothered cry. The light was poor and the shadows played tricks with his eyes. He stepped forward, peering strangely at her, then halted.

"Margherita!" he whispered; then in a shaking voice, "My God!"

"Yes," she said, quietly, "it is I."

He touched her gently, staring as if bereft of his senses. He felt himself swept by a tremendous excitement. It struck him dumb; it shook him; it set the room to whirling dizzily. The place was no longer ill-lit and shabby, but illumined as if by a burst of light. And through his mad panic of confusion he saw her standing there, calm, tawny, self-possessed.

"Caro Norvin! You have found me, indeed," he heard her say. "I wondered when the day would come."

"You—you!" he choked. His arms were hungry for her, his heart was melting with the wildest ecstasy that had ever possessed it. She was clad as he often remembered her, in a dress which partook of her favorite and inseparable color, her hair shone with that unforgettable luster; her face was the face he had dreamed of, and there was no shock of readjustment in his recognition of her. Rather, her real presence made the cherished mental image seem poor and weak.

"I came to see Miss Fabrizi. Why are *you* here?" He glanced at the door as if expecting an interruption.

"I am she."

"Contessa!"

"Hush!" She laid her fingers upon his lips. "I am no longer the Contessa Margherita. I am Vittoria Fabrizi."

"Then—you have been here—in New Orleans for a long time?"

"More than a year."

"Impossible! I—You—It's inconceivable! Why have we never met?"

"I have seen you many times."

"And you didn't speak? Why, oh, why, Margherita?"

"My friend, if you care for me, for my safety and my peace of mind, you must not use that name. Collect yourself. We will have explanations. But first, remember, I am Vittoria Fabrizi, the nurse, a poor girl."

"I shall remember. I don't understand; but I shall be careful. I don't know what it all means, why you—didn't let me know." In spite of his effort at self-control he fell again into a delicious bewilderment. His spirits leaped, he felt unaccountably young and exhilarated; he laughed senselessly and yet with a deep throbbing undertone of delight. "What are names and reasons, anyhow? What are worries and hopes and despairs? I've found you. You live; you are safe; you are young. I feared you were old and changed—it has seemed so long and—and my search dragged so. But I never ceased thinking and caring—I never ceased hoping—"

She laid a gentle hand upon his arm. "Come, come! You are upset. It will all seem natural enough when you know the story."

"Tell me everything, all at once. I can't wait." He led her to a low French *lit de repos* near by, and seated himself beside her. Her nearness thrilled him with the old intoxication, and he hardly heeded what he was saying. "Tell me how you came to be Vittoria Fabrizi instead of Margherita Ginini; how you came to be here; how you knew of my presence and yet—Oh, tell me everything, for I'm smothering. I'm incoherent. I—I—"

"First, won't you explain how you happened to come looking for me?"

He gathered his wits to tell her briefly of Myra Nell, feeling a renewed sense of strangeness in the fact that these two knew each other. She made as if to rise.

"Please!" he cried; "this is more important than Miss Warren's predicament. She's really delighted with her adventure, you know."

"True, she is in no danger. There is so much to tell! That which has taken four years to live cannot be told in five minutes. I—I'm afraid I am sorry you came."

"Don't destroy my one great moment of gladness."

"Remember I am Vittoria Fabrizi—"

"I know of no other name."

"Lucrezia is here, also, and she, too, is another. You have never seen her. You understand?"

He nodded. "And her name?"

"Oliveta! We are cousins."

"I respect your reasons for these changes. Tell me only what you wish."

"Oh, I have nothing to conceal," she said, relieved at his growing calmness. "They are old family names which I chose when I gave up my former life. You wonder why? It is part of the story. When Martel died the Contessa Margherita died also. She could not remain at Terranova where everything spoke of him. She was young; she began a long quest. As you know, it was fruitless, and when in time her ideas changed she was born to a new life."

"You have—abandoned the search?"

"Long ago. You told me truly that hatred and revenge destroy the soul. I was young and I could not understand; but now I know that only good can survive—good thoughts, good actions, good lives."

"And is the Donna Teresa here?"

Vittoria shook her head. "She has gone—back, perhaps, to her land of sunshine, her flowers, and her birds and her dream-filled mountain valleys. It was two years ago that we lost her. She could not survive the change. I have—many regrets when I think of her."

"You know, of course, that I returned to Sicily, and that I followed you?"

"Yes. And when I learned of it I knew there was but one thing to do."

"I was unwise—disloyal there at Terranova." She met his eyes frankly, but made no sign. "Is that why you avoided me?"

"Ah, let us not speak of that old time. When one severs all connections with the past and begins a new existence, one should not look back. But I have not lost interest in you, my friend, I have learned much from Myra Nell; seeing her was like seeing you, for she hardly speaks of any one else. Many times we nearly met—only a moment separated us—you came as I went, or I came in time barely to miss you. You walked one street as I walked another; we were in the same crowds, our elbows touched, our paths crossed, but we never chanced to meet until this hour. Now I am almost sorry—"

"But why—if you have forgiven me; how could you be so indifferent? You must have known how I longed for you."

Her look checked him on the brink of a passionate avowal.

"Does my profession tell you nothing?" she asked.

"You are a—nurse. What has that to do with it?"

"Do you know that I have been with the Sisters of Mercy? I—I am one of them."

"Impossible!"

"In spirit at least. I shall be one in reality, as soon as I am better fitted."

"A nun!" He stared at her dumbly, and his face paled.

"I have given all I possess to the Order excepting only what I have settled upon Oliveta. This is her house, I am her guest, her pensioner. I am ready to take the last step—to devote my life to mercy. Now you begin to understand my reason for waiting and watching you in silence. You see it is very true that Margherita Ginini no longer exists. I have not only changed my name, I am a different woman. I am sorry," she said, doing her best to comfort him—"yes, and it is hard for me, too. That is why I would have avoided this meeting."

"If you contemplate this—step," he inquired, dully, "why have you left the hospital?"

"I am not ready to take Orders. I have much to—overcome. Now I must prepare Oliveta to meet you, for she has not changed as I have, and there might be consequences."

"What consequences?"

"We wish to forget the past," she said, non-committally. When she returned from her errand she saw him outlined blackly against one of the long windows, his hands clasped behind his back, his head low as if in meditation. He seemed unable to throw off this spell of silence as they drove to the La Branche home, but listened contentedly to her voice, so like the low, soft music of a cello.

After he left her it was long before he tried to reduce his thoughts to order. He preferred to dwell indefinitely upon the amazing fact that he at last had found her, that he had actually seen and touched her. Finally, when he brought himself to face the truth in its entirety, he knew that he was deeply disappointed, and he felt that he ought to be hopeless. Yet hope was strong in him. It blazed through his very veins, he felt it thrill him magically.

When he fell asleep that night it was with a smile upon his lips, for hope had crystallized into a baseless but none the less assured belief that he would find a way to win her.

# XVI.
# QUARANTINE

Blake arose like a boy on Christmas morning. He thrilled to an extravagant gladness. At breakfast the truth came to him—he was young! For the first time he realized that he had let himself grow up and lose his illusions; that he had become cynical, tired, prosaic, while all the time the flame of youth was merely smouldering. Old he was, but only as a stripling soldier is aged by battle; as for the real, rare joys of living and loving, he had never felt them. Myra Nell had appealed to his affection like a dear and clever child, and helped to keep some warmth in his heart. But this was magic. The sun had never been so bright, the air so sweet to his nostrils, the strength so vigorous in his limbs.

He had become so accustomed to the mysterious letters by this time that he had grown to look for them as a matter of course, and he was not disturbed when, on arriving at his office, he found one in his mail. Heretofore the writer had been positive in his statements, but now came the first hint of uncertainty.

"I cannot find Belisario Cardi," he wrote. "His hand is over all, and yet he is more intangible than mist. I am hedged about with difficulties and dangers which multiply as the days pass. I can do no more, hence the task devolves upon you. Be careful, for he is more desperate than ever. It is your life or his.

**"ONE WHO KNOWS."**

It was as daunting a message as he could have received—the withdrawal of assistance, the authoritative confirmation of his fears—yet Blake's spirit rose to meet the exigency with a new courage. It occurred to him that if Maruffi, or whoever the author was, had exhausted his usefulness, perhaps Vittoria could help. She had spent much time in her search for this very Cardi, and might have learned something of value concerning him. Oliveta, too, could be of assistance. He felt sure that the knowledge of his own peril would be enough to enlist their aid, and he gladly seized upon the thought that a common interest would draw him closer to the woman he loved.

He arrived at the La Branche house early that afternoon, and found young Rilleau sitting on a box beneath Myra Nell's window, with the girl herself embowered as before in a frame of roses.

"Any symptoms yet?" Norvin inquired, agreeably.

"Thousands! I'm slowly dying."

Lecompte nodded dolefully. "Look at her color."

"No doubt it's the glow from those red roses that I see in her cheeks."

"It's fever," Miss Warren exclaimed, indignantly. She took a hand-glass from her lap and regarded her vivid young features. "Smallpox attacks people differently. With me the first sign is fever." She had parted her abundant hair and swept it back from her brow in an attempt to make herself look ill, but with the sole effect of enhancing her appearance of abounding health. Madame la Branche's best black shawl was drawn about her plump and dimpled shoulders. Assuming a hollow tone, she inquired: "Do you see any other change in me?"

"Yes. And I rather like that way of doing your hair."

"Vittoria says I look like a picture of Sister Dolorosa, or something."

"Is Miss Fabrizi in?"

"In? How could she be out? Isn't she a dear, Norvin? I knew you'd meet some day."

"Does she play whist?"

"Of course not, silly. She's—nearly a nun. But we sat up in bed all night talking. Oh, it's a comfort to have some one with you at the last, some one in whom you can confide. I can't bear to—to soar aloft with so much on my conscience. I've confessed *everything.*"

"What's to prevent her from catching the disease and soaring away with you?"

"She's a nurse. They're just like doctors, you know, they never catch anything. Is that hideous watchman still at his post?"

"Yes. Fast asleep, with his mouth open."

"I hope a fly crawls in," said the girl, vindictively; then, in an eager whisper: "Couldn't you manage to get past him? We'd have a lovely time here for a week."

Rilleau raised his voice in jealous protest.

"And leave me sitting on my throne? Never! I'm giving this box-party for you, Myra Nell."

"Oh, you could come, too."

"I respect the law," Norvin told her; but Lecompte continued to complain.

"I don't see what you're doing here at this time of day, anyhow, Blake, Have you no business responsibilities?"

"I'm a member of the Contagion Club; I've a right to be here."

"We were discussing rice, old shoes, and orange blossoms when you interrupted," the languid Mr. Rilleau continued. "Frankly, speaking as a friend, I don't see anything in your conversation so far to interest a sick lady. Why don't you talk to the yellow-haired nurse?"

"I intend to."

"Vittoria is back in the kitchen preparing my diet," said Myra Nell. "She's making fudge, I believe. I—I seem to crave sweet things. Maybe it's another symptom."

"It must be," Blake acknowledged. "I'll ask her what she thinks of it." With a glance at the slumbering guard he vaulted the low fence and made his way around to the rear of the house.

He heard Vittoria singing as he came into the flower-garden, a low-pitched Sicilian love-song. He called to her, and she came to a window, smiling down at him, spotless and fresh in her stiff uniform.

"Do you know that you're trespassing and may get into trouble?" she queried.

"The watchman is asleep, and I had to speak to you."

"No wonder he sleeps. Myra Nell holds the poor fellow responsible for all her troubles, and those young men have nearly driven him insane."

"Is there any danger of smallpox, really?"

"Not the slightest. This quarantine is merely a matter of form. But that child—" She broke into a frank, sweet laugh. "She pretends to be horribly frightened. All the time she is acting—the little fraud!"

Norvin flushed a bit under her gaze.

"I had no chance to talk to you last night."

"And you will have no chance now." Vittoria tipped her chin the slightest bit.

"I must see you, alone."

"Impossible!"

"To-night. You can slip away on some pretext or other. It is really important."

She regarded him questioningly. "If that is true I will try, but—I cannot meet you at Oliveta's house. Besides, you must not go into that quarter alone at night."

"What do you mean?" he inquired, wondering how she could know of his danger.

"Because—no American is safe there now. Perhaps I can meet you on the street yonder."

"I'll be waiting."

"It may be late, unless I tell Myra Nell."

"Heaven above! She'd insist on coming, too, just because it's forbidden."

"Very well. Now go before you are discovered."

During the afternoon his excitement increased deliciously, and that evening he found himself pacing the shaded street near the La Branche home, with the eager restlessness of a lover.

It was indeed late when Vittoria finally appeared.

"Myra Nell is such a chatterbox," she explained, "that I couldn't get her to bed. Have you waited long?"

"I dare say. I'm not sure."

"This is very exciting, is it not?" She glanced over her shoulder up the ill-lighted street. Rows of shade trees cast long inky blots between the corner illuminations; the houses on either side sat well back in their yards, increasing the sense of isolation. "It is quite a new experience for me."

"For me, too."

"I hope we're not seen. Signore Norvin Blake and a trained nurse! Oh, the comment!"

"There's a bench near by where we can sit. Passers-by will take us for servants."

"You are the butler, I am the maid," she laughed.

"I am glad you can laugh," he told her. "You were very sad, there at Terranova."

"I've learned the value of a smile. Life is full of gladness if we can only bring ourselves to see it. Now tell me the meaning of this. I knew it must be important or I would not have come." Back of the bench upon which she had seated herself a jessamine vine depended, filling the air with perfume; the night was warm and still and languorous; through the gloom she regarded him with curiosity.

"I hate to begin," he said. "I dread to speak of unpleasant things — to you. I wish we might just sit here and talk of whatever we pleased."

"We cannot sit here long on any account. But let me guess. It is your work against — those men."

"Exactly. You know the history of our struggle with the Mafia?"

"Everything."

"I am leading a hard fight, and I think you can help me."

"Why do you think so?" she asked, in a low voice. "I have given up my part. I have no desire for revenge."

"Nor have I. I do not wish to harm any man; but I became involved in this through a desire to see justice done, and I have reached a point where I cannot stop or go back. It started with the arrest of Gian Narcone. You know how Donnelly was killed. They took his life for Narcone's, and he, too, was my — dear friend."

"All this is familiar to me," she said, in a strained tone.

"I will tell you something that no one knows but myself, I have a friend among the Mafiosi, and it is he, not I, who has brought the murderers of Mr. Donnelly to an accounting."

"You know him?"

"Yes. At least I think I do."

"His — name?" She was staring at him oddly.

"I feel bound not to reveal it even to you. He has told me many things, among them that Belisario Cardi is alive, is here, and that it is he who worked all this evil."

"What has all this to do with me?" she inquired. "Have I not told you that I gave my search into other hands?"

"It was Cardi who killed—one whom we both loved, one for whose life I would have given my own; it was Cardi who destroyed my next-best friend, a simple soul who lived for nothing but his duty. Now he has threatened my life also—does that count for nothing with you?"

She leaned forward, searching his face earnestly. "You are a brave man. You should go away where he cannot harm you."

"I would like very much to," he confessed, "but I am too great a coward to run away."

"And why do you tell me this?"

"I need your help. My mysterious friend can do no more; he has said so. I'm not equal to it alone."

"Oh," she cried, as if yielding to a feeling long suppressed, "I did so want to be rid of it all, and now you are in danger—the greatest danger. Won't you give it up?"

He shook his head, puzzled at her vehemence. "I don't wish to drag you into it against your will, but Oliveta lives there among her countrypeople. She must know many things which I, as an outsider, could never learn. I—need help."

There was a long silence before the girl said:

"Yes, I will help, for I am still the same woman you knew in Sicily. I am still full of hatred. I would give my life to convict Martel's assassins; but I am fighting myself. That is why I have gone to live with Oliveta until I have conquered and am ready to become a Sister."

"Please don't say that."

"Oliveta, you know, is alone," she went on, with forced composure, "and so I watch over her. She is to be married soon, and when she is safe, then I think I can return to the Sisters and live as I long to. It will be a good match, much better than I ever hoped for, and she loves, which is even more blessed to contemplate." Vittoria laid her hands impulsively upon his arm. "Meanwhile I cannot refuse such aid as I can give you, for you have already suffered too much through me. You *have* suffered, have you not?"

"It has turned my hair gray," he laughed, trying not to show the depth of his feeling. "But now that I know you are safe and well and happy, nothing seems to matter. Does Myra Nell know who you are?"

"No one knows save you and Oliveta. If that child even dreamed—" She lifted her slender hands in an eloquent gesture. "My secret would be known in an hour. Now I must go, for even housemaids must observe the proprieties."

"It's late. I think I had better see you safely home."

"I dare say our watchman has found himself a comfortable bed—"

"The slumbers of night-watchmen are notoriously deep."

"And Papa La Branche has finished his solitaire. There is no danger."

No one was in sight as they stole in through the driveway to the servants' door. She gave him her hand, and he pressed it closely, whispering:

"When shall I see you again?"

"After the quarantine. I can do nothing until then."

"You will go back to Oliveta's house?"

"Yes, but you must never come there, even in daylight." She thought for a moment while he still retained her hand. "I will instruct you later—" She broke off suddenly, and at the same instant Blake heard a stir in the darkness behind him.

Vittoria drew him quickly into the black shadows of the rear porch, where they stood close together, afraid to move until the man had passed. The kitchen gallery was shielded by a latticework covered with vines, and Blake felt reasonably safe within its shelter. He was beginning to breathe easier when a voice barely an arm's-length away inquired, gruffly:

"Who's there?"

He would have given something handsome to be out of this foolish predicament, which he knew must be very trying to his companion. But the fates were against him. To his horror, the man struck a match and mounting the steps to the porch flashed it directly into his face.

"Good evening," said Blake, with rather a weak attempt at assurance.

"What are you doing here?" the guard demanded. "Don't you know that this house is quarantined?"

"I do. Kindly lower your voice; there are people asleep."

The fellow's eyes took in the girl in her stiffly starched uniform before the match burned out and darkness engulfed them once more.

"I'm not a burglar."

"Humph! I don't know whether you are or not."

"I assure you," urged Vittoria.

"Strike another match and I'll prove to you that I'm not dangerous." When the light flared up once more Norvin selected a card from his case and handed it to the watchman. "I am Norvin Blake, president of the Cotton Exchange."

But this information failed of the desired effect.

"Oh, I know you, but this ain't exactly the right time to be calling on a lady."

Vittoria felt her companion's muscles stiffen.

"I will explain my presence later," he said, stiffly; then, turning to Vittoria, "I am sorry I disturbed this estimable man. Good night."

"Just a minute," the watchman broke in. "You needn't say good night."

"What do you mean?"

"This house is quarantined for smallpox."

"Well?"

"Nobody can come or go without the doctor's permission."

"I understand that."

"Now that you're here, I reckon you'll stay."

Miss Fabrizi uttered a smothered exclamation.

"You're crazy!" said Blake, angrily.

"Yes? Well, that's my instructions."

"I haven't been inside."

"That don't make any difference; the lady has."

"It's absurd. You can't force—"

"'Sh-h!" breathed Vittoria.

Some one had entered the kitchen at their back. A light flashed through the window, the door opened, and Mr. La Branche, clad in a rusty satin dressing-gown and carpet slippers, stood revealed, a lamp in his hand.

"I thought I heard voices," he said. "What is the trouble?"

"There's no trouble at all, sir," Blake protested, then found himself absurdly embarrassed.

Vittoria and the guard both began to speak at once, and at length she broke into laughter, saying:

"Poor Mr. Blake, I fear he has been exposed to contagion. It was necessary for him to talk with me on a matter of importance, and now this man tells him he cannot leave."

But from Papa La Branche's expression it was evident that he saw nothing humorous in the situation.

"To talk with you! At this hour!"

"I'm working for the Board of Health, and those are my orders," declared outraged authority.

"It was imperative that I see Miss Fabrizi; the blame for this complication is entirely mine," Norvin assured the old creole.

The representative of the Board of Health inquired, loudly: "Didn't the doctors tell you that nobody could come or go, Mr. La Branche?"

"They did."

"But, my dear man, this is no ordinary case. Now that I have explained, I shall go, first apologizing to Mr. La Branche for disturbing him."

"No, you won't"

The master of the house stepped aside, holding his light on high.

"Miss Fabrizi is my guest," he said, quietly, "so no explanations are necessary. This man is but doing his duty, and, therefore, Mr. Blake, I fear I shall have to offer you the poor hospitality of my roof until the law permits you to leave."

"Impossible, sir! I—"

"I regret that we have never met before; but you are welcome, and I shall do my best to make you comfortable." He waved his hand commandingly toward the open door.

"Thank you, but I can't accept, really."

"I fear that you have no choice."

"But the idea is ridiculous, preposterous! I'm a busy man; I can't shut myself up this way for a week or more. Besides, I couldn't allow myself to be forced upon strangers in this manner."

"If you are a good citizen, you will respect the law," said La Branche, coldly.

"Bother the law! I have obligations! Why—the very idea is absurd! I'll see the health officers and explain at once—"

The old gentleman, however, still waited, while the watchman took his place at the top of the steps as if determined to do his duty, come, what might.

Norvin found Vittoria's eyes upon him, and saw that beneath her self-possession she was intensely embarrassed. Evidently there was nothing to do now but accept the situation and put an end to the painful scene at any sacrifice. Once inside, he could perhaps set himself right; but for the present no explanations were possible. He might have braved the Board of Health, but he could not run away from Papa La Branche's accusing eye. Bowing gravely, he said:

"You are quite right, sir, and I thank you for your hospitality. If you will lead the way, I will follow."

The two culprits entered the big, empty kitchen, then followed the rotund little figure which waddled ahead of them into the front part of the house.

# XVII.
## AN OBLIGATION IS MET

Montegut La Branche paused in the front hall at the foot of the stairs.

"It is late" he said; "no doubt Mademoiselle wishes to retire."

"I would like to offer a word of explanation," Norvin ventured, but Vittoria interposed, quietly:

"Mr. La Branche is right—explanations are unnecessary." Bowing graciously to them both, she mounted the stairs into the gloom above, followed by the old Creole's polite voice:

"A pleasant sleep, Mademoiselle, and happy dreams." Leading the way into the library, he placed the lamp upon a table, then, turning to his unbidden guest, inquired, coldly, "Well?"

His black eyes were flashing underneath his gray brows, and he presented a fierce aspect despite his gown, which resembled a Mother Hubbard, and his slippers, which flapped as he walked.

"I must apologize for my intrusion," said Norvin. "I wish you to understand how it came about."

"In view of your attentions to my wife's cousin, it was unfortunate that you should have selected this time, this place, for your—er—adventure."

"Exactly! I'm wondering how to spare Miss Warren any annoyance."

"I fear that will be impossible. She must know the truth."

"She must not know; she must not guess."

"M'sieu!" exclaimed the old man. "My wife and I can take no part in your intrigues. Myra Nell is too well bred to show resentment at your conduct, no matter what may be her feelings."

Norvin flushed with exasperation, then suddenly felt ashamed of himself. Surely he could trust this chivalrous old soul with a part of the truth. Once his scruples were satisfied, the man's very sense of honor would prevent him from even thinking of what did not concern him.

"I think you will understand better," he said, "when you have heard me through. I can't tell you everything, for I am not at liberty to do so. But you know, perhaps, that I am connected with the Committee of Justice."

"I do."

"You don't know the full extent of the task with which I am charged, however."

"Perhaps not."

"Its gravity may be understood when you know that I have been marked for the same fate as Chief Donnelly."

The old man started.

"My labors have taken me into many quarters. I seek information through many channels. It was upon this business, in a way, that I came to see Miss Fabrizi."

"I do not follow you."

"She is a Sicilian. She knows much which would be of value to the Committee and to me. It was necessary for me to see her alone and secretly. If the truth were known it would mean her—life, perhaps."

The Creole's bearing altered instantly.

"Say no more. I believe you to be a man of honor, and I apologize for my suspicions."

"May I trust you to respect this confidence?"

"It is sealed."

"But this doesn't entirely relieve the situation. I can't explain to Madame La Branche or to Miss Myra Nell even as much as I've explained to you."

"Some day will you relieve me from my promise of secrecy?" queried the old man, with an eager, bird-like glance from his bright eyes.

"Assuredly. As soon as we have won our fight against the Mafia."

"Then I will lie for you, and confess later. I have never lied to my wife, M'sieu—except upon rare occasions," Mr. La Branche chuckled merrily. "And even then only about trifles. So, the result? Absolute trust; supreme confidence on her part. A happy state for man and wife, is it not? Ha! I am a very good liar, an adept, as you shall see, for I am not calloused by practice and therefore liable to forgetfulness. With me a lie is always fresh in my mind; it is a matter of absorbing interest, hence I do not forget myself. Heaven knows the excitement of nursing an innocent deceit and of seeing it grow and flower under my care will be most welcome, for the monotony of this abominable confinement—But I must inquire, do you play piquet?"

"I am rather good at it," Norvin confessed, whereat Papa La Branche seemed about to embrace him.

"You are sent from heaven!" he declared. "You deliver me from darkness. Thirty-seven games of Napoleon to-day! Think of it! I was dealing the thirty-eighth when you came. But piquet! Ah, that is a game, even though my angel wife abominates it. We have still five days of this hideous imprisonment, so let us agree to an hour before lunch, an hour before dinner, then—um-,—perhaps two hours in the evening at a few cents a game, eh? You agree, my friend?" The little man peered up timidly. "Perhaps—but no, I dare say you are sleepy, and it *is* late."

"I should enjoy a game or two right now," Norvin falsified. "But first, don't you think we'd better rehearse our explanation of my presence?"

"A good idea. You came to see me upon business. I telephoned, and you came like a good friend, then—let me see, I was so overjoyed to see a new face that I rushed forth to greet you, and behold! that scorpion, that loathsome reptile outside pronounced you infected. He forced you to enter, even against my protestations. It was all my fault. I am desolated with regrets. Eh? How is that? You see nature designed me for a rogue."

"Excellent! But what is our important business?"

"True. Since I retired from active affairs I have no business. That is awkward, is it not? May I ask in what line you are engaged?"

"I am a cotton factor."

"Then I shall open an account with you. I shall give you money to invest. Come, there need be no deceit about that; I shall write you a check at once."

"That's hardly necessary, so long as we understand each other."

But Mr. La Branche insisted, saying:

"One lie is all that I dare undertake. I have told two at the same time, but invariably they clashed and disaster resulted. There! I trust you to make use of the money as you think best. But enough! What do women know of business? It is a mysterious word to them. Now— piquet!" He dragged Norvin to a seat at a table, then trotted away in search of cards, his slippers clap-clapping at every step as if in gleeful applause. "Shall we cut for deal, M'sieu? Ah!" He sighed gratefully as he won, and began to shuffle. "With four hours of piquet every day, and a lie upon my conscience, I feel that I shall be happy in spite of this execrable smallpox."

Myra Nell's emotions may be imagined when, on the following morning, she learned who had broken through the cordon while she slept.

"Lordy! Lordy!" she exclaimed, with round eyes. "He said he'd do it; but I didn't think he really would."

She had flounced into Vittoria's room to gossip while she combed her hair.

"Mr. La Branche says it's all his fault, and he's terribly grieved," Miss Fabrizi told her. "Now, now! Your eyes are fairly popping out."

"Wouldn't your eyes pop out if the handsomest, the richest, the bravest man in New Orleans deliberately took his life in his hands to see you and be near you?"

"But he says it was important business which brought him." Vittoria smiled guiltily.

"Tell that to your granny! You don't know men as I do. Have you really seen him? I'm not *dreaming*?"

"I have seen him, with these very eyes, and if you were not such a lazy little pig you'd have seen him, too. Shall you take your breakfast in your room, as usual?" Vittoria's eyes twinkled.

"Don't tease me!" Miss Warren exclaimed, with a furious blush. "I—I love to tease other people, but I can't stand it myself. Breakfast in my room, indeed! But of course I shall treat him with freezing politeness."

"Why should you pretend to be offended?"

"Don'tyouunderstand?Thisisboundtocausegossip.Why,theideaof Norvin Blake, the handsomest, the richest—"

"Yes, yes."

"The idea of his getting himself quarantined in the same house with *me*, and our being here together for days—maybe for *months!* Why, it will create the loveliest scandal. I'll never dare hold up my head again in public, *never*. You see how it must make me feel. I'm compromised." Myra Nell undertook to show horror in her features, but burst into a gale of laughter.

"Do you care for him very much?"

"I'm crazy about him! Why, dearie, after *this*—we're—we're almost married! Now watch me show him how deeply I'm offended."

But when she appeared in the dining-room, late as usual, her frigidity was not especially marked. On the contrary, her face rippled into one smile after another, and seizing Blake by both hands, she danced around him, singing:

"You did it! You did it! You did it! Hurrah for a jolly life in the pest-house!"

Madame La Branche was inclined to be shocked at this behavior, but inasmuch as Papa Montegut was beaming angelically upon the two young people, she allowed herself to be mollified.

"I couldn't believe Vittoria," Myra Nell told Norvin. "Don't you know the danger you run?"

Mr. La Branche exclaimed: "I am desolated at the consequences of my selfishness! I did not sleep a wink. I can never atone."

"Quite right," his wife agreed. "You must have been mad, Montegut. It was criminal of you to rush forth and embrace him in that manner."

"But, delight of my soul, the news he bore! The joy of seeing him! It unmanned me." The Creole waved his hands wildly, as if at a loss for words.

"Oh, you fibber! Norvin told me he'd never met you," said Myra Nell.

"Eh! Impossible! We are associates in business; business of a most important—But what does that term signify to you, my precious ladybird? Nothing! Enough, then, to say that he saved me from disaster. Naturally I was overjoyed and forgot myself."

His wife inquired, timidly, "Have your affairs gone disastrously?"

"Worse than that! Ruin stared us in the face until *he* came. Our deliverer!"

Blake flushed at this fulsome extravagance, particularly as he saw Myra Nell making faces at him.

"Fortunately everything is arranged now," he assured his hostess. But this did not satisfy Miss Warren, who, with apparent innocence, questioned the two men until Papa La Branche began to bog and flounder in his explanations. Fortunately for the men, she was diverted for the moment by discovering that the table was set for only four.

"Oh, we need another place," she exclaimed, "for Vittoria!"

The old lady said, quietly: "No, dear. While we were alone it was permissible, but it is better now in this way."

Myra Nell's ready acquiescence was a shock to Norvin, arguing, as it did, that these people regarded the Countess Margherita as an employee. Could it be that they were so utterly blind?

He was allowed little time for such thoughts, however, since Myra Nell set herself to the agreeable task of unmasking her lover and confounding Montegut La Branche. But Cousin Althea was not of a suspicious nature, and continued to beam upon her husband, albeit a trifle vaguely. Then when breakfast was out of the way the girl added to Norvin's embarrassment by flirting with him so outrageously that he was glad to flee to Papa Montegut's piquet game.

At the first opportunity he said to Vittoria: "I feel dreadfully about this. Why, they seem to think you're a—a—servant! It's unbearable!"

"That is part of my work; I am accustomed to it." She smiled.

"Then you *have* changed. But if they knew the truth, how differently they'd act!"

"They must never suspect; more depends upon it than you know."

"I feel horribly guilty, all the same."

"It can make no difference what they think of me. I'm afraid, however, that you have—made it—difficult for Myra Nell."

"So it appears. I didn't think of her when I entered this delightful prison."

"You had no choice."

"It wasn't altogether that. I wanted to be near you, Vittoria."

Her glance was level and cool, her voice steady. "It was chivalrous to try to spare me the necessity of explaining. The situation was trying; but we were both to blame, and now we must make the best of it. Myra Nell's misunderstanding is complete, and she will be unhappy unless you devote yourself to her."

"I simply can't. I think I'll keep to myself as much as possible."

"You don't know that girl," Vittoria said. "You think she is frivolous and inconsequent, that she has the brightness of a sunbeam and no more substance; but you are mistaken. She is good and true and steadfast underneath, and she can feel deeply."

Blake found that it was impossible to isolate himself. Mr. La Branche clung to him like a drowning man; his business affairs called him repeatedly to the telephone; Myra Nell appropriated him with all the calm assurance of a queen, and Madame La Branche insisted upon seeing personally to his every want. The only person of whom he saw little was Vittoria Fabrizi.

His disappearance, of course, required much explaining and long conversations with his office, with his associates, and with police headquarters, where his plight was regarded as a great joke. This was all very well; but there were other and unforeseen consequences.

Bernie Dreux heard of the affair with blank amazement, which turned into something resembling rage. His duty, however, was plain. He packed a valise and set out for the quarantined house like a man marching to his execution; for he had a deathly horror of disease, and smallpox was beyond compare the most loathsome.

But the Health Department had given strict orders, and he was turned away; nay, he was rudely repulsed. Crushed, humiliated, he retired to his club, and there it was that Rilleau found him, steeped in melancholy and a very insidious brand of Kentucky Bourbon.

When Lecompte accused Blake of breaking the rules of the game, the little bachelor rose resolutely to his sister's defense.

"Norvin's got a perfect right to protect her," he lied, "and I honor him for it."

"You mean he's engaged to her?" Rilleau inquired, blankly.

Bernie nodded.

"Well, so am I, so are Delevan and Mangny, and the others."

"Not this way." Mr. Dreux's alcoholic flush deepened. "He thought she was in danger, so he flew to her side. Mighty unselfish to sacrifice his business and brave the disease. He did it with my consent, y'understand? When he asked me, I said, 'Norvin, my boy, she needs you.' So he went. Unselfish is no word for it; he's a man of honor, a hero."

Mr. Rilleau's gloom thickened, and he, too, ordered the famous Bourbon. He sighed.

"I'd have done the same thing; I offered to, and I'm no hero. I suppose that ends us. It's a great disappointment, though. I hoped — during Carnival week that she'd—Well, I wanted her for my real queen."

Bernie undertook to clap the speaker on the shoulder and admonish him to buck up; but his eye was wavering and his aim so uncertain that he knocked off Mr. Rilleau's hat. With due apologies he ran on:

"She couldn't have been queen at all, only for him. He made it possible."

"I had as much to say about it as he did."

Bernie whispered: "He lent me the money, y'understand? It was all right, under the circumstances, everything being settled but the date, y'understand?"

Rilleau rose at last, saying: "You're all to be congratulated. He is the best fellow in New Orleans, and there's only one man I'd rather see your sister marry than him; that's me. Now I'm going to select a present before the rush commences. What would you think of an onyx clock with gold cupids straddling around over it?"

"Fine! I'm sorry, old man—I like you, y'understand?" Bernie upset his chair in rising to embrace his friend, then catching sight of

August Kulm, who entered at the moment, he made his way to him and repeated his explanations.

Mr. Kulm was silent, attentive, despairing, and spoke vaguely of suicide, whereupon Dreux set himself to the task of drowning this Teutonic instinct in the flowing bowl.

"I don't know what has happened to the boys," Myra Nell complained to Norvin, on the second day after his arrival. "Lecompte was going to read me the Rubaiyat, and Raymond Cline promised me a bunch of orchids; but nobody has shown up."

"It's jealousy," he said, lightly.

"I suppose so. Of course it was nice of you to compromise me this way—it's delicious, in fact—but I didn't think it would scare off the others."

"You think I have compromised you?"

"You know you have, *terribly*. I'm engaged to all of them— everybody, in fact, except you—"

"But they know my presence here is unintentional."

"Oh! *Is* it, really?" She laughed.

"Don't you believe it is?"

"Goodness! Don't spoil all my pleasure. If ever I saw two cringing, self-conscious criminals, it's you and Papa Montegut. Men are so deceitful. Heigh-ho! I thought this was going to be splendid, but you play cards all day with Mr. La Branche while I die of loneliness."

"What would you like me to do?" he faltered.

"I don't know. It's very dull. Couldn't you sally forth and drag in Lecompte or Murray or Raymond?" She looked up with eyes beaming. "Bernie was furious, wasn't he?"

Mr. La Branche came trotting in with the evening newspaper in his hand. "It's in the paper," he chuckled. "Those reporters get everything."

"What's in the paper?" Myra Nell snatched the sheet from his hand and read eagerly as he went trotting out again with his slippers applauding every step. "Oh, Lordy!"

Blake read over her shoulder, and his face flushed.

"Norvin, we're really, truly engaged, now. See!" After a pause, "And you've never even asked me."

There was only one thing to say.

"Myra Nell," he began, "I want you—Will you—"

"Oh, you goose, you're not taking a cold shower!"

"Will you do me the honor to be my wife?"

She burst into delightful laughter. "So you actually have the courage to propose? Shall I take time to think it over, or shall I answer now?"

"Now, by all means."

"Very well, of course I—won't."

"Why not?" he exclaimed, with a start.

"The idea! You don't mean it!"

"I do."

"Why, Norvin, you're old enough to be my father."

"Oh, no, I'm not."

"Do you think I could marry a man with gray hair?"

"It all gets gray after a while."

"No. I'll be engaged to you, but I'll never marry any one, never. That would spoil all the fun. This very thing shows how stupid it must be; the mere rumor has scared the others away."

"You're a Mormon."

"I'm not. I'll tell you what I'll do; if I ever marry any one, I'll marry you."

"That's altogether too indefinite."

"I don't see it. Meanwhile we're engaged, aren't we?"

"If that's the case—" He reached uncertainly for her hand, and pressed it. "I—I'm very happy!"

She waited an instant, watching him shyly, then said: "Now I must show this to Vittoria. But—please don't look so frightened."

The next instant she was gone. When Miss Fabrizi entered her room, a half-hour later, it was to find her with her eyes red from weeping.

As for Norvin, he had risen to the occasion as best he could. He loved Myra Nell sincerely, tenderly, in a big-brotherly way; he would have gone to any lengths to serve her, yet he could not feel toward her as he felt toward Vittoria Fabrizi. He nerved himself to stand by his word, even though it meant the greatest sacrifice. But the thought agonized him.

Nor was he made more easy as time went on, for Mr. and Mrs. La Branche took it for granted that he was their cousin's affianced lover; and while the girl herself now bewildered him with her shy, inviting coquetry, or again berated him for placing her in an unwelcome position, he could never determine how much she really cared.

When the quarantine was finally lifted he walked out with feelings akin to those of a prisoner who has been reprieved.

# XVIII.
## BELISARIO CARDI

After his enforced idleness Blake was keen to resume his task, yet there was little for him to do save study the one big problem which lay at the root of the whole matter.

The evidence against the prisoners was in good shape; they were indicted, and the trial date would soon be set. They had hired competent lawyers and were preparing for a desperate fight. Where the necessary money came from nobody seemed to know, although it was generally felt that a powerful influence was at work to free them. The district attorney expressed the strongest hopes of obtaining convictions; but there came disturbing rumors of alibis for the accused, of manufactured evidence, and of overwhelming surprises to be sprung at the last moment. Detectives were shadowed by other detectives, lawyers were spied upon, their plans leaked out; witnesses for the State disappeared. Opposing the authorities was a master hand, at once so cunning and so bold as to threaten a miscarriage of justice.

This could be none other then Belisario Cardi, yet he seemed no nearer discovery than ever. Norvin had no idea how to proceed. He could only wait for some word from his new ally, Vittoria Fabrizi. It might be that she would find a clue, and he feared to complicate matters by any premature or ill-judged action. Meanwhile, he encountered the results of Bernie Dreux's garrulity. He found himself generally regarded as Myra Nell's accepted suitor, and, of course, could make no denial. But when he telephoned to the girl herself and asked when he might call he was surprised to hear her say:

"You can't call at all Why, you've ruined all my enjoyment as it is! There hasn't been a man in this whole neighborhood since I came home. Even the policeman takes the other side of the street."

"All the more reason why I should come."

"I won't have you hanging around until I get my Carnival dresses fitted. Oh, Norvin, you ought to see them. There's one-white brocaded peau de soie, all frills and rosebuds; the bodice is trimmed with pearl passementerie, and it's a dear." After a moment's hesitation she added: "Norvin dear, what does it cost to rent the front page of a newspaper?"

"I don't know. I don't think it can be done."

"I wondered if you couldn't do it and—deny our engagement."

"Do you want to break it?" He could hardly keep the eagerness out of his voice.

"Oh, no! But I'd like to deny it until after the Carnival. Now don't be offended. I'll never get my dances filled if I'm as good as married to you. Imagine a queen with an empty programme. I just love you to pieces, of course, but I can't allow our engagement to interfere with the success of the Carnival, can I?"

"Don't you know this is a thing we can't joke about?"

"Of course I do. It has taught me a good lesson."

"What?"

"I'll never be engaged to another man."

"Well! I should hope not. Do you intend to marry me, Myra Nell?"

"I don't know. Sometimes I think I will, then again I'm afraid nobody'd ever come to see me if I did. I'll get old, like you."

"I'm not old."

"We'd both have gray hair and—I can't talk any more. Here comes Bernie with an armful of dresses and a mouthful of pins. If he coughs I'll be all alone in the world. No, you can't see me for a week. I don't even want to hear from you except—"

"What?"

"Well, the strain of dress-fitting is tremendous. I'm nearly always hungry—ravenous for nourishment."

"You mean you're out of candy, I suppose?"

"Practically. There's hardly a whole piece left. They've all been nibbled."

Blake did not know whether to feel amused or ashamed. He was relieved at the girl's apparent carelessness, yet this half-serious engagement had put Myra Nell in a new light. He could not think of their relations as really unchanged, and this was inevitable since his sentiment for her was genuine. The grotesqueness of the affair—even Myra Nell's own attitude toward it—seemed a violation of something sacred.

But nothing could subdue the joy he felt in his growing intimacy with Vittoria, whom he managed to see frequently, although she never permitted him to come to Oliveta's house. Little by little her reserve melted, and more and more she seemed to forget her intention of devoting herself to a religious life, while fears for her friend's safety appealed to the deep mother instinct which had remained latent in her.

She was unable, however, even with Oliveta's assistance, to put any information in his way, and Blake could think of no better plan than to try once more to sound Caesar Maruffi. If Caesar had really written the letters, it would be strange if he could not be induced to go farther, despite his obvious fear of Cardi. It was unbelievable that a man who knew so much about the Mafia was really in ignorance of its leader's identity, and Blake was convinced that if he acted diplomatically and seized the right occasion he could bring the fellow to unbosom himself.

Discarding all thought of his own safety, he went often to the Red Wing Club. But he found Caesar wary, and he dared not be too abrupt. Time and again he was upon the verge of speaking out, but something invariably prevented, some inner voice warned him that the man's mood was unpropitious, that his extravagant caution was not yet satisfied. He allowed the Sicilian to feel him out to his heart's content, and, at last, seeing that he made no real progress, he set out one evening resolved to risk all in an effort to reach some definite understanding.

He was delayed in reaching the foreign quarter, and the dinner-hour was nearly over when he arrived at the cafe. Maruffi was there, as usual, but he had finished his meal and was playing cards with some of his countrymen, swarthy, eager-faced, voluble fellows whose chatter filled the place. They greeted Norvin politely as he seated himself near by, then went on with their amusement as he ordered and ate his dinner. He was near enough to hear their talk, and to catch an occasional glimpse of the game, so that he was not long in finding that they played for considerable stakes. They were as earnest as school-boys, and he watched their ever-changing expressions with interest, particularly when he discovered that Maruffi was in hard luck. The big Sicilian sat bulked up in a corner, black, silent, and sinister, his scowling brows bespeaking his rage. Occasionally he growled a curse, then sent the waiter scurrying with an order. Other Italians were drawn to the scene and crowded about the players.

When Norvin had finished his meal he sat back to smoke and idly sip his claret, thinking he would wait until the game broke up, so that he might get Caesar to himself and perhaps put the issue to the test. He began to study the fellow's face, thinking what force, what passion lay in it, puzzling his brain for some means of enlisting that energy upon his side. But as fortune continued to run against Maruffi, he began to fear that the time was not favorable.

What a picture those laughing, hawk-like men formed, surrounding the black, resentful merchant! Martel Savigno could have drawn a group like that, he mused, for he had a rare appreciation of his own people, no matter what might be said of his talent. He had done some very creditable Sicilian sketches; in fact, Norvin had one framed in his room. What a pity the Count had been stricken in the first years of his promise! What a ruthless hand it was that had destroyed him! What a giant mind it was which had kept all Sicily in terror and scaled its lips!

In that very group yonder there probably was more than one who knew the evil genius in person, and yet they were held in a thralldom of fear which no offer of riches could break. What manner of man was this Cardi? What hellish methods did he follow to wield such despotism? Those card-players were impudent, unscrupulous blades, as ready to gamble with death as with their jingling coins, and yet they dared not lift a hand against him.

Blake saw that the game had reached a point of unusual intensity; the players were deeply engrossed; the spectators had fallen silent, with bright eyes fixed upon the mounting stakes. When the tension broke Norvin saw that Caesar had lost again, and smiled at the excited conversation which ensued. There was a babble of laughter, of curses, of expostulation, shafts of badinage flew at the Sicilian merchant. In the midst of it he raised a huge, hairy fist and brought it down, smiting the table until the coins, the cards, and the glasses leaped. His face was distorted; his voice was thick with passion.

"*Silenzio!*" he growled, with such imperative fury that the others fell silent; then hoarsely: "I play my own game, and I lose. That is all! You are like old wives with your advice. It is my accursed luck, which will some day bring me to the gallows. Now deal!"

That same nausea which invariably seized Norvin Blake in moments of extreme excitement swept over him now. His whole body went cold, the knot of figures faded from his vision, he heard the noisy voices as if from a great distance. A giant hand had reached forth and gripped him, halting his breath and his heart-beats. The room swam dizzily, in a haze.

He found, an instant later, that he had risen and was gripping the table in front of him as if for support. He had upset his goblet of wine, and a wide red stain was spreading over the white cloth. To him it was the blood of Martel Savigno. He stared down at it dazedly, his eyes glazed with horror and surprise.

As the crimson splotch widened his heart took up its halting labors, then began to race, faster and faster, until he felt himself smothering; his frame was swept with tremors. Then the raucous voices grew louder and louder, mounting into a roar, as if he were coming out from a swoon, and all the time that red blotch grew until he could see no other color; it blurred the room and the quarreling gamblers; it steeped the very air. He was still deathly sick, as only those men are whose blood sours, whose bones and muscles disintegrate at the touch of fear.

He did not remember leaving the place, but found the cool night air fanning fresh upon his face as he lurched blindly down the dark street, within his eyes the picture of a scowling, black-browed visage; in his ears that hoarse, unforgettable command, "*Silenzio!*"

A single word, burdened with rage and venom, had carried him back over the years to a certain moment and a certain spot on a Sicilian mountain-side. The peculiar arrogance, the harsh vibrations of that voice permitted no mistake. He saw again a ghost-gray road walled in with fearful shadows, and at his feet two silent, twisted bodies dimly outlined against the dust. A match flared and Ricardo Ferara grinned up into the night beneath his grizzled mustache, Narcone, the butcher, his hands still wet, was whining for the blood of the American. He heard Martel Savigno call, heard the young Count's voice rise and break in a shriek, heard a thunder of hoofs retreating into the blackness. Sicilian men were peering into his face, talking excitedly; through their chatter came that same voice, imperative, furious, filled with rage, and it cried:

"*Silenzio!*"

There was no mistaking it. The veil was ripped at last.

Blake recalled the dim outlines of that burly, bull-necked figure as it had leaped into brief silhouette against the glare of the blazing match, that night so long ago, and then he cried out aloud in the empty street as he realized how complete was the identification. He remembered Donnelly's vague prediction five minutes before he was stricken:

"If what I suspect is true, it will cause a sensation,"

A sensation indeed! The surprise, the realization of consequences, was too overpowering to permit coherent thought. This Maruffi, or Cardi, or whoever he might prove to be, was tremendous. No wonder he had been hard to uncover. No wonder his power was absolute. He had the genius of a great general, a great politician, and a great criminal, all in one, and he was as pitiless as a panther, more deadly than a moccasin. What influence had perverted such intellect into a weapon of iniquity? What evil of the blood, what lesion of the brain, had distorted his instincts so monstrously?

Caesar Maruffi, rich, respected, honored! It was unbelievable.

Blake halted after a time and took note of the surroundings into which his feet had led him. He was deep in the foreign quarter, and found, with a start, that he had been heading for Vittoria Fabrizi's dwelling as if guided by some extraneous power. By a strong exercise of will he calmed himself. What he needed above all things was counsel, some one with whom he could share this amazing discovery. Perhaps his presence here was a sign; at any rate, he decided to follow his first impulse, so hastened onward.

Inside the house his brain cleared in a measure, as he waited; but his agitation must have left plain traces, for no sooner had Vittoria appeared than she exclaimed:

"My friend! Something has happened."

He rose and met her half-way. "Yes. Something tremendous, something terrible."

"It was unwise of you to come here—you may be followed. Tell me quickly what has made you so indiscreet?"

"I have found Belisario Cardi."

She paled; her eyes flamed.

"Yes—it's incredible." His voice shook. "I know the man well, that's the marvel of it. I've trusted him; I've rubbed shoulders with him; I went to him to-night to enlist his aid." He paused, realizing for the first time that the mystery of those letters was now deeper than ever. If Maruffi had not written them, who then? "He's the best and richest Italian in the city. God! The thing is appalling."

"He must go to justice," said Vittoria, quietly. "His name?"

"Caesar Maruffi!"

The girl's eager look faded into one of blank dismay.

"No!" she said, strangely. "No!"

"Do you know him?"

In a daze she nodded; then cast a hurried, frightened look over her shoulder.

"Madonna mia! Caesar Maruffi!" Disbelief and horror leaped into her eyes. "You are mad! Not Caesar. I do not believe it."

"Caesar, *Caesar*." he cried. "Why do you call him that? Why do you doubt? What is he to you?"

She drew away with a look that brought him to his senses.

"There is no mistake," he mumbled. "He is Cardi. I know it. I—"

"Wait, wait; don't tell me." She went groping uncertainly to the door. "Don't tell me yet."

A moment later he heard her call:

"Oliveta! Come quickly, sorella mia. A friend. Quickly!"

Oliveta—recognizably the same girl that he had known in Sicily— entered with her black brows lifted in anxious inquiry, her dark eyes wide with apprehension.

"Some evil has befallen; tell me!" she said, wasting no time in greeting.

"No. Nothing evil," Blake assured her.

"Our friend has made a terrible discovery," said Vittoria, in a faint voice. "I cannot believe—I—want you to hear, carina." She motioned to Norvin.

"I have been seeking our enemy, Belisario Cardi, and—I have found him."

Oliveta cried out in fierce triumph: "God be praised! He lives; that is enough. I feared he had cheated us."

"Listen!" exclaimed Vittoria, in such a tone that the peasant girl started. "You don't understand."

"I understand nothing except that he lives. His blood shall wash our blood. That is what we swore, and I have never forgotten, even though you have. He shall go to meet his dead, and his soul shall be accursed." She spoke with the same hysterical ferocity as when she had cursed her father's murderer in the castello of Terranova.

"He calls himself Caesar Maruffi," Blake told her.

There was a pause, then she said, simply: "That is a lie."

"No, no! I saw him that night. I saw him again to-night."

"It cannot be."

"That is what I have said," concurred Vittoria, with strange eagerness. "No, no—it would be too dreadful."

Mystified and offended, Blake defended his statement forcibly. "Believe it or not, as you please, it is true. That night in Sicily he came among the brigands who held me prisoner. They were talking excitedly. He cried, 'Silenzio!' in a voice I can never forget. To-night he was gambling, and he lost heavily. He was furious; his friends began to chatter, and he cried that word again! I would know it a thousand years hence. I saw it all in a flash. I saw other things I had failed to grasp—his size, his appearance. I tell you he is Belisario Cardi."

"God help me!" whispered the daughter of Ferara, crossing herself with uncertain hand. She was staring affrightedly at Vittoria. "God help me!" She kept repeating the words and gesture.

Blake turned inquiringly to the other woman and read the truth in her eyes.

"Good Lord!" he cried. "He is her—"

She nodded. "They were to be married."

Oliveta began speaking slowly to her foster sister. "Yes, it is indeed true. I have suspected something, but I dared not tell you all—the things he said—all that I half learned and would not ask about. I was afraid to know. I closed my eyes and my ears. Body of Christ! And all the time my father's blood was on his hands!"

Vittoria appealed helplessly to Blake. "You see how it is. What is to be done?"

But his attention was all centered upon Oliveta, whose face was changing curiously.

"His blood!" she exclaimed. "I have loved that infamous man. His hands—" She let her gaze fall to her own, as if they too might be stained from contact.

"Does Maruffi know who you really are?" he asked.

Vittoria answered; "No. She would have told him soon; we were waiting until we had run down those men. You see, it was largely through her that I worked. Those things which I could not discover she learned from—him. It was she who secured the names of Di Marco and Garcia and the others."

Sudden enlightenment brought a cry from him.

"You! Then you wrote those letters! You are the 'One Who Knows'?"

Vittoria nodded; but her eyes were fixed upon the girl.

Oliveta was whispering through white lips: "It is the will of God! He has been delivered into my hands."

"I am beginning to—"

"Wait!" Vittoria did not withdraw her anxious gaze. After an instant she inquired, gently, "Oliveta, what shall we do?"

"There is but one thing to do."

"You mean—"

"I have been sent by God to betray him." Her face became convulsed, her voice harsh. "I curse him, living and dead, in the name of my father, in the name of Martel Savigno, who died by his hand. May he pray unheard, may he burn in agony for a thousand thousand years. Take him to the hangman, Signore. He shall die with my curse in his ears."

"I can't bring him to justice," Blake confessed. "I know him to be the assassin, but my mere word isn't enough to convict him. I have no way of connecting him with the murder of Chief Donnelly, and that is what he must answer for."

Oliveta's lips writhed into a tortured smile. "Never fear, I shall place the loop about his neck where my arms have lain. He has told me little, for I feared to listen. But wait! Give me time."

Vittoria cried in a shocked voice: "Child! Not—that,"

"It was from him I learned of Gian Narcone and his other friends; now I shall learn from his own mouth the whole truth. He shall weave the rope for his own destruction. Oh, he is like water in my hands, and I shall lie in his arms—"

"Lucrezia! You can't touch him—knowing—"

"I will have the truth, if I give myself to him in payment, if I am damned for eternity. God has chosen me!"

She broke down into frightful sobs. With sisterly affection the other woman put her arms about her and tried to soothe her. At length she led her away, but for a long time Norvin could hear sounds of the peasant girl's grief. When Vittoria reappeared her face was still pale and troubled.

"I can do nothing with her. She seems to think we are all divine instruments."

"Poor girl! She is in a frightful position. I'm too amazed to talk sensibly. But surely she won't persist."

"You do not know her; she is like iron. Even I have no power over her now, and I—fear for the result. She is Sicilian to the core, she will sacrifice her body, her soul, for vengeance, and that—man is a fiend."

"It's better to know the truth now than later."

"Yes, the web of chance has entangled our enemies and delivered them bound into our hands. We cannot question the wisdom of that power which wove the net. Oliveta is perhaps a stronger instrument than I; she will never rest until her father is avenged."

"The strangest part is that you are the 'One Who Knows,' You told me you had given up the quest."

"And so I had. I was weary of it. My life was bleak and empty. I could not return to Sicily, because of the memories it held. We came South in answer to the call of our blood, and I took up a work of love instead of hate, while Oliveta found a new interest in this man, who was wonderful and strong and fierce in his devotion to her. I attained to that peace for which I had prayed. Then, when I was nearly ready for my vows, my foster sister learned of Gian Narcone and came to me. We talked long together, and I finally yielded to her demands— she is a contadina, she never forgets—and I wrote that first letter to Mr. Donnelly. I feared you might see and recognize my handwriting, so I bought one of those new machines and learned to use it. What followed you know. When we discovered that the Mafia had vowed to take Chief Donnelly's life in payment for Narcone's, we were forced to go on or have innocent blood upon our hands.

"The Chief was killed in spite of our warnings, and then you appeared as the head of his avengers—you—my truest friend, the brother of Martel. I knew that the Mafia would have your life unless you crushed it, and in a sense I was responsible for your danger. It seemed my duty to help break up this accursed brotherhood, much as I wished that the work might fall to other hands. Oliveta was eager for the struggle, and while she fought for her vengeance, I—I fought to save you."

"You did this for *me!*" he cried, falteringly.

"Yes. My position at the hospital, my occupation made it easy for me to learn many things. It was I who discovered the men who actually killed Chief Donnelly; for Normando, after his injury, was brought there and I attended him. I learned of his accomplices, where the boy, Gino Cressi, was concealed, and other things. Lucrezia was a spy here among her countrypeople, and Caesar was forever dropping bits of information, though we never dreamed who he was."

She went to the long French window, and, shading her eyes with her hands, peered down into the dark street.

"Then you have—thought of me," he urged. "You thought of me even before we were drawn together by this net of chance?"

"You have seldom been out of my thoughts," she told him, quietly. "You were my only friend, and I live a lonely life." Turning with a wistful smile, she asked: "And have you now and then remembered that Sicilian girl you knew so long ago?"

His voice was unruly; it broke as he replied: "Your face is always before me, Contessa. I grew very tired of waiting, but I always felt that I would find you."

She gave him her two hands. "The thought of your affection and loyalty has meant much to me; and it will always mean much. When I have entered upon my new life and know that you are happy in yours—"

"But I never shall be happy," he broke out, hoarsely.

She stopped him with a grave look.

"Please! You must go now. I will show you a way. So long as Cardi is at liberty you must not return; the risks are too great for all of us. As Oliveta learns the truth I shall advise you. Poor girl, she needs me tonight. Come!"

She led him through the house, down a stairway into the courtyard, and directed him into a narrow passageway which led out to the street behind. "Even this is not safe, for they may be waiting." She laid her hand upon his arm and said, earnestly, "You will be careful?"

"I will."

He fought down the wild impulse to take her in his arms. As he skulked through the gloom, searching the darkest shadows like a criminal, his fear was gone, and in his heart was something singing joyously.

# XIX.
## FELICITE

"You're just the man I'm looking for," Bernie Dreux told Norvin, whom he chanced to meet on the following morning. "I've made a discovery."

"Indeed! What is it?"

"Hist! The walls have ears." Bernie cast a glance over his shoulder at the busy, sunlit street and the hurrying crowds. "Come!" With a melodramatic air he led Blake into a coffee-house near by. "You can't guess it!" he exclaimed, when they were seated.

"And what's more, I won't try. You're getting too mysterious, Bernie."

"I've found him."

"Whom?"

"The bell-cow; the boss dago; the chief head-hunter; Belisario Cardi!"

Blake started and the smile died from his lips. Dreux ran on with some heat:

"Oh, don't look so skeptical. Any man with intelligence and courage can become as good a detective as I am. I've found your Capo-Mafia, that's all."

"Who is he?"

"You won't believe me; but he's well thought of. You know him; O'Neil knows him. He's generally trusted."

Norvin began to suspect that by some freak of fortune his little friend had indeed stumbled upon the truth. Dreux was leaning back in his chair and beaming triumphantly.

"Come, come! What's his name?"

"Joe Poggi."

"Poggi? He's the owner of that fruit-stand you've been watching."

"Exactly! Chief Donnelly suspected him."

"Nonsense!" Norvin's face was twitching once more. "Poggi is on the force; he's a detective, like you."

"Come off!" Bernie was shocked and incredulous.

"Have you shadowed him for months without learning that he's an officer?"

"I—I—He's the fellow, just the same."

"Oh, Bernie, you'd better stick to the antique business."

Mr. Dreux flushed angrily. "If he isn't one of the gang," he cried, "what was he doing with Salvatore di Marco and Frank Garcia the night after Donnelly's murder? What's he doing now with Caesar Maruffi if he isn't after him for money?"

Blake's amusement suddenly gave place to eagerness.

"Maruffi!" he exclaimed. "What's this?"

"Joe Poggi is blackmailing Caesar Maruffi out of the money to defend his friends. He was at di Marco's house an hour before Salvatore's arrest. I saw him with Garcia and Bolla and Cardoni more than once."

"Why didn't you tell this to O'Neil?"

"I tried to, but he wouldn't listen. When I said I was a detective he laughed in my face, and we had a scene. He told me I couldn't find a ham at a Hebrew picnic. Since then I've been working alone. Poggi has been lying low lately, but—" Bernie hesitated, and a slight flush stole into his cheeks. "I've become acquainted with his wife—we're good friends."

"And what have you learned from her?"

"Nothing directly; but I think she's acting as her husband's agent, collecting blackmail to hire lawyers for the defense. Poor Caesar! he's rich, and Poggi is bleeding him. Since Joe is on the police force he knows every thing that goes on. No wonder you can't break up the Mafia!"

"By Jove!" said Norvin. "I was warned of a leak in the department. But it couldn't be Poggi!"

He began to question Bernie with a peremptoriness and rapidity that made the little man blink. Mingled with much that was grotesque and irrelevant, he drew out a fairly credible story of nocturnal meetings between the Italian detective and Caesar Maruffi, which, taken in connection with what he already knew, was most disturbing.

"How did you come to meet Mrs. Poggi?" he inquired, at last.

The question brought that same flush to Mr. Dreux's cheeks.

"She found I was following her one day," he explained, "so I told her I was smitten by her beauty. I got away with it, too. Rather clever, for an amateur, eh?"

"Is she good-looking?"

Bernie nodded. "She's an outrageous flirt, though, and—oh, what a temper!" He shuddered nervously. "Why, she'd stick a knife into me or bite my ears off if she suspected. She's insanely jealous."

"It's not a nice position for you."

"No. But I've something far worse than her on my hands—Felicite. She's more to be feared than the Mafia."

"Surely Miss Delord isn't dangerous."

"Isn't she?" mocked the bachelor. "You ought to see—" He started, his eyes fixed themselves upon the entrance to the cafe with a look of horror, he paled and cast a hurried glance around as if in search of a means of escape. "Here she is now!"

Norvin turned to behold Miss Delord approaching them like an arrow. She was a tiny creature, but it was plain that she was out in all her fighting strength. Her pretty face was dark with passion, her eyes were flashing, and they pierced her lover with a terrible glance as she paused before him, crying furiously:

"Well? Where is she?"

"Felicite," stammered Dreux, "d-don't cause a scene."

Miss Delord stamped a ridiculously small foot and cried again, oblivious of all save her black jealousy:

"Where is she, I say? Eh? You fear to answer. You shield her, perhaps." A plump brown hand darted forth and seized Bernie by the ear, giving it a tweak like the bite of a parrot.

"Ouch!" he exclaimed, loudly. "Felicite, you'll ruin us!"

A waiter began to laugh in smothered tones.

"Tell me," stormed the diminutive fury. "It is time we had a settlement, she and I. I will lead you to her by those ass's ears of yours and let her hear the truth from your own mouth."

"Miss Delord, you do Bernie an injustice," Norvin said, placatingly.

She turned swiftly. "Injustice? Bah! He is a flirt, a loathsome trifler. What could be more abominable?"

"Felicite! D-don't make a scene," groaned the unhappy Dreux, nursing his ear and staring about the cafe with frightened, appealing eyes.

"Bernie was just—"

"You defend him, eh?" stormed the creole girl. "You are his friend. Beware, M'sieu, that I do not pull your ears also. I came here to unmask him."

"Please sit down. You're attracting attention."

"Attention! Yes! But this is nothing to what will follow. I shall make known his depravity to the whole city, for he has sweethearts like that King Solomon of old. It is his beauty, M'sieu! Listen! He loves a married woman! Imagine it!"

"Felicite! For Heaven's sake—"

"A dago woman by the name of Piggy. But wait, I shall make her squeal. Piggy! A suitable name, indeed! He follows her about; he meets her secretly; he adores her, the scoundrel! Is it not disgusting? But I am no fool. I, too, have watched; I have followed them both, and I shall scratch her black face until it bleeds, then I shall tell her husband the whole truth."

Miss Delord paused, out of breath for the moment, while Bernie pawed at her in a futile manner. Beads of perspiration were gathering upon his brow and he seemed upon the verge of swooning. As if from habit, however, he reached forth a trembling hand and deftly replaced a loose hairpin, then tucked in a stray lock which Felicite's vehemence had disarranged.

"Y-your hat's on one side, my dear," he told her.

She tossed her head and drew away, saying, "Your touch contaminates me—monster!"

Blake drew out a chair for her; his eyes were twinkling as he said, "Won't you allow him to explain?"

"There is nothing to explain, since I know everything. See! His tongue cleaves to the roof of his mouth. He quails! He cannot even lie! But wait until I have told the Piggy's husband—that big, black ruffian—then perhaps he will find his voice. Ah, if I had found that woman here there would have been a scene, I promise you."

"Help me—out," gasped Mr. Dreux, and Norvin came willingly to his friend's rescue.

"Bernie loves no one but you," he said.

"So? I glory in the fact that I loathe him."

"Please sit down."

"No!" Miss Delord plumped herself down upon the edge of the proffered seat, her toes bardy touching the floor.

"I'm—working Mrs. Poggi," Bernie explained. "I'm a—detective."

"What new falsehood is this?"

"No falsehood at all," Norvin told her. "He is a detective—a very fine one, too—and he has been working on the Mafia case for a long time. It has been part of his work to follow the Poggis. Please don't allow your jealousy to ruin everything."

"I am not jealous. I merely will not let him love another, that is all—But what is this you say?" Her velvet eyes had lost a little of their hardness; they were as round as buttons and fixed inquiringly upon the speaker.

"You must believe me," he said, impressively, "though I can't tell you more. Even of this you mustn't breathe a word to any one. Mr. Dreux has had to permit this misunderstanding, much against his will, because of the secrecy imposed upon him."

With wonderful quickness the anger died out of Felicite's face, to be replaced by a look of sweetness.

"A detective!" she cried, turning to Bernie. "You work for the public good, at the risk of your life? And that dago woman is one of the Mafia? What a noble work! You forgive me?"

Instantly Mr. Dreux's embarrassment left him and he assumed a chilling haughtiness.

"Forgive you? After such a scene? My dear girl, that's asking a good deal."

Felicite's lips trembled, her eyes, as they turned to Norvin, held such an appeal that he hastened to reassure her.

"Of course he forgives you. He's delighted that you care enough to be jealous."

Bernie grinned, whereupon his peppery sweetheart exploded angrily:

"You delight in my unhappiness, villain! You enjoy my sufferings! Very well! You have flirted; I shall flirt You drive me to distraction; I shall behave accordingly. That Antoine Giroux worships me and would buy a ring for me to-morrow if I would consent."

"I'll murder him!" exclaimed Dreux, with more savagery than his friend believed was in him.

"Now, don't start all over again," Blake cautioned them. "You are mad about each other—"

"Nothing of the sort," declared Felicite.

"At least Bernie worships you."

The girl fell silent and beamed openly upon her lover.

"Why don't you two end this sort of misunderstanding and—marry?"

Miss Delord paled at this bold question. Dreux gasped and flushed dully, but seemed to find no words.

"That is impossible," he said, finally.

"It's nothing of the sort," urged Blake. "You think you're happy this way, but you're not and never will be. You're letting the best years of your lives escape. Why care what people say if you're happy with each other and unhappy when apart?"

To his surprise, the girl turned upon him fiercely. "Do not torture Bernie so," she cried. "There are reasons why he cannot marry. I love him, he adores me; that is enough." Two tears gathered and stole down her smooth cheeks. "You are cruel to hurt him so, M'sieu."

"Bernie, you're a coward!" Blake said, with some degree of feeling, but the girl flew once more to her lover's defense.

"Coward, indeed! His bravery is unbelievable. Does he not risk his life for this miserable Committee of yours? He has the courage of a thousand lions."

"I admire your loyalty—and of course it's really not my affair, although—Why don't you go out to the park where the birds are singing, and talk it all over? Those birds are always glad to welcome lovers. Meanwhile I'll look into the Poggi matter."

Bernie was glad enough to end the scene, and he arose with alacrity; but his face was very red and he avoided the eye of his friend. As for Miss Delord, now that her doubts were quelled, she was as sparkling and as cheerful as an April morning.

If Bernie Dreux supposed that his troubles for the day had ended with that stormy scene in the cafe, he was greatly mistaken. He had promised Felicite that he would fly to her with the coming of dusk, and that neither the claims of duty nor of family should keep him from her side. But that evening Myra Nell seized upon him as he was cautiously tiptoeing past her door on his way out. The tone of her greeting gave him an unpleasant start.

"I want to talk with you, young man," she said.

Now nobody, save Myra Nell, ever assumed the poetic license of calling Bernie "young man," and even she did so only upon momentous occasions. A quick glance at her face confirmed his premonition of an uncomfortable half-hour.

"I haven't a cent, really," he said, desperately.

"This isn't about money." She was very grave. "It is something far more serious."

"Then what can it be?" he inquired, in a tone of mild surprise.

But she deigned no explanation until she had led him into the library, waved him imperiously to a seat upon the hair-cloth sofa, and composed herself on a chair facing him. Reflecting that he was already late for his appointment, he wriggled uncomfortably under her gaze.

"Well?" she said, after a pause. Something in her bearing caused his spirits to continue their downward course. Her brow was furrowed with a somber portent.

"Yes'm," he said, nervously, quite like a small schoolboy whose eyes are fixed upon the sunshine outside.

"I've heard the truth."

"Yes'm," he repeated, vaguely.

"Needless to say I'm crushed,"

Bernie slowly whitened as the meaning of his sister's words sank in. He seemed to melt, to settle together, and his eyes filled with a strange, hunted expression.

"What are you talking about?" he demanded, thickly.

"You know, very well."

"Do I?"

She nodded her head.

"This is the first disgrace which has ever fallen upon us, and I'm heartbroken."

"I don't understand," he protested, in a voice so faint she could scarcely hear him. But his pallor increased; he sat upon the edge of the couch, clutching it nervously as if it had begun to move under him. He really felt dizzy. Myra Nell had a bottle of smelling-salts in her room, and he thought of asking her to fetch it.

"Even yet I can't believe it of you," she continued. "The idea that you, my protector, the one man upon whom I've always looked with reverence and respect; you, my sole remaining relative.... The idea that you should be entangled in a miserable intrigue.... Why, it's appalling!" Her lips quivered, tears welled into her eyes, seeing which the little man felt himself strangling.

"Don't!" he cried, miserably. "I didn't think you'd ever find it out." "I seem to be the only one who doesn't know all about it." Myra Nell shuddered.

"I simply couldn't help it," he told her. "I'm human and I've been in love for years."

"But think what people are saying."

He passed a shaking hand over his forehead, which had grown damp. "One never realizes the outcome of these things until too late. I hoped you'd never discover it. I've done everything I could to conceal it."

"That's the terrible part—your double life. Don't you know it's wrong, wicked, vile? I can't really believe it of you. Why, you're my own brother! The honor of our name rests upon you. The—the idea that you should fall a victim to the wiles of a low, vulgar—"

Bernie stiffened his back and his colorless eyes flashed.

"Myra Nell, she's nothing like that!" he declared. "You don't know her."

"Perhaps. But didn't you think of me?" He nodded his head. "Didn't you realize it meant my social ruin?" Again he nodded, his mind in a whirl of doubts and fears and furious regrets. "Nobody'll care to marry me now. What do you think Lecompte will say?"

"What the devil has Lecompte to do with it? You're engaged to Norvin Blake."

"Oh, yes, among the others."

Bernie was too miserable to voice the indignation which such flippancy evoked in him. He merely said:

"Norvin isn't like the others. It's different with him; he compromised you."

"Yes. It was rather nice of him, but do you think he'll care to continue our engagement after this?"

"Oh, he's known about Felicite for a long time. Most of the fellows know. That's what makes it so hard."

This intelligence entirely robbed Myra Nell of words; she stared at her half-brother as if trying to realize that the man who had made this shocking admission was he.

"Do you mean to tell me that your friends have known of this disgrace?" she asked at length.

Bernie nodded. "Of course it seems terrible to you, Myra Nell, for you're innocent and unworldly, and I'm rather a dissipated old chap. But I'm awfully lonely. The men of my own age are successful and busy and they've all left me behind; the young ones don't find me interesting. You see, I don't know anything, I can't do anything, I'm a failure. Nobody cares anything about me, except you and Felicite I found a haven in her society; her faith in me is splendid. To her I'm all that's heroic and fine and manly, so when I'm with her I begin to feel that I'm really all she believes, all that I hoped to be once upon a time. She shares my dreams and I allow myself to believe in her beliefs."

"And yet you must realize that your conduct is shocking?"

"I suppose I do."

"You must know that you're an utterly immoral person?" He nodded. "You're my protector, Bernie; you're all I have. I'm a poor motherless girl and I lean upon you. But you must appreciate now that you're quite unfit to act as my guardian."

The little man wailed his miserable assent. His half-sister's reproachful eyes distracted him; the mention of her defenseless position before the world touched his sorest feeling. It was almost more than he could stand, He was upon the verge of hysterical breakdown, when her manner suddenly changed.

Her eyes brightened, and, rising swiftly, she flung herself down beside him upon the sofa, where he still sat clutching it as if it were a bucking horse. Then, curling one foot under her, she bent toward him, all eagerness, all impulsiveness. With breathless intensity she inquired:

"Tell me, Bunnie, is she pretty?"

"Very pretty, indeed," he said, lamely.

"What's she like? Quick! Tell me all about her. This is the wickedest thing I ever heard of and I'm *perfectly* delighted."

It was Bernie's turn to look shocked. He arose indignantly. "Myra Nell! You paralyze me. Have you no moral—"

"Rats!" interrupted Miss Warren, inelegantly. "I've let you preach to me in the past, but never again. We've the same blood in us, Bunnie. If I were a man I dare say I'd do the most terrible things—although I've never dreamed of anything so fiercely awful as this."

"I should hope not," he gasped.

"So come now, tell me everything. Does she pet you and call you funny names and ruffle your hair the way I do?"

Bernie assumed an attitude of military erectness. "It's bad enough for me to be a reprobate in secret," he said, stiffly, "but I sha'n't allow my own flesh and blood to share my shame and gloat over it."

The girl's essential innocence, her child-like capacity for seeing only the romance of a situation in which he himself recognized real dishonor, made him feel ashamed, yet he was grateful that she took the matter, after all, so lightly. His respite, however, was of short duration. Failing to draw him out on the subject which held her interest for the moment, Myra Nell followed the beckoning of a new thought. Fixing her eyes meditatively upon him, she said, with mellow satisfaction:

"It seems we're both being gossiped about, dear."

"You? What have *you* been doing?" he demanded, in despair.

"Oh, I really haven't done anything, but it's nearly as bad. There's a report that Norvin Blake is paying all my Carnival bills, and naturally it has occasioned talk. Of course I denied it; the idea is too preposterous."

Bernie, who had in a measure recovered his composure, felt himself paling once more.

"Amy Cline told me she'd heard that he actually bought my *dresses*, but Amy is a catty creature. She's mad over Lecompte, you know; that's why I encourage him; and she wanted to be Queen, too, but la, la, she's so skinny! Well, I was furious, naturally—" Miss Warren paused, quick to note the telltale signs in her brother's face. "Bernie!" she said. "Look me in the eye!" Then—"It is true!"

Her own eyes were round and horrified, her rosy cheeks lost something of their healthy glow; for once in her capricious life she was not acting.

"I never dreamed you'd learn about it," her brother protested. "When Norvin asked me if you'd like to be Queen I forbade him to mention it to you, for I couldn't afford the expense. But he told you in spite of me, and when I saw your heart was set on it—I—I just couldn't refuse. I allowed him to loan me the money."

"Bernie! Bernie!" Myra Nell rose and, turning her back upon him, stared out of the window into the dusk of the evening. At length she said, with a strange catch in her voice, "You're an anxious comfort, Bernie, for an orphan girl." Another moment passed in silence before he ventured:

"You see, I knew he'd marry you sooner or later, so it wasn't really a loan." He saw the color flood her neck and cheek at his words, but he was unprepared for her reply.

"I'll never marry him now; I'll never speak to him again."

"Why not?"

"Can't you understand? Do you think I'm entirely lacking in pride? What kind of man can he be to *tell* of his loan, to make it public that the very dresses which cover me were bought with his money?" She turned upon her half-brother with clenched hands and eyes which were gleaming through tears of indignation. "I could *kill* him for that."

"He didn't tell," Bernie blurted out.

"He must have. Nobody knew it except you—" Her eyes widened; she hesitated. "You?" she gasped.

It was indeed, the hour of Bernie's discomfiture. Myra Nell was his divinity, and to confess his personal offense against her, to destroy her faith in him, was the hardest thing he had ever done. But he was gentleman enough not to spare himself. At the cost of an effort which left him colorless he told her the truth.

"I'd been drinking, that day of the quarantine. I thought I'd fix it so he couldn't back out."

Myra Nell's lips were white as she said, slowly, measuring him meanwhile with a curious glance:

"Well, I reckon you fixed it right enough; I reckon you fixed it so that neither of us can back out." She turned and went slowly upstairs, past the badly done portraits of her people which stared down at her in all their ancient pride. She carried her head high before them, but, once in her room, she flung herself upon her bed and wept as if her heart were breaking.

Fortunately for Norvin Blake's peace of mind, he had no inkling of Bernie's indiscretion nor of any change in Myra Nell. His work now occupied his mind to the exclusion of everything else. While anxiously waiting for some word from Oliveta he took up, with O'Neil, the investigation of Joe Poggi, the Italian detective. Before definite results had been obtained he was delighted to receive a visit from Vittoria Fabrizi, who explained that she had risked coming to see him because she dared not trust the mails and feared to bring him into the foreign quarter.

"Then Oliveta has made some progress?" he asked, eagerly.

"Yes."

"Good! Poor girl, it must be terribly hard for her to play such a part."

"No one knows how hard it has been. You would not recognize her, she has changed so. Her love, for which we were so deeply thankful, has turned into bitter hate. It was a long time before she dared trust herself with Maruffi, for always she saw the blood of her father upon his hands. But she is Sicilian, she turned to stone and finally welcomed his caresses. Ah! that man will suffer for what he has made her endure."

Blake inquired, curiously, "Does he really love her?"

"Yes. That is the strangest part of the whole affair. It is the one good thing in his character, the bit of gold in that queer alloy which goes to make him up. Perhaps if he had met her when he was younger, love would have made him a different man. In her hands he is like wax; he is simple, childlike; he fawns upon her, he would shower her with gifts and attentions; yet underneath there is that streak of devilish cunning."

"What has he told, so far?"

"Much that is significant, little that is definite. We have pieced his words together, bit by bit, and uncovered his life an inch at a time. It was he who paid the blood money to di Marco and Bolla—thousand dollars."

"A thousand dollars for the life of Dan Donnelly!"

The Countess lowered her yellow head. "They in turn hired Larubio, Normando, and the rest. The chain is complete."

"Then all that remains is to prove it, link by link, before arresting him."

"Is not Oliveta's word sufficient proof?"

"No." Blake paced his office silently, followed by the anxious gaze of his caller. At length he asked, "Will she take the stand at the trial?"

"Heaven forbid! Nothing could induce her to do so. That is no part of her scheme of vengeance, you understand? Being Sicilian, she will work only in her own way. Besides—that would mean the disclosure of her identity and mine."

"I feared as much. In that case every point which Maruffi confesses to her must be verified by other means. That will not be easy, but I dare say it can be done."

"The law is such a stupid thing!" exclaimed Vittoria. "It has no eyes, it will not reason, it cannot multiply nor add; it must be led by the hand like a blind old man and be told that two and two make four. However, I have a plan."

"I confess that I see no way. What do you advise?"

"These accused men are in the Parish prison, yes? Very well. Imprison spies with them who will gain their confidence. In that way we can verify Maruffi's words." "That's not so easily done. There is no certainty that they would make damaging admissions."

"Men who dwell constantly with thoughts of their guilt feel the need of talking. The mind is incapable of continued silence; it must communicate the things that weigh it down. Let the imprisoned Mafiosi mingle with one another freely whenever ears are open near by, and you will surely get results." Seeing him frown in thought, she continued, after a moment, "You told me of a great detective agency — one which sent that man Corte here to betray Narcone."

"Yes, the Pinkertons. I was thinking of them. I believe it can be done. At any rate, leave it to me to try, and if I succeed no one shall know about it, not even our own police. When our spies enter the prison, if they do, it will be in a way to inspire confidence among the Mafiosi. Meanwhile, do you think you are entirely safe in that foreign quarter?"

"Quite safe, although the situation is trying. I have felt the strain almost as deeply as my unfortunate sister."

"And when it is all over you will be ready for your vows?"

Her answer gave no sign of the hesitation he had hoped for and half expected.

"Of course."

He shook his head doubtfully. "Somehow, I—I feel that fate will keep you from that life; I cannot think of you as a Sister of Mercy." In spite of himself his voice was uneven and his eyes were alight with the hope which she so steadfastly refused to recognize.

As she rose to leave she said, musingly, "How strange it is that this master of crime and intrigue should betray himself through the one good and unselfish emotion of his life!"

"Samson was shorn of his strength by the fingers of a woman," he said.

"Yes. Many good men have been betrayed by evil women, but it is not often that evil men meet their punishment through good ones. And now—a riverderci."

"Good-by, for a few days." He pressed his lips lightly to her fingers.

# XX.
# THE MAN IN THE SHADOWS

Late one day, a fortnight after her visit to Blake's office, Vittoria returned from a call upon Myra Nell Warren, to find Oliveta in a high state of apprehension. The girl, who had evidently kept watch for her, met her at the door, and inquired, nervously:

"What news? What have you heard?"

"Nothing further, sorella mia."

"Impossible! God in Heaven! I am dying! This suspense—I cannot endure it longer."

Vittoria laid a comforting hand upon her.

"Courage!" she said. "We can only wait. I too am torn by a thousand demons. Caesar has gone, but no one knows where."

Oliveta shuddered. "We are ruined. He suspects."

"So you have said before, but how could he suspect?"

"I don't know, yet judge for yourself. I worm his secrets from him at the cost of kisses and endearments; I hold him in my arms and with smiles and caresses I lead him to betray himself. Then, suddenly, without warning or farewell, he vanishes. I tell you he knows. He has the cunning of the fiend, and your friend Signore Blake has blundered." Oliveta's face blanched with terror. She clung to her companion weakly, repeating over and over: "He will return. God help us, he will return."

"Even though he knows the truth, which is far from likely, he would scarcely dare to come here," Vittoria said, striving with a show of confidence which she did not feel to calm her foster sister.

"You do not know him as I do. You do not know the furies which goad him in his anger."

In spite of herself Vittoria felt choked again by those fears which during the days since Maruffi's disappearance she had with difficulty controlled. She knew that the net had been spread for him in all caution, yet he had slipped through it. Whether he had been warned or whether mere chance had taken him from the city at the last moment, neither she, nor Blake, nor the Chief of Police had been able to learn. All had been done with such secrecy that, except a bare half-dozen trusted officers, no one knew him to be even suspected of a part in the Mafia's affairs. Norvin had been quick to sense the possible danger to the two women, and had urged them to accept his protection; but they had convinced him that such a course had its own dangers, for in case the Mafioso was really unsuspicious the slightest indiscretion on their part might frighten him. Therefore they had insisted upon living as usual until something more definite was known.

This afternoon Vittoria had received a message from Myra Nell, requesting, or rather demanding, her immediate attendance. She had gone gladly, hoping to divert her mind from its present anxieties; but the girl had talked of little except Norvin Blake and the effect had not been calming.

Oliveta soon discovered that her sister was in a state to receive rather than give consolation.

"Carissima, you are ill!" she said with concern.

Vittoria assented. "It is my eyes—my head. The heat is perhaps as much to blame as our many worries." She removed her hat and pressed slender fingers to her throbbing temples, while Oliveta drew the curtains against the fierce rays of a westering sun. Later, clad in a loose silken robe, Vittoria flung herself upon the low couch and her companion let down her luxuriant masses of hair until it enveloped her like a cloud. She lay back upon the cushions in grateful relaxation, while Oliveta combed and brushed the braids, soothing her with an occasional touch of cool palms or straying fingers.

"How strange that both our lives should have been blighted by this man!" the peasant girl said at length.

"'Sh-h! You must not think of him so unceasingly," Vittoria warned her.

"One's thoughts go where they will when one is sick and wearied. I have grown to hate everything about me—the people, the life, the country."

"Sicily is calling you, perhaps?"

Oliveta answered eagerly, "Yes! You, too, are unhappy, my dearest. Let us go home. Home!" She let her hands fall idle and stared ahead of her, seeing the purple hills behind Terranova, the dusty gray-green groves of olive-trees, the brilliant fields of sumach, the arbors bent beneath their weight of blushing fruit. "I want to see the village people again, my father's relatives, old Aliandro, and the Notary's little boy—"

"He must be a well-grown lad, by now," murmured Vittoria. "Aliandro, I fear, is dead. But it is a long road to Terranova; we have—changed."

"Yes—everything has changed. My happiness has changed to misery, my hope to despair, my love to hate."

"Poor sister mine!" Vittoria sympathized. "Be patient. No wound is too deep for time to heal. The scar will remain, but the pain will disappear. I should know, for I have suffered."

"And do you suffer no longer? It has been a long time since you mentioned—Martel."

For a moment Vittoria remained silent, her eyes closed. When she replied it was not in answer to the question. "I can never return to Sicily, for it would awaken nothing but distress in me. But there is no reason why you should not go if you wish. You have the means, while all that I had has been given to the Sisters."

Oliveta cried out at this passionately. "I have nothing. That which you gave me I hold only for you. But I would not go alone; I shall never leave you."

"Some time you must, my dear. Our parting is not far off."

"I am not sure." The peasant girl hesitated. "Deep in your heart, do you hope to find peace inside the walls of that hospital?"

"Yes—peace, at least; perhaps contentment and happiness also."

"That is impossible," said Oliveta, at which Vittoria's hazel eyes flew open.

"Eh? Why not?"

"Because you love this Signore Blake!"

"Oliveta! You are losing your wits."

"Perhaps! But I have not lost my eyes. As for him, he loved you even in Sicily."

"What then?"

"He is a fine man. I think you could hear an echo to the love you cherished for Martel, if you but listened."

Vittoria gazed at her foster-sister with a look half tender and half stern. Her voice had lost some of its languid indifference when she replied:

"Any feeling I might have would indeed be no more than an echo. I—am not like other women; something in me is dead—it is the power to love as women love. I am like a person who emerges from a conflagration, blinded; the eyes are there, but the sight is gone."

"Perhaps you only sleep, like the princess who waited for a kiss—"

Vittoria interrupted impatiently: "No, no! And you mistake his feelings. I attract him, perhaps, but he loves Miss Warren and has asked her to marry him. What is more, she adores him and—they were made for each other."

"She adores him!" echoed the other. "Che Dio! She only plays at love. Her affections are as shifting as the winds."

"That may be. But he is in earnest. It was he who gave her this social triumph—he made her Queen of the Carnival. He even bought her dresses. It was that which caused her to send for me this afternoon. Heaven knows I was in no mood to listen, but she chattered like a magpie. As if I could advise her wisely!"

"She is very dear to you," Oliveta ventured.

"Indeed, yes. She shares with you all the love that is left in me."

"I think I understand. You have principles, my sister. You have purposely barred the way to your fairy prince, and will continue sleeping."

Vittoria's brow showed faint lines, but whether of pain or annoyance it was hard to tell.

Oliveta sighed. "What evil fortune overhangs us that we should be denied love!"

"Please! Let us speak no more of it." She turned her face away and for a long time her companion soothed her with silent ministrations. Meanwhile the dusk settled, the golden flames died out of the western windows, the room darkened. Seeing that her patient slept, Oliveta arose and with noiseless step went to a little shrine which hung on the wall. She knelt before the figure of the Virgin, whispering a prayer, then lit a fresh candle for her sister's pain and left the room, partly closing the door behind her.

She had allowed the maid-servant to go for the afternoon, and found, upon examination, that the day's marketing had been neglected. There was still time, however, in which to secure some delicacies to tempt Vittoria's taste so she flung a shawl over her dark hair and descended softly to the street.

A little earlier on this same afternoon, as Norvin Blake sat at work in his office, the telephone bell roused him from deep thought. He seized the instrument eagerly, hoping for any news that would relieve the tension upon his nerves. For uncertainty as to Maruffi's whereabouts had weighed heavily upon him, especially in view of the possible danger to the woman he loved and to her devoted companion. The voice of O'Neil came over the wire, full-toned and distinct:

"Hello! Is this Blake?" —and then, "We've got Maruffi!"

"When? Where?" shouted Norvin.

"Five minutes ago; at his own house. Johnson and Dean have been watching the place. He went with them like a lamb, too. They've just 'phoned me that they're all on their way here."

"Good! Do you need me?"

"No! See you later. Good-by!"

The Acting Chief slammed up his receiver, leaving his hearer stunned at the suddenness of this long-awaited denouement.

Maruffi taken! His race run! Then this was the end of the fight! A ferocious triumph flooded Norvin's brain. With Belisario Cardi in the hands of the law the spell of the Mafia was broken. Savigno and Donnelly were as good as avenged. He experienced an odd feeling of relaxation, as if both his body and brain were cramped and tired with waiting. Then, realizing that the Countess and Oliveta must have suffered an even greater strain, he set out at once to give them the news in person.

As he turned swiftly into Royal Street he encountered O'Connell, who, noting his haste and something unusual in his bearing, detained him to ask the cause.

"Haven't you heard?" exclaimed Norvin. "Maruffi's captured at last."

"You don't mean it!"

"Yes. O'Neil told me over the wire not ten minutes ago."

O'Connell fell into step with him, saying, incredulously: "And he came without a fight? Lord! I can't believe it."

"Nor I. I expected trouble with him."

"Sure! I thought he was a bad one, but that's the way it goes sometimes. I reckon he saw he had no chance." The officer shook his red head. "It's just my blamed luck to miss the fun." O'Connell was one of the few who had been first trusted with the news of Maruffi's identity, and for the past fortnight he had been casting high and low for the Sicilian's trail. Ever since that October night when he had supported Donnelly in his arms as the life ebbed from the Chief, ever since he had knelt on the soft banquette with the sting of powder smoke in his nostrils, he had been obsessed by a fanatical desire to be in at the death of his friend's murderers. He left Blake at his destination and hurried on toward St. Phillip Street in the vague hope that he might not be too late to take a hand in some part of the proceedings.

Blake's hand was upon Oliveta's bell when the door opened and she confronted him. Her start, her frightened cry, gave evidence of the nervous dread under which she labored.

"Don't be afraid, Oliveta," he said, quickly. "I come with news— good news."

She swayed and groped blindly for support. He put out his hand to sustain her, but she shrank away from him, saying, faintly: "Then he is captured? God be praised!"

In spite of the words, her eyes filmed over with tears, a look of abject misery bared itself upon her face.

"Where is the Countess?"

"Above—resting. Come; she, too, will rejoice."

"Let me take her the news. You were going out, and—I think the air will do you good. Be brave, Oliveta; you have done your share, and there's nothing more to fear."

She acquiesced dully; her olive features were ghastly as she felt her way past him; she walked like a sick woman.

He watched her pityingly for a moment, then mounted the stairs. As he laid his hand upon the door it gave to his touch and he stood upon the threshold of the parlor. Vittoria's name was upon his lips when, by the dim evening light which came through the drawn curtains and by the faint illumination from the solitary shrine candle, he saw her recumbent form upon the couch.

She was lying in an attitude of complete relaxation, her sun-gilded hair straying in long thick braids below her waist, Those tawny ropes were of a length and thickness to bind a man about the body. Her lips were slightly parted; her lashes lay like dark shadows against her ivory cheeks.

He was swept by a sudden awed abashment. The impulse to retreat came over him, but he lacked the will. The longing which had remained so strong in him through years of denial, governing the whole course of his life, blazed up in him now and increased with every heartbeat. He found that without willing it he had come close to the couch. The girl's slim hand lay upon the cushions, limply upturned to him; it was half open and there sprang through him an ungovernable desire to bury his lips in its rosy palm. He knelt, then quailed and recovered himself. At the same instant she stirred and, to his incredulous delight, whispered his name.

A wild exultation shot through him. Why not yield to this madness, he asked himself, dizzily. The long struggle was over now. For this woman's sake he had repeatedly played the part of bravery in a fever of fear. He had done what he had done to make himself worthy of her, and now, at the last, he was to have nothing—absolutely nothing, except a memory. Against these thoughts his notions of honorable conduct hastily and confusedly arrayed themselves. But he was in no state to reason. The same enchantment, half psychic, half physical, ethereal yet strongly human, that had mastered him in the old Sicilian days, was at work upon him now. Dimly he felt that so mighty and natural a thing ought not to be resisted. He stood stiffly like a man spellbound.

It may have been Oliveta's accusation that affected the course of the sleeping woman's thoughts, it may have been that she felt the man's nearness, or that some influence passed from his mind to hers. However it was, she spoke his name again, her fingers closed over his, she drew him toward her.

He yielded; her warm breath beat upon his face; then the last atoms of self-restraint fled away from him like sparks before a fierce night wind. A fiery madness coursed through his veins as he caught her to him. Her lips were fevered with sleep. For a moment the caress seemed real; it was the climax of his hopes, the attainment of his longings. He crushed her in his arms; her hair blinded him; he buried his face in it, kissing her brow, her cheek, the curve where neck and shoulder met, and all the time he was speaking her name with hoarse tenderness.

So strangely had the fanciful merged into the real that the girl was slow in waking. Her eyelids fluttered, her breast rose and fell tumultuously, and even while her wits were struggling back to reality her arms clung to him. But the transition was brief. Her eyes opened, and she stiffened as with the shock of an electric current. A cry, a swift, writhing movement, and she was upon her feet, his incoherent words beating upon her ears but making no impression upon her brain.

"*You!* God above!" she cried.

She faced him, white, terror-stricken, yet splendid in her anger. She was still dazed, but horror and dismay leaped quickly into her eyes.

"Margherita! You called me. You drew me to you. It was your real self that spoke—I know it."

"You—kissed me while—I slept!"

He paled at the look with which she scorched him, then broke out, doggedly:

"You wanted me; you drew me close. You can't undo that moment—you can't. My God! Don't tell me it was all a mistake. That would make it unendurable. I could never forgive myself."

She hid her face with a choking cry of shame. "No, no! I didn't know—"

He approached and touched her arm timidly. "Margherita," he said, "if I thought you really did not call me—if I were made to believe that I had committed an unpardonable offense against your womanhood and our friendship—I would go and kill myself. But somehow I cannot believe that. I was beside myself—but I was never more exalted. Something greater than my own will made me do as I did. I think it was your love answering to mine. If that is not so—if it is all a delusion—there is nothing left for me. I have played my part out to the end. My work is done, and I do not see how I can go on living."

There was an odd mingling of pain and rapture in the gaze she raised to his. It gave him courage.

"Why struggle longer?" he urged, gently. "Why turn from love when Heaven wills you to receive it and learn to be a woman? I was in your thoughts and you longed for me, as I have never ceased, all these years, to hunger for you. Please! Please! Margherita! Why fight it longer?"

"What have you done? What have you done?" she whispered over and over. She looked toward the open door as if with thought of escape or assistance, and despite his growing hope Blake was miserable at sight of her distress.

"How came you here, alone with me?" she asked at length. "Oliveta was here only a moment ago."

"I came with good news for both of you. I met Oliveta as she went out, and when I had told her she sent me to you. Don't you understand, dear? It was good news. Our quest is over, our work is done, and God has seen fit to deliver our enemy—"

She flung out a trembling hand, while the other hid itself in the silk and lace at her breast.

"What is this you tell me? Maruffi? Am I still dreaming?"

"Maruffi has been arrested."

"Is it possible?—this long nightmare ended at last like this? Maruffi is arrested? You are safe? No one has been killed?"

"It is all right. O'Neil telephoned me and I came here at once to tell you and Oliveta."

"When did they find him? Where?"

"Not half an hour ago—at his house. We have been watching the place ever since he disappeared, feeling sure he'd have to return sooner or later, if only for a moment. He is under lock and key at this instant."

Blake attributed a stir in the hall outside to the presence of the maid-servant; Margherita, whose eyes were fixed upon him, failed to detect a figure which stood in the shadow just beyond the open door.

"Does he know of our part in it—Oliveta's part?" she asked.

"O'Neil didn't say. He'll learn of it shortly, in any event. Do you realize what his capture means? I—hardly do myself. For one thing, there's no further need of concealment. I—I want people to know who you are. It seems hardly conceivable that Belisario Cardi has gone to meet his punishment, but it is true. Lucrezia has her revenge at last. It has been a terrible task for all of us, but it brought you and me together. I don't intend ever to let you go again, Margherita. I loved you there in Sicily. I've loved you every moment, every hour—"

Blake turned at the sound of a door closing behind him. He saw Margherita start, then lean forward staring past him with a look of amazement, of frightened incredulity, upon her face. Some one, a man, had stepped into the dim-lit room and was fumbling with the lock, his eyes fixed upon them, meanwhile, over his shoulder. The light from the windows had faded, the faint illumination from the taper before the shrine was insufficient fully to pierce the gloom. But on the instant of his interruption all triumph and hope, all thoughts of love, fled from Norvin's mind, bursting like iridescent bubbles, at a touch. The flesh along his back writhed, the hair at his neck lifted itself; for there in the shadow, huge, black, and silent, stood Caesar Maruffi.

# XXI.
## UNDER FIRE

Blake heard Margherita's breath release itself. She was staring as if at an apparition. His mind, working with feverish speed, sought vainly to grasp the situation. Maruffi had broken away and come for his vengeance, but how or why this had been made possible he could not conceive. It sufficed that the man was here in the flesh, sinister, terrible, malignant as hell. Blake knew that the ultimate test of his courage had come.

He felt the beginnings of that same shuddering, sickening weakness with which he was only too familiar; felt the strength running out from his body as water escapes from a broken vessel. He froze with the sense of his physical impotency, and yet despite this chaos of conflicting emotions his inner mind was clear; it was bitter, too, with a ferocious self-disgust.

There was a breathless pause before Maruffi spoke.

"Lucrezia Ferara!" he said, hoarsely, as if wishing to test the sound of the name. "So Oliveta is the daughter of the overseer, and you are Savigno's sweetheart." His words were directed at Margherita, who answered in a thin, shrill, broken voice:

"What—are you doing—here?"

"I came for that wanton's blood. Give her to me."

"Oliveta? She is—gone."

The Sicilian cursed. "Gone? Where?"

"Away. Into the street. You—you cannot find her."

"Christ!" Maruffi reached upward and tore open the collar of his shirt.

Blake spoke for the first time, but his voice was dead and lifeless.

"Yes. She's gone. You're wanted. You must go with me!"

Maruffi gave a snarling, growling cry and his gesture showed that he was armed. Involuntarily Blake shrank back; his hand groped for his hip, but, half-way, encountered the pile of silken cushions upon which Margherita had been lying; his fingers sank into them nervously, his other hand gripped the carven footboard of the couch. He had no weapon. He had not dreamed of such a necessity.

In this imminent peril a new fear swept over him greater than any he had ever known. It was not the fear of death. It was something far worse. For the moment, it seemed to him inevitable that Margherita Ginini should, at last, learn the truth concerning him, should see him as he was that night at Terranova. Swift upon the heels of his long-deferred declaration of love would come the proof that he was a craven. Then he thought of her danger, realizing that this man was quite capable in his fury of killing her, too, and he stiffened in every fiber. His cowardice fell away from him like a rotten garment, and he stood erect.

Maruffi, it seemed, had not heard his last words, or else his mind was still set upon Oliveta. "Gone!" he exclaimed. "Then I shall not see her face grow black within my fingers—not yet. God! How I ran!" He cursed again. "But I shall not fare so badly, after all." He stirred, and with his movement Blake flew to action. Swiftly, with one sweep of his right hand, he brought the silken cushions up before his breast and lunged at his enemy. At the same instant Maruffi fired.

In the closed room the detonation was deafening; it rattled the windows, it seemed to bulge the very walls. Blake felt a heavy blow which drove the floss-filled pillows against his body with the force of a giant hammer, it tore them from his grip, it crushed the breath from his lungs and spun him half around. Seeing that he did not fall, Maruffi cocked and fired a second time without aiming, but his victim was upon him like a tiger and together they crashed back against the wall, locked in each other's arms.

Blake's will propelled him splendidly. All that indecision with which fear works upon the mind had left him, but the old contraction of his nerves still hampered his action. The blaze from Maruffi's second shot half blinded him and its breath smote him like a blow.

"Two!" he counted, wonderingly. A pain in his left side, due to that first sledge-hammer impact, was spreading slowly, but he had crossed the room under the belching muzzle of the revolver and was practically unharmed.

There began a struggle—the more terrible since it was unequal—in which the weaker man had to drive his body at the cost of tremendous effort. Blake was like a leader commanding troops which had begun to retreat. But more power came to him under the spur of action and the pressing realization that he must give Margherita a chance to get safely away. If he could not wrest the weapon from Maruffi's hands he knew that he must receive those four remaining bullets in his own body. He rather doubted that he could take that weight of lead.

He shouted to her to run, while he wrestled for possession of the gun. He had flung his right arm about his adversary's body, his other hand gripped his wrist; his head was pressed against Maruffi's chest. The weapon described swift circles, jerking parabolas and figures as the men strained to wrest it from each other. Maruffi strove violently to free his imprisoned hand, and in doing so he discharged the revolver a third time. The bullet brought a shower of plaster from the ceiling, and Blake counted with fierce exultation,

"Three!"

He gasped his warning to the woman again, then twined his leg about his antagonist's in a wrestler's hold, striving mightily to bear Maruffi against the wall. But Caesar was like an oak-tree. Failing to move him, Blake suddenly flung himself backward, with all his weight, lifting at the same instant in the hope of a fall. In this he was all but successful. The two reeled out into the room, tripped, went to their knees, then rose, still intertwined in that desperate embrace. The odd, stiff feeling in Blake's side had increased rapidly; it began to numb his muscles and squeeze his lungs. His eyes were stinging with sweat and smoke; his ears were roaring. As they swayed and turned he saw that Margherita had made no effort to escape and he was seized with an extraordinary rage, which for a brief time renewed his strength.

She was at the front window crying for help.

"Jump! For—God's sake, jump!" he shouted, but she did not obey. Instead she ran toward the combatants and seized Maruffi's free arm, in a measure checking his effort to break the other man's hold. Her closeness to danger agonized Blake, the more as he felt his own strength ebbing, under that stabbing pain in his side. He centered his force in the grip of his left hand, clinging doggedly while the Sicilian flung his two assailants here and there as a dog worries a scarf.

Blake fancied he heard a stamping of feet in the hall outside and the sound of voices, of heavy bodies crashing against the door. Maruffi heard it, too, for with a bellow of fury he redoubled his exertions. A sweep of his arm flung the girl aside; with a mighty wrench of his body he carried Blake half across the room, loosening his hold. Then he seized him by the throat and forced his head back.

The shouting outside was increasing, the pounding was growing louder. Blake's breath was cut off and his strength went swiftly; his death grip on the Sicilian's body slackened. As he tore at the fingers which were throttling him, his left hand slipped, citing to Maruffi's sleeve, and finally began clawing blindly for the weapon. The next moment he was hurled aside, so violently that he fell, his feet entangled in the cushions with which he had defended himself against the first shot.

He rose and renewed his attack, hearing Margherita cry out in horror. This time Maruffi took deliberate aim, and when he fired the figure lurching toward him was halted as if by some giant fist.

"Four!" Blake counted. He was hit, he knew, but he still had strength; there were but two more shots to come. Then he was dazed to find himself upon his knees. As if through a film he saw the Italian turn away and raise his weapon toward the girl, who was wrenching at the door.

"Maruffi!" he shouted. "Oh, God!" then he closed his eyes to shut out what followed. But he heard nothing, for he slipped forward, face down, and felt himself falling, falling, into silence and oblivion.

As O'Connell made his way toward St. Phillip Street he nursed a growing resentment at the news Norvin Blake had given him. His feeling toward Caesar Maruffi had all the fierceness of private hatred, calling for revenge, and he considered himself ill-used in that he had not even been permitted to witness the arrest. He knew Maruffi's countrymen would be likely to make a demonstration, and he was grimly desirous of being present when this occurred.

As he neared the heart of the Italian section he saw a blue-coated officer running toward him.

"What's up?" he cried. "Have the dagoes started something?"

"Maruffi was pinched, but he got away," the other answered. "Johnson is hurt, and—"

O'Connell lost the remaining words, for he had broken into a run.

A crowd had gathered in front of a little shop where the wounded policeman had been carried to await the arrival of an ambulance, and even before O'Connell had heard the full story of the escape Acting-Chief O'Neil drove up behind a lathered horse. He leaped from his mud-stained buggy, demanding, hoarsely:

"Where is he—Maruffi?"

Officer Dean, Johnson's companion, met him at the door of the shop.

"He made his break while I was 'phoning you," he answered.

"Hell! Didn't you frisk him?" roared the Chief.

"Sure! But we missed his gun."

"Caesar carries it on a cord around his neck—nigger-fashion," briefly explained O'Connell.

Dean was running on excitedly: "I heard Johnson holler, but before I could get out into the street Maruffi had shot him twice and was into that alley yonder. I tried to follow, but lost him, so I came back and sent in the alarm."

The Acting Chief cursed under his breath, and with a few sharp orders hurried off the few officers who had reached the scene. Then as an ambulance appeared he passed into the room where Johnson lay. As he emerged a moment later O'Connell drew him aside.

"Maruffi won't try to leave town till it's good and dark," he said. "He's got a girl, and I've an idea he'll ask her to hide him out."

"It was his girl who turned him up—she and Blake—"

O'Connell cried, sharply: "Wait! Does he know she did that? If he does, he'll make for her, sure."

"That may be. Those two women are all alone, and I'd feel better if they were safely out of the way. I'll leave you there on the way back."

An instant later they were clattering over the uneven flags while their vehicle rocked and bounded in a way that threatened to hurl them out.

Even before they reached their destination they saw people running through the dusk toward the house in which the two girls lived and heard a shot muffled behind walls. O'Neil reined the horse to his haunches as the shrill cry of a woman rang out above them, and the next moment he and O'Connell were inside, rushing up the stairs with headlong haste. They were brought to a stop before a bolted door from behind which came the sounds of a furious struggle.

"Blake! Norvin Blake!" shouted O'Connell.

"Break it down!" O'Neil ordered. He set his back against the opposite wall, then launched himself like a catapult. The patrolman followed suit, but although the panels strained and split the heavy door held.

"By God! he's in there!" the Chief cried, as he set his shoulder to the barrier for a second time. "Once more! Together!" Through a crevice which had opened in the upper panels they caught a glimpse of the dimly lighted room. What they saw made them struggle like madmen.

Another shot sounded, and O'Neil in desperation inserted his fingers in the opening and tore at it. Through the aperture O'Connell saw Maruffi run to an open window at the rear, then pause long enough to snatch the taper from its sconce at the foot of the little shrine and, stooping, touch its flame to the long lace curtains. They promptly flashed into a blaze. Parting them, he bestrode, the sill, lowered himself outside, and disappeared. It was an old but effective ruse to delay pursuit.

"Quick! He's set fire to the place," O'Connell gasped, and dashed down the hall.

A tremendous final heave of O'Neil's body cleared his way, a few strides and he was at the window, ripping the blazing hangings down and flinging them into the court below. When he turned it was to behold in the dim twilight Vittoria Fabrizi kneeling beside Blake. Her arms were about him, her yellow hair entwined his figure.

"A light! Somebody get a light!" the Chief roared to those who had followed him up the stairs, then seeing a lamp near by he lit it hurriedly, revealing the full disorder of the room. He knelt beside Vittoria, who drew the fallen man closer to her, moaning something in Italian which O'Neil could not understand. But her look told him enough, and, rising, he ordered some one to run for a doctor. Strangers, white-faced and horrified, were crowding in; the sound of other feet came from the stairs outside, questions and explanations were noisily exchanged. O'Neil swore roundly at the crowd and drove it ahead of him down into the street, where he set a man to guard the door. Then he returned and helped the girl examine her lover's wounds. Her fingers were steady and sure, but in her face was such an abandonment of grief as he had never seen, and her voice was little more than a rasping whisper. They were still working when the doctor came, followed a moment later by a disheveled, stricken figure of tragedy which O'Neil recognized as Oliveta.

At sight of her foster-sister the peasant girl broke into a passion of weeping, but Vittoria checked her with an imperious word, meanwhile keeping her tortured eyes upon the physician. She waited upon him, forestalling his every thought and need with a mechanical dexterity that bore witness to her training, but all the while her eyes held a pitiful entreaty. Not until she heard O'Neil call for an ambulance did she rouse herself to connected speech. Then she exclaimed with hysterical insistence:

"You shall not take him away! I am a nurse; he shall stay here. Who better than I could attend to him?"

"He can stay here if you have a place for him," said the doctor. O'Neil drew him aside, inquiring, "Will he live?"

The doctor indicated Vittoria with a movement of his head. "I'm sure of it. That girl won't let him die."

The news of that combat traveled fast and far and it came to Myra Nell Warren among the first. Despite the dreadful false position in which Bernie had placed her with respect to Norvin, the girl had but one thought and that was to go to her friend. She could not endure the sight of blood, and her somewhat child-like imagination conjured up a gory spectacle. She was afraid that if she tried to act as nurse she would faint or run away when most needed. But she was determined to go to him and to assist in any way she could. It was not consistent with her ideas of loyalty to shrink from the sight of suffering even though she could do nothing to relieve it.

When she mounted the stairs to Oliveta's living-quarters she was pale and agitated, and she faltered on the threshold at the sight of strangers. Within were a newspaper reporter, a doctor, the Chief of Police, the Mayor of the city, while outside a curious throng was gathered. Seeing Miss Fabrizi, she ran toward her, sobbing nervously.

"Where is he, Vittoria? Tell me that he's—safe!"

Some one answered, "He's safe and resting quietly."

"T-take me to him."

A spasm stirred Vittoria's tired features; she petted the girl with a comforting hand, while Mayor Wright said, gently:

"It must have been a great shock to you, Myra Nell, as it was to all of us, but you may thank God he has been spared to you."

The reporter made a note upon his pad, and began framing the heart interest of his story. Here was a new and interesting aspect of an event worth many columns.

Vittoria led the girl toward her room, but outside the door Myra Nell paused, shaking in every limb.

"You—you love him?" asked the other woman.

The look which Miss Warren gave her stabbed like a knife, and when the girl had sunk to her knees beside the bed, with Blake's name upon her lips, Vittoria stood for a long moment gazing down upon her dazedly.

Later, when she had sent Myra Nell home and silence lay over the city, Norvin's nurse stole into the great front room where she had experienced so much of gladness and horror that night, and made her way wearily to the little image of the Virgin. She noted with a start that the candle was gone, so she lit a new one and, kneeling for many minutes, prayed earnestly for strength to do the right and to quench the leaping, dazzling flame which had been kindled in her heart.

# XXII.
# A MISUNDERSTANDING

Several days later Vittoria Fabrizi led Bernie Dreux into the room where Norvin lay. The little man walked on tiptoe and wore an expression of such gloomy sympathy that Blake said:

"Please don't look so blamed pious; it makes me hurt all over."

Bernie's features lightened faintly; he smiled in a manner bordering upon the natural.

"They wouldn't let me see you before. Lord! How you have frightened us!"

"My nurse won't let me talk."

Blake's eyes rested with puzzled interrogation upon the girl, who maintained her most professional air as she smoothed his pillow and admonished him not to overtax himself. When she had disappeared noiselessly, he said:

"Well, you needn't put a rose in my hand yet awhile. Tell me what has happened? How is Myra Nell?"

"She's heartbroken, of course. She came here that first night; but the smell of drugs makes her sick."

"I suppose Maruffi got away?"

Dreux straightened in his chair; his face flushed proudly; he put on at least an inch of stature. "Haven't you heard?" he inquired, incredulously.

"How could I hear anything when I'm doctored by a deaf-mute and nursed by a divinity without a tongue?"

"Maruffi was captured that very night. Sure! Why, the whole country knows about it." Again a look of mellow satisfaction glowed on the little man's face. "My dear boy, you're a hero, of course, but—there—are—others."

"Who caught him?"

"I did."

"*You!*" Norvin stared in open-mouthed amazement.

"That's what I said. I—me—Mr. Bernard Effingwell Dreux, the prominent cotillion leader, the second-hand dealer, the art critic and amateur detective. I unearthed the notorious and dreaded Sicilian desperado in his lair, and now he's cooling his heels in the parish prison along with his little friends."

"Why—I'm astonished."

"Naturally! I found him in Joe Poggi's house. Mr. Poggi also languishes in the bastille."

"How in the world—"

"Well, it's quite a story, and it all happened through the woman—" Bernie flushed a bit as he met his companion's eye. "When I told you about Mrs. Poggi I didn't exactly go into all the intimate—er—details. The truth is she became deeply interested in me. I told you how I met her—Well, she wasn't averse to receiving my attentions—Heavens, no! She ate 'em up! Before I knew it I found myself entangled in an intrigue—I had hold of an electric current and couldn't let go. When I didn't follow her around, she followed me. When I didn't make love, she did. She learned about Felicite, and there was—Excuse me!" Bernie rose, put his head cautiously outside the door to find the coast clear, then said: "Hell to pay! I tried to back out; but you can't back away from some women any more than you can back away from a prairie fire." He shook his head gloomily. "It seems she wasn't satisfied with Poggi; she had ambitions. She'd caught a glimpse of the life that went on around her and wanted to take part in it. She thought I was rich, too—my name had something to do with it, I presume—at any rate, she began to talk of divorce, elopement, and other schemes that terrorized me. She was quite willing that I murder her husband, poison her relatives, or adopt any little expedient of that kind which would clear the path for our true love. I was in over my depth, but when I backed water she swam out and grabbed me. When I stayed away from her she looked me up. I tried once to tell her that I didn't really care for her—only once." The memory brought beads of sweat to the detective's brow. "Between her and Felicite I led a dog's life. If I'd had the money I'd have left town.

"I'd been meeting her on street corners up to that point; but she finally told me to come to the house while Poggi was away—it was the day you were hurt. I rebelled, but she made such a scene I had to agree or be arrested for blocking traffic. She carries a dagger, Norvin, in her stocking, or somewhere; it's no longer than your finger, but it's the meanest-looking weapon I ever saw. Well, I went, along about dark, determined to have it out with her once for all; but those aristocrats during the French Revolution had nothing on me. I know how it feels to mount the steps of the guillotine.

"The Poggi's parlor furniture is upholstered in red and smells musty. I sat on the edge of a chair, one eye on her and the other taking in my surroundings. There's a fine crayon enlargement of Joe with his uniform, in a gold frame with blue mosquito-netting over it to disappoint the flies—four ninety-eight, and we supply the frame—done by an old master of the County Fair school. There's an organ in the parlor, too, with a stuffed fish-hawk on it.

"She seemed quite subdued and coy at first, so I took heart, never dreaming she'd wear her dirk in the house. But say! That woman was raised on raw beef. Before I could wink she had it out; it has an ivory hilt, and you could split a silk thread with it. I suppose she didn't want to spoil the parlor furniture with me, although I'd never have showed against that upholstery, or else she's in the habit of preparing herself for manslaughter by a system of vocal calisthenics. At any rate, we were having it hot and heavy, and I was trying to think of some good and unselfish actions I had done, when we heard the back door of the cottage open and close, then somebody moving in the hall.

"Mrs. Poggi turned green—not white—green! And I began to picture the head-lines in the morning papers! 'The Bachelor and the Policeman's Wife,' they seemed to say. It wasn't Poggi, however, as I discovered when the fellow called to her. He was breathing heavily, as if he had been running. She signaled me to keep quiet, then went out; and I heard them talking, but couldn't understand what was said. When she came back she was greener than ever, and told me to go, which I did, realizing that the day of miracles is not done. I fell down three times, and ran over a child getting out of that neighborhood."

Blake, who had listened eagerly, inquired:

"The man was Maruffi?"

"Exactly! I got back to the club in time to hear about his arrest and escape and your fight here. The town was ringing with it; everybody was horrified and amazed. What particularly stunned me was the news that Maruffi, not Poggi, was the head of the Mafia; but my experience in criminal work has taught me to be guided by circumstances, and not theory, so when I learned more about Caesar's escape I fell to wondering where he could hide. Then I recalled his secret meetings with Joe Poggi and that scalding volcano of emotion from whom I had just been delivered. Her fright, when she let me out, something familiar in the voice which called to her, came back, and—well, I couldn't help guessing the truth. Maruffi was in the house of one of the officers who was supposed to be hunting him."

"But his capture?"

"Simple enough. I went to O'Neil and told him. We got a posse together and went after him. We descended in such force and so suddenly that he didn't have a chance to resist. If I'd known who he was at first I'd have tried to take him single-handed."

"Then it's well you didn't know." Blake smiled.

"What bothers me," Dreux confessed, "is how Mrs. Poggi regards my action. I—I hate to appear a cad. I'd apologize if I dared."

Vittoria appeared to warn Dreux that his visit must end. When the little man had gone Norvin inquired:

"You knew of Maruffi's arrest?"

"Oh, yes!"

"Why didn't you tell me?"

"You were in no condition to hear news of importance."

"Is that why you have been so silent?"

"Hush! You have talked quite enough for the present."

"You act strangely—differently," he insisted.

"I am your nurse. I am responsible for your recovery, so I do as I am ordered."

"And you haven't changed?" he inquired, wistfully.

"Not at all, I am quite the same—quite the same girl you knew in Sicily!" He did not relish her undertone, and wondered if illness had quickened his imagination, if he was forever seeing more in her manner, hearing more in her words than she meant. There was something intangibly cold and distant about her, or seemed to be. During the first feverish hours after his return to consciousness he had seen her hanging over him with a wonderful loving tenderness—it was that which had closed his wounds and brought him back toward health so swiftly; but as his brain had cleared and he had grown more rational this vision had disappeared along with his other fancies.

He wondered whether knowledge of his pseudo-engagement to Myra Nell had anything to do with her manner. He knew that she was in the girl's confidence. Naturally, he himself was not quite at his ease in regard to Miss Warren. The rumor about his advancing the money for her Carnival expenses had been quieted through Bernie's efforts, and the knowledge of it restricted to a necessary few. Although Myra Nell had refused his offers of marriage and treated the matter lightly, he could not help feeling that this attitude was assumed or exaggerated to cover her humiliation—or was it something deeper? It would be terrible if she really cared for him in earnest. Her own character protected her from scandal. The breaking-off of his supposed engagement with her could not hurt her—unless she really loved him. He closed his eyes, cursing Bernie inwardly. After a time he again addressed Vittoria.

"Tell me," he said, "how Maruffi came to spare you. My last vision was of him aiming—"

"He had but four shots."

"Four?"

"Yes, he had used two in his escape from the officers—before he came here."

"I see! It was horrible. I felt as if I had failed you at the critical moment, just as I failed—"

"As you failed whom?"

"Martel!" The word sounded in his ears with a terrible significance; he could hardly realize that he had spoken it. He had always meant to tell her, of course, but the moment had taken him unawares. His conscience, his inmost feeling, had found a voice apart from his volition. There was a little silence. At length she said in a low, constrained tone.

"Did you fail—him?"

"I—I did," he said, chokingly; and, the way once opened, he made a full and free confession of his craven fear that night on the road to Terranova, told her of the inherent cowardice which had ever since tortured and shamed him, and of his efforts to reconstruct his whole being. "I wanted to expiate my sin," he finished, "and, above all, I have longed to prove myself a man in your sight."

She listened with white, set face, slightly averted. When she turned to him at last, he saw that her eyes were wet with tears.

"I cannot judge of these matters," she said. "You—you were no coward the other night, amico mio. You were the bravest of the brave. You saved my life. As for that other time, do not ask me to turn back and judge. You perhaps blame yourself too much. It was not as if you could have saved Martel. It is rather that you should have at least tried—that is how you feel, is it not? You had to reckon with your own sense of honor. Well, you have won your fight; you have become a new person, and you are not to be held responsible for any action of that Norvin Blake I knew in Sicily, who, indeed, did not know his own weakness and could not guard against it. Ever since I met you here in New Orleans I have known you for a brave, strong man. It is splendid—the way in which you have conquered yourself—splendid! Few men could have done it. Be comforted," she added, with a note of tenderness that answered the pleading in his eyes—"there is no bitterness in my heart."

"Margherita," he cried, desperately, "can't you—won't you—"

"Oh," she interposed, peremptorily, "do not say it. I forbid you to speak." Then, as he fell silent, she continued in a manner she strove to make natural: "That dear girl, Myra Nell Warren, has inquired about you daily. She has been distracted, heartbroken. Believe me, caro Norvin, there is a true and loving woman whom you cannot cast aside. She seems frivolous on the surface, I grant you. Even I have been deceived. But at the time of Mr. Dreux's dreadful faux pas she was so hurt, she grieved so that I couldn't but believe she felt deeply."

Norvin flushed dully and said nothing.

Vittoria smiled down upon him with a look that was half maternal in its sweetness.

"All this has been painful for you," she said, "and you have become over-excited. You must not talk any more now. You are to be moved soon."

"Aren't you going to be my nurse any more?"

"You are to be taken home."

His hand encountered hers, and he tried to thank her for what she had done, but she rose and, admonishing him to sleep, left the room somewhat hurriedly.

In the short time which intervened before Norvin was taken to his own quarters Vittoria maintained her air of cool detachment. Myra Nell came once, bringing Bernie with her, much to the sick man's relief; his other friends began to visit him in rapidly increasing numbers; he gradually took up the threads of his every-day life which had been so rudely severed. Meanwhile, he had ample time to think over his situation. He could not persuade himself that Vittoria had been right in her reading of Myra Nell. Perhaps she had only put this view forward to shield herself from the expression of a love she was not ready to receive. He could not believe that he had been deluded, that there was in reality no hope for him.

Mardi Gras week found him still in bed and unable to witness Myra Nell's triumph. During the days of furious social activity she had little time to give him, for the series of luncheons, of pageants, of gorgeous tableaux and brilliant masked balls kept her in a whirl of rapturous confusion, and left her scant leisure in which to snatch even her beauty sleep.

Since she was to be the flower of the festival, and since her beauty was being saved for the grand climax of the whole affair, she had no idea of sacrificing it. Proteus, Momus, the Mistick Krewe of Comus, and the other lesser societies celebrated their distinctive nights with torch and float and tableau; the city was transformed by day with bunting and flags, by night it was garlanded with fire; merrymakers thronged the streets, their carnival spirit entered into every breast. It was a glad, mad week of gaiety, of dancing, of laughter, of flirting and love-making under the glamour of balmy skies and velvet torch-lit nights; and to the pleasure of the women was added the delicious torture of curiosity regarding those mysterious men in masks who came through a blaze of fire and departed, no one knew whither.

As the spirit of the celebration mounted, Myra Nell abandoned herself to it; she lived amid a bewilderment of social obligations, through which she strove incessantly to discover the identity of her King. Finding herself unsuccessful in this, her excitement redoubled. At last came his entrance to the city; the booming cannon, the applauding thousands, his royal progress through the streets toward the flower-festooned stand where she looked down upon the multitude. Miss Warren's maids of honor were the fairest of all this fair city, and yet she stood out of that galaxy as by far the most entrancing.

Her royal consort came at length, a majestic figure upon a float of ivory and gold; he took the goblet from her hand; he pledged her with silent grace while the assembled hordes shouted their allegiance to the pair. She knew he must be very handsome underneath his mask; and he was bold also, in a quite unkingly way, for there was more in his glance than the greeting of a monarch; there was ardent love, a burning adoration which thrilled her breast and fanned her curiosity to a leaping flame. This was, indeed, life, romance, the purple splendor for which she had been born. She could scarcely contain herself until the hour of the Rex ball, when she knew her chance would come to match her charm and beauty against his voiceless secrecy. She was no longer a make-believe queen, but a royal ruler, beloved by her subjects, adored by her throne-mate. Then the glittering ball that followed!—the blazing lights, the splendid pantomime, the great shifting kaleidoscope of beauteous ladies and knightly men in gold and satin and coats of mail! And, above all, the maddening mystery of that king at her side whose glances were now melting with melancholy, now ablaze with eagerness, and whose whispered words, muffled behind his mask, were not those of a monarch, but rather those of a bold and audacious lover! He poured his vows into her blushing ear; he set her wits to scampering madly; his sincere passion, together with the dream-like unreality of the scene, intoxicated her. Who could he be? How dared he say these things? What faint familiar echo did his voice possess? Which one of her many admirers had the delightful effrontery to court her thus ardently beneath a thousand eyes? He was drunk with the glory of this hour, it seemed, for he whispered words she dared not listen to. What preposterous proposals he voiced; what insane audacity he showed! And yet he was in deadly earnest, too. She canvassed her many suitors in her mind, she tried artfully to trap him into some betrayal; the game thrilled her with a keen delight. At last she realized there was but one who possessed such brazen impudence, and told him she had known him from the first, whereat he laughed with the abandon of a pagan and renewed the fervor of his suit.

Blake learned from many sources that Myra Nell had made a gorgeous Queen. The papers lauded her grace, her beauty, the magnificence of her costumes. Bernie was full of it and could talk of nothing else when he dropped in as usual.

"She's all tired out, and I reckon she'll sleep for a week. I hope so, anyhow."

"I'm sorry I couldn't see her, but I'm glad I escaped the Carnival. The Mardi Gras is hard enough on the women; but it kills us men."

"I should say so. Look at me—a wreck." After a moment he added: "You think Myra Nell is all frivolity and glitter, but she isn't; she's as deep as the sea, Norvin. I can't tell you how glad I am that you two—" Blake stirred uneasily. "I—I admire you tremendously, for you're just what I wanted to be and couldn't. I'm talking foolishly, I know, but this Carnival has made me see Myra Nell in a new light; I see now that she was born for joy and luxury and splendor and—and those things which you can give her. She's been a care to me. I've been her mother; I've actually made her dresses—but I'm glad now for all my little sacrifices." Two tears gathered and trickled down Mr. Dreux's cheeks, while Blake marveled at the strange mixture of qualities in this withered little beau. Bernie's words left him very uncomfortable, however, and the hours that followed did not lessen the feeling.

Although Myra Nell sent him daily messages and gifts—now books, now flowers, now a plate of fudge which she had made with her own hands and which he was hard put to dispose of—she nevertheless maintained a shy embarrassment and came to see him but seldom. When she did call, her attitude was most unusual: she overflowed with gossip, yet she talked with a nervous hesitation; when she found his eyes upon her she stammered, flushed, and paled; and he caught her stealing glances of miserable appeal at him. She was very different from the girl he had known and had learned to love in a big, impersonal way. He attributed the change to his own failure in responding to her timid advances, and this made him quite unhappy.

Nor did he see much of Vittoria, although Oliveta came daily to inquire about his progress.

He was up and about in time for the Mafia trial; but his duties in connection with it left him little leisure for society, which he was indeed glad to escape. New Orleans, he found, was on tiptoe for the climax of the tragedy which had so long been its source of ferment; the public was roused to a new and even keener suspense than at any time—not so much, perhaps, by the reopening of the case as by the rumors of bribery and corruption which were gaining ground. A startling array of legal talent had appeared for the defense; the trial was expected to prove the greatest legal battle in the history of the commonwealth.

Maruffi, with his genius for control, had assumed an iron-bound leadership and laughed openly at the possibility of a conviction. He had struck the note of persecution, making a patriotic appeal to the Italian populace; and the foreign section of the city seethed in consequence.

On the opening day the court-room was packed, the halls and corridors of the Criminal Court building were filled to suffocation, the neighboring streets were jammed with people clamoring for admittance and hungry for news from within. Then began the long, tedious task of selecting a jury. Public opinion had run so high that this was no easy undertaking. As day after day went by in the monotonous examination and challenge of talesmen, as panel after panel was exhausted with no result, not only did the ridiculous shortcomings of our jury system become apparent, but also the fact that the Mafia had, as usual, made full use of its sinister powers of intimidation. In view of the atrocious character of the crime and the immense publicity given it, those citizens who were qualified by intelligence to act as jurors had of necessity read and heard sufficient to form an opinion, and were therefore automatically debarred from service. It became necessary to place the final adjudication of the matter in the hands of men who were either utterly indifferent to the public weal or lacked the intelligence to read and weigh and think.

A remarkable wave of humanity seemed to have overwhelmed the city. Four out of every five men examined professed a disbelief in capital punishment, which, although it merely covered a fear of the Mafia's antagonism, nevertheless excused them for cause. Day after day this mockery went on.

As the list of talesmen grew into the hundreds and the same extraordinary antipathy to hanging continued to manifest itself, it occasioned remark, then ridicule. It would have been laughable had it not been so significant. The papers took it up, urging, exhorting, demanding that there be a stiffening of backbone; but to no effect. More than this, the Mafia had reigned so long and so autocratically, it had so shamefully abused the courts in the past, that a large proportion of honest men declared themselves unwilling to believe Sicilian testimony unless corroborated, and this prevented them from serving.

A week went by, and then another, and still twelve men who could try the issue fairly had not been found. Some few had been accepted, to be sure, but they were not representative of the city, and the list of talesmen who had been examined and excused on one pretext or another numbered fully a thousand.

Meanwhile, Maruffi smiled and shrugged and maintained his innocence.

# XXIII.
# THE TRIAL AND THE VERDICT

Blake did not attend these tiresome preliminaries, although he followed them with intense interest, the while a sardonic irritation arose in him. Chancing to meet Mayor Wright one day, he said:

"I'm beginning to think my original plan was the best after all."

"You mean we should have lynched those fellows as they were taken?" queried the Mayor, with a smile.

"Something like that."

"It won't take long to fix their guilt or innocence, once we get a jury."

"Perhaps—if we ever get one. But the men of New Orleans seem filled with a quality of mercy which isn't tempered with justice. Those who haven't already formed an opinion of the case are incompetent to act as intelligent jurors. Those who could render a fair judgment are afraid."

"You don't think there's any chance of an acquittal!"

"Hardly! And yet I hear the defense has called two hundred witnesses, so there's no telling what they will prove. You see, the prosecution is handicapped by a regard for the truth, something which doesn't trouble the other side in the least."

"Suppose they should be acquitted?"

"It would mean the breakdown of our legal system."

"And what would happen?"

Blake repeated the question, eyeing the Mayor curiously.

"Exactly! What would happen? What ought to happen?"

"Why, nothing," said the other, nervously. "They'd go free, I suppose. But Maruffi can't get off—he resisted an officer."

"Bah! He'd prove that Johnson assaulted him and he acted in self-defense."

"He'd have to answer for his attack upon you."

Norvin gave a peculiarly disagreeable laugh. "Not at all. That's the least of his sins. If the law fails in the Donnelly case I sha'n't ask it to help me."

But his pessimism gave way to a more hopeful frame of mind when the jury was finally impaneled and sworn and the trial began. The whole city likewise heaved a sigh of relief. The people had been puzzled and disgusted by the delay, and now looked forward to the outcome with all the keener eagerness to see justice done. Even before the hour for opening, the streets around the Criminal Court were thronged; the halls and lobbies were packed with a crowd which gave evidence of a breathless interest. No inch of space in the court-room was untenanted; an air of deep importance, a hush of strained expectancy lay over all.

Norvin found himself in a room with the other witnesses for the State, a goodly crowd of men and women, whites and blacks, many of whom he had been instrumental in ferreting out. From beyond came the murmur of a great assemblage, the shuffling of restless feet, the breathing of a densely packed audience. The wait grew tedious as witness after witness was summoned and did not return. At last he heard his own name called, and was escorted down a narrow aisle into an inclosure peopled with lawyers, reporters, and court officials, above which towered the dais of the judge, the throne of justice. He mounted the witness-stand, was sworn, and seated himself, then permitted his eyes to take in the scene. Before him, stretching back to the distant walls, was a sea of faces; to his right was the jury, which he scanned with the quick appraisal of one skilled in human analysis. Between him and his audience were the distinguished counsel, a dozen or more; and back of them eleven swarthy, dark-visaged Sicilian men, seated in a row. At one end sat Caesar Maruffi, massive, calm, powerful; at the other end sat Gino Cressi, huddled beside his father, his pinched face bewildered and terror-stricken.

A buzz of voices arose as the crowd caught its first full glimpse of the man who had so nearly lost his life through his efforts to bring these criminals to justice. Upon Maruffi's face was a look of such malignant hate that the witness stiffened in his chair. For one brief instant the Sicilian laid bare his soul, as their eyes met, then his cunning returned; the fire died from his impenetrable eyes; he was again the handsome, solid merchant who had sat with Donnelly at the Red Wing Club. The man showed no effect of his imprisonment and betrayed no sign of fear.

Norvin told his story simply, clearly, with a positiveness which could not fail to impress the jury; he withstood a grilling cross-examination at the hands of a criminal lawyer whose reputation was more than State-wide; and when he finally descended from the stand, Larubio, the cobbler, the senior Cressi, and Frank Normando stood within the shadow of the gallows. Normando he identified as the man in the rubber coat whose face he had clearly seen as the final shot was fired; he pointed out Gino Cressi as the picket who had given warning of the Chief's approach, then told of his share in the lad's arrest and what Gino had said. Concerning the other three who had helped in the shooting he had no conclusive evidence to offer; nevertheless, it was plain that his testimony had dealt a damaging blow to the defense. Yet Maruffi's glance showed no concern, but rather a veiled and mocking insolence.

As Blake passed out, young Cressi reached forth a timid hand and plucked at him, whispering:

"Signore, you said they would not hurt me."

"Don't be afraid. No one shall harm you," he told the boy, reassuringly.

"You promise?"

"Yes."

Cressi snatched his son to his side and scowled upward, breathing a malediction upon the American.

Inasmuch as the assassination had been carefully planned and executed at a late hour on a deserted street, it was popularly believed that very little direct testimony would be brought out, and that a conviction, therefore, would rest mainly upon circumstantial evidence; but as the trial progressed the case against the prisoners developed unexpected strength. Had Donnelly fallen at the first volley, his assailants would, in all probability, never have been identified, but he had stood and returned their fire for a considerable time, thus allowing opportunity for those living near by to reach their windows or to run into the street in time to catch at least a glimpse of the tragedy. Few saw more than a little, no one could identify all six of the assailants; but so thoroughly had the prosecution worked, so cunningly had it put these pieces together, that the whole scene was reproduced in the court-room. The murderers were singled out one by one and identified beyond a reasonable doubt.

One witness had passed Larubio's shop a few minutes before the shooting and had recognized the cobbler and his brother-in-law, Gaspardo Cressi. He also pointed out Normando and Paul Rafiro, both of whom he knew by sight.

From an upper window of a house near by another man who had been awakened by the noise saw Normando and Celso Fabbri in the act of firing. A woman living opposite the cobbler's house peered out into the smoke and flare in time to see Adriano Dora kneeling in the middle of the street. He was facing her; the light was fairly good; there could be no mistake. Various residents of the neighborhood had similar tales to tell, for, while no one had seen the beginning of the fight, a dozen pairs of eyes had looked out upon the finish, and many of these had recorded a definite picture of one or more of the actors. A gentleman returning from a lodge-meeting had even found himself on the edge of the battle, and had been so frightened that he ran straight home. He had learned, later, the significance of the fray, and had told nobody about his experience until Norvin Blake had traced him out and wrung the story from him. He feared the Mafia with the fear of death; but descending from the stand he pointed out four of the assassins—Normando, Fabbri, Rafiro, and Dora. He had seen them in the very act of firing.

A watchman on duty near by saw the boy Gino running past a moment before the shooting began; then, as he hurried toward the disturbance, he met Normando, Dora, and Rafiro coming toward him. The first of these carried a shotgun, which dropped into the gutter as he slipped and fell. The weapon and the suit of clothes Normando had worn were produced and identified. It transpired that this witness knew Paul Rafiro well, and for that reason had refused to tell what he knew until Norvin Blake had come to him and forced the words from his lips.

So it ran; the chain of evidence grew heavier with every hour. It seemed that some superhuman agency must have set the stage for the tragedy, posting witnesses at advantageous points. People marveled how so many eyes had gazed through the empty, rainy night; it was as if a mysterious hand had reached out of nowhere and brought together the onlookers, one by one, willing and unwilling, friend and enemy alike.

A more conclusive case than the State advanced against the six hired murderers during the first few days would be hard to conceive, and the public began to look for equally conclusive proof against the master ruffian and his lieutenants; but through it all Maruffi sat unperturbed, guiding the counsel with a word or a suggestion, in his bearing a calm self-assurance.

Then came a surprise which roused the whole city. From out of the parish prison appeared another Italian, a counterfeiter, who had recently been arrested, and who proved to be a Pinkerton detective "planted" among the Mafiosi for a purpose. Larubio had been a counterfeiter in Sicily—it was in the government prison that he had learned his cobbler's trade; and out of the fullness of his heart he had talked—so the detective swore—concerning these foolish Americans who sought to stay the hand of La Mafia. Nor had he been the only one to commit himself. Di Marco, Garcia, and the other two lieutenants turned livid as the stool-pigeon confronted them with their own words.

On the heels of this came the crowning dramatic moment of the trial.

Normando broke down and tried to confess in open court. He was a dull, ignorant man, with a bestial face and a coward's eye. This unexpected treachery, his own complete identification, had put an intolerable strain upon him. Without warning, he rose to his feet in the crowded court-room and cried loudly in his own tongue:

"Madonna mia! I do not want to die! I confess! I confess!"

Norvin Blake, who had been watching the proceedings from the audience, leaped from his seat as if electrified; other spectators followed, for even among those who could not understand the fellow's words it was seen that he was breaking. Normando's ghastly pallor, his wet and twitching lips, his shaking hands, all told the story.

Confusion followed. Amid the hubbub of startled voices, the stir of feet, the interruption of counsel, the wretch ran on, repeating his fear of death and his desire to confess, meanwhile beating his breast in hysterical frenzy.

Of all the Americans present perhaps Norvin alone understood exactly what the Sicilian was saying and why consternation had fallen upon the other prisoners. Larubio went white; a blind and savage fury leaped into Maruffi's face; the other nine wilted or stiffened according to the effect fear had upon them.

A death-like hush succeeded the first outbreak, and through Normando's gabble came the judge's voice calling for an interpreter. There was no need for the crier to demand silence; every ear was strained for the disclosures that seemed imminent.

Blake was forcing himself forward to offer his services when the wretch's wavering eyes caught something in the audience and rested there. The death sign of the Brotherhood was flashed at him; he halted. His tongue ran thickly for a moment; then he sank into his chair, and, burying his head in his hands, began to rock from side to side, sobbing and muttering. Nor would he say more, even when a recess was declared and he was taken into the judge's chambers. Thereafter he maintained a sullen, hopeless silence which nothing could break, glaring at his captors with the defiance of a beast at bay. But the episode had had its effect; it seemed that no one could now doubt the guilt of the prisoners.

The assurance of conviction grew as it was proven that Maruffi himself had rented Larubio's shop and laid the trap for Donnelly's destruction. Step by step the plot was bared in all its hideous detail. The blood money was traced from the six hirelings up through the four superiors to Caesar himself. Then followed the effort to show a motive for the crime—not a difficult task, since every one knew of Donnelly's work against the Mafia. Maruffi's domination of the Society was harder to bring out; but when the State finally rested its case, even Blake, who had been dubious from the start, confessed that American law and American courts had demonstrated their efficiency.

During all this time his relations with Vittoria remained unchanged. She and Oliveta eagerly welcomed his reports of the trial; but she never permitted him to see her alone, and he felt that she was deliberately withdrawing from him. He met her only for brief interviews. Of Myra Nell, meanwhile, he saw nothing, since, with characteristic abruptness, she had decided to visit some forgotten cousins in Mobile.

Of all those who followed the famous Mafia trial, detail by detail, perhaps no one did so with greater fixity of interest than Bernie Dreux. He reveled in it, he talked of nothing else, his waking hours were spent in the courtroom, his dreams were peopled with Sicilian figures. He hung upon Norvin, his hero, with a tenacity that was trying; he discussed the evidence bit by bit; he ran to him with every rumor, every fresh development. As the prosecution made its case his triumph became fierce and fearful to behold; then when the defense began its crafty efforts he grew furiously indignant, a mighty rage shook him, he swelled and choked with resentment.

"What do you think?" he inquired, one day. "They're proving alibis, one by one! It's infamous!"

"It will take considerable Sicilian testimony to offset the effect of our witnesses," Blake told him.

But Dreux looked upon the efforts of the opposing lawyers as a personal affront, and so declared himself.

"Why, they're trying to make you out a liar! That's what it amounts to. The law never intended that a gentleman's word should be disputed. If I were the judge I'd close the case right now and instruct the sheriff to hang all the prisoners, including their attorneys."

"They'll never be acquitted."

Bernie shook his head morosely.

"There's a rumor of jury-fixing. I hear one of the talesmen was approached with a bribe before the trial."

"I can scarcely believe that."

"I'll bet it's true just the same. If I'd known what they were up to I'd have got on the jury myself. I'd have taken their money, then I'd have fixed 'em!"

"You'd have voted for eleven hemp neckties, eh?"

"I'd have hung each man twice."

Although Blake at first refused to credit the rumors of corruption, the following days served to verify them, for more than one juryman confessed to receiving offers. This caused a sensation which grew as the papers took up the matter and commented editorially. A leading witness for the State finally told of an effort to intimidate him, and men began to ask if this was destined to prove as rotten as other Mafia cases in the past. A feeling of unrest, of impatience, began to manifest itself, vague threats were voiced, but the idea of a bribed or terrorized jury was so preposterous that few gave credence to it. Nevertheless, the closing days of the trial were weighted heavily with suspense. Not only the city, but the country at large, hung upon the outcome. So strongly had racial antipathy figured that Italy took note of the case, and it assumed an international importance. Biased accounts were cabled abroad which led to an uneasy stir in ministerial and consular quarters.

During the exhaustive arguments at the close of the trial Norvin and Bernie sat together. When the opening attorneys for the prosecution had finished, Dreux exclaimed, triumphantly:

"We've got 'em! They can't escape after that."

But when the defense in turn had closed, the little man revealed an indignant face to his companion, saying:

"Lord! They're as good as free! We'll never convict on evidence like that."

Once more he changed, under the spell of the masterly State's attorney, and declared with fierce exultance:

"What did I tell you? They'll hang every mother's son of 'em. The jury won't be out an hour."

The jury was out more than an hour, even though press and public declared the case to be clear. Yet, knowing that the eyes of the world were upon her, New Orleans went to sleep that night serene in the certainty that she had vindicated herself, had upheld her laws, and proved her ability to deal with that organized lawlessness which had so long been a blot upon her fair name.

Soon after court convened on the following morning the jury sent word that they had reached a verdict, and the court-room quickly filled. Rumors of Caesar Maruffi's double identity had gone forth; it was hinted that he was none other than the dreaded Belisario Cardi, that genius of a thousand crimes who had held all Sicily in fear. This report supplied the last touch of dramatic interest.

Blake and Bernie were in their places before the prisoners arrived. Every face in the room was tense and expectant; even the calloused attendants felt the hush and lowered their voices in deference. Every eye was strained toward the door behind which the jury was concealed. There came the rumble of the prison van below, the tramp of feet upon the hollow stairs, and into the dingy, high-ceilinged hall of justice filed the accused, manacled and doubly guarded. Maruffi led, his black head held high; Normando brought up the rear, supported by two officers. He was racked with terror, his body hung like a sack, a moisture of foam and spittle lay upon his lips. When he reached the railing of the prisoners' box he clutched it and resisted loosely, sobbing in his throat; but he was thrust forward into a seat, where he collapsed.

The judge and the attorneys were in their places when a deputy sheriff swung open the door to the jury-room and the "twelve good men and true" appeared. As if through the silence of a tomb they went to their stations while eleven pairs of black Sicilian eyes searched their downcast features for a sign. Larubio, the cobbler, was paper-white above his smoky beard; Di Marco's swarthy face was green, like that of a corpse; his companions were frozen in various attitudes of eager, dreadful waiting. The only sound through the scuff and tramp of the jurors' feet was Normando's lunatic murmuring. As for the leader of the band, he sat as if graven in stone; but, despite his iron control, a pallor had crept up beneath his skin.

Blake heard Bernie whisper:

"Look! They know they're lost."

"Gentlemen of the jury, have you agreed upon a verdict?" came the voice of the judge.

The foreman rose. "We have."

He passed a document up to the bench, and silently the court examined it.

The seconds were now creeping minutes. Normando's ceaseless mumbling was like that of a man distraught by torture. A hand was used to silence him. The spectators were upon their feet and bent forward in attention; the cordon of officers closed in behind the accused as if to throttle any act of desperation.

The judge passed the verdict down to the minute clerk, who read in a clear, distinct, monotonous tone:

"Celso Fabbri, Frank Normando, mistrial. Salvatore di Marco, Frank Garcia, Giordano Bolla"—the list of names seemed interminable—"Gaspardo Cressi, Lorenzo Cardoni, Caesar Maruffi"—he paused for an instant while time halted—"not guilty."

After the first moment of stunned stupefaction a murmur of angry disapproval ran through the crowd; it was not loud, but hushed, as if men doubted their senses and were seeking corroboration of their ears. From the street below, as the judgment was flashed to the waiting hundreds, came an echo, faint, unformed, like the first vague stir that runs ahead of a tempest.

The shock of Norvin Blake's amazement in part blurred his memory of that dramatic tableau, but certain details stood out clearly afterwards. For one thing he heard Bernie Dreux giggling like an overwrought woman, while through his hysteria ran a stream of shocking curses He saw one of the jurors rise, yawn, and stretch himself, then rub his bullet head, smiling meanwhile at the Cressi boy. He saw Caesar Maruffi turn full to the room behind him and search for his own face. When their eyes met, a light of devilish amusement lit the Sicilian's visage; his lips parted and his white teeth gleamed, but it was no smile, rather the nervous, rippling twitch that bares a wolf's fangs. His color had come flooding back, too; victory suffused him with a ruddy, purple congestion, almost apoplectic. Then heads came between them; friends of the prisoners crowded forward with noisy congratulations and outstretched palms; the rival attorneys were shaking hands.

Blake found himself borne along by the eddying stream which set out of the court-room and down into the sunlit street, where the curbs were lined with uplifted faces. Dreux was close beside him, quite silent now. A similar silence brooded over the whole procession which emerged from the building like a funeral cortege. When the moments brought home the truth to its members they felt, indeed, as if they came from a house of death, for they had seen Justice murdered, and the chill was in their hearts.

But there was something sinister in the hush which gagged that multitude.

Many readers will doubtless recall, even now, the shock that went through this country at the conclusion of the famous New Orleans Mafia trial of twenty years ago. They will, perhaps, remember a general feeling of surprise that an American jury would dare, in the face of such popular feeling and such apparently overwhelming evidence, to render a verdict of "not guilty." In some quarters the farcical outcome of the trial was blamed upon Louisiana's peculiar legal code. But the truth is our Northern cities had not at that time felt the power of organized crime. New York, for instance, had not been shaken by an interminable succession of dynamite outrages nor terrorized by bands of Latin-born Apaches who live by violence and blackmail; therefore, the tremendous difficulty of securing convictions was not appreciated as it is to-day.

There was a universal suspicion that the last word concerning the New Orleans affair had not been written, so what followed was not entirely a surprise.

# XXIV.
# AT THE FEET OF THE STATUE

Two hours after the verdict there was a meeting of the Committee of Justice, and that night the evening papers carried the following notice:

**"MASS-MEETING"**

"All good citizens are invited to attend a mass-meeting to-morrow morning at 10 o'clock at Clay Statue, to take steps to remedy the failure of justice in the Donnelly case. Come prepared for action."

It was signed by the fifty well-known men who had been appointed to represent the people. That incredible verdict had caused a great excitement; but this bold and threatening appeal brought the city up standing. It caused men who had been loudly cursing the jury to halt and measure the true depth of their indignation. There was no other topic of conversation that night; and when the same call appeared in the morning papers, together with a ringing column headed,

**"AWAKE! ARISE!"**

it stirred a swift and mighty public sentiment. Never, perhaps, in any public press had so sanguinary an appeal been issued.

"Citizens of New Orleans," it read in part, "when murder overrides law and justice, when juries are bribed and suborners go unwhipped, it is time to resort to your own indefeasible right of self-preservation. Alien bands of oath-bound assassins have set the blot of a martyr's blood upon your civilization. Your laws, in the very Temple of Justice, have been bought, suborners have loosed upon your streets the midnight murderers of an officer in whose grave lies the majesty of American law.

"Rise in your might, people of New Orleans! Rise!"

A similar note was struck by editorials, many of them couched in language even stronger and more suited to fan the public rage. The recent trial was called an outrageous travesty on justice; attention was directed to the damnable vagaries of recent juries which had been impaneled to try red-handed Italian murderers.

"Our city is become the haven of blackmailers and assassins, the safe vantage-ground for Sicilian stilletto bands who slay our legal officers, who buy jurors, and corrupt sworn witnesses under the hooded eyes of Justice. How much longer will this outrage be permitted?" So read a heavily typed article in the leading journal.

A wave of fierce determination ran through the whole community.

Margherita Ginini was waiting at Blake's place of business when he arrived, after a night of sleepless worry. She, too, showed evidence of a painful vigil; her hand was shaking as she held out a copy of the morning paper, inquiring:

"What is the meaning of this?"

"It means we're no longer in Sicily," he said.

"You intend to—kill those men?"

"I fear something like that may occur. The question will be put up to the people, plainly."

She clutched the edge of his desk, staring at him with wide, tragic eyes.

"Your name heads the list. Did—you do this?"

"I am the chairman of that committee. I did my part."

"But the law declares them innocent," she gasped—"all but two, and they can be tried over again."

"The law!" He smiled bitterly. "Do you believe that?"

"I believe they are guilty—who can doubt it? But this lawlessness—this mad cry for revenge—it is against all my beliefs, my religion. Oh, my friend, can't you stop it? At least take no part in it—for my sake."

His look was hard, yet regretful,

"For your sake I would give my life gladly," he said, "but there are times when one must act his destined part. That verdict holds me up to the public as a perjurer; but that is a small matter. Oh, I have had my scruples; I have questioned my conscience, and deep in my heart I see that there is only one way. I'd be a hypocrite if I denied it. I'm wrong, perhaps, but I can't be untrue to myself."

"We know but a part of the truth," she urged, desperately. "God alone knows it all. You saw three men—there are others whom you did not see."

"They were seen by other eyes quite as trustworthy as mine."

She wrung her hands miserably, crying:

"But wait! Guilty or innocent, they have appeared in judgment, and the law has acquitted them. You urge upon the people now a crime greater than theirs. Two wrongs do not make a right. Who are you to raise yourself above that power which is supreme?"

"There's a law higher than the courts."

"Yes, one; the law of God. If our means have failed, leave their punishment to Him."

He shook his head, no trace of yielding in his eyes.

"One man was killed, and yet you contemplate the death of eleven!"

"Listen," he cried, "this cause belongs to the people who have seen their sacred institutions debauched. If I had the power to sway the citizens of New Orleans from the course which I believe they contemplate, I doubt that I could bring myself to exercise it, for it is plain that the Mafia must be exterminated. The good of the city, the safety of all of us, demands it." He regarded her curiously. "Do you realize what Maruffi's freedom would mean to you and Oliveta?"

"We are in God's hands."

"It would require a miracle to save you. Caesar would have my life, too; he told me as much with his eyes when that corrupted jury lifted the fear of death from his heart."

"So!" cried the girl. "You fear him, therefore you take this means of destroying him! You goad the public and your friends into a red rage and send them to murder your enemy."

Her hysteria was not proof against the look which leaped into his eyes—the pallor that left him facing her with the visage of a sick man.

"During the last five years," he said, slowly, "I've often tried to be a man, but never until last night have I succeeded fully. When I signed that call to arms I felt that I was writing Maruffi's death-warrant. I hesitated for a time, then I put aside all thoughts of myself, and now I'm prepared to meet this accusation. I knew it would come.

The world — my world — knows that Maruffi's life or mine hinges on his liberty; if he dies by the mob to-day, that world will call me coward for my act; it will say that I roused the passions of the populace to save myself. Nevertheless, I was chosen leader of that committee, and I did their will — as I shall do the will of the people."

"The will of the people! You know very well that the people have no will. They do what their leaders tell them."

"My name is written. I am sorry that I cannot do as you wish."

"But surely you do not deceive yourself," she insisted. "This is wrong, oh, so inconceivably, so terribly wrong! You do not possess the divine power to bestow life. How then can you dare to take it? By what possible authority do you decree the destruction of your fellow-men whom the law has adjudged innocent?"

"By the sovereign authority of the public good. By the inherited right of self-protection."

"You would shoot them down, like caged animals?"

"Those eleven individuals have ceased to exist as men. They represent an infection, a diseased spot which must be cut out. They stand for disorder and violence; to free them would be a crime, to give them arms to defend themselves would be merely to increase their evil."

"There is a child among them, too; would you have his death upon your conscience?"

"I told Gino he should come to no harm, and, God willing, he sha'n't."

"How can you hope to stem the rage of a thousand madmen? A mob will stop at no half measures. There are two men among the prisoners who are entitled to another trial. Do you think the people will spare them if they take the others?" He shrugged his shoulders doubtfully, and she shuddered. "You shall not have the death of those defenseless men upon your soul!" she cried. "Your hands at least shall remain clean."

"Please don't urge me," he said.

"But I do. I ask you to take no part in this barbarous uprising."

"And I must refuse you."

She looked at him wildly; her face was ashen as she continued:

"You have said that you love me. Can't you make this sacrifice for me? Can't you make this concession to my fears, my conscience, my beliefs? I am only a woman, and I cannot face this grim and awful thing. I cannot think of your part in it."

The look she gave him went to his heart.

"Margherita!" he cried, in torture; "don't you see I have no choice? I couldn't yield, even if the price were—you and your love. You wouldn't rob me of my manhood?"

"I could never touch hands which were stained with the blood of defenseless men—not even in friendship, you—understand?"

"I understand!" For a second time the color left his face.

Her glance wavered again, she swayed, then groped for the door, while he stood like stone in his tracks.

"Good-by!" he said, lifelessly.

"Good-by!" she answered, in the same tone. "I have done my part. You are a man, and you must do yours as you see it. But may God save you from bloodshed."

Long before the hour set for the gathering at Clay Statue the streets in that vicinity began to fill. Men continued on past their places of business; shops and offices remained closed; the wide strip of neutral ground which divided the two sides of the city's leading thoroughfare began to pack. Around the base of the monument groups of citizens congregated until the cars were forced to slow down and proceed with a clangor of gongs which served only as a tocsin to draw more recruits. Vehicles came to a halt, were wedged dose to the curbs, and became coigns of vantage; office windows, store-fronts, balconies, and roof-tops began to cluster with a human freight.

After a week of wind and rain the sun had risen in a sky that was cloudless, save for a few thin streaks of shining silver which resembled long polished rapiers or the gleaming spear-points of a host still hidden below the horizon. The fragrance of shrubs and flowers, long dormant, weighted the breeze. It was a glorious morning, fit for love and laughter and little children.

Nor did the rapidly swelling assemblage resemble in any measure a mob bent upon violence. It was composed mainly of law-abiding business men who greeted each other genially; in their grave, intelligent faces was no hint of savagery or brutality. All traffic finally ceased, the entire neighborhood was massed and clotted with waiting humanity; then, as the hour struck, a running salvo of applause came from the galleries and a cheer from the street when a handful of men was seen crowding its way up to the base of the statue. It was composed of a half-dozen prominent men who had been identified with the Committee of Justice; among them was Norvin Blake. A hush followed as one of them mounted the pedestal and began to speak. He was recognized as Judge Blackmar, a wealthy lawyer, and his well-trained voice filled the wide spaces from wall to wall; it went out over the sea of heads and up to the crowded roof-tops.

He told of the reasons which had inspired this indignation meeting; he recounted the history of the Mafia in New Orleans, and recalled its many outrages culminating in the assassination of Chief Donnelly.

"Affairs have reached such a crisis," said he, "that we who live in an organized and civilized community find our laws ineffective and are forced to protect ourselves as best we may. When courts fail, the people must act. What protection is left us, when our highest police official is slain in our very midst by the Mafia and his assassins turned loose upon us? This is not the first case of wilful murder and supine justice; our court records are full of similar ones. The time has come to say whether we shall tolerate these outrages further or whether we shall set aside the verdict of an infamous and perjured jury and cleanse our city of the ghouls which prey upon it. I ask you to consider this question fairly. You have been assembled, not behind closed doors, nor under the cloak of darkness, but in the heart of the city, in the broad light of day, to take such action as honest men must take to save their homes against a public enemy. What is your answer?"

A roar broke from all sides; an incoherent, wordless growling rumbled down the street. Those on the outskirts of the assemblage who had come merely from curiosity, or in doubt that anything would be accomplished, began to press closer.

A restless murmur, broken by the cries of excitable men, arose when the second speaker took his place. Then as he spoke the temper of the people began to manifest itself undeniably. The crowd swayed and cheered; certain demands were voiced insistently; a wave of intense excitement swept it as it heard its desires so boldly proclaimed.

As the heaving sea is lashed to fury by the wind, the people's rage mounted higher with every sentence of the orator; every pause was greeted with howls. Men stared into the faces around them, and, seeing their own emotions mirrored, they were swept by an ever-increasing agitation. There was a general impulse to advance at once upon the parish prison, and knots of stragglers were already making in that direction, while down from the telegraph-poles, from roofs and shed-tops men were descending. All that seemed lacking for a concerted movement was a leader, a bold figure, a ringing voice to set this army in motion.

Blake had been selected to make the third address and to put the issue squarely up to the people; but, as he wedged his way forward to enact his role, up to the feet of the statue squirmed and wriggled a figure which assumed the place just vacated by the second speaker.

It was Bernie Dreux, but a different Bernie from the man his amazed friends in the crowd thought they knew. He was pale, and his limbs shook under him, but his eyes blazed with a fire which brought a hush of attention to all within sight of him. Up there against the heroic figure of Henry Clay he looked more diminutive, more insignificant than ever; but oddly enough he had attained a sudden dignity which made him seem intensely masterful and alive. For a moment he paused, erect and motionless, surveying that restless multitude which rocked and rumbled for the distance of a full city square in both directions; then he began. His voice, though high-pitched from emotion, was as clear and ringing as a trumpet; it pierced to the farthest limits of the giant audience and stirred it like a battle signal. The blood of his forefathers had awakened at last; and old General Dreux, the man of iron and fire and passion, was speaking through his son.

"People of New Orleans," he cried, "I desire neither fame nor name nor glory; I am here not as one of the Committee of Public Safety, but as a plain citizen. Let me therefore speak for you; let mine be the lips which give your answer. Fifty of our trusted townsmen were appointed to assist in bringing the murderers of Chief Donnelly to justice. They told us to wait upon the law. We waited, and the law failed. Our court and our jury were debauched; our Committee comes back to us now, the source from which it took its power, and acknowledges that it can do no more. It lays the matter in our hands and asks for our decision. Let me deliver the message: Justice must be done! Dan Donnelly must be avenged to-day!"

The clamor which had greeted the words of the previous speakers was as nothing to the titanic bellow which burst forth acclaiming Dreux's.

"This is the hour for action, not for talk," he continued, when he had stilled them. "The Anglo-Saxon is slow to anger, and because of that the Mafia has thrived among us; but once he is aroused, once his rights are invaded and his laws assailed, his rage is a thing to reckon with. Our Committee asks us if we are ready to take justice into our own hands, and I answer, Yes!"

A chaos of waving arms and of high-flung hats, a deafening crash of voices again answered.

"Then our speakers shall lead us. Judge Blackmar shall be the first in command; Mr. Slade, who spoke after him, shall be second, and I shall be the third in authority. Arm yourselves quickly, gentlemen, and may God have mercy upon the souls of those eleven murderers."

He leaped lightly down, and the great assemblage burst into motion, streaming out Canal Street like a storming army. It boiled into side streets and through every avenue which led in the direction of the prison. At each corner it gathered strength; every thoroughfare belched forth reinforcements; hundreds who had entertained no faintest notion of taking part fell in, were swallowed up in the seething tide, and went shouting to the very gates of the jail.

Once that tossing river of humanity had been given force and direction its character changed; it became a mailed dragon, it suddenly blossomed with steel. Peaceful, middle-aged men who had stood beside the monument buttoned up in peculiarly bulky overcoats were now marching silently with weapons at their shoulders.

Strangest of all, perhaps, was the greeting this army received on every side. The flotsam and jetsam which swirled along in its eddies or followed in its wake cheered, howled, and danced deliriously; men, women, and children from doorways and galleries raised their voices lustily, and applauded as if at some favorite carnival parade. In notable contrast was the bearing of the armed men themselves; they marched through the echoing streets like a regiment of mutes.

# XXV.
# THE APPEAL

On the iron balcony of a house in the vicinity of the parish prison the two Sicilian girls were standing. Across from them loomed the great decaying structure with its little iron-barred windows and its steel-ribbed doors behind which lay their countrymen. From inside came the echo of a great hammering, as if a gallows were being erected; but the square and the streets outside were quiet.

"What time is it now?" Oliveta had repeated this question already a dozen times.

"It is after ten."

"I hear nothing as yet, do you?"

"Nothing!"

"We could hear if it were not for that dreadful pounding yonder in the jail."

"Hush! They are building barricades."

The peasant girl gasped and seized the iron railing in front of her.

"Madonna mia! I am dying. Do you think Signore Blake will yield to your appeal and turn the mob?"

"I'm afraid not," said Vittoria, faintly.

"He can do more than any other, for he is powerful; they will listen to him. If Caesar should escape! I am shamed through and through to have loved such a man, and yet to have him killed like a rat in a hole! I pray, and I know not what I pray for—my thoughts are whirling so. Do you hear anything from the city?"

"No, no!"

There was a moment's pause.

"Those barricades will not allow them to enter, even if our friend does not persuade them to disperse."

"I have heard there is sometimes shooting." Vittoria shuddered. "It is terrible for men to become brutes."

"The time is growing late," Oliveta quavered.

There was another period of silence while they strained their ears for the faintest sound, but the fresh breeze wafted nothing to them. On a neighboring gallery two housewives were gossiping; a child was playing on the walk beneath, and his piping laughter sounded strangely incongruous. From across the way rose that desultory pounding as spikes were driven home and beams were nailed in place. Through a grated aperture in the prison wall an armed man peered down the street.

"Caesar is cunning," Oliveta broke out. "He is not one to be easily caught. He is brave, too. Ah, God! how I loved him and how I have hated him!" Ever since Maruffi's capture she had remained in a frame of mind scarcely rational, fluctuating between a silent, sullen mood of revenge and a sense of horror at her betrayal of the man who had once possessed her whole heart.

"It can't be that you still care for him?"

"No, I loathe him, and if he escapes he would surely kill me. Yet sometimes I wish it." She began mumbling to herself. "Look!" she cried, suddenly. "What is this?"

A public hack came swinging into view, its horses at a gallop. It drew up before the main gate of the prison, a man leaped forth and began pounding for admittance. Some one spoke to him through a grating.

"What does he say?" queried the peasant girl.

"I cannot hear. Perhaps he comes to say there is no—Mother of God! Listen!"

From somewhere toward the heart of the city came a faint murmur.

"It is the rumble of a wagon on the next street," gasped Oliveta.

The sound died away. The girls stood frozen at attention with their senses strained. Then it rose again, louder. Soon there was no mistaking it. A whisper came upon the breeze, it mounted into a long-drawn humming, which in turn grew to a steady drone of voices broken by waves of cheering. It gathered volume rapidly, and straggling figures came running into view, followed by knots and groups of fleet-footed youths. The driver of the carriage rose on his box, looked over his shoulder, then whipped his horses into a gallop and fled. As he did so a slowly moving wagon laden with timbers turned in from a side street. It was driven by a somnolent negro, who finally halted his team and stared in dull lack of comprehension at what he saw approaching.

By now the street beneath the girls was half filled with people; it echoed to a babble of voices, to the shuffle and tread of a coming multitude, and an instant later out of every thoroughfare which fronted upon the grim old prison structure streamed the people of New Orleans.

"See! They are unarmed!" Oliveta's fingers sank into her sister's wrist.

Then through the press came a body of silent men, four abreast and shoulder to shoulder. The crowd opened to let them through, cheering frenziedly. They wore an air of sober responsibility; they carried guns, and looked to neither right nor left. Directly beneath the waiting women they passed, and at their head marched Norvin Blake and Bernie Dreux together with two men unknown to the girls.

Vittoria leaned forward horror-stricken, and although she tried to call she did not hear her voice above the confusion; Oliveta clutched her, murmuring distractedly.

The avenues were jammed from curb to curb; telegraph-poles, lamp-posts, trees held a burden of human forms; windows and house-tops were filling in every direction; a continuous roar beat thunderously against the prison walls.

The army of vigilantes drew up before the main gate, and a man smote it with the butt of his shotgun, demanding entrance. The crowd, anticipating a volley from within, surged back, leaving them isolated. A dozen bluecoats struggled to clear the sidewalks next the structure, but they might as well have tried to stem a rising tide with their naked hands; they were buffeted briefly, then swallowed up.

In answer to a command, the armed men scattered, surrounding the building with a cordon of steel; then the main body renewed its assault. But the oaken barrier, stoutly reinforced, withstood them gallantly, and a brief colloquy occurred, after which they made their way to a small side door which directly faced the two women across the street. This was not so heavily constructed as the front gate and promised an easier entrance; but it was likewise locked and barred. Then some one spied the wagon and its load of timbers, now hopelessly wedged into the press, and a rush was made toward it. A beam was raised upon willing shoulders, and with this as a battering-ram a breach was begun.

Every crash was the signal for a shout from the multitude, and when the door finally gave way a triumphant roar arose. The armed men swarmed into the opening and disappeared one by one, all but two who stood with backs to the door and faced the crowd warningly. It was evident that some sort of order prevailed among them, and that this was more than an unorganized assault.

Through the close-packed ranks, on and on around the massive pile, ran the word that the vigilantes were within; it was telegraphed from house-top to house-top. Then a silence descended, the more sinister and ominous because of the pandemonium which had preceded it.

Thus far Vittoria and her companion had seen and heard all that occurred, for their position commanded a view of both fronts of the building; but now they had only their ears to guide them.

"Come, let us leave now! We have seen enough." Vittoria cried, and strove to drag Oliveta from her post. But the girl would not yield, she did not seem to hear, her eyes were fixed with strained and fascinated horror upon that shattered aperture which showed like a gaping wound. Her bloodless lips were whispering; her fingers, where they gripped the iron railing, were like claws.

"Quickly! Quickly!" moaned Vittoria. "We did not come to see this monstrous thing. Oliveta, spare yourself!" In the silence her voice sounded so loudly and shrilly that people on the adjoining balcony turned curious, uncomprehending faces toward her.

Moment after moment that hush continued, then from within came a renewed hammering, hollow, measured; above it sounded the faint cries of terrified prisoners. This died away after a time, and some one said:

"They're into the corridors at last. It won't be long now."

A moment later a dull, unmistakable reverberation rolled forth like the smothered sound of a subterranean explosion; it was followed by another and another—gunshots fired within brick walls and flag-paved courtyards.

It shattered that sickening, unending suspense which caused the pulse to flutter and the breath to lag; the crowd gave tongue in a howl of hoarse delight. Then followed a peculiar shrilling chorus—that familiar signal known as the "dago whistle"—which was like the piercing cry of lost souls. "Who killa da Chief?" screamed the hoodlums, then puckered their lips and piped again that mocking signal. As the booming of the guns continued, now singly, now in volley, the maddened populace squeezed toward that narrow entrance through which the avengers had disappeared; but they were halted by the guards and forced to content themselves by greeting every shot with an exultant cry. The streets in all directions were tossing and billowing like the waves of the sea; men capered and flung their arms aloft, shrieking; women and children waved their aprons and kerchiefs, sobbing and spent with excitement. It was a wild and grotesque scene, unspeakably terrible, inhumanly ferocious.

Through it the two Sicilian girls clung to each other, fainting, revolted, fascinated. When they could summon strength they descended to the street and fought their way out of the bedlam.

Norvin Blake was not a willing participant in the lynching, although he had gone to the meeting at Clay Statue determined to do what he considered his duty. He had felt no doubt as to the outcome of the mass-meeting even before he saw its giant proportions, and even before it had sounded its approval of the first speaker's words, for he knew how deeply his townspeople were stirred by the astounding miscarriage of justice. At the rally of the Committee on the afternoon previous it had been urged to proceed with the execution at once, and the counsel of the more conservative had barely prevailed. Blake knew perhaps better than his companions to what lengths the rage of a mob will go, and he confessed to a secret fear of the result. Therefore, although he marched in the vanguard of the storming party, it was more to exercise a restraining influence and to prevent violence against unoffending foreigners, than to take part in the demonstration. As for the actual shedding of blood, his instinct revolted from it, while his reason recognized its necessity and defended it.

Bernie Dreux's amazing assumption of dictatorship had relieved him of the duty of heading the mob, a thing for which he was profoundly grateful. When the main body of vigilantes had armed itself, he fell in beside his friend with some notion of helping and protecting him. But the little man proved amply equal to the occasion. He was unwaveringly grim and determined It was he who faced the oaken gate and demanded entrance in the name of the people; it was he who suggested the use of the battering-ram; and it was he who first fought his way through the breach, at the risk of bullets from within. Blake followed to find him with his fowling-piece at the head of the prison captain, and demanding the keys to the cells.

The posse had gained a partial entrance, but another iron-ribbed door withheld them from the body of the prison, and there followed a delay while this was broken down. Meanwhile, from within came the sound of turning locks and of clanging steel doors, also a shuffling of many feet and cries of mortal terror, which told that the prisoners had been freed to shift for themselves in this extremity.

In truth, a scene was being enacted within more terrible than that outside, for as the deputies released the prisoners, commanding them to save themselves if they could, a frightful confusion ensued. Not only did the eleven Sicilians cry to God, but the other inmates of the place who feared their crimes had overtaken them joined in the appeal. Men and women, negroes and whites, felons and minor evil-doers, rushed to and fro along the galleries and passageways, fighting with one another, tearing one another from places of refuge, seeking new and securer points of safety. They huddled in dark corners; they crept under beds, beneath stairways, and into barrels. They burrowed into rubbish piles only to be dragged out by the hair or the heels and to see their jealous companions seize upon these sanctuaries.

Terror is swiftly contagious; the whole place became a seething pit of dismay. Some knelt and prayed, while others trampled upon them; they rose from their knees to beat with bleeding fists upon barred doors and blind partitions; but as their fear of death increased and the chorus of their despair mounted higher there came another pounding, nearer, louder—the sound of splitting wood and of rending metal. To escape was impossible; to remain was madness; of hiding-places there was a fearful scarcity.

The regulators came rushing into the prison proper, with footsteps echoing loudly through the barren corridors. Out into the open court they swarmed, then up the iron stairways to the galleries that ringed it about, peering into cells as they went, ousting the wretched inmates from remotest corners. But the chamber in which they knew their quarry had been housed was empty, so they paused undecided, while from all sides came the smothered sounds of terror like the mewling and squeaking of mice hidden in a wall.

Suddenly some one shouted, "There they are!" and pointed to the topmost gallery, which ran in front of the condemned cells. A rush began, but at the top of the winding stairs another grating barred the way. Through this, however, could be seen Salvatore di Marco, Giordano Bolla, and the elder Cressi. The three Sicilians had fled to this last stronghold, slammed the steel door behind them, and now crouched in the shelter of a brick column. Some one hammered at the lock, and the terrified prisoners started to their feet with an agonized appeal for mercy. As they exposed themselves to view a man fired through the bars. His aim was true; Di Marco flung his arms aloft and pitched forward on his face. Crazed by this, his two companions rushed madly back and forth; but they were securely penned in, and appeal was futile. Another shot boomed deafeningly in the close confines of the place, and Cressi plunged to his death; then Bolla followed, his bloody hands gripping the bars, his face upturned in a hideous grimace, and his eyes, which stared through at his slayers, glazing slowly.

Down the ringing stairs marched the grim-featured men who had set themselves this task, and among them Bernie Dreux strode, issuing orders. The weapon in his hand was hot, his shoulder was bruised, for he had long been unaccustomed to the use of firearms.

Then began a systematic search of the men's department of the prison; but no new victims were discovered, only the ordinary prisoners who were well-nigh speechless with fright.

"Where are the others?" went up the cry, and some one answered:

"On the women's side."

The band passed through to the adjoining portion of the double building, and, keys having been secured, the rapidity of their search increased. Into the twin courtyard they filed; then while some investigated the cookhouse others climbed to the topmost tier of cells. As the quest narrowed, six of the Sicilians, who had lain concealed in a compartment on the first floor, broke out in a desperate endeavor to escape, but they were caught between the opposing ranks, as in the jaws of a trap. The cell door clanged to behind them; they found themselves at bay in the open yard. Resistance was useless; they sank to their knees and set up a cry for mercy. They shrieked, they sobbed, they groveled; but their enemies were open to no appeal, untouched by any sense of compunction. They were men wholly dominated by a single fixed idea, as merciless as machines.

There followed a nightmare scene; a horrid, bellowing uproar of voices and detonations, of groans and prayers and curses. The armed men emptied their weapons blindly into that writhing tangle of forms, and as one finished he stepped back while another took his place. The prison rocked with the din of it; the wretches were shot to pieces, riddled, by that horizontal hail which mowed and mangled like an invisible scythe. Now a figure struggled to its feet only to become the target for a fusillade; again one twisted in his agony only to be filled with missiles fired from so short a range that his garments were torn to rags. The pavement became wet and slippery; in one brief moment that section of the yard became a shambles.

Then men went up and poked among the bodies with the hot muzzles of their rifles, turning the corpses over for identification; and as each stark face was recognized a name went echoing out through the dingy corridors to the mob beyond.

Larubio, the cobbler, had attempted a daring ruse. The firing had ceased when up out of that limp and sodden heap he rose, his gray hair matted, his garments streaming. They thrust their rifles against his chest and killed him quickly.

Nine men had died by now, and only two remained, Normando and Maruffi. The former was found shortly, where he had squeezed himself into a dog-kennel which stood under the stairs; but the vigilantes, it seemed, had had enough of slaughter, so he was rushed into the street, where the crowd tore him to pieces as wolves rend a rabbit. Even his garments were ripped to rags and distributed as ghastly souvenirs.

Norvin Blake had been a witness to only a part of this brutality, but what he had seen had sickened him, and had increased his determination to find Gino Cressi. He shared not at all in the sanguinary exaltation which possessed his fellow-townsmen; instead he longed for the end and hoped he would be able to forget what he had seen. He would have fled but for his fear of what might happen to the Cressi boy. Corridor after corridor he searched, peering into cells, under cots, into corners and crannies, while through the cavernous old building the other hunters stormed. He was hard pressed to keep ahead of them, and when he finally found the lad they were close at his heels.

They came upon him with the lad clinging to his knees, and a shout went up.

"Here's the Cressi kid. He gave the signal; let him have it!"

But Norvin turned upon them, saying:

"You can't kill this boy."

"Step aside, Blake," ordered a red-faced man, raising and cocking his weapon.

Norvin seized the rifle-barrel and turned it aside roughly. The two stared at each other with angry eyes.

"He's only a baby, don't you understand? Good God! You have children of your own."

"I—I—" The fellow hesitated. "So he is. Damnation! What has come over me?" He lowered his gun and turned against the others who were clamoring behind him. "This is—awful," he murmured, shakingly, when the crowd had passed on. "I've done all I intend to." He flung his rifle from him with a gesture of repugnance, and went out of the cell.

Norvin continued to stand guard over his charge while the search for Maruffi went on, for he dared not trust these men who had gone mad. Thus he did not learn that his arch enemy had been taken until he saw him rushed past in the hands of his captors. Caesar had fought as best he could against overwhelming odds, and continued to resist now in a blind fury; but a rope was about his neck, at the end of which were a dozen running men; a dozen gun-butts hustled him on his way to the open air. Blake closed the cell door upon Gino Cressi and followed, drawn by a magnetic force he could not resist.

The main gate of the prison opened before the rush of that tangled, growling handful of men, and they swept straight out into the turmoil that filled the streets. An instant later Maruffi was beset by five thousand maniacs; he was kicked, he was beaten, he was spat upon, he was overwhelmed by an avalanche of humanity. His progress to the gallows was a short but a terrible one, marked by a series of violent whirlpools which set through that river of people. The uproar was deafening; spectators screamed hoarsely, but did not hear their voices.

From where Blake paused beside the gate he traced the Sicilian's progress plainly, marveling at the fellow's vitality, for it seemed impossible that any human being could withstand that onslaught. A coil of rope sailed upward, a negro perched in a tree passed it over a limb, and the next instant the head and shoulders of the Capo-Mafia rose above the dense level of standing forms. He was writhing horribly, but, seizing the rope with his hands, he drew himself upward; his blackened face glared down upon his executioners. The grinning negro kicked at the dark head beneath him, once, twice, three times, so violently that he lost his balance and fell, whereupon a bellowing shout of laughter arose more terrible than any sound heretofore. Still the Sicilian clung to the rope which was strangling him. Then puffs of smoke curled up in the sunshine, and the crowd rolled back upon itself, leaving the gibbet ringed with armed men. Maruffi's body was swayed and spun as if by invisible hands; his fingers slipped; he settled downward.

Blake turned and hid his face against the cold, damp walls, for he was very sick.

# XXVI.
# AT THE DUSK

Within two days the city had regained its customary calm. It had, in fact, settled down to a more placid mood than at any time since the murder of Chief Donnelly. Immediately after the lynching the citizens had dispersed to their homes. No prisoners except the Mafiosi had been harmed, and of those who had been sought not one had escaped. The damage to the parish prison did not amount to fifty dollars. Through the community spread a feeling of satisfaction, which horror at the terrible details of the slaughter could not destroy. There was nowhere the slightest effort at dodging responsibility; those who had led in the assault were the best-known citizens and openly acknowledged their parts. It was realized now, even more fully than before the event, that the course pursued had been the only one compatible with public safety; and, while every one deplored the necessity of lynchings in general, there was no regret at this one, shocking as it had been.

This state of mind was reflected by the local press, and, for that matter, by the press of all the Southern cities where the gravity of the situation had become known, while to lend it further countenance, the Cotton Exchange, the Board of Trade, and the Chamber of Commerce promptly passed resolutions commending the action of the vigilance committee. There was some talk of legal proceedings; but no one took it seriously, except the police, who felt obliged to excuse their dereliction. Of course, the stir was national—international, indeed, since Italy demanded particulars; but, serene in the sense of an unpleasant duty thoroughly performed, New Orleans did not trouble to explain, except by a bare recital of facts.

In spite of the passive part he had played, Blake was perhaps more deeply affected by the doings at the prison than any other member of the party, and during the interval that followed he did not trust himself to see Vittoria. There was a double reason for this, for he not only recalled their last interview with consternation, but he still had a guilty feeling about Myra Nell. On the second afternoon after the lynching Bernie Dreux dropped in to tell him of his sister's return from Mobile.

"She read that I took a hand in the fuss," Bernie explained, "but, of course, she has no idea I did so much actual shooting. When she told me she was going to see you this afternoon, I came to warn you not to expose me."

"Do you regret your part?"

"Not the least bit. I'm merely surprised at myself."

"You surprised all your friends," Blake said, with a smile. "You seem to have changed lately."

In truth, the difference in Dreux's bearing was noteworthy, and many had remarked upon it. The dignity and force which had enveloped the little beau for the first time when he stood before the assembled thousands still clung to him; his eyes were steady and bright and purposeful; he had lost his wavering, deprecatory manner.

"Yes, I've just come of age," he declared, with some satisfaction. "I realize that I'm free, white, and twenty-one, for the first time. I'm going to quit idling and do something."

"What, for instance?"

"Well, I'm going to marry Felicite, to begin with, then maybe some of my friends will give me a job."

"I will," said Blake.

"Thanks, but—I'd rather impose on somebody else at the start. I want to make good on my own merits, understand? I've lived off my relatives long enough. It's just as bad to let the deceased members of your family support you as to allow the live ones—"

"Bernie!" Blake interrupted, gravely. "I'm afraid I won't marry Myra Nell."

"You think she won't have you, eh? She has been acting queerly of late; but leave it to me."

Norvin was spared the necessity of further explanation by the arrival of the girl herself. Miss Warren seemed strangely lacking in her usual abundance of animal spirits; she was obviously ill at ease, and the sight of her brother did not lessen her embarrassment. During the brief interchange of pleasantries her eyes were fixed upon Blake with a troubled gaze.

"We—I just ran in for a moment," she said, and seemed upon the point of leaving after inquiring solicitously about his health.

"My dear," said Bernie, with elaborate unction, "Norvin and I have just been discussing your engagement."

Miss Warren gasped and turned pale; Blake stammered.

With a desperate effort the girl inquired:

"D—do you love me, Norvin?"

"Of course I do."

"See!" Bernie nodded his satisfaction.

"Oh, Lordy!" said Myra Nell. "I—can't marry you, dear."

"What?" Blake knew that his expression was changing, and tried to stifle his relief.

As for Bernie, he flushed angrily, and his voice rang with his newly born determination.

"Don't be silly. Didn't he just say he loved you? And, for heaven's sake, don't look so scared. We won't devour you."

"I can't marry him," declared the girl, once more.

"Why?"

"Be-because I'm already married! There! Jimmy! I've been trying to get that out for a month."

Dreux gasped. "Myra Nell! You're crazy!"

She nodded, then turned to Blake with a look of entreaty, "P-please don't kill yourself, dear? I couldn't help it."

"Why, you poor frightened little thing! I'm delighted! I am indeed," he told her, reassuringly.

"Don't you care? Aren't you going to storm and—and raise the dickens?" she queried. "Maybe this is your way of hiding your despair?"

"Not at all. I'm glad—so long as you're happy."

"And you're not mad with anguish nor crushed with—Why, the idea! I'm perfectly *furious!* I ran away because I was afraid of you, and

I haven't seen my husband once, not once, do you understand, since we were married. Oh, you—*brute!*"

By this time Dreux had recovered his power of speech, and yelled in furious voice:

"Who is the reptile?"

There came a timid rap, the office door opened, and Lecompte Rilleau inserted his head, saying gently:

"Me! I! I'm it!"

Blake rose so suddenly that his chair upset, whereupon Rilleau, who saw in this abrupt movement a threat, propelled himself fully into view, crying with determination:

"Here! Don't you touch her! She's mine! You take it out of me!"

Blake's answering laugh seemed so out of character that the bridegroom took it as merely a new phase of insanity, and edged in front of his wife protectingly.

"I wanted to come in at first and break the news, but she wouldn't let me," he explained.

"You have a weak heart. You—you mustn't fight!" implored Myra Nell; but Lecompte only shrugged.

"That's all a bluff." Then to Norvin: "I'll admit it *was* a mean trick, and I guess my heart really might have petered out if she'd married you; but I'm all right now, and you can have satisfaction."

"I don't know whether to be angry or amused at you children," Norvin told them. "Understand, once for all, that our engagement wasn't serious. There have been a lot of mistakes and misunderstandings—that's all. Now tell us how and when this all happened."

"Y-yes!" echoed Bernie, who was still dazed.

Myra Nell seemed more chagrined than relieved.

"It was perfectly simple," she informed them. "It happened during the Carnival. I—never heard a man talk the way he did, and I was really worried about his heart. I said no—for fifteen minutes, then we arranged to be married secretly. When it was all over, I was frightened and ran away. You're such a deep, desperate, unforgiving person, Norvin. I—I think it was positively horrid of you."

"Good Lord!" breathed her brother. "What a perverted sense of responsibility!"

"Are we forgiven?"

"It's all right with me, if it is with Norvin," said Bernie, somewhat doubtfully.

"Forgiven?" Blake took the youthful pair by the hands, and in his eyes was a brightness they had never seen. "Of course you are, and let me tell you that you haven't cornered all the love in the world. I've never cared but for one woman. Perhaps you will wish me as much happiness as I wish you both?"

"Then you have found your Italian girl?" queried Myra Nell, with flashing eagerness.

"Vittoria!"

"Vittoria!" Miss Warren shrieked. "Vittoria—a *countess!* So, she's the one who spoiled everything?"

"Gee! You'll be a count," said Rilleau.

There followed a period of laughing, incoherent explanations, and then the beaming bridegroom tugged at Myra Nell's sleeve, saying:

"Now that it's all over, I'm mighty tired of being a widower."

She flung her arms about his neck and lifted her blushing face to his, explaining to her half-brother, when she could:

"I don't know what you'll do without some one to look after you, Bernie, but—it's perfectly grand to elope."

Dreux rose with a grin and winked at Norvin as he said:

"Oh, don't mind me. I'll get along all right." And seizing his hat he rushed out with his thin face all ablaze. When Blake was finally alone, he closed his desk and with bounding heart set out for the foreign quarter. His day had dawned; he could hardly contain himself. But, as he neared his goal, strange doubts and indecisions arose in his mind; and when he had reached Oliveta's house he passed on, lacking courage to enter. He decided it was too soon after the tragedy at the parish prison to press his suit; that to intrude himself now would be in offensively bad taste. Then, too, he began to reason that if Margherita had wished to see him she would have sent for him—all in all, the hour was decidedly unpropitious. He dared not risk his future happiness upon a blundering, ill-timed declaration; therefore he walked onward. But no sooner had he passed the house than a thousand voices urged him to return, in this the hour of the girl's loneliness, and lay his devotion at her feet. Torn thus by hesitation and by the sense of his unworthiness, he walked the streets, hour after hour. At one moment he approached the house desperately determined; the next he fled, mastered by the fear of dismissal. So he continued his miserable wanderings on into the dusk.

Twilight was settling when Margherita Ginini finished her packing. The big living-room was stripped of its furnishings; trunks and cases stood about in a desolate confusion. There was no look of home or comfort remaining anywhere, and the whole house echoed dismally to her footsteps. From the rear came the sound of Oliveta's listless preparations.

Pausing at an open window, Margherita looked down upon the street which she had grown to love—the suggestion of darkness had softened it, mellowed it with a twilight beauty, like the face of an old friend seen in the glow of lamplight. The shouting of urchins at play floated upward, stirring the chords of motherhood in her breast and emphasizing her loneliness. With Oliveta gone what would be left? Nothing but an austere life compressed within drab walls; nothing but sickness and suffering on every side. She had begun to think a great deal about those walls of late and—The bells of a convent pealed out softly in the distance, bringing a tightness to her throat. In spite of herself she shuddered. Those laughing children's voices mocked at her empty life. They seemed always to jeer at that hungry mother-love, but never quite so loudly as now. She remembered surprising Norvin Blake at play with these very children one day, and the half-abashed, half-defiant light in his eyes when he discovered her watching him. Thinking of him, she recalled just such another twilight hour as this when, in a whirl of shamed emotion, she had been compelled to face the fact of her love. A sudden trembling weakness seized her at the memory, and she saw again those cold gray walls, which never echoed to the gleeful crowing of babes or the thrilling merriment of little voices. In that brief hour of her awakening life had opened gloriously, bewilderingly, only to close again, leaving her soul bruised and sore with rebellion.

She crossed the floor listlessly in answer to a knock, for the repeated attentions of her neighbors, although sincere and touching, were intrusive; then she fell back at sight of the man who entered.

The magic of this evening hour had brought him to her in spite of all his fears; but his heart was in his throat, and he could hardly manage a greeting. As he passed the threshold of the disordered room he looked round him in dismay.

"What is this?" he asked.

"Oliveta is going home to Sicily. It is our parting."

"And you?"

"To-morrow—I go to the Sisters."

"No, no!" he cried, in a voice which thrilled her. "I won't let you. For hours I've been trying to come here—Dearest, don't answer until you know everything. Sometimes I fear I was the one who was dreaming at that moment when you confessed you loved me, for it is all so unreal—But my love is not unreal. It has lived with me night and day since that first moment at Terranova—I couldn't speak before, but all these years seem only hours, and I've been living in the gardens of Sicily where you first smiled at me and awoke this love. You asked me to take no part—I had to refuse—I've tried to make a man of myself, not for my own sake, not for what the world would say, but for you—"

In the tumult of feeling that his words aroused she held fast to one thought.

"What—what about Myra Nell?" she gasped.

"Myra Nell is married!"

The curling lashes which had lain half closed during his headlong speech flew open to display a look of wonderment and dawning gladness.

"Yes," he reiterated. "She is married. She has been married ever since the Carnival, and she's very happy. But I didn't know. I was tied by a miserable misunderstanding, so I couldn't come to you honestly until today. And now—I—I'm—afraid—"

"What do you fear?" she heard herself say. The breathless delight of this moment was so intense that she toyed with it, fearing to lose the smallest part. She withheld the confession trembling upon her lips which he was too timid to take for granted, too blind to see.

"Can you take me, in spite of my wretched cowardice back there in Sicily? I would understand, dear, if you couldn't forget it, but—I love you so—I tried so hard to make myself worthy—you'll never know how hard it was—I couldn't do what you asked me, the other day, but, thank God, my hands are clean."

He held them out as if in evidence; then, to his great, his never-ending surprise, she came forward and placed her two palms in his. She stood looking gravely at him, her surrender plain in the curve of her tremulous lip, the droop of her faltering, silk-fringed lids.

Knowledge came to him with a blinding, suffocating suddenness which set his brain to reeling and wrung a rapturous cry from his throat.

After a long time he felt her shudder in his arms.

"What is it, heart of my life?" he whispered, without lifting his lips from her tawny cloud of hair.

"Those walls!" she said. "Those cold, gray walls!"

A sob rose, caught, then changed to a laugh of deep contentment, and she nestled closer.

Children's voices were wafted up to them through the fragrant, peaceful dusk, and the two fell silent again, until Oliveta came and stood beside them with her face transfigured.

"God be praised!" said the peasant girl, as she put her hands in theirs. "Something told me I should not return to Sicily alone."

### THE END